Look for Brenda Novak's next novel
In Seconds
available September 2011

To Doris—

BRENDA NOVAK

INSIDE

Enjoy!

Brenda Novak

MIRA®

Recycling programs
for this product may
not exist in your area.

ISBN-13: 978-0-7783-2993-0

INSIDE

Copyright © 2011 by Brenda Novak, Inc.

For questions and comments about the quality of this book please contact us at Customer_eCare@Harlequin.ca.

www.MIRABooks.com

Printed in U.S.A.

To Investigative Officer David Doglietto.
Thanks for taking a large chunk of your day off to
give me a tour of Soledad Prison (which was fascinating),
for answering all my questions and emails, for reading this
book when it was in manuscript form and correcting my
mistakes, and for teaching me so much about what it's
really like "inside." Your knowledge and follow-through was
so helpful—and your generosity is inspiring. Thanks, Dog

Dear Reader,

I rarely watch TV. I don't have anything against it. For me, it's all about opportunity cost. If I'm watching television, I can't be doing other things that are more important to me. So I miss out on even the most popular shows. For instance, I've never seen *Seinfeld, Friends, Sex and the City, Survivor* or *Lost.* I missed *Prison Break,* too, until I went to Utah to visit my daughter and she insisted on showing it to me on DVD. "You'll *love* it," she said, and she was right. I found the characterization, plotting, acting and dialogue fantastic. I was so captivated, in fact, that I rented every season and watched the whole thing. But, when it was all over, I decided there was one thing about *Prison Break* I would've done differently, and that was the romance between the two lead characters. The writers took a very minimalist approach and yet, for me, it was the most interesting part of the whole show.

So...I decided to write my own romance set inside the high-risk, high-conflict world of a maximum security prison, and I chose one of the most notorious prisons in America—Pelican Bay in Northern California (California's Siberia). With such a backdrop, I needed some very special characters, and I think I managed that with Peyton and Virgil. Virgil is probably one of the most tortured heroes I've created and yet I fell instantly in love with him. I hope you will, too.

I always enjoy hearing from readers. Feel free to write to me at P.O. Box 3781, Citrus Heights, CA 95611 or via email at www.brendanovak.com. If you have a computer, be sure to sign up for my mailing list so I can alert you when I have a new book coming out and you can take advantage of all the monthly giveaways and other freebies. Every May I hold an annual online auction for diabetes research at my website, so log on and register for that, too. So far, together with all the generous people who have supported me, we've raised over $1 million—and we're not done yet!

I'd like to extend a special thank-you to Michelle Thomas. Not only has she supported my writing, she's been a huge support to my efforts to raise money for diabetes research. Her name appears as a character in this novel because she was generous enough to purchase the privilege in my last auction.

I hope you enjoy the story!

Brenda Novak

1

Isolation is the sum total of wretchedness to a man.
                                            —Thomas Carlyle

Peyton Adams eyed the three men who'd driven to
the public library with her from the prison, as well as
the two they'd secretly come to meet. She knew what
she had to say wouldn't be popular, especially with the
warden, who was growing desperate enough to try anything, but she felt duty-bound to express her opinion.
"I say no. It's too risky. Maybe if we put him in the Security Housing Unit we could protect him, but not in
general population. No way."

Simeon Bennett, the person whose life she was attempting to save, sat across the conference table and
hardly seemed grateful for her intervention. "You disagree?" she said when he narrowed his ice-blue eyes.

"I'm confident I can complete the assignment or I
wouldn't be sitting here," he said.

An employee of Department 6, a company she'd never
heard of but which was apparently a private security
contractor out of L.A., he looked as tough as any inmate
she'd seen in the sixteen years she'd been working corrections. Somewhere in the neighborhood of six feet four

inches tall and two hundred and twenty-five pounds, he could've been hewn out of stone. With biceps and pecs that bulged beneath his carefully ironed dress shirt, and his blond hair shaved in a precise military haircut, he had an intimidating appearance. But it would take a lot more than muscle and a malevolent stare to survive inside Pelican Bay if he happened to spook the wrong inmate.

"I don't think you understand what it's like." She motioned at the door, which they'd just closed, to signify the prison, even though it was eight miles northeast of the library and shrouded in fog on such a cold January day.

It was plain that he wanted to argue with what she'd said but, for whatever reason, he leashed the impulse. Maybe he was saving up for the final salvo. Rick Wallace, an associate director at the California Department of Corrections and Rehabilitation and the man who'd brought him, took up the argument instead.

"I know what we're proposing is unprecedented, but the problems at Pelican Bay are reaching critical proportions. Something's got to be done. The director is determined to uncover and prosecute whoever's responsible for murdering Judge Garcia." Forever conscious of his appearance, he straightened his expensive yet conservative tie. "Secretary Hinckley and the governor are both behind him on this. What with various newspapers around the state taking up the cry that Pelican Bay is a headquarters for gang violence, we've got to act and act decisively." A heavy-looking gold ring flashed as he motioned to Simeon. "Mr. Bennett understands the risks involved. Although he's in the private sector, he's been working in the criminal justice world for the past decade or so. I say we give him a shot."

The tranquility of the library seemed to mock Peyton's agitation as she stood. "It's great that he has some experience at—where did you say?—this Department 6, but I'm sure nothing he's done in the past could prepare him for this. Besides, do you think he can handle the job alone?"

Simeon rocked back and gazed up at her with enough cool reserve to make her believe he was already an inmate, but maintained his silence.

"He won't be alone," Wallace said. "He'll have your full support, right?"

"You mean what little I can give him from the administration building, *right?* Once he's been knifed I can certainly see that he gets medical care, but—"

Wallace snapped open the slim leather briefcase he'd carried in with him. "Are you telling me you can't keep the inmates in your prison safe, Chief Deputy Warden?"

"Prisons are built to keep those on the *outside* safe, and that's where I suggest Mr. Bennett stay," she replied. "If he's dropped into our population and asks too many of the wrong questions, he won't live through the first week. And even if he does—"

"Your objection has been noted, Peyton." Finally deigning to speak, Warden Fischer cut her off and indicated that she should return to her seat. He'd been at the helm of California's most notorious supermax for only three years but, at sixty-one, he'd been in corrections twice as long as she had. He'd worked at Corcoron and San Quentin before Pelican Bay, was a personal friend of Arnold Schwarzenegger, the governor who'd appointed him, and ruled his prison with an iron fist. A product of the get-tough-on-crime sentiment that'd swept across the nation in the '70s and '80s—the precursor to prisons like

Pelican Bay—Fischer wasn't well liked by either staff or inmates. Stocky, with a barrel chest, bowed legs and a scratchy voice, he reminded her of a grizzled hermit. But Peyton did her best to ignore his rough edges. As far as she was concerned, he confused rehabilitation with punishment. She was merely biding her time until he retired. As second in command, she hoped to take his place, at which point she planned to guide the prison in a much more enlightened direction.

"Rosenburg, what do *you* think?" The warden turned to the much younger man on his left.

Senior Investigator of the prison's four-member police force, Officer Frank Rosenburg was in his late thirties and wore a police uniform instead of a suit. Charged with monitoring all drug and gang activity, as well as investigating any other crime perpetrated in or originating from Pelican Bay—including homicide, money laundering, bank robberies, home invasions, even prostitution—Rosenburg and his men had their hands full. With 3,343 inmates incarcerated in the supermax, most of whom were level four—"the worst of the worst," to use a catchphrase Peyton had heard ad nauseam since accepting her position there six months ago—the ratio of investigators to inmates definitely wasn't optimal.

The Security Housing Unit, or SHU, was supposed to level the playing field. Approximately 1,200 of Pelican Bay's inmates resided in complete isolation with no break from their eight-by-twelve-foot concrete cells except for one hour a day when they were allowed to pace, alone, in a cement box the size of a racquetball court. Despite being constantly monitored and having no privileges, they managed to run extensive criminal organizations that affected people inside *and* outside the prison.

Fingering his dark brown goatee, Frank scowled. "You know how it is, boss. We're working our asses off, but it takes hours and hours each day just to go through inmate communications. The bad guys are winning. I believe the Hells Fury are responsible for the death of Judge Garcia. Detric Whitehead or someone else put out the hit. Garcia was about to preside at Chester Wellington's trial, and the Hells Fury didn't want that. But I can't explain exactly how they pulled it off. And proving it? That'll be even tougher."

"So you like this idea," Warden Fischer prompted.

Barely five feet eight inches, an inch taller than Peyton, Frank glanced at Simeon. It was clear he *didn't* like the idea, but in deference to the corrections department, he was trying not to reject it out of hand. "I'd rather hire a few more officers who'd work under my command so we could handle this in-house."

"There's no money to hire additional staff. You know that." The warden drummed his yellowed fingernails on the table.

"We could ally ourselves with the Santa Rosa police, set up another task force, like they did for Operation Black Widow," Frank said.

The warden had begun to chuckle before Frank could even get the words out. "*That's* your answer? Operation Black Widow encompassed thirty government agencies, including the FBI. It took nearly three years and was one of the largest, most expensive investigations of a U.S. gang to date. If this state doesn't have the funds to hire a few more cops, it sure doesn't have the funds for another Operation Black Widow. You can bet the feds won't bankroll it. They have too many of their own problems right now."

Not pleased with this response, Frank sat taller.

"What we can't afford is a misstep. If we screw up, the Hells Fury will gain even more power. I don't have to tell you they're growing at an unprecedented rate, on both sides of the fence."

Wallace jumped in again. "Operation Black Widow succeeded because of an informant. That's what kicked off the whole thing, and that's what we're missing here. Without information—names, dates, places—we have nothing except a new gang that's quickly taking over Pelican Bay and moving into the streets of Northern California."

"Maybe we can get someone to flip," Peyton said. "Someone who's about to be paroled and wants to enjoy his freedom instead of becoming a foot soldier in some street regiment for the Hells Fury, which will only land him back in prison."

Relief eased the worry in Rosenburg's face. "Buzz Criven is due out next month. If we could offer him a deal—"

"Even if you offer him a deal and he accepts it, there's no guarantee he'd keep up his end." Warden Fischer pinched his nostrils, pulled and let go—one of his less attractive habits. "You know what's at stake for him, how those bastards lie."

"That's why I'm suggesting we create a mole," Wallace said.

But at what cost? Peyton wondered. Since when was a human life worth less than the expense of an ordinary investigation? If Simeon Bennett thought he'd be trusted by the Hells Fury just because he was white and appeared to be a fellow inmate, he was sadly mistaken. Gangs didn't work that way.

"Blood in, blood out. That's the code gangs live by, at least most of the gangs in Pelican Bay." She focused exclusively on Simeon. "You know what that means, don't you?"

Placing his hands on the table, he clasped them in front of him. They had enough knicks and scars to suggest he'd been in more than a few fights, but it was the words *love* and *hate* tattooed on his knuckles that caught Peyton's eye. Obviously he wasn't a typical cop—technically he wasn't a cop at all—but that didn't mean he'd be safe housed with convicted rapists, murderers and gangbangers.

"What, you want to give me some sort of gang quiz?" he asked. "Make sure I know the lingo?"

She straightened the jacket of her suit, a navy blue pinstripe with a pencil skirt she'd bought on her last trip to San Francisco. "You're saying you're willing to stab someone to get in? Because if *that's* true, I'll reserve a cell for you this minute."

He winked at her. "Now we're getting somewhere."

Peyton felt her mouth drop open. "*This* is who you want to put inside our prison?" she said to Wallace.

"Perfect, isn't he?" he replied with a grin.

To avoid an angry, knee-jerk reaction, she made a pretense of smoothing her hair, which was, as always, sleekly arranged in a tight knot at her nape—an efficient style that enabled her to feel slightly fashionable, despite working in a world where fashion played no part. "You *liked* his response?"

As calm, cool and collected as a politician, even when he was under fire, Wallace met her gaze with a level stare. "I think he's believable. And that's what we need."

In an effort to be as clear as possible, she leaned forward. "The point I was trying to make is this: it takes more than *words* to pass a gang initiation."

"Simeon and I have already discussed it," he responded. "We could stage certain…events. It'll require some cooperation from you, of course, but we can make a stabbing or…whatever else appear real."

Peyton picked up a pen someone else had left on the table to punctuate her words. "You don't get it. You can't choose who you stab. The Hells Fury set the mark."

"We'll figure it out." Wallace looked at Fischer as if to say, *Are you going to let her continue to fight us?* and Fischer spoke again, but he didn't rebuke Peyton. He seemed more interested in clarification.

"The department will pay for the investigation?"

Wallace hurried to confirm it. "That's correct. Why not? It'll be a bargain compared to what we'll need just to stop the bleeding if we don't head off this problem."

The warden was under constant pressure to trim the operating budget—every warden was, especially with the economic problems facing California. This state had a higher percentage of its population locked up than any other and was struggling to support what it had created. But Peyton didn't believe saving money justified jeopardizing a man's life, even if that man was foolhardy enough to get involved in such a dangerous operation. She hoped the fifth person at the table—Joseph Perry, one of the associate wardens below her and the third man who'd ridden over with her to meet Wallace and Bennett—would speak up as she had. If he agreed with her, maybe Fischer would listen.

But she should've known better than to count on Perry. When she arched an eyebrow at him, asking for his opinion, he shoved his wire-rimmed glasses higher and remained mum.

"You don't have anything to say?" she pressed.

With a sniff—he battled constant allergies—he

finally spoke in a characteristically nasal voice. "I, ah, I suppose it can work."

In other words, he didn't give a damn if it didn't. It wasn't his neck on the line.

Peyton turned to the warden. "At least take some time to think this over, sir."

"That's exactly what I've been doing." Fischer studied Simeon. "You sure you've got the balls for this, son?"

One side of his mouth twisted in the semblance of a grin, Bennett rolled up his sleeve to expose a tattoo that looked like a prisoner ID number.

"You're an ex-con?" Peyton cried.

Bennett didn't rush to explain. Buttoning his sleeve, he nodded.

"Oh, that's great." She leaned back so she could cross her legs. "That really makes me feel I can rely on you." What inmate tattooed his prison number on his arm? Only a very belligerent one....

He didn't seem to find her sarcasm warranted. "Considering your reservations, I'm more worried about being able to rely on *you*."

Peyton would have offered a retort, but the warden spoke before she could. "Why'd they put you behind bars?"

"Murder one." His gaze never wavered from her face, even though she wasn't the one who'd asked the question. He was interested in her reaction. Too stunned to speak, she gaped at him.

Rosenburg's chair raked the carpet as he shoved himself away from the table. "How long were you in?"

Simeon had read her shock and repugnance; Peyton could tell. His lips maintained that mocking grin, but this time he looked at Frank when he answered. "Nearly six years."

"What happened to Mr. Bennett was…unfortunate," Wallace said. "But, thanks to evidence that surfaced well after his conviction, he was exonerated."

Exonerated. For a moment, that word held no meaning for Peyton. Simeon Bennett had become a regular ex-con to her—probably because he seemed every bit as hardened as the men in her prison. Before Wallace's explanation could reverse that image, she had to walk herself through the definition. *He didn't do it.* Of course. He wouldn't be sitting here, working for the CDCR if he'd *murdered* someone.

But *six years?* For a crime he didn't commit? She couldn't believe he'd be willing to put himself back in such a vulnerable position. To make his pretense credible, they wouldn't be able to show him any favoritism or give him time off. Going undercover in Pelican Bay would be very close to going inside for real.

"If you think that convinces me you're ideal for this job, you're wrong," Peyton told him.

He had to speak over Wallace in order to respond. "And why is that, Chief Deputy?"

"Something so tragic…it has to have made…changes in who you are."

A muscle flexed in his cheek. "Which would make me damaged goods. Is that what you're saying?"

She looked at the warden, Frank, even Joe, for support, but got avid curiosity instead. "It could."

Simeon's jaw jutted forward. "I assure you I've passed all my psych evals…with flying colors."

Wallace handed them each a manila envelope. "You'll find Mr. Bennett's résumé inside. Given the unusual nature of his background, I assumed you'd have some questions. We want you to feel completely comfortable with what we've got planned—well, as comfortable as any of us can feel under the circumstances. But rest assured that we've done our homework. We're calling this Operation Inside, and we expect it to be a success."

"We..." Peyton repeated.

"The *department.*"

His emphasis was intended to make a point: it wouldn't be too beneficial to piss off her employer. But she couldn't justify worrying more about her career than a man's *life*.

Peyton shifted her gaze to Simeon's knuckles. *Love. Hate.* Which emotion dominated the other? Did he even know from one minute to the next? "Where'd you do the time?"

"In the federal system."

He could've elaborated but, once again, didn't. Was it because he didn't want her poking around in his past, checking up on him? If so, that defensiveness bothered Peyton. A man who'd spent six years in prison for murder could have a lot of dark secrets, despite being exonerated and despite having worked in the private sector for some time.

"How long have you been out?" the warden asked.

The contempt Simeon wore like an army jacket grew more apparent. He didn't like talking about this, didn't like being questioned. "Ten years."

"And you've been with Department 6 ever since?"

"I became a cop, then moved to the private sector, but I've been with Department 6 for most of that time."

"So you went in at...what?" Peyton asked.

His eyebrows slid up. "Eighteen."

That was young. Peyton could only imagine how such an experience had affected him. "Your family must've been heartsick."

He wasn't fooled by the sympathy in her voice. He

knew she was digging for additional information, maybe even some assurances and explanations. But he refused to accommodate her. "Yeah, they were pretty broken up about it."

This man already had her guessing at what was going on behind the mask of his G.I. Joe face. She prayed that the giant chip on his shoulder, if not his background, would motivate Warden Fischer to rethink his willingness to go along with the department's plan. But without bothering to open his manila folder, Fischer stood and extended his hand to Wallace.

"We'll do all we can to keep him safe. When will he go in?"

Shit. Peyton ground her teeth in frustration. Fischer was going for it.

"We were hoping he could arrive just after the other transfers next Tuesday," Wallace said as they clasped hands. "During a busy afternoon like that he shouldn't stand out."

It was Friday now, which meant this investigation would begin in four days.... And, as far as Peyton was concerned, such a handsome man would always stand out.

"No problem. We frequently get singles," Fischer said.

Frank stood and rested his hands on his utility belt. "What will his story be?"

Wallace responded. "His central file will indicate that he was convicted of killing his stepfather. The closer we stick to the truth, the more convincing it'll be."

"The *truth?*" Peyton echoed.

Although she and Wallace had gotten along on every other visit, today his lips pursed whenever she spoke. "That's what he went in for originally."

A shiver crawled up her spine. Not only had Bennett been convicted of murder, he'd been convicted of killing someone very close to him. That made her uncomfortable, whether the jury had been mistaken or not. There had to have been a reason he was convicted in the first place.

When Simeon's piercing blue eyes lingered on Peyton yet again, she sensed that he understood the revulsion she was feeling—that he expected it and resented it at the same time.

"Who really killed your stepfather?" she asked.

When he merely smiled, Wallace filled in the blank. "His uncle. He's being held at Solano State in California, awaiting trial. He also has a mother in L.A., where he was raised, who might've put her brother up to it. There's some circumstantial evidence to suggest it, but no real proof, so she's never been charged. The only other member of the family is a younger sister who is now a divorced mother of two, if that helps. Any other information you might need, Chief Deputy?"

Yes—a lot. If his mother had persuaded her brother to kill her husband, how was it that *Simeon* had gone to prison? Wouldn't his mother have come forward to stop it? Did she just let it happen? Or had she and her brother framed him? Question after question sped through Peyton's mind. But she saw no point in pursuing the answers. Warden Fischer was going to do this with or without her agreement. Why make their mutual boss any angrier? She'd heard the sarcasm in Wallace's response. "No," she said.

"We'll be ready for him on Tuesday, then." The warden motioned toward the door as if he expected Wallace to leave before him, but Wallace didn't budge.

"One more thing."

At his somber tone, everyone perked up.

"Bennett's true identity and everything else about Operation Inside is top secret. *Everything*. Do you understand?"

"You have nothing to worry about," Fischer assured him. "When we get back to the prison, I'll make sure every member of my staff understands the sensitivity of the situation and their responsibility regarding it."

"No." Wallace shook his head. "You won't tell your staff. The only people who can know are the ones in this room."

Fischer scratched his sagging jowls. He seemed to be catching on to what Peyton had understood all along. "You're saying we can't even tell the C.O.s working in gen pop?"

"That's what I'm saying."

"Then…how will they protect him?"

Parting his jacket, Wallace hooked his thumbs inside his belt as if posing for *GQ*. He wanted to be director of the CDCR someday. He'd never actually voiced that aspiration, not to Peyton, but it was obvious from the way he tried to impress those above him and how unyielding he could be to those below. "They won't do more for him than they would for any other inmate," he said.

"But—" At last the warden started to argue, only to be overruled.

"Treating him differently, pulling him aside to ask how things are going, showing him respect the others aren't entitled to—that's what will get him killed. One knowing look could be enough."

The warden buttoned his coat. "The way you've got it set up doesn't provide much support."

As Peyton had already mentioned.…

"It's our only choice," Wallace said. "We can't risk a leak."

"I promise you, my staff is completely trustworthy," Fischer insisted.

Wallace's wedding band wasn't nearly as impressive as the heavy gold and diamond ring he'd bought to celebrate his recent promotion. Once again, Peyton noticed it as he lifted his hand to gain everyone's attention before the warden could add anything else. "There are 1,400 employees at this prison. I'm not accusing anyone, but we all know that drugs, messages, weapons come in and out. For that to occur as frequently as it does, some of your staff have to be acting as facilitators. One word of warning to the Hells Fury and…well, I don't have to tell you how fast the truth would spread and what could happen as a result."

A frown creased Fischer's heavily lined face. "So this investigation will include convicts and employees alike?"

"That remains to be seen, doesn't it?" Releasing his belt, Wallace closed his briefcase. Then he and Simeon Bennett walked out.

Peyton heard their car start while she, Fischer, Rosenburg and Perry stood staring at one another. Finally the warden asked Rosenburg and Perry to excuse them for a moment, and the two men went out to wait in the van.

Bracing for a tirade, Peyton leaned against the door she'd shut on the heels of Rosenburg. She thought her boss was about to chew her out for being uncooperative during the meeting. He generally didn't hesitate to let her know if he disapproved of her behavior. Because they were so different in their philosophies, that happened more often than she would've liked. But this time he surprised her.

"You don't like the idea of this investigation, do you, Peyton?"

She'd already made that clear. "No, sir."

"You don't think Bennett can handle it?"

"I'm not sure anyone can. You know what it'll be like if he's labeled a snitch. The Hells Fury won't demand proof. Suspicion will be enough. I'm afraid we'll have blood on our hands before the week is out."

He sat on the edge of the table. "One way or another, it's going to turn into a can of worms," he admitted. "But...if he *could* break the stranglehold of the Hells Fury, everyone will be better off."

She couldn't deny that. Measuring her words so she could speak the truth without undermining her integrity, she said, "It would be nice to put a stop to Detric Whitehead and his organization, yes."

"We have no choice except to comply. You understand that, don't you?"

After being in heels all day, her feet were beginning to hurt, but she resisted the urge to sit down. She didn't want to appear tired or weak. She worked in a prison, had to prove herself every single day. "And why is that, sir?"

"You heard Wallace. He presented his plan as if we had some input, but we didn't. The decision was made before he ever asked us to meet him here. Even the governor is set on it."

Securing the flap of Wallace's manila envelope, she bit back the accusation that he could've tried harder to refuse. "So...what do you suggest we do?"

"We go along with the damn investigation, as agreed. But there's no need for two of us to spearhead this thing. I've given it my blessing. Now I want you to run with it."

Apprehension clawed at Peyton's stomach. Why would he turn such a sensitive investigation over to her? "Would you mind clarifying that, sir?"

"I've got more than I can handle on my plate already. You'll take over from here."

Irritated by a strand of hair that'd fallen from the knot at her nape, she tucked it behind her ear. "Which means…what, exactly? I'll be the liaison?"

"That's right. You'll meet with Bennett whenever it's safe to do so, and you'll relay his progress to Wallace. This is your baby. All of it."

But *she* was the one who had a problem with the operation. And she'd just strained her relationship with Wallace, to say nothing of alienating Bennett. Why would—?

And then it dawned on her. Warden Fischer was purposely distancing himself. He was as nervous about this investigation as she was and didn't want to be anywhere nearby if it blew up in their faces.

Now she understood why he'd invited her to attend such a clandestine meeting, even though she was far from the patsy Joseph Perry was. She was his "fall guy." He could pacify the Department of Corrections by acquiescing to their wishes, and sidestep the blame if it all went to hell.

"Do I have any choice?" she asked.

He smoothed down his sparse white hair. "Not unless you'd prefer to tender your resignation."

Peyton drew a steadying breath. As tempting as that sounded at the moment, she'd invested sixteen years in her career. She wasn't about to throw it all away without a fight. Especially when there was a chance, albeit a small one, that Bennett could come through and make them both heroes.

She imagined the pale blue eyes of the man who'd sat across the conference table from her. She wasn't sure she'd ever seen irises that exact shade of blue, certainly none that so closely resembled shards of ice.... "No, sir."

Fischer smiled. "Glad to hear it. Good luck to you and Bennett," he said, and left her standing in the conference room.

Dropping her head in her hands, Peyton cursed Fischer and his reluctance to take responsibility for what had just happened.

Was Bennett as good as Wallace thought?

She hoped so—because if he went down, so did she.

2

Wallace had provided a one-page background sketch on Simeon Bennett, nothing more. Peyton understood the need for secrecy, the danger of putting too much in writing, but this supposed "bio" revealed nothing they hadn't been told. It was a formality, a pretense, and that made her uncomfortable. She spent five days a week with some of the most cunning liars, thieves and murderers in California. She knew when she was being played, and that was what the meeting at the library had felt like.

What was the CDCR trying to pull? She'd never dreamed she'd have to worry about the people on *her* side of the law, especially those in the chain of command above her.

A soft knock sounded at her office door.

Peyton slid the sheet of paper she'd been reading back into the envelope, then stuck it under some files on her desk. "Come in."

Shelley, her administrative assistant, poked her curly brown head into the room. "I'm heading home. Is there anything you'd like me to do before I go?"

Peyton glanced at the clock. Four-thirty already? She was so busy the days flew by. Maybe that was why she didn't have much of a love life—in addition to the fact that she refused to date anyone who worked at the prison, which ruled out most of the men in Crescent City. "No, thank you. I'll see you on Monday."

Shelley paused. "Uh-oh."

"What's the matter?" Peyton asked.

"You've got 'the crease of concern.'"

To keep her hands occupied, Peyton straightened her stapler, pen holder, calendar. "The crease of concern?"

"Yep." She pointed to her own forehead. "Right there. You get it whenever you're worried. What's wrong?"

Peyton smiled to clear away that crease. Regardless of how she felt about what the department was doing, she wouldn't risk Bennett's life by letting on that something unusual was afoot. "Just another inmate in gen pop claiming to be suicidal."

"What does his psych report say?"

"That he's a malingerer."

"A what?"

"Faking it," Peyton clarified.

Stepping into the room, Shelley crossed her arms over her large breasts, which strained against a dress that was far too tight, and leaned against the wall. "What's he in for?"

Briefly allowing herself to be distracted by the business she'd been dealing with before Warden Fischer's little meeting eight miles away, Peyton took a sip of the coffee that'd nearly grown cold on her desk. "Molesting three boys."

"Then he's in the hat, isn't he?"

In the hat meant he was marked to be beaten or killed by other inmates. Rapists, molesters and child murderers weren't well liked, even in prison. "I'm not so sure that's the only reason he's saying he wants to exit the land of the living," she said.

Bracelet jangling as she walked, Shelley approached the chairs on the other side of Peyton's desk. "Come on, you know how many of these guys try to get themselves into the Psychiatric Services Unit. But with only one hundred and twenty-eight beds, you can't send them all there. I'd put him back in gen pop."

"Without a second thought?"

She adjusted her dress, which had started to ride up. "Why not?"

"What if he really goes through with it? What if he hangs himself in his cell? Would you want to be responsible for that?"

"No." Straightening, she hitched up her giant handbag. "That's why *you* get paid the big bucks."

Big bucks? Peyton made $120,000 year, but money didn't help her sleep at night. She'd been so idealistic when she'd chosen this profession, so certain she'd be able to make a difference. But, more often than not, there wasn't a good answer to the dilemmas she faced. She couldn't put this guy, Victor Durego, in the SHU. The SHU was reserved for behavioral problems; keeping inmates in total isolation cost taxpayers an exorbitant amount of money. If Victor had no mental disorder, she couldn't keep him in the PSU, either. It didn't make sense to waste the valuable time of the mental health professionals who worked there or take up a slot that was legitimately needed by someone else. For a week or two, she could move him into the Transitional Housing Unit, where they put the gangbangers who decided to debrief, but returning Victor to general population would leave him vulnerable to what had made him claim he was suicidal in the first place—probably another inmate who'd threatened him.

"There's always the other philosophy," Shelley said.

Peyton pushed the coffee to one side so she wouldn't be tempted by it. "What philosophy?"

"That a guy who molests children deserves whatever he gets."

She knew Shelley wasn't alone in her ambivalence toward Victor's safety. But Peyton believed it was humanity that separated the caregivers from the inmates. If the caregivers appointed themselves judge, jury and executioner, they were no better than the people they imprisoned. "As far as I know, physical injury wasn't part of his sentence. And we don't have the right to embellish it."

"I'm just saying.… You can't see into the future. What he did landed him in prison. Now that he's here, all you can do is make the call and hope for the best."

Shelley was right on that count. Peyton had made many such "calls." Some turned out as she'd hoped. Others didn't. Which was why the responsibility weighed so heavily.

"I should get going," her assistant said. "Good luck with it."

"Thanks." Peyton waved. Then the door closed, leaving her alone with Victor's file, a stack of others on which she had to make some decision or other and the manila envelope on Simeon Bennett.

Removing Simeon's bio, she read it again. Then she got on her computer and searched the internet for "Department 6, Los Angeles."

A webpage came up. It provided only general information, as she'd expected, but there was a contact number.

If she pretended to know Simeon and asked for him by name, maybe she could figure out if he at least worked where he said he did....

A man answered on the second ring. "Department 6."

Peyton curled the nails of her free hand into her palm. She was using her cell phone so her name would've appeared on caller ID, but that beat letting him know she was calling from a prison. "Is Simeon Bennett there?"

"Who?"

"Simeon Bennett. B-E-N-N-E-T-T. I met him at a club last weekend. I have an ex-boyfriend who…who's scaring me." She drew a deep breath in an effort to make the lie more convincing. "Simeon said he worked for a private security company that could protect me. He said I should call him at this number if my ex kept harassing me."

"I'm sorry, but I've never heard of a Simeon Bennett," the man responded.

And yet he was supposed to have worked there for most of the past ten years?

"Would you like to speak to someone else? Protection is definitely a service we offer."

"No. Thanks, anyway," she said, and hung up.

Just as she'd thought. Bennett didn't work for Department 6. So what *had* he been doing? And what about the rest of his résumé? Was any of it true? Had she even been given his real name?

She got up and crossed to the credenza, where she picked up the last photograph ever taken of her and her father. At four years old, she stood hugging his leg outside their middle-class home in Citrus Heights, a suburb of Sacramento. Shortly after a neighbor snapped that picture, he'd gone to prison for embezzling the money to pay for her mother's cancer treatments. Because of him, Grace had survived an additional quarter of a century, but after serving five years, with only three weeks left on his sentence, he was stabbed—and died in minutes.

Her father was the reason she'd gone into corrections. Knowing him and the reality of his story convinced Peyton to look at convicts as individuals with unique backgrounds, situations and desires, just like other human beings. Sometimes mitigating circumstances led a man to do the unthinkable. It wasn't fair to make snap judgments or lump them all together. Now that she was reaching positions with enough authority to make significant changes, she wouldn't allow Fischer, or the department, to set her up for failure by sending her into some dangerous investigation without all the facts. She'd worked too hard to get where she was.

So how would she learn exactly what they had planned? Although she'd seen the prisoner number on Bennett's arm, she'd been so shocked by what it signified that she hadn't thought to memorize it. She could recall only the first four digits. Otherwise, she might've been able to use that to obtain further information.

Maybe she wouldn't need it. Wallace hadn't done much to cover his tracks. He was so used to being in charge, so arrogant and sure no one at the prison would bother to check on anything he said, he hadn't even invented a fictional company for Bennett's previous employer. Or chosen an organization that wasn't as easy to locate.

Setting her father's picture back in its place, she

grabbed her purse and flung her jacket over her shoulder. She'd figure out who Bennett really was, or she wouldn't let him into the prison on Tuesday. Maybe her determination would end her career, but she'd go down swinging.

In the notes Wallace had given him on Operation Black Widow, Crescent City had been called "California's Siberia" by one defense attorney. Now that he'd seen it for himself, Virgil had to agree. Nearly four hundred miles from both San Francisco and Sacramento, and eight hundred miles from Los Angeles, it was only accessible via narrow, winding roads clogged with RVs, or a small airstrip with very few flights. Dense forests of giant, old-growth redwoods hemmed it in on one side—silent, massive and pungent. An angry, churning Pacific Ocean stretched to eternity on the other.

But it wasn't just the physical isolation that made this part of the California coast different from the hot sun and toes-in-the-sand party beaches down south. It was the climate. Foggy and chilly, with trees shaped by the wind, this tiny dot on the map seemed every bit as lonely as a barren field of ice. The only major difference was the lush beauty.

There shouldn't be a prison here, he decided. Especially a supermax as notorious for harsh discipline, even abuse, as Pelican Bay. It was too much of a contradiction.

Chief Deputy Warden Peyton Adams was also too much of a contradiction. He pictured her blond hair pulled into a knot at her nape, the wide brown eyes that'd stared out at him with such quick perception, the satiny skin that made her look too young to hold the authority she did, the lines of her suit, which was practical yet stylish. Had he met her anywhere else, he would've guessed she worked behind the makeup counter at Neiman Marcus or sold upscale women's clothing.

Hiding ruthless power behind such a pretty face seemed the ultimate lie.

But he'd been told that lie before, hadn't he? By his own mother....

"So what do you think?" Wallace piped up as he drove them from Jedediah Smith Redwoods State Park, a sight Simeon had wanted to see, to a restaurant for dinner.

Virgil didn't care for Wallace. Smug, cocky and shallow, he wasn't particularly likable. There were moments when, without provocation, Simeon had to fight the impulse to break his jaw, and that upset him as much as everything else going on in his life. He hadn't always struggled with authority. The resentment that simmered just below his skin was a product of the years he'd spent in prison dealing with corrections officers who'd been created from the same mold, and was no doubt influenced by The Crew, the gang he'd had to clique up with to survive. "About what?"

"The meeting."

He adjusted the hat and glasses Wallace had provided for their trip to the state park, in case they were spotted by an off-duty corrections officer who might later recognize him. "It went more or less as I expected." Except for the beautiful chief deputy warden who'd been so unfriendly to their plan. Like the stunning vistas that appeared without warning, she'd come as a complete surprise. He couldn't imagine someone like her working at a prison.

"So you can handle it?"

"Do I have any choice?"

Wallace shifted beneath his stare. "No, I guess you don't."

The old-fashioned business signs they passed, like the one in front of the local gift shop, made Virgil feel as if they'd detoured onto the set of *Happy Days*. But that sign and others similar to it were merely one facet of this place, holdouts from an earlier era. Overall, Crescent City had become a mixed bag. Heads bent against the constant drizzle, rednecks mingled with artisans. Old, weather-beaten buildings soldiered on amid the typical fast-food joints seen everywhere else in the country. And, at the harbor in the small bay—the only calm in a restless sea—fishing boats bobbed next to shiny new recreational craft.

He took in every detail as if he hadn't seen anything like it in years. Because, other than on the long drive from Sacramento this morning, he hadn't. He'd read all the books, leaflets, newsletters and pamphlets he could lay his hands on when he was inside, but experiencing a place like this made a real and very different impact. He especially enjoyed the salt-laden air and the smell of the loamy earth and towering trees.

While Wallace parked at Raliberto's Tacos on M Street, Virgil wished he could've visited Crescent City back when it was teeming with lumberjacks and salmon fishermen. It would have felt innocent then. But, according to Wallace, who'd picked him up at the airport in Sacramento, it was only because of Pelican Bay that Crescent City had survived. In the early '80s, the salmon fishing had died and thirteen of the seventeen sawmills went out of operation. The prison, which opened in '89, supplied much-needed jobs. Now nearly half the town's population resided behind bars and most of the other half worked in a capacity related to that.

"You as hungry as I am?" Wallace continued to strive for camaraderie.

"Hungry enough." Virgil yanked on the heavy jacket intended to hide his build and got out. "You staying all weekend?"

"I haven't decided." The car chirped as he locked it and came around the front. "Is that necessary?"

"If you think it's your presence that's keeping me here, you're delusional."

Shoving his hands in his pockets, Wallace jingled his change. "Look, I don't like this any more than you do. But my job's on the line and—"

Virgil broke in with an incredulous laugh. "You're worried about your *job?* I have a lot more at risk than that, so stop whining. It's this simple—you take care of Laurel, I'll do my part."

"A U.S. marshal will arrive at her door on Monday."

"Does she know that?"

"Not yet."

"Then I want to tell her."

"You can't contact her. And *we're* not going to advise her, either." He held up a hand before Virgil could protest. "We don't want her to do or say anything that might tip off your *friends,* do we?"

Friends… The Crew had once been his friends. Now they were his greatest enemy. Good thing there weren't any Crew members at Pelican Bay. Of course, if there were, he wouldn't be doing this. As with most gangs, they were connected to a specific region—mostly L.A., with an offshoot in Arizona. "What if Monday's not soon enough?"

With a sigh, Wallace shook his head. "Fine. I'll leave

first thing in the morning, get her moved and be back on Tuesday to effect your 'transfer.'"

Three whole days of freedom. It wasn't a lot. Especially when he had to lie low and make sure he wasn't noticed. But it was something. Simeon couldn't wait.

Ducking into the restaurant to keep his suit from getting wet, Wallace turned to see why he hadn't followed. But there was no one in their immediate vicinity, so as far as Virgil was concerned, Wallace could wait all day. He'd go in when he was good and ready. For now, all he wanted was to stand in the rain.

Removing the bogus glasses, he tilted back his head, closed his eyes and let the drops fall on his face.

Whenever staff who worked for the department came to Crescent City, they stayed at a garden-style motel of twenty-four rooms called the Redwood Inn. Peyton knew this because she'd gone out to dinner with Wallace and various others three times in the past and had driven them back to the motel twice when they'd had too much to drink. She'd even had a room there herself when she'd been sent to interview for her current position. She assumed that was where she'd find Bennett. Habits were tough to break.

"Hey, look who it is!" Michelle Thomas, who managed the inn, smiled brightly when Peyton walked into the lobby. Peyton had first met Michelle, who was three years younger, six months ago when she'd stayed here. They'd been friends ever since. Together with two other women, divorcées like Michelle, they got together every week, usually for dinner. Once in a while, on special occasions, they drove to Sacramento or San Francisco to go dancing.

"What are you doing here?" Michelle wanted to know. "I wasn't expecting you."

"Looking for Rick Wallace from the Department of Corrections. Has he checked in?"

No doubt Michelle was well aware that she had a couple of guests from the CDCR. The rooms were on a master account. "Yeah, earlier this afternoon. He rented two rooms, fifteen and sixteen. I saw him go into sixteen, if you want to knock. But I don't think he's there. He and whoever he's with—some guy who waited in the car—left shortly after they got here, and—" she walked over to study the parking lot through the front door "—I don't see his car."

"They might've gone out to eat."

"That'd be my guess, too. Would you like to leave a message?"

"No, that's okay. I'll call him later. I just...I need to use the restroom. Then I'll be on my way." She headed down the hall that went past the closet where the maids returned their towel carts and hung their smocks. Peyton had visited Michelle here often enough to know the motel routine. But she'd never dreamed that knowledge would come in handy. "We still on for dinner tomorrow night?" she called back.

"Far as I know," Michelle replied. "Have you talked to Jodie or Kim?"

"Not yet. Why don't you give them a call?"

There wasn't another soul in the lobby, so Peyton knew Michelle wouldn't hesitate to make a personal call, even though she was on duty. She had the run of the place; she'd been working here for a decade and would probably still be here in another decade. Her ex-husband, a corrections officer at the prison, lived a block to the north. As much as Michelle craved the big city, with its greater possibilities for love and employment, she didn't want to take her kids from their father.

Peyton stood inside the bathroom until she could hear Michelle on the phone. Then she cracked open the door and waited until her friend moved out of sight before slipping into the maid's closet, where she helped herself to one of the master keys clipped to a smock. As she dropped it in her purse, she peered out to make sure Michelle wasn't watching for her and reentered the lobby as soon as her friend turned in the other direction.

"Everybody coming for dinner tomorrow?" she asked.

Deeply engrossed in conversation, Michelle looked up and motioned for her to be quiet. "That's okay. If you can't make it, you can join us next week."

"Who is it?" Peyton mouthed.

"Jodie," Michelle mouthed back.

Knowing Wallace and Bennett could return any minute, Peyton hurried to the door. "I'm dying to get out of these heels. Call me later and let me know what's going on," she said, and hustled out.

After driving around the block, Peyton parked, turned off her phone and locked it and her purse, everything except the card key, in her trunk. Then she went back to the motel.

As she ducked into a small alcove where she couldn't be seen from the parking lot or the lobby, she had to ask herself if she was really going through with this. So far, she hadn't done anything too daring. Michelle trusted her, so taking the key had been easy. Putting it back would be just as easy. But the risk escalated from here....

What if she got caught?

Hoping to slow her galloping heart, Peyton pressed

a hand to her chest and closed her eyes. *Think! Are you crazy?*

No. She was determined not to be used. And that meant she had to know who Bennett was and why he was lying. If she did get caught in his room, she'd simply go on the offensive, tell Rick what she'd learned by calling Department 6. Best-case scenario, he'd believe she was acting to protect the warden, the staff and the inmates at Pelican Bay, as well as the CDCR. Worse case, he'd call the cops and have her arrested for breaking and entering.

But she couldn't imagine he'd want the publicity involved in such a scandal, not when he was trying to launch a top-secret investigation. Chances were greater that he wouldn't do anything—especially because she was only trying to find out what he should've told her from the beginning.

Anyway, she wouldn't get caught. The maids were gone for the day, Michelle was likely still on the phone, there was no one in the parking lot and it was raining. Who'd see her? All she had to do was move fast.

Using her hand to shelter her face, she walked the short distance during which she'd be visible from the street as confidently as if she was approaching her own room. It seemed to take longer than it should have, but she was fine until she reached number fifteen. Then the key card she'd taken from the maid's closet wouldn't work.

Alarm poured through her as she swiped it again. Fortunately, this time she heard the tumbler fall.

Thank God, she breathed, and stepped inside.

The drapes, pulled closed, shut out what was left of the evening light, making the darkness, which smelled faintly of cologne or shampoo, crowd in on her. The scent was appealing but foreign enough to unnerve her. After scrambling to turn on the light, she saw that the beds were, for the most part, untouched. A bedraggled-looking duffel bag sat on the carpet. Stepping over it, she went to make sure the bathroom was empty.

It was. She saw a shaving kit on the sink—the source of the smell. The ironing board was out, too, suggesting Simeon had ironed his blue shirt, his dark slacks or both. He'd probably shaved, as well, and brushed his teeth. A tube of toothpaste and a toothbrush resided on the small ledge above the sink.

"At least you have good hygiene." Talking to herself kept her nerves under control, but now that she was inside, she was once again filled with purpose. If there was anything here to help her figure out what was going on, she'd find it. Then she'd get the hell out....

Kneeling beside his bag, she removed a stack of clothing, all neatly folded and smelling like the shaving lotion in the bathroom. At the bottom, she discovered several letters. Addressed to ADX Florence, a federal penitentiary in a remote, unincorporated part of Fremont County, Colorado, the envelopes bore the name Virgil Skinner, but they had the prisoner ID number she'd seen tattooed on Bennett's arm—99972-506. At least, she assumed it was the same number, since it started with 9997.

So did this mean Simeon Bennett *wasn't* his real name? That was her guess. And the letters weren't dated a decade earlier. The one she held in her hand had been sent a month ago.

"What the heck?" Opening the first envelope, she took out a picture of a beautiful woman with long blond hair and eyes that appeared to be as blue as Bennett's... or Skinner's. Kneeling in some sort of park, she had an

arm around two children—a girl who looked about three
and a boy of maybe five. There was no writing on the
back identifying the subjects, but a date stamp on the
front indicated it had been taken recently.

Curious to learn who the woman was and what she
meant to Bennett/Skinner—could she be his wife?—
Peyton began to read.

Virgil—
I'm so excited to think you'll be coming home. I
can't tell you how much I miss you. We're going
to live the most boring, safest lives in the whole
world. And it'll all begin in a couple of weeks.
God, it's been so long since I've felt bored *or* safe.
I can hardly wait.

To answer your question, Mom is still calling
me, begging me to believe her. I won't, of course.
As far as I'm concerned, she deserves to be locked
up along with Gary. But she's the least of my worries right now. I'm pretty sure I'm being watched.
There's a white Ford Fusion that keeps driving by
my house. Sometimes, early in the morning, I'll
see it sitting out front. None of my neighbors own
a car like that.

I know what you're thinking—that it has
to be Tom. But it doesn't feel that way. I'm pretty
sure he's finally happy in his new relationship. He
doesn't even care about seeing the kids anymore,
makes no effort whatsoever.

So…do you think I'm being paranoid?
Maybe I am.…

Anyway, prison mail takes forever. I'm not
even sure you'll get this before you're released, so
I'll close for now. Just know that I love you and

miss you and it doesn't matter what happened in the past. We'll build a new future.

Love, Laurel

Virgil? Who was Virgil? Judging by the prisoner number, Virgil had to be Simeon. But, if so, this letter proved he hadn't gotten out of prison nearly as long ago as she'd been told at the library.

Did Wallace know? He had to, didn't he? So why would he pretend it'd been ten years since Bennett's release? And what else had they lied about—besides Bennett's name and what he'd been doing?

There were other letters from the same person who, according to the return address, lived in Colorado. Toward the bottom of the stack, Peyton found letters from another woman living in Los Angeles. She guessed it was his mother, but couldn't tell for sure. The letters hadn't been opened and she couldn't open them without making it obvious that someone had been through his bag.

Voices, coming from outside the door, interrupted her search.

"No need to wake me before you go."

That was Bennett. Skinner. Wallace answered from farther away. She couldn't tell what he said. She was too busy shoving as much as she could back into the bag to concentrate on listening.

Then she heard the key in the lock.

Shit! Now what? She couldn't get under the bed. There wasn't enough space.

Looking for another alternative, she darted around the ironing board toward the bathroom. But as she glanced back to see if he was opening the door, she spotted one of the letters lying on the carpet. It must've fallen in her rush to replace everything.

Knowing she had to grab it, that there wasn't a chance he'd miss something so out of place, she dashed back....

3

Having been out of prison for less than a week, Virgil hadn't quit looking over his shoulder, marking the exits in a room, remaining aware of the people around him. He *couldn't* stop, not if he wanted to stay alive. As soon as the leadership of The Crew figured out that he'd switched sides, they'd send a couple of foot soldiers to kill him. So he'd started putting a piece of dental floss in motel doors if he planned to return.

Wallace had laughed when he saw him do it. He'd said, "They couldn't have tracked you all the way up here. Not yet." That had to be why the government wasn't in any big hurry to take Laurel into custody. They didn't understand how quickly The Crew might react, how fast they'd go after anyone connected to Virgil, anyone he loved, if they couldn't reach him.

Virgil never assumed he'd be safe. If he died, there'd be no one to protect his sister. His service to the department was all he had to trade on her behalf. And right now he was damn glad he'd gone to the trouble of using that floss—because it was gone.

Someone had been in his room.

Maybe the management had sent over a maintenance man to fix a leaky faucet or running toilet. Or a maid had checked to make sure he had his full complement of towels. It *could* be either of those things—but didn't *have* to be.

He considered making Wallace aware that there might be trouble. But the associate director's TV was already blaring. He didn't carry a gun and was probably worthless in a fight. And Simeon didn't want him to know he had a weapon.

Setting his bag of groceries on the ground, he clutched the steak knife he'd stolen from the restaurant in his left hand. Fortunately, he was ambidextrous enough that he often fought with his left just to throw his opponent, who was more often right-handed, off balance. It wasn't much, especially if he was facing two or three people, but today his experience and prison tactics were all he had.

Fully expecting a bullet to come whizzing out from the interior, he ducked as he threw open the door. But nothing happened. When the door merely shut, he didn't know what to think. Especially because that floss hadn't just slipped to the ground; whoever had gone into his room had tracked it inside. In the split second the door had swung wide, he'd spotted it lying on the carpet.

Not only that, the light was on, even though Virgil had turned it off.

He couldn't imagine a maid would be that sloppy. But a maintenance man? Maybe.

Propping the door open with his groceries so he could get out fast if he had to, he crept inside. If someone was waiting for him, he couldn't see who. Or where. The chair was tucked under the desk. There was no space under the beds. And only a very skinny man would be able to conceal himself in such a tiny closet. The door of that closet stood open, anyway, from when he'd taken out the ironing board.

Whoever it was had to be in the bathroom.

Pressing his back to the wall so his reflection wouldn't be visible in the mirror, he listened for movement and heard...nothing. Then, just as he was about to step inside, he caught a slight rustling.

The shower curtain...

His intruder was in the tub.

Peyton's chest seized the second Virgil threw back the shower curtain and hauled her toward him. She twisted her ankle struggling to stay on her feet despite her high heels, but the scream that built in her throat never escaped. He had her on the carpet outside the bathroom with a knife to her throat so fast she could barely whimper.

"What the hell are you doing in my room?" he growled, pinning her beneath him.

Snippets of the many nightmares she'd had since starting work in corrections flashed through her mind as she stared helplessly up at him. He'd just been released from ADX Florence, could be as dangerous as anyone at Pelican Bay. She halfway expected him to slit her throat, but he cursed and threw the knife to one side instead.

"What the hell are you doing in my room?" he asked again, only this time, in many ways, it was a different question. There wasn't an edge of menace in his voice anymore. He was irritated and angry, yes, but she no longer felt that her life was in danger. He got up and backed toward the wall, but once he realized she didn't have the strength to stand, he came forward again and offered to help her.

Shaking too badly to reach up, Peyton waved him off. She doubted she could put any weight on her ankle even if she could get to her feet. "I was…" She managed to shove herself into a sitting position and almost finished with, *I was sure you were going to kill me*. That was all she could think, over and over, as if she'd hit her head instead of her shin when he'd dragged her from the tub. But why repeat the obvious?

In an effort to make sure she didn't, she closed her eyes and kept her mouth shut, too.

"Um, don't freak out, but…you've got a little cut," he said.

Peyton wiped the moisture from her neck and stared down at the red on her fingertips—blood. "Who are you?" she whispered. "Who are you *really?*"

He didn't answer. He went to get a washcloth, then bent down next to her so he could press it against her injury.

The scent of his aftershave filled her nostrils, much stronger now that he was so close. And the beauty of his eyes was even more riveting. "Why are you in Crescent City?" she asked, taking the washcloth so he could let go.

He went into the bathroom and came out holding the letter she'd tried to retrieve.

"If you've read my mail, you know."

Propping herself against the wall for support, she tried to decipher what was going on. "Virgil Skinner? That's your real name?"

He walked over and pulled the groceries inside so the door could close. "Yes."

As she'd guessed. "Are you…on parole?"

"Sort of," he admitted.

Sort of wasn't enough. "After sixteen years in corrections, I've never heard of anyone being 'sort of' on parole."

"I was exonerated in my stepfather's killing."

Take another deep breath. "But…they have something else on you."

"Yes."

"What is it?"

"What I did on the inside."

Oh, hell… "Are we talking murder?"

When he didn't respond, she knew she'd guessed correctly and the thought of that made her queasy. "I see."

"No, you don't." Bitterness oozed through those three small words, but he didn't attempt to justify or explain his actions. He acted as if it would be futile to even try, that she wouldn't believe him no matter what.

He was seasoned, all right.

Pulling the washcloth away, she studied the size of the red streak to determine how badly she'd been cut. Her injury wasn't life-threatening, but it stung. "How long were you really in?"

He guided the cloth back to her neck. "Fourteen years."

A lot more than six.… "How old are you?"

"Thirty-two."

Four years younger than she was. "That means you went in when you were…eighteen."

"Like I told you before."

"So it wasn't *all* lies."

"Not all of it."

He'd spent nearly half his life in prison. The tragedy of that didn't escape her. Neither did the fact that he'd gone in as an innocent young man, wrongly accused, and been shaped into a killer. How was that for proof that the penal system wasn't working?

Her skirt had bunched up around her thighs. She smoothed it down, but he didn't seem to notice. "Why did Wallace say you worked for Department 6?"

"He used them on another investigation, and he knew they were mostly retired military with some trained civilians. He figured it would make a believable background. I certainly don't look like a regular cop."

"No." She had to clear her throat to boost the volume of her voice. "But…I still don't understand. Why all the lies?"

His thigh muscles contracted as he crouched in front of her. He had so much physical strength—but that wasn't the only thing that made him intimidating. Anger, determination, even resentment, rolled off him like sweat. And, come Tuesday, she was going to be responsible for his safety and the safety of those she put him in contact with.…

He was answering her question. Yanking her gaze from his thighs, she struggled to pay closer attention.

"We're trying to protect the only family I have left."

"Your mother?"

"I don't claim her."

"Then your sister."

He chucked the envelope onto the desk. "Yes."

"Why? What do you need to protect her from?"

"From the gang I joined when I was inside. When they realize I'm walking away, they're going to make sure I pay, and if they can't get to me, they'll kill her, maybe even her children."

"So you're debriefing." Debriefing meant disassociating and divulging everything he knew about the gang to which he'd belonged. It also meant agreeing to testify.

"Not exactly. I have nothing to say about The Crew. I'm merely trading my services for a new identity—for myself and my sister."

"You're using what you learned about gangs by being a member of one to infiltrate the Hells Fury?" Where he had no loyalties.

"Basically."

She searched for the knife he'd held to her throat and saw it lying in the corner of the room. "But…Wallace doesn't trust me? Or Fischer? He felt he couldn't confide in us?"

"Trust entails a certain amount of…risk. I don't take risks. Unless I have to," he added begrudgingly.

"So you insisted on a new identity."

"That's right."

Apparently they cared so much about his request, and felt so beholden to him for endangering his life, they'd slapped together a "résumé" that hadn't even fooled her. Nice of them… "So what makes you think you can be successful?"

"The Crew isn't that different than the Hells Fury. I can get in."

Peyton's head was starting to hurt as badly as her ankle. It was the stress. And she hadn't eaten since breakfast. Sometimes she just got too busy. "Prison gangs are racially based. Does that mean you're a supremacist, a *racist?*"

"I'm a *survivalist*." The wryness in his voice told her as much as his words that it'd been a practical decision. Joining a gang often had nothing to do with believing in the ideology. It was about having protection when you needed it, about living to see the next day in a racially charged environment where survival would be nearly impossible without allies. In prison, you either conquered or were conquered.

She knew which side a man like Virgil would choose to be on. He'd conquer or die trying.

He, more than anyone, would know the stakes involved in what they had planned. And yet he was going back inside—as an informant. He couldn't possibly put himself in a more untenable position.

Then Peyton remembered the letters she'd found in his bag and the suspicion his sister had conveyed about being watched and everything became a little clearer. The Department of Corrections had found a man they could bend to their will because he had someone he hoped to protect. If he managed to gather the information necessary to bring down the Hells Fury, he and his sister would get new identities—for real—which would also give him a clean slate. Apparently they hadn't charged him for whatever he'd done on the inside. Maybe they couldn't; maybe they didn't have the evidence they needed for a conviction. But they were still holding it over his head.

And if he didn't succeed? What would it matter? He wasn't a police officer with a family and a community behind him who'd demand action and answers in response to his murder. He was just another gangbanger, and they could prove it. That made him expendable.

"You can't get what you want by informing on The Crew?"

"No. I won't give up any member of The Crew."

"You still feel certain…loyalties?"

"I honor my word. It's that simple."

"How do you know you won't find friends—people you won't want to rat out—in the Hells Fury?"

"Because I don't need a friend. What I need is a fresh start."

"So you're working against the Hells Fury instead as…some kind of compromise?"

"Exactly. From the way they're growing, and the control they're exerting, they're just as big a threat as The Crew. And I haven't given *them* my word—on anything. They're fair game."

So…he'd be a fraudulent gang member—a "buster"—when it came to the Hells Fury. But that was just as dangerous as snitching on his own gang. Maybe more dangerous because he'd be locked up with the men on whom he was informing and they'd feel very little loyalty to one so new.

Peyton cringed at the memory of what the Hells Fury had done to Edward Garraza, the last brother they'd suspected of turning "traitor." A corrections officer had found him in the laundry with his toes and fingers cut off and his eyes plucked out.

"That can be hazardous to your health," she said.

His eyebrows slid up. "Since when did anybody care about that?"

He knew the score. That was partly what bothered her about Virgil Skinner. Keen intelligence showed in his eyes, in his bearing. At a minimum, he was smarter than the average gang member, many of whom had little or no education. He'd likely been swept up by events he couldn't control, and they'd carried him fourteen years down a path he never would've chosen. Which hardly seemed fair. No more so than being forced to make the sacrifice he was now making as a result.

Peyton climbed carefully to her feet. Her ankle hurt, but she hadn't twisted it so badly that she couldn't stand. It would be fine in a few days. "Why were you incarcerated in a federal institution?"

"Because I was prosecuted federally." He grimaced. "Tougher sentencing laws. Otherwise, maybe I would've met you sooner, since I'm from L.A."

The return address on the letter from his sister had indicated Colorado Springs. "But your sister's in Colorado?"

"That's right. She left L.A. to be able to visit me on a regular basis."

"She sounds nice. I hope the government's putting her in the Witness Protection Program immediately." Because he was right. If he left The Crew, they'd put out a hit and "torpedo"—send someone to shoot—his loved ones. The fact that they were watching Laurel so overtly meant they were trying to scare her—and keep Virgil mindful of his allegiances and his duty to support them in their criminal activities. Those could include murdering someone, charging taxes for drug deals going down on what they considered *their* turf or robbing a bank.

"They're going to move her soon. Now I just need to do my part."

Which wouldn't be easy and it might even be impossible. "Blood in, blood out," she murmured. No wonder he'd reacted the way he had when she'd said that before. He knew the meaning of those words far better than she could've imagined.

A bitter smile curved his lips. "Blood in, blood out."

Peyton felt such sadness for the dreams his sister had expressed in her letter. *We're going to live the most boring, safest lives in the whole world,* she'd written, and just the opposite was true.

"Do you think your mother had anything to do with the murder of her husband?"

"I'd bet my life on it."

That explained why he hadn't opened her letters. "A pretty unequivocal response. What makes you think—"

"And that's all I'll say on the subject," he interrupted.

Peyton could see why he might not be eager to discuss it. She didn't need to know any more, anyway. She'd already figured out what she deemed important.

After their little tussle, her hair was too messy to walk outside and risk running into Michelle. Pulling out the elastic, she shook it loose so she could redo it. "You're not the luckiest man in the world, are you?"

He leaned against the wall and watched her from beneath half-lowered eyelids. "No. But I haven't done myself any favors, either."

At least he accepted responsibility for his actions.

"So where do we go from here?" he asked. "Are you planning to march over to Wallace's room and try to blow up this deal? Because you won't succeed. The department isn't going to back off. They have me right where they want me, and they're going to take full advantage of it."

The more she complained and raised hell, the less chance Skinner would have of keeping a lid on what he was doing. She felt it was safer to say nothing. For now, anyway.

"No. I'm not even going to tell him I know." She limped into the bathroom, tossed the bloody cloth in the sink and examined the cut on her neck in the mirror. "Whether or not you tell him is up to you, since you're the one putting your life on the line. But I want you to understand one thing."

When he came to the doorway, he blocked it and she instantly felt trapped. "What's that?"

Her injury was just a nick, nothing serious. "Fischer has put me in charge of this operation, so...you'd better play nice."

"Which means...?"

"No games. You trust me, tell me everything as soon as you possibly can, and I'll work to protect you."

"Why'd Fischer put you in charge?"

Using her fingers to groom her long hair into some semblance of order, she created another knot at her nape. "It's what he does when he encounters anything too... volatile."

"You got stuck with the assignment no one else wanted."

"Basically."

"I feel sorry for you."

Sarcasm. "I won't apologize for caring about my job." Taking another look at the cut on her neck, she dabbed at the fresh blood. "Just know that, for the time being, I'm the only friend you've got."

His gaze slid down her body. Either he'd noticed she was favoring her ankle and wondering if she was seriously hurt, or he was trying to intimidate her by reminding her that she was, after all, no match for his strength. "How friendly do we want to be?"

She rolled her eyes at the suggestiveness in his voice. Then she turned on the faucet and dampened a clean washcloth so she could remove the blood from her suit before it stained. "You nearly slit my throat. That's hardly an aphrodisiac."

"You broke into my motel room. There are people who might see that as…somewhat Freudian."

"Which gives you an excuse to come on to me?"

He lifted his large hands. "Hey, I'm just playing my part, right? Isn't that what you'd expect from a guy who's been without a woman for fourteen years?"

She studied him in the mirror. "'Without a woman' doesn't necessarily mean you haven't been sexually active."

"I've never had sex with a man, if that's what you're implying. But you're not going to bed with me, so what does it matter?"

After hanging the cloth on the towel bar, she turned to face him. "If you knew that already, why'd you ask?" she said, but she could guess easily enough. He wasn't used to being around a woman, let alone working with one, not since he'd been incarcerated, and this was his way of establishing some boundaries between them. After more than a decade of being forced to adhere to strict rules governing every interaction, he was probably uncomfortable with so much freedom. She understood the psychology, but still found the behavior fascinating.

"I asked so you could quit pretending," he replied.

"Excuse me? Pretending what?"

"To look at me like a human being. I'm garbage, right? A beautiful woman like you, someone with a normal life and so much…*promise,* has no interest in gutter trash like me. I'm nothing to you."

"Fortunately, I don't know *exactly* what you've done. And I don't want to know. Since we'll be working together, I'd rather not let that form the basis of my opinion."

"Hiding from my history won't change who and what I am."

He was the one pointing that out? That said a lot about him, evoked a certain amount of respect, however grudging. "What's the problem, *Simeon?* Afraid I'll expect you to act like an honorable man?"

"Honorable?" He chuckled under his breath. "I'm not worried about that. Just making a few things clear."

"Well, there's no need to draw such a solid line between us."

"Because you're not likely to forget who and what I am?"

"Because you're not interested in me in the first place."

He leaned his shoulder against the door frame. "Why do you say that?"

"You don't like authority figures."

Reaching around her, he grabbed the cloth. Then his chest came within an inch of her breasts as he wiped the cut on her neck. She could tell he expected her to flinch. He was trying to prove she *wasn't* really willing to treat him like any other man, despite her words.

But she didn't jerk away, and that seemed to surprise him. Judging by the expression on his face, it also piqued his interest.

"Tell me how I'm not interested in you again?" he murmured.

"Stop testing me. I work with convicts every day. I won't spook just because you stand close."

Strong emotion flashed in his eyes as he took hold of her arm. "Maybe you should be more frightened than you are," he said from between gritted teeth. "You have no idea what I'm capable of."

If he wanted to hurt her, he would've done it when

he held the knife. So why was he dead set on displaying himself in the worst possible light? To make sure she wouldn't give him a chance to prove he could be so much better?

She wanted to ask, but didn't. She knew she'd be stupid to tempt him into revealing how terrible he could be. Besides, she preferred to keep her distance. He made her uneasy. But not because she feared him. Just the opposite, in fact. She saw something decent and worthy in him regardless of all he'd been through, all he'd said and done—which was dangerous in its own right. Feeling empathy or anything else for a man caught in this type of no-win situation could only lead to heartbreak.

"Next time you proposition someone, you might show some tenderness," she said, and stared at his fingers, which were still wrapped tightly around her arm.

"Some women like it rough," he said, but he let go simply because she'd indicated she wanted him to, and that made her smile. He was what she thought he was—essentially a good man.

"You can't always play it safe," she responded.

"Play it safe?" he echoed.

She removed her high heels so she could walk without stressing her ankle and squeezed past him. "Someday you might actually want to feel something that goes beyond the physical."

He didn't follow her. "That won't be any day soon."

Considering what he had to face in the coming weeks, that day might *never* come. But she didn't see any reason to state the obvious. "Get some sleep," she said, but then she spotted the groceries and remembered that he'd used them to prop open the door.

Hesitating, she turned back. "How'd you figure out I was here before you even entered the room?"

"I pay attention to detail," he said, and this time when his gaze dropped to her legs, she got the impression he wanted her to know he was enjoying the view.

4

Peyton Adams had done much more than break into his motel room; she'd blindsided him. The raw, jagged emotions she inspired—desire, regret, frustration, sadness and hope—slammed into one another as if there wasn't room inside Virgil to hold them all. There probably wasn't, not with the hate, anger and resentment already simmering in his heart.

You can't always play it safe.... Someday you might actually want to feel something that goes beyond the physical, she'd said. But she didn't understand. After what he'd been through, it would be a *relief* to limit his experiences to tangible, concrete exchanges.

Anything more than that fed the yearning he felt for all the comforts and experiences a normal man would crave, and that was his greatest enemy. Anything more brought up the "what could have beens" and the "if onlys" and the "whys" that burned in his gut. Anything more made his existence unbearable.

The only way to survive in his world, at least without going mad, was to stop *wanting.* Wanting made him weak.

Dropping onto the bed, he covered his eyes with one arm while trying to regain the calm, cool, decisive control that had taken him this far. Getting out of prison after so long and facing all the changes that required had been a lot harder than he'd anticipated. The opportunity to *finally* touch, taste, feel, smell and see the outside world had made him greedy. He wanted to grab what he could, experience as much real living as possible before it was too late. And finding a beautiful woman in his room, especially one who knew what he was and didn't seem to be afraid, only heightened that desperate urge.

But he wouldn't think about Peyton anymore. It didn't matter how pretty she was. Who was she to him? No one. Just a woman—a woman he'd be a fool to even *like*. He couldn't afford distractions, hopes or disappointments. Only if he managed to do the impossible would his sister and her children have a chance at the life they deserved, and he wanted that for Laurel, Mia and Jake more than all the things he wanted for himself.

Lifting his arm, he eyed the phone, wishing he could call Laurel. He knew she had to be upset, even frantic with worry, and that made him agitated, too. But Wallace was right. He couldn't put her mind at ease. Not yet. When she'd arrived at the prison to get him, she would've been told that someone else had picked him up and that was all she could know until Wallace had her safely tucked away, with a new identity, somewhere else in the country.

Just a few more days, he told himself. As soon as Wallace called to say she was in protective custody, he'd explain.

The relief he felt then would have to carry him through the months ahead....

The Ford Fusion was back. Laurel spotted it in the pale yellow light of the streetlamp near her neighbor's house, and the nagging anxiety she'd experienced so often of late began to churn in her stomach. The acidic burn suggested her ulcer was coming back. The doctor had warned her that could happen. He'd insisted she relax, calm down. But how could she calm down when her brother was missing? When she was being watched, even followed, by two men she'd never seen before? She had children to protect.

Were these strangers somehow involved in Virgil's disappearance? She'd thought that collecting her brother from prison would be the easiest part of the past fourteen years. But it hadn't gone as planned. When she'd arrived, he'd already left, and no one seemed to know where he was.

Had he slipped away because he knew these men would be waiting for him? *Were* they waiting for him? What else could they want? They'd started coming by around the time she'd first learned he'd be exonerated.

If only she'd hear from him.

Fearing he might be dead, she struggled to hold back the tears that seemed to burn behind her eyes all the time now. She and Virgil had been through too much for his life to end so soon. They deserved the chance to recover what they could of the years they'd lost.

Forever conscious of the car across the street, she returned her attention to the window. She needed to call the police again. Yesterday they'd sent out a patrol unit. The officer had run the men off and warned them not to return, yet here they were. They didn't frighten easily.

Maybe they'd be arrested this time.

She'd just pulled her cell phone out of her pocket when a noise from behind caused her to whirl around. A man of about twenty-seven stood in her living room.

He'd shaved his head, although a small patch of hair grew from his chin. He wore baggy jeans and an over-large T-shirt that hung on his muscular body and even his face was tattooed. His physical appearance was frightening enough; the gun he held in his right hand made him downright terrifying.

"Throw your phone over here." He motioned with the muzzle.

If she did as he asked, she wouldn't be able to summon help. But if she didn't, he'd kill her and the noise would wake Mia and Jake.

She imagined them stumbling from their beds to find her dead on the floor, and tossed it away, hoping she'd be able to placate him. "Who are you?" she whispered.

Only five foot nine or so, the intruder seemed almost as wide as he did tall. A gold tooth flashed when he talked, but his eyes had no sparkle. They reminded her of shark eyes—dark, flat and dull. "I'll ask the questions. Where is he?"

Her heart pushed the blood through her body at a dizzying pace. "Who?"

"Skin."

She prayed he'd keep his voice down. "Who's Skin? I don't know anyone by that name."

"Virgil Skinner. You know *that* name, don't you?"

That he believed Virgil to be alive gave her a glimmer of hope. It meant this man, whoever he was, hadn't killed him, and neither had those people outside on the street—whoever *they* were.

"Where is he?" he demanded again.

"I have no clue."

"He better not be dropping the flag."

She didn't know how to respond to that, wasn't even sure what it meant. "Excuse me?"

"I don't want to jack you up. I'll blow you away if I have to, though, so you might want to work with me."

He was high or drunk or both. She could tell by the way he kept twitching. His eyes darted between her and the door as if he expected the cops to come charging through at any moment.

Assuming he'd fire before he left, she covered her mouth to stifle the sound of her fear. "I'm trying," she whispered through her fingers. "I just...don't understand."

"That's why, if I have to kill you, I'm going to carve Skin's eyes out and serve them to him on a platter. Tell him that."

Oh, God... "I *c-can't* tell him. I don't know where he is. I swear it."

The lightning bolts that served as his eyebrows shot together. "What if I don't believe you?"

That was the million-dollar question—and she'd never been more frightened to learn an answer. "It's the truth. I went to p-pick him up last week at the—" her tongue felt thick and unwieldy as she forced it to form words "—at the prison, but he n-never came out."

"He must've called, told you not to worry," he prodded.

Tears spilled over her lashes as she shook her head.

"You're telling me you haven't heard from him?"

"I'm afraid he's d-dead." Her voice caught on a sob.

The man studied her for a second and finally lowered the gun. "Go ahead and cry, Laurel, because if he's on the run he might as well be dead."

The burning in her stomach grew worse. "He's been exonerated. Why would he run?"

"You don't need to know that. You just need to know this—if you hear from him, tell him Ink stopped by lookin' for him. Tell him he's got one more chance. He calls Pretty Boy by noon tomorrow, anything…unpleasant can still be avoided. If not, you'll all die."

"Mommy?"

Laurel's breath lodged in her throat. Mia stood at the entrance to the room, rubbing her eyes and yawning. "Who are *you?*" she asked, wrinkling her nose as if she didn't like what she saw.

Grinning at her reaction, the intruder showed her his gold tooth, then waved her forward with his gun.

"No, Mia!" Laurel cried. But it was no use. He reached out and grabbed her before she could back away. Then he put the gun to her head.

"Are you tellin' me the truth? Huh? Are you still gonna say you don't know where your brother is? Because I'll shoot her. You know I will."

Laurel's lungs pumped like pistons but she couldn't seem to suck in the oxygen she needed. "N-no!" she gasped, fighting just to speak. "I d-don't know! Please!"

Her veracity must've shown through her terror, because he released Mia. He shoved her away so hard she fell, but at least he didn't shoot her.

"*Now* I believe you," he said with a laugh. Then he saluted her and went out the way he must've come in.

By the time Laurel scooped up her daughter and managed to stop shaking enough to dial 9-1-1, he was long gone. So was the car across the street. The officer who arrived fifteen minutes later found the imprint of a man's boot in her plants at the back door, but that was it.

* * *

Peyton normally loved Saturdays—and tried to enjoy this one. Since she was off work, she rambled around the house a bit, did some reading, cleaned out the fridge, caught up on correspondence she'd brought home from the prison and iced her injured ankle, which was still a little swollen. But she couldn't concentrate. All she could think about was Virgil Skinner, who was in the worst situation she could imagine, or soon would be. Picturing him sitting over at the Redwood Inn with a small quantity of clothing, a few prized letters from his sister (not to mention the less-prized letters from what sounded like a terrible mother) and a steak knife bothered her. He'd already suffered so much. What else would he have to endure?

She didn't like the idea of someone being wrongfully imprisoned for any length of time, let alone fourteen years. It didn't seem fair that he couldn't walk away and try to forget. But if she expressed that sentiment to Warden Fischer or even Wallace, she knew how they'd respond. They hated people like her, who still felt compassion. Believing she was weak or misguided made it easier to cope with the difficult decisions they had to confront almost daily, helped justify their callousness. But she didn't care what they said. Was it so bad to be worried about the safety and survival of a fellow human being? People weren't pawns....

And yet she understood the need, on occasion, to use them as such. Police and prison officials had to have some way of fighting the gang problem. Recent estimates suggested seventy percent of the prison population was affiliated with a gang. They couldn't allow the Hells Fury to gain any more power than they already possessed. If the "good guys" didn't do *something*,

something like this, how else would the HF be stopped? Getting convictions required information, and there weren't a lot of gang members who'd talk. They knew what would happen if they did.

Propping her foot on the couch, Peyton surfed through several channels on TV, but nothing held her interest. So she tossed the remote aside and grabbed her cell phone instead.

"Redwood Inn." It was Michelle. Peyton recognized her voice.

"Hey, it's me. You're still there? I thought you'd be off."

"My assistant manager called in sick. But I bet he's fine. He wasn't happy that I scheduled him, said he had a lot to do around the house. I think this is his way of getting back at me."

"Sorry, kiddo."

"Lee has the kids today, too. I could've had a few hours to myself for a change. But I'll live. What's going on with you? I tried to reach you last night but you didn't answer."

"I twisted my ankle, so I took some painkillers and went to bed." She'd actually gone back to the prison, pulled the arrest history of every inmate she suspected of being a member of the Hells Fury and made notes she hoped would be helpful to Virgil and the investigation. But she couldn't tell Michelle that.

"How'd you hurt your ankle?"

Peyton's mind flashed to that moment when Virgil had hauled her out of his shower. "Climbing the stairs to my front door."

"Those stairs are so steep," Michelle complained. "They're dangerous."

But they provided an incredible view of the sea.

Peyton loved her small, cabinlike home, and the deck was her favorite part of it. "They're fine as long as you watch where you're going."

"Are you on crutches?"

"Not quite."

"So will you be coming to dinner?"

"Dinner's still on?"

"Of course."

"What did Jodie and Kim say?"

"Jodie's fighting with her ex and doesn't feel she can leave the kids. But Kim's coming."

Peyton wanted to say she'd go. But she couldn't take the time, not when she only had three days to prepare Virgil. She got the impression that Wallace planned to toss him inside and let him learn it all from the ground up, but she felt Virgil's stint at Pelican Bay could be shortened if she gave him a crash course on who was who inside the Hells Fury and what to expect from them. Now that she was in charge of the investigation, at least the on-site part, she had every reason to make sure it ran smoothly, and that was what she intended to do. Skinner wouldn't be killed on *her* watch.

"I wish I could, but I should stay off my ankle. I'm behind at the prison, anyway, and had to bring some paperwork home with me."

"You work too hard, you know?"

"That's what it takes."

"Come on, I can't believe you're bailing out."

Knowing how much Michelle counted on the escape their evenings provided, Peyton felt a twinge of guilt. But she wouldn't be good company. Not tonight. She was too distracted, too caught up in what would be happening at the prison on Tuesday. "I'm sorry."

"Okay. We'll miss you, but—" Michelle sighed "—I guess it's not a big deal."

"Have fun."

"We will. Someone just walked in. I have to go."

"Wait—will you put me through to Rick Wallace's room?"

"Mr. Wallace is gone." Michelle sounded surprised.

Wincing, Peyton lowered her foot to the carpet. "He left? Already?"

"You thought he'd stay for the weekend?"

"He told me he might."

"Nope. Checked out this morning. But he said he'd see me in a few days, if that helps."

Peyton remembered the groceries Virgil had brought into his room last night. Maybe Wallace had left, but Virgil was still around. "Fine. Try room fifteen instead."

"You got it."

There was a click and the phone began to ring.

After five rings, Peyton expected her call to transfer to an automated message service, but then she heard a gruff hello.

"Hey," she said.

A moment of silence ensued. "Is this my new *friend?*" he asked at length.

"Your new…work associate for lack of a better term. But don't pretend you can't use a friend. What are you doing?"

"Just got out of the shower."

Although she tried to banish the image, she pictured him standing at the nightstand in a towel—or maybe nothing at all. "You slept in?"

"Went hiking."

Leaning her head back against the sofa, she stared

up at her wood-plank ceiling, stained a beautiful ma-
hogany color, and the fan that hung from one of the raf-
ters. "How do you like the area?"

"I've never seen anything like it."

"It's magnificent, isn't it?" Peyton smiled as she
imagined Virgil experiencing the redwoods for the first
time. "What are your plans for this afternoon?"

"I've got a TV."

He'd probably had a TV in prison and would again,
as long as he behaved himself. "Get dressed. I'm coming
to get you."

"Because…?" He sounded genuinely confused.

"We've got work to do."

"Chief Deputy Adams—"

"Yes?"

"It'd be better if you just…let me do my thing."

She toyed with the ends of her hair. "Why's that, Mr.
Skinner?"

"There's no reason for you to invest in what's going
to happen."

Leaning forward, she smoothed the area rug that covered this part of the hardwood floor. "There is if it's
happening at my prison."

"But what I'm doing…it isn't really under your ju-
risdiction. I thought you understood that. The meeting
at the library…it was just Wallace's attempt to be diplomatic. A courtesy."

"I realize the department's calling the shots on this,
but I'm responsible for you while you're at Pelican Bay."
Getting up, she hobbled toward her bedroom, which
wasn't easy to reach with a swollen ankle. It was at the
bottom of a narrow, winding staircase, like a cabin one
might find on a boat. "Besides, *you're* investing in it,

aren't you?" she said. Did he truly think he should do it alone?

"*I* have a compelling reason."

"Making sure an undercover operative for the Department of Corrections doesn't get killed is *my* compelling reason. From Tuesday on, I'll be responsible for you. I'm sorry if you've got a problem with that, but I plan to do my job."

He cursed under his breath. "You shouldn't be working at a prison."

Tired of hearing that comment, in one form or another, from almost everyone she met—*You work at a prison? I didn't know they hired women like you. The guys must* love *you*—Peyton injected irritation into her voice. "Why not?"

He didn't back off. "You already know the answer to that question."

Clinging to the handrail, she took each stair with caution so she wouldn't tumble down. "Because I'm a woman?"

"Because you're a constant reminder of everything a convict's missing."

"Really? Is that *all* I do?"

"All that matters."

Convicts lived in such a male world, one filled with so much testosterone, they often lost a certain…modern sensibility. Peyton was used to it. But that didn't mean she liked the discrimination it bred. "Quit with all the sexist bullshit."

"It's the truth—from someone who knows. You don't think half the men in that prison are fantasizing about you when they close their eyes?"

Stopping at the foot of the stairs, she decided to hit back. "Is that what *you* dreamed about last night?"

When he laughed softly, she knew he wasn't going to deny it. She also realized she was allowing the conversation to drift into dangerous territory, and tried to reel it back in. "Anyway, last I checked, you weren't in personnel. So until you take over the country and do away with the Equal Rights Amendment, spare me your opinions on hiring women."

"I'm not talking about *all* women."

"Oh, so you're not a complete jerk. You'd only refuse the ones you deemed too young or attractive or interesting or...whatever? And how, exactly, would you implement such standards, Mr. Skinner? Who would get to determine which female was too good-looking and which wasn't? Because if a job is open to one woman, it's open to all women. Beauty is subjective."

"Your beauty isn't."

As angry as he'd made her, she was also perversely flattered. She wanted him to find her attractive, because she found him to be one of the handsomest men she'd ever seen. "I'll take that as a compliment," she said. "So are you interested in getting out of the motel today or not?"

She'd left him nowhere to go with the argument he'd started—she suspected purposely—and he seemed to realize it quickly enough. "What do you have planned?"

She moved into her bedroom and began searching through her closet, trying to decide what to wear. "An educational seminar."

"There's only one problem."

"What's that?"

"We can't be seen together."

"I've got that covered. When I get there, I'll call your room and let the phone ring once. Come around the block. I'll be waiting in a white Volvo SUV."

She removed the sweats she'd been wearing. "And, Virgil?"

"What?"

"Bring the hat and glasses. Leave the knife at the motel."

"Sorry," he said. "The knife goes where I do. It's not much, but…it's all I've got."

She supposed he could've lied to her and brought it anyway. "Fine, but just so you know, I have plenty of steak knives. If someone attacks you, feel free to use one of mine."

"You're taking me to your *house?*"

Finding the jeans she wanted, she held the phone between her shoulder and ear while putting them on. "Do you know of a better place?"

"Yeah. *Here.*"

"No. The manager's a good friend."

This distracted him. "Is that how you broke into my room? I should sue."

Peyton couldn't help smiling at the grumble in his voice. "I got the worst of it. Anyway, I think you have bigger problems to worry about. And she didn't *give* me the key. I stole it."

"Do you still have it?"

"You're afraid I might come back?"

He hesitated. "Would you want me to have a key to *your* room?"

Part of her actually wanted to say yes, which was why her voice grew solemn. "I took it back. I said I found it on the floor at a restaurant, and she thought one of the maids accidentally carried it off the premises." Fortunately, Michelle had been more exasperated than angry so Peyton didn't have to feel bad for getting a maid in trouble. It would've been difficult to place blame, anyway. The smocks were used interchangeably.

"She fell for that?"

"Completely."

"I should rat you out."

"If only you could show your face."

"No one would have to see you come here. We could sneak you in," he said.

"No. If Michelle saw us, she'd ask all kinds of questions." Especially if she got a good look at him. "And we can't go to a restaurant. I'm too familiar to the community, since so many people work at the prison. We'd definitely attract attention."

"That's your logic for taking me home?"

She pulled a sweater from its hanger. "That's it."

"Peyton—"

His use of her first name took her off guard. Both the inmates and staff at the prison called her Chief Deputy Adams, as he'd done only moments ago. "What?"

"There are people who want me dead. You read that letter, you know what they're doing to my sister. If they've found me, if they're watching me, they could follow us—"

"They haven't found you."

"How do you know?"

Deciding to wear her hair down for a change, she ran a brush through it. "Because you'd already be dead."

His silence implied that he agreed, but he hadn't given up arguing with her. "There *is* one other thing."

"What's that?"

"I was just released from prison, remember?"

"I'm not likely to forget."

"It doesn't bother you—make you afraid?"

"According to what I've been told, you were innocent."

"That doesn't mean I *remained* innocent. You're the one who suggested I've become...warped."

She remembered the comment she'd made in the meeting. "Have you ever raped or killed a woman, Virgil?" she asked.

"No."

"Would you if you had the chance?"

"I had the chance yesterday, didn't I?"

She set her brush on the vanity. "Exactly."

His voice deepened. "But I'd be lying if I said I didn't want you."

The flutter in her stomach surprised her even more than his unexpected admission. She'd been propositioned by a lot of inmates in her day. She'd reacted with annoyance, revulsion, fear, sometimes amusement, but she'd never felt breathtaking excitement. She couldn't imagine why she'd feel it now, except that it'd been a long time for her, too. Maybe not fourteen years, but two or three. And since Crescent City offered so little in the way of romantic possibility, the future didn't seem very promising.

"What you want is a woman, any woman," she said. "That's hardly flattering."

"Maybe not *any* woman," he responded.

She grinned at the wry note in his voice. "Humor, from an intense guy like you?"

"When everything's a matter of life and death you tend to get serious very fast."

"I understand. I'm serious, too, about bringing down the Hells Fury. That means we need to get to work— and I can't show you pictures over the phone. I guess we could rent a motel room in a different city, where we wouldn't have to worry about being spotted, but I don't see how that would be an improvement. If we're going to be alone it might as well be here."

"As long as you know not to trust me too much, we'll be fine."

"Correct me if I'm wrong, but you just said you wouldn't hurt me. At least, I think that's what you meant."

"I won't hurt you. But if you give me the opportunity to do the opposite, I'm taking it."

Oh, God… He thought he was putting her on notice, scaring her off. He probably figured that if he destroyed any chance he had before they were even together, he wouldn't get his hopes up. But, in reality, he was offering her some of the thrills that'd been so conspicuously missing from her life. "Then I'll be careful to keep my signals clear."

"That's all I ask."

Now she was worried, but more because of how she might react to him than how he might react to her. "See you in a few minutes."

5

Virgil was fairly certain that what he stood to lose outweighed what he stood to gain. Driving himself crazy wanting what he couldn't have had never seemed wise. While in prison, he'd watched other men torture themselves over missing this or that and he made a point of not being so stupid. But he was only human. And, as the chief deputy warden led him up the stairs to her front door, moving slowly because of her ankle, her ass was right at eye level. He couldn't help admiring it. He'd been seventeen when he'd had his last sexual encounter—with the girl he took to the homecoming dance. They'd dated a few weeks, lost their virginity to each other, continued to experiment for a month or so and that was the extent of it. It probably hadn't been the best sex in the world, but he would've had no experience at all if not for that short period. Three months later he'd been arrested.

Her name was Carrie. He'd dreamed of her soft thighs and breasts a lot since then, but as he aged those dreams had become so old and tired they were as ineffectual as a threadbare shirt. They certainly weren't as stimulating as a flesh-and-blood woman, especially a woman who looked like Peyton Adams.…

As soon as they reached an elevated deck from which

he could see the Pacific Ocean, he circumvented her so he could focus on something that didn't make him instantly hard. Like the barbecue, the picnic table, the trees towering all around or the wind chimes that hung from the eaves and tinkled in the breeze.

"This is nice." He noted the rhythmic wash of the waves. The ocean sounded even closer than it was. "Peaceful."

"I like it."

The house behind him had a wall of windows. He was eager to look in, but only because he wanted to learn more about this woman who seemed so out of place in the prison system.

Once he'd acknowledged the reason for his interest, he knew he'd be a fool to feed his curiosity. He crossed to the banister instead of letting her lead him directly inside. There was no point in getting to know her. Even if he ended up liking her, she'd never feel the same way. He was an ex-con. The fact that he'd been wrongly imprisoned was irrelevant. He'd lost the most important years of his life, the years during which most other men built a foundation that allowed them to support a family. Other than the few classes he'd taken while incarcerated, he had no college education, no career—just a lot of experiences guaranteed to keep him up at night.

It'd be easier, smarter, *better,* to immediately rule out what his body insisted might be attainable.

"How long have you lived here?" he asked.

"Since I started at Pelican Bay six months ago."

"So Crescent City is pretty new to you."

"Yeah."

"Where did you come from?"

She approached the banister at the other end. "I grew

up in Sacramento, where I worked at Folsom Prison for fifteen years."

"Do you have family in Sacramento?"

Hugging herself to ward off the cold advancing with the fog, she kicked a pinecone off the deck. "Some. An aunt and a few cousins."

Quit asking her questions. None of it matters.

And yet he wanted to know. "Any siblings?"

"I was an only child."

He closed his eyes, breathed in the scent of the forest. "Where are your parents?"

To keep the wind from whipping her hair into her face, she anchored it behind her ears. "They're both dead."

The sadness in her voice undermined his resolve. "I'm sorry."

"Things happen." For a moment, she seemed lost in her memories. Standing still, staring out to sea, she reminded him of the female figurehead on an old wooden sailing ship. Beautiful, lonely but serene. A bare-breasted woman was supposed to shame nature and calm the seas. He'd read that somewhere. He'd also read that a live female on board was considered bad luck.

He felt as if he'd just discovered a stowaway on his own vessel. Would Peyton prove to be a blessing or a curse?

Maybe seeing her bare-breasted would help him decide....

"How'd you lose them?" he asked when she didn't elaborate.

"My mother had ovarian cancer. She went into remission for quite a while, over twenty-five years, but... it came back in the end. She died twenty-nine months ago."

She counted by months, not years. The pain was still fresh.

Zipping his sweatshirt, he sat on the picnic table. He'd left the hat and glasses he'd worn from the motel in Peyton's car. There was no need for them out here. She didn't have neighbors. "And your father?"

"Died in prison."

Virgil walked over to her. "Your father was a *convict?*"

"He spent five years behind bars."

"What for?"

She continued to fight the wind. "It's a long story."

In other words, she didn't want to get into it. "How'd he die?"

Her gaze remained anchored on the horizon. "How do most people die in prison?"

"Someone shanked him?"

A slight nod confirmed it.

Virgil wanted to touch her, to comfort her, if he could, but he didn't know how. Except for what he'd said to his sister in his letters, he hadn't had much experience with tenderness, not in fourteen years. And, as an eighteen-year-old boy who'd had only one rather tentative sexual relationship, a less than reliable mother and four step-fathers, he hadn't had the best example. "How old was he?"

"Thirty-one."

A year younger than he was. She'd lost him early. "That's too soon to die," he said, but he'd seen it, plenty of times.

"He was a good man."

A convict who was also a good man? Virgil didn't believe there was any way to be both. He'd tried. But Peyton's belief in her father gave him hope that, accurately or not, his sister might be able to remember him in the same light. "Is your dad the reason you went into corrections?"

Peyton offered him a fleeting smile. "That, and I thought I could make a difference."

Holding his breath for fear she'd think he was coming on to her, he covered her hand with his. "Maybe you are," he said, then forced himself to let go and turn away. "I guess we'd better get started, huh?"

"This is Buzz Criven." Peyton slid the picture onto her dining table.

Instead of sitting next to her, Virgil had chosen the seat across from her. Ever since he'd touched her, briefly, while they were out on the deck, he'd been careful to keep his distance, so careful that he stepped wide just to avoid brushing up against her.

Peyton told herself she should be glad of his caution. He was showing her respect. But the way he behaved had the opposite effect. His reluctance made her crave physical contact, if only to see how he might react to it.

Lifting the picture, Virgil studied its subject. "Rosenburg mentioned him in the meeting yesterday. He's getting out soon."

"But he'll be inside for the next thirty days. I'm thinking it might be smart to make him your cell mate. Maybe, since he's a short-timer, he'll be more prone to recruit you right away, to help you along, to talk about his activities, that sort of thing."

"He has power inside?"

"Some. Like the Nuestra Family, the Hells Fury have modeled their organization after the military. Buzz would be considered a captain."

He put down the picture. "Who's the general?"

"We believe it's Detric Whitehead. We've kept him in the SHU for the past ten years, trying to curb his activities, but somehow he manages to get his orders wherever he needs them to go. This man—" she pulled out another picture "—Weston Jager, or Westy as they call him, is pretty far up the chain of command. He's in gen pop, so you'll meet him when you go in. If it wasn't Whitehead who put out the hit on Judge Garcia, it could've been Weston."

Virgil rubbed his chin with the knuckles of his left hand. "These guys are skinheads?"

"The Hells Fury are actually a hybrid—part racist skinhead, part street gang and part prison gang. In recent years, they haven't been as worried about their supremacist ideology as making a profit from their illegal activities. Without strong leadership—and the opposition posed by the Nuestra Family, which unifies them—I would've expected them to divide into two camps, the way Public Enemy Number 1 did years ago, with the true supremacists on one side and the crime-for-profit supporters on the other. But…that hasn't happened. Whitehead keeps them tough and focused."

"Are there any PEN1 in Pelican Bay?"

He hadn't met her eyes since they sat down, and that bothered Peyton. She didn't know why. Maybe it wounded her ego that he could ignore her so easily. "There were, but that was a few years ago. For the most part, the Hells Fury have absorbed them, as well as all the other smaller white gangs."

He thumbed through the photographs and stats she'd collected on the known members of the Hells Fury. "Their activities are mostly drug-related?"

"They don't limit themselves. They're involved in

drugs, yes, but also assault, murder, attempted murder, prostitution. Even white-collar crimes like fraud, counterfeiting and identity theft."

"Where'd they get their start?"

"In the Texas prison system, in the mid-eighties. They've grown considerably since then."

He looked up, caught her eye, but glanced away. "I can't believe they've been able to gain such a stronghold here, of all places. According to Wallace, everyone knows this is Nuestra Family turf."

"That's partly why the Fury have grown so fast. Operation Black Widow made a sizable dent in the NF. Since then, anyone hoping to keep them in check, anyone who needs protection from them, joins the Hells Fury."

"And what's the NF's reaction to having another gang rise up to challenge them?"

She noticed a scar on his forearm. Long and jagged, it looked as if it came from a defensive wound. She couldn't help wondering when he'd received it. "They're not happy, as you might've guessed. These two gangs are always on the brink of war. We keep them apart as much as possible, but that doesn't stop the violence. It seems as if someone from one side or the other is getting assaulted practically every day."

He spread out the profiles of the most important members. "What's the death toll?"

"This year?" She sat back. "A handful, which is damn good considering there've been nearly a hundred assaults since January. It says a lot about our medical staff."

His gaze met hers again and finally held. She wasn't sure what he was thinking, but suddenly the men in the Hells Fury felt no more dangerous than their pictures. She was mesmerized by Virgil's eyes. The pain inside them was unsettling and yet it seemed at home there, even added an unfathomable quality that made him all the more mysterious.

Clearing his throat, he went back to the materials strewn in front of him. "What symbols do they use?"

"As with most supremacist groups, you'll see the swastika. More specific to the Hells Fury is the *HF* or a pitchfork." She fished out a picture of a man with *HF* inked in fancy script on his pectoral muscle. "The letters *fury* might be tattooed on the knuckles or across the back." She showed him that, too. "But their most consistent symbol seems to be a satanic *S* that looks more like a lightning bolt." She couldn't find the photograph she'd planned to bring of the *S,* so she drew it. "I heard one man say it represents the Destroyer."

"It's also the weapon of Zeus," he muttered.

"You're familiar with Greek mythology?"

"I've checked out a few books."

"Not what I'd expect you to read."

"I didn't have a lot of choices. If it was available to me, I read it. What're their colors?"

"Orange and black. Ghoulish, huh?"

It was growing late, and Peyton was getting hungry. She could send these files to the motel with Virgil, let him finish on his own. Or she could invite him to dinner and they could continue together.

She didn't see any reason either of them had to spend the evening alone. "I was going to make some pesto pasta tonight. Would you like to join me?"

She expected an eager response. What man who'd been eating prison rations for fourteen years would turn down a home-cooked meal? A chance to eat all he wanted? But he surprised her by rising to his feet. "No, thank you. I should get back."

He'd spoken as curtly as though he had an important meeting, but she knew he had nothing scheduled. Nothing until Tuesday. "You're choosing whatever you've got in that grocery bag Wallace provided over my garlic bread and pasta?"

"There's no need for you to put yourself out."

"Cooking for two isn't much different than cooking for one."

"I'm fine. Thank you."

Refusing to lower his guard, he'd started already walking toward the door.

"Are you trying to prove a point, Virgil?"

He stopped. "What point would that be?"

"That you don't need anyone? That you don't want anyone? That you're fine on your own?"

"I *am* fine on my own."

She pursed her lips. "A simple dinner might threaten that? Threaten *you?*"

"Maybe. In any case, I've already warned you."

"Warned me." To be careful of the signals she sent him, he meant. She shook her head and laughed. "To a man who's been in prison for so long I probably look pretty good. But don't let that confuse you. *Any* woman would look good."

"Quit acting as if I can't tell the difference between you and someone else, as if I have no taste, no ability to discriminate. I've had other opportunities. Once I established who and what I was, the only person who ever came on to me in prison was a woman. She would've spread her legs at the snap of my fingers."

Peyton pushed her chair back. "How's that, if you were housed in a male prison?"

He shoved his hands into his pockets. "She wasn't a prisoner."

"So it was a staff member?"

"A C.O."

"Did you take what she offered?"

"Hell, no. She got off on passing herself around to as many men as she could, mostly prison scum. Who knew what diseases she carried? I could never be desperate enough to sleep with her."

It wasn't difficult to imagine a female C.O. taking an interest in a man like Virgil Skinner. He'd caught *her* eye, hadn't he? "Who was she?"

"Doesn't matter."

"Staff having sex with inmates, that's against the law."

He shrugged. "Don't look at me to rat her out."

"Why not? It doesn't sound as if you're too impressed with her."

"No, but I live and let live, unless I don't have any other choice."

Prison rules. What remained of the values, for lack of a better word, he'd developed on the inside. Peyton recognized it easily. "So, if you don't need me, why are you running?"

As he chuckled under his breath, his eyes ranged over her. "What do you care if I leave? Aren't there enough other men to admire you in Crescent City?"

"Stop it. I'm not trying to— Never mind." Getting up, she scooped her car keys off the table. "If you'd rather go back to the motel and eat alone, fine. I'll take you." She made a move to stalk past him, but he caught her by the arm, and when she looked up, into his face, she realized he wasn't nearly as unimpassioned as he'd implied.

"You know what I want from you," he said. "If you want it, too, you don't have to make me dinner. You don't have to view me as an equal. Hell, you don't have to do anything at all. Just ask."

He was determined to maintain the upper hand, at least when it came to any personal interaction between them. But what he didn't understand was that she couldn't justify such a shallow encounter. She'd never had one before; no way was she starting now. She wasn't angling for a thrill, although there *was* that aspect. For some reason, she craved a real encounter with this man, something as honest as meeting him had been unexpected. "I'm not interested in a quick tumble."

"Who said it had to be quick?" He sent her a lazy grin. "We've got all weekend. And despite my past, I'm clean, if that's what you're worried about. They tested me before my release."

"Good to know, but I can't accept your terms. Although not for the reasons you think."

Two grooves formed between his eyebrows. "Then what do you want from me?"

His close proximity made her feel…odd, breathless, aroused. "Does it have to be so complicated? I want you to stay for dinner. That's what I invited you to do, isn't it?"

When his eyes lowered to her chest, she knew he was anything but unaffected. "If I stay, it won't be for dinner."

Their eyes met again and she saw what she hadn't been able to see before—vulnerability, maybe even confusion, beneath a shield of male pride. That he hated feeling as needy as he did made her want to touch him and be touched by him all the more, if only to provide him with some comfort after what he'd been through. But she couldn't respond to the emotions he evoked in her. She barely knew him. And even though the CDCR hadn't officially hired him, she *was* working with him. As a woman trying to be successful in a man's world, a woman who already had the odds stacked against her, she'd always been careful to maintain her professionalism. So why, out of nowhere, was she tempted to indulge herself? With *him?*

"Then I'm taking you home," she said.

"That's what I thought." He responded with a careless smile, but that didn't fool her. He was disappointed.

And so was she.

6

"They also use a pendulum," Peyton said as she drove. She was trying to get her mind back on business, back on the reason they'd gotten together in the first place, and stem the rush of hormones.

Virgil glanced over at her. "What are you talking about?"

He hadn't spoken since they'd left. Gripping the steering wheel tighter, she drew a deep breath. "The Hells Fury. You asked me about their symbols. I didn't mention the pendulum, but they use that symbol, too. I'm guessing it represents the passage of time, the steady march toward death."

"Like in 'The Pit and the Pendulum.'"

"You're familiar with it?"

Leaning his head back on the seat, he closed his eyes. "'I was sick—sick unto death with that long agony; and when they at length unbound me, and I was permitted to sit, I felt that my senses were leaving me. The sentence—the dread sentence of death—was the last of distinct accentuation which reached my ears.'"

"I'll take that as a yes." The fact that he'd memorized the opening suggested he'd identified with the story in some way, but that came as no surprise, considering his situation. She turned down the radio. "That must've been uplifting material to read in prison."

"I read it in high school, too."

"So…you graduated?"

"I would have if my murder trial hadn't interfered," he said dryly. "I was in my senior year when they carted me off."

Because it'd grown dark, Peyton had less fear that they might be spotted by someone who would later point a finger at "Simeon" and blow his cover. His glasses sat in his hat on the console between them. She was glad he could relax, but the quiet of the countryside they passed on their way into town made her feel as if they were just as isolated as they'd been at her house. "Did you get your G.E.D.?"

"Not for several years. I was too busy trying to get myself D.O.A."

"D.O.A. is dead on arrival."

"I know."

She slowed for a traffic light. "You were suicidal?"

"Not in the classic sense. Just self-destructive, fatalistic. I was looking for trouble, and I expected the trouble I found to be the kind that would put me out of my misery for good."

"It wouldn't be easy to deal with being falsely imprisoned."

"I was consumed by rage." His hand curled into a fist. Obviously the rage hadn't left him. But if his mother and uncle had betrayed him as badly as it appeared, he had every right to feel angry. Peyton couldn't think of anything that would cut a child more deeply. "Is that when you joined The Crew?"

"Yes."

The light turned green, so she gave her SUV some

gas. "Why'd you pick them and not some other gang, like the Aryan Brotherhood?"

He stared out the window, toward the whitecaps of the sea. "The Crew is an offshoot of the AB. My first cellie was a member."

"Thanks to the Hells Fury, The Crew doesn't have much of a presence at Pelican Bay."

"I know. You're lucky. They're worse than all the other gangs."

"I doubt any gang could be worse than the Hells Fury. They live for violence. But I'll take your word for it." Peyton found herself less than eager to reach the motel. "So did your cellie actively recruit you?"

"He didn't have to. He knew, once I'd had enough ass whippings, I'd come to him. And he was right. After a few months, I was burning to take out a few of the bastards who'd jacked me up. The Crew seemed the perfect network to help me do that."

"The other inmates were giving you trouble?"

"That's a euphemism if ever I heard one," he said with a laugh. "I was getting the shit kicked out of me almost every day by big gorilla-like guys who were at least a decade older and had been pumping iron for years." His lips slanted in a bitter smile, as if he was picturing it all. "That was quite a rude awakening after attending a nice suburban high school. But it wasn't until one guy—a deviant called Bruiser—tried to make a bitch out of me that I actually joined The Crew."

Making a "bitch" or a "punk" out of him was basically turning him into a sex slave. His youth and good looks would've made him particularly vulnerable to such "daddies," and every prison had them—men who used sex to punish or control. Peyton did her best to keep that type of behavior out of Pelican Bay. The entire staff did.

But she knew it went on despite their efforts. Too many inmates pretended that whatever relationships they had were mutually agreeable. Reporting the abuse could get them maimed or killed, so they refused to take the risk, which made it very difficult to punish the offenders. Virgil was telling her that, at eighteen, he'd chosen to die fighting rather than become someone's "bitch" or "punk."

They'd arrived at the street where she had to let him out. "The 'blood out' thing didn't bother you?"

"I thought I was going to die either way. And I was getting used to blood, mine and everyone else's. Being able to fight was all there was to take pride in. Once I learned how, I decided to be the best, the one everyone else feared. I didn't think about the future. As far as I was concerned, I didn't have one." She stopped when she reached the corner and he opened his door. "I wish I'd considered what my actions would mean to Laurel. But I was so…in the moment. Venting my anger and taking revenge—that was all that mattered."

Now that he'd matured and calmed down, he'd do anything to change that; she could tell. But even if he could go back, she wasn't sure he'd be able to take a different path. Not with his temperament and determination. "You're still here, right? The Crew must've given you the protection you needed."

"They did at first. But after a while protection wasn't the point. My reputation was enough to keep me from being ambushed. It was the friendships I enjoyed. They were my only family for fourteen years. That's what I'll miss."

If he thought she'd be shocked to hear him speak kindly of men who belonged to a violent criminal organization, he was wrong. She knew why gangs formed, how close they could become. It wasn't always for nefarious reasons. Some poor souls simply had nothing else, nothing better, anyway. "What will they do when they realize you're out?"

"It'll be a hell of a lot worse than a B.O.S., if that's what you're thinking. I know too much."

"A B.O.S.?"

"Beat on sight. I've been gone almost a week. They're probably already on my trail."

Peyton let the car idle. "Some people don't understand how you can love someone who does terrible things. They don't understand the complexity of human nature, on both sides of a relationship like that."

"Most of the men in The Crew are the worst people I've ever known. I hated them then. I hate them now." He put on the hat and glasses, even though he was unlikely to run into anyone who'd be able to see him clearly enough to identify him later. "But there were a few others—" his voice changed, grew soft "—men I admired and considered my brothers."

And yet even these "brothers" would very likely kill him if they ever found him. Which meant he'd be betrayed by his family again.

He closed the door as if that was that, but she lowered the passenger's side window. "Virgil?"

When he turned back, she nearly told him that she'd seen contradictions like the one he'd mentioned and empathized with the conflict he must be feeling. But he didn't need her empathy. If she couldn't allow herself to be a closer friend—or whatever—to him, she'd only become another contradiction, one more person guaranteed to let him down.

"Never mind. I hope you enjoy your dinner."

He studied her for a moment. "It was nice just looking at you," he said.

Peyton waited for him to laugh or shrug or indicate in some other way that he wasn't quite sincere, but he didn't. She was pretty sure he'd paid her a legitimate compliment, no censure or challenge or sarcasm involved. But by the time she believed it, he was too far away for her to respond.

Shifting the transmission into gear, she drove off but kept one eye on her rearview mirror until she could no longer see him. "You're an interesting man, Virgil Skinner," she murmured. A small part of her—maybe even a big part—wished she could've been irresponsible enough to sleep with him.

But she hadn't become chief deputy warden by being irresponsible.

The last thing Rick Wallace wanted was to fly back to Colorado. Thanks to the long drive from Crescent City, he'd spent only a few hours with his wife and kids. But he needed to make sure Laurel Hodges and her children remained safe. If anything happened to her, Skinner would lose his motivation, and if Skinner lost his motivation, the whole operation would fall apart.

Mercedes, his wife, walked into the bedroom carrying a basketful of laundry and frowned when she saw him. "What are you doing in a suit?"

Having just showered and dressed, he straightened his tie. "I'm heading to the airport."

"What?" She dumped the laundry onto the bed. It used to be that she had all the housework done by the weekend, so she could devote her time to him, but that'd changed. Nowadays when he asked her about the state of the house, she said there wasn't much reason to keep

it perfect when she and the kids were the only ones who ever saw it. She said even when he *was* home he walked past them as if they were inanimate objects and not real people, always thinking about his work.

Hoping to finish getting ready before she could really lay into him, he slipped into the bathroom. He didn't like it when Mercedes was upset. That nasty edge to her voice ground on his nerves, making him wonder why he'd ever married her. If not for the kids, they probably would've split up years ago. But since they had children, that wasn't an option. Growing up, he'd suffered through the divorce of his own parents and had promised himself that he'd never make the mistakes they had. And he wouldn't. Especially considering the financial consequences....

"I'm sorry," he muttered, but he'd said it so many times it was an automatic response that no longer held any meaning for either of them.

"Today, when you said you left Crescent City because you missed us and wanted to be with us, I thought..."

He glanced at her in the mirror, saw her nostrils flare.

"Well, I assumed you were home for the rest of the weekend. And you *know* I thought that."

The last sentence dripped with accusation. In order to sidestep a major blowout, he decided to play dumb. "So? What are you getting at?"

"I'm wondering why you weren't courteous enough to disabuse me of that notion."

Because she would've started pouting and might've refused him sex.

"Rick?" Mercedes prompted when he didn't respond.

Here we go again.... "I didn't know I'd have to leave tonight."

It was easier to lie, but he'd been too obvious about it. The disappointment he'd created by setting her up for this reversal made her pounce.

"That's not true," she snapped, coming to the door.

He didn't bother arguing. "Sorry."

Ignoring his second empty apology, she blocked his path and he realized it hadn't been very smart to let her box him in. "Can't we have even a partial weekend as a family?" she asked.

"We had dinner. That was more than we would've had if I'd stayed in Crescent City."

"Dinner? You think I should be happy with one meal together in a whole week?"

"We had more than a meal."

She rolled her eyes at his meaningful grin. "You were home just long enough to lift my nightgown so you could get off, and now you're leaving."

He should've gone to the trouble of pleasuring her. Then maybe she wouldn't be acting like this. But he'd been so preoccupied.... "Better your nightgown than someone else's, right?" He chuckled as if he was joking, but the anger that flashed in her eyes told him he'd been made on that, too.

"What are you saying?"

He sobered. "I'm saying that at least I still come home for it." *Usually.* "That's something."

"It's not enough. Not anymore."

"Come on, Mercedes." He hung his head, implying that he felt bad, but he didn't. Not really. They fought so often, he'd grown numb. "Please?"

"Please, what? Please don't ask for anything? Please don't expect you to behave like a husband? Please don't demand that you do your part in our relationship or as the father of this family?"

Jerking his head up, he shot her a look that said he was tired of hearing the same old complaints. "I don't have time for this. I'm going to miss my plane."

She didn't move out of the way. "I want you to quit your job."

He gaped at her. "Are you kidding? How would we pay the bills?"

"You could find something else."

"Nothing that'll pay what I'm making now!"

"Then I'll go to work, too. I need to get out, anyway, make a change. I'd do anything to fix what's wrong. Our children need to see more of their father. *I* need…" She let her words dangle, probably because she knew how selfish they sounded. "I can't take the neglect, Rick."

"Neglect?" He grimaced. "If you want to get off and I'm not around, use a damn dildo. Maybe you need to grow up and start fulfilling yourself a little bit instead of relying on me."

"I'm not talking about sex!"

"Then what are you talking about? You think it's *my* fault we're having trouble? How do you know it's not you? Maybe you don't like that I have to work so much, but I don't like that you're so needy. It makes my skin crawl."

He actually shuddered. The minute that registered on her face, he wished he could take it back. It was the stress—the pressure he was under. Maybe Mercedes had gained some weight, and maybe she'd let herself go in other ways. He couldn't help finding her drab and worn compared to the women who caught his eye. Compared to Peyton, who particularly appealed to him. But he still loved her. Didn't he?

"I wasn't needy until I married you," she said. "You made me like this." He heard their youngest daughter come into the living room then, yelling "Daddy!" and Mercedes dropped her voice. "And sometimes I hate you for it."

"You *hate* me?"

He expected her to deny it. He'd taken her words out of context. She hadn't really said she hated *him*. But she didn't attempt to correct him; she stood there, glaring at him through those hazel eyes that seemed years older than when he'd looked into them last.

"Mercedes?" he prompted.

"I hate what you've turned me into," she finally declared.

The tears that streamed down her cheeks made it possible for him to breathe again. She didn't mean it. It wasn't as if she'd ever *leave* him. "We'll talk about it when I get back, okay? I promise. And…and maybe we'll get counseling." She'd been begging him to go to a therapist for more than a year. Maybe if he gave her that hope, she'd calm down and he'd be free to do what he had to do before dealing with his marriage.

"If we don't get help, we won't make it," she told him dully, and turned, like a tired old hag in her sloppy sweats, to do the laundry.

Rick knew he should put his arms around her, comfort her, tell her he still loved her and offer a sincere apology. He could see how she'd feel used. When they made love, he pretended she was someone else, someone more attractive. And lately that someone had been Peyton. Fantasizing about another woman wasn't the best thing for their relationship. He owed Mercedes more. But he couldn't bring himself to touch her right now. He kept seeing Peyton's bright eyes, beautiful face and perfect figure, and the contrast between them was just too great; he was losing all desire for his own wife.

Or maybe it was Mercedes's fault for not taking better care of herself. If she was more attractive, he'd want her—as long as she could stop acting like a bitch when he needed a little understanding.

Regardless, they'd have to solve their problems later. If he didn't make this flight, Laurel might not survive the night. Then he wouldn't have the option to quit; he'd be fired.

"Listen, I—I'll call you later, okay? I wouldn't go tonight if I had any choice, but…something big is going on at work. Something that came down from the governor himself. This isn't optional. It's flattering that they've chosen me to implement it. And I would've told you I had to leave except…I knew it would upset you and I didn't want to deal with the backlash. You can understand that, can't you? I'm so tired of fighting."

"You can't be any more tired of it than I am," she said.

"Daddy?" Ruby came to their bedroom. "You're leaving again?" she asked, and the disappointment in her voice and on her face so mirrored her mother's he could barely bring himself to swipe a kiss across her cheek.

"I'll be back soon, princess," he said, and went to tell his other daughter goodbye.

7

Peyton wanted to know more about the crime for which Virgil Skinner had lost fourteen years of his life. She also wanted to know more about his mother and his uncle and what they'd done to help or hurt him.

Figuring there had to be some details about him in the media, a piece on his exoneration if not the crime, she went online and began to search. Because he'd been incarcerated in Colorado, she first visited the website of the *Denver Post* and was pleasantly surprised to find an article dated two weeks ago.

> ### Convicted Murderer Exonerated
> ### After Fourteen Years
> Virgil Skinner, thirty-two, was only eighteen when he was convicted for the murder of his stepfather, Martin Crawley, who was forty-six at the time. Given a life sentence for shooting Crawley with Crawley's own gun, which was kept in the house, Skinner wasn't expected to see a parole board for thirty years.
>
> Enter Innocent America, an organization based in Los Angeles dedicated to freeing Americans wrongly convicted of crimes. "There are

other organizations dedicated to exonerating, almost exclusively through DNA testing, wrongly convicted individuals," said Lisa Higgleby, staff attorney for IA. "We're here for all the rest. Barring DNA proof, it's very difficult to get a conviction overturned, but a far greater percentage of people are faced with this type of case than one that can be cleared through the use of science." According to Higgleby, the primary causes of wrongful conviction include witness misidentification, an incompetent or inadequate defense, the use of jailhouse informants and prosecutorial/police misconduct or mistakes.

For Skinner, however, it was the testimony of the one person he should have been able to trust—his mother—that sealed his fate. "If not for the way my mother protected my uncle, and herself, my brother would not have gone to prison and lost such a big chunk of his life," said Laurel Hodges, Skinner's sister, a divorced mother of two who has fought diligently for her brother's freedom. It was Hodges who contacted Innocent America and convinced them to take a look at his case.

"Laurel's faith in her brother was unyielding. I absolutely couldn't tell her no," said Higgleby. "But this case would never have reached a happy resolution without Geraldine Lawson." Ex-wife to Skinner's uncle, Lawson came forward with information about the night Crawley was killed that caused police to reopen the investigation.

Gary Lawson has since been charged with Martin Crawley's murder and is being held without bail in Los Angeles while awaiting trial. Skinner's own mother is suspected of asking her brother to carry out the murder, but no charges have yet been filed against her.

Comfortably dressed in sweats again now that she was back from taking Virgil to the motel, Peyton read the article twice, then searched the internet with *Ellen Crawley* and *Ellen Lawson,* in case she'd gone back to her maiden name, *Geraldine Lawson, Martin Crawley, Virgil Skinner,* even *Laurel Hodges* as keywords. But other than a short piece in the *L.A. Times* mentioning Ellen and Gary's implication in the fourteen-year-old shooting, she came up empty-handed. During regular business hours, she could probably get hold of someone in the federal system who might agree to run his prisoner ID number. But since he'd been released, that might not give her much. She already knew where he'd been incarcerated, at least at the end of his sentence, and for how long. What she wanted was the rest of Virgil's story....

Leaning back, she glanced at the clock. Nearly nine. Not terribly late. She wondered if she'd be able to reach Wallace. She hadn't planned to tell him that she knew Bennett wasn't who she'd been told he was. But now that Rick had left Crescent City, maybe they could have a private conversation. She had Wallace's cell number in her electronic phonebook. He'd given it to her more than a month ago, when they'd met for dinner to discuss the growing gang problem. He hadn't suggested anything like what they were doing with Virgil, but she guessed he'd been thinking about developing Operation Inside even then.

She brought up his contact information while walking into the living room, where she could pace in front of the wall of windows that looked out onto the dark ocean.

He answered almost immediately. "Don't tell me something's wrong."

She realized what he must've thought, hearing from her so late and so unexpectedly. "No, nothing."

"Then what's up?"

"I need to talk to you."

"At nine o'clock on a Saturday night?"

"Sorry, but I'm glad you're available."

"I'm not…not really. I'm at the airport, waiting in the security line. You've got maybe ten minutes. So what's going on? Is it Bennett?"

"Don't you mean Skinner?"

He went silent. Then he said, "How'd you find out?"

Being purposely vague to avoid an outright lie, she kept it simple. "I did some research."

He didn't question her further. Was it because he knew he hadn't put any work into that sketchy bio? "Skinner's the one who wanted to use a false name," he explained. "I was just trying to accommodate him, for safety reasons."

His safety wasn't worth doing a better job?

"Otherwise, I would've told you."

She stared up at the stars, which seemed far brighter here on the coast than they ever had in Sacramento. "I see."

"Are you…upset?"

"No, but I do feel entitled to some answers."

Obviously relieved that she was taking his deception so well, he became less stressed and more congenial. "What do you want to know?"

"Why don't we start with this—why was he tried

in the federal system? Was it only because of tougher sentencing? Or was there more?"

"As far as I know, that was it."

As Virgil had indicated. "That was a consideration for an eighteen-year-old boy?"

"A kid who'd murdered his stepfather in cold blood. Or so they believed."

"It sucks to be wrong when you've thrown the book at someone, doesn't it?" She knew it wasn't Rick's mistake, but she couldn't help blaming him because she could tell he didn't really care what had happened to Skinner.

"Cut the sarcasm, Peyton. How about feeling sorry for the victim and the victim's family for a change?"

The typical security announcement came over the PA in the background. She waited before continuing, so he'd be able to hear her. "Why do I have to choose between them? In this case, the 'perpetrator' was as much a victim as anyone else."

"Yeah, well, we're not social workers. And if it makes you feel any better, the fact that Skinner was charged federally could turn out to be very fortunate for him."

Only Wallace could shrug off so many years of someone else's pain. "How can *any* of this turn out to be fortunate for him?"

"When it's over, he'll stand to receive $700,000."

Rick was referring to the Justice for All Act, which provided settlements to those proven to be falsely imprisoned. But $700,000, as large as it sounded in a lump sum, wasn't a lot. Time served was one thing; the experiences Virgil would never forget and how they'd shape his future was another.

"If he'd stayed in the state system, he'd get quite a bit less," Wallace was saying. "At one hundred bucks a day, California pays more than most states. But that's still a

couple hundred thousand less than what he should get
from the feds."

He'll stand *to receive...* Should *get from the feds...*
Wallace wasn't making any promises, and Peyton knew
why. A lot could happen before that sum was ever paid.
Even without all the complications of Virgil's current
predicament, even if he'd never acted out in prison, there
was a possibility the money would never come. The government could appeal it, force him to fight an extended
legal battle. She'd seen compensation funds tied up for
years. "That's supposed to make me feel better?"

"Oh, shit. You drive me nuts, you know that?"

She wanted to ask, *Why? Because I have a conscience?* but knew that would be going too far. Instead,
she tried to remain on topic. "I'm just saying Skinner's
sister could probably use the money."

"You're saying it to the wrong person. I have no
power in the federal system. You know that."

"Whoever negotiated this deal—the director or the
governor—might be able to grease the way."

"Maybe they're not too inclined to stick their necks
out. He went in an innocent boy, but he didn't play nice
with others while he was inside. He's a loose cannon.
The only reason he's remotely pliable is because of his
sister."

The stab of defensiveness she felt further irritated
Peyton. "Wouldn't *you* be bitter?"

"Hey, I'm touched by your desire to champion the
underdog, but I don't have time for it today. I'm the fa-
cilitator, not the decision maker."

He had the ear of the decision maker, though. He just
didn't care.

"I'll talk to you later," he said.

"Wait! What'd he do?" Peyton made it a habit not to

read C-files, if she could help it. Knowing what a convict had done made it more difficult not to judge or fear. But she was too curious about Skinner; she had to ask.

"Our boy was pretty handy with a blade."

Her mind flashed to the knife Skinner had held to her throat. She wondered if Wallace even knew he had it, and guessed not. "He killed another inmate?"

"Two to be precise."

"Two?" she repeated, shocked in spite of her expectations.

"You ask Skinner, he'll tell you it was self-defense. They jumped him. But there are witnesses who claim otherwise."

Thinking of what she'd just read and had already known—that jailhouse witnesses were one of the reasons a certain percentage of innocent people were locked up—she had to ask, *"Reliable* witnesses?"

"Depends on who you talk to. But he shouldn't have had a shank to begin with."

Maybe he didn't feel safe. Maybe he knew he might get jumped…. "Was he ever charged?"

"No."

Then the D.A. didn't have enough evidence for a conviction. But she was willing to bet they'd threatened to bring charges. "Someone offered him a deal?"

"If he turned informant and agreed to take down the Hells Fury, the past would stay in the past."

"I see. And if he didn't, he'd face the possibility of another trial."

"That's right. Even if he hired a good attorney and was able to avoid more prison time, he'd still have a record—"

"If they managed to convict him."

He ignored her interruption. "And little hope of

compensation for time already served. That's no place to start a new life."

No, it wasn't. She headed to the kitchen, washed an apple and took it into the living room. "He's not doing this for the compensation money, you know."

"Like I said, his sister's the only reason he's tractable."

"Is she in real danger?"

"As real as it gets. Skinner could help the authorities get convictions against most of The Crew. But he won't do it. He has this…twisted sense of honor. Says he won't break his word or stab his friends in the back for any reason."

Skinner's "twisted" honor seemed more admirable than what she'd seen of Wallace's, but she choked back what she wanted to say and took advantage of the chance to gather more information.

"Then why are they worried?"

"They can't trust that. They have to assume the worst. And they don't let anyone walk away."

"What I don't get is this—how did the CDCR get hold of him?"

"We had a problem. The feds had a solution. We don't work in a vacuum."

Security asked him for his ID. She waited for him to deal with that before continuing. "So…what's happening here is a favor, a loaner, from the feds?"

"It's basically a way for *everyone* to get what they want."

The noise level surrounding him grew louder; she guessed he'd reached the X-ray machines. "At Skinner's expense."

"No, not at his expense. He's getting something out of it, too."

"A promise to forget what he might or might not have done in prison. And maybe some money."

"I don't know what all is involved. The secretary didn't give me details. Anything else? Because I've got to go. I'll miss my flight if I don't hustle."

"Just one more thing."

"What's that?"

A fresh surge of jostling came across the line. "Fischer."

"What about him?"

She threw the apple into the air and caught it. "He doesn't know Bennett isn't Bennett."

"Your point?"

"I'd like to keep it that way."

"Why?"

"For the same reason Skinner requested it in the first place. Safety. The fewer people who know his real name, the better off he'll be." And the better able *she'd* be to protect him.

"Go ahead and go around me," she heard him say, and imagined him stepping out of line. "Now that you know, I'm not sure that's the best way to proceed."

He was already thinking about how it might reflect on him if the truth surfaced later. Always looking out for himself.… "Weren't you the one talking about how easily word of this could leak? If the Hells Fury figure out that something suspicious is going on, even if there's no name associated with it, no specific target they can go after, they'll be defensive and more secretive than ever, which will only make his job harder."

"You're saying we can't trust *Fischer?*"

"I'm saying he'll tell Frank and Joe, and who knows how many they might confide in. Even if they share it with just their wives it could get around. You know what Crescent City is like. Shop talk. Everywhere. At Little League. At the hair salon. At the grocery store. I want to give Bennett—Skinner—what he was hoping to achieve by using a false identity to begin with, that's all."

"But if Fischer finds out and starts to raise hell…"

"He won't."

"Find out? Or raise hell?" he asked dryly.

Two squirrels zipped along her deck. "If he doesn't find out, he won't have any reason to raise hell."

Wallace told some other people to go around him. "Fine. Keep it to yourself if that's what you want," he said. "But if it comes out later that you knew all along and he gets mad because I didn't tell him, I'll explain that you were the one who decided not to pass on the information."

"Fine. Save your own ass," she said. "I wouldn't expect more from you." She'd never spoken to him like that before. The words had tumbled out before she could stop them.

He bristled just as she expected. "Welcome to the real world. You want to work in corrections you'll have stand on the front lines like the rest of us."

As if *he'd* ever been on the front lines. The son of a congressman, he'd gotten a leg up thanks to friends of Daddy's; he'd never actually worked in a prison. "I have no problem with that," she said. "Fischer put me in charge of this, anyway."

There was a slight pause as he digested what she'd told him, but he didn't respond to it. "You're a pain in the ass, you know that?" he said, and then he was gone.

8

It was going to be a long night. After spending a couple of hours at the water's edge, where he'd eaten a peanut butter and jelly sandwich while staring out to sea, Virgil returned to his motel room and settled in with the TV on and Peyton's files at hand. He figured he'd study until he was too tired to continue and, eventually, he might be able to sleep. He knew how to survive an endless night. He'd endured plenty of them in prison. Until he'd managed to establish himself in the pecking order, he'd been so terrified he'd scarcely dared close his eyes. Only by refusing to back down, even if he was getting his ass kicked, had he earned any respect.

If he could adapt to that environment, he could adapt to anything, couldn't he? One would think so. But all the coping skills he'd developed wouldn't transfer to this latest challenge. Getting out had filled him with too much hope. Hope that he'd be able to break the grip The Crew had on him. Hope that he could forget the past decade and a half and live a normal life. Hope that his sister would be safe, that she could raise her children in peace.

And that wasn't all he wanted. Not since meeting Peyton Adams. She'd entered his mind so many times since she'd dropped him off, it made him angry with himself and with her. All through dinner, such as it was, he'd been thinking about how soft her skin had looked—especially when she had her hair slicked back and was wearing that no-nonsense business suit—how tempting he found the curves beneath her tight-fitting sweater and those faded blue jeans, and how much he admired her basic decency. She wasn't like the other wardens and C.O.s he'd met. Some of them were good people, too. Eddie Glover had made a world of difference for him at Florence. But Peyton had a certain sensibility no one else possessed....

He craved more—of her time, her attention, *her*—but he knew that wouldn't be wise for either of them.

How had he let her get under his skin so quickly?

Maybe that wasn't *too* odd. Even Wallace found her attractive. He'd mentioned how pretty she was before they'd met her at the library, had joked about wanting to get in her pants. He'd obviously thought talking so crudely was the best way to relate to an ex-con, but Virgil hadn't been impressed.

The phone rang.

Hoping it was his sister, or Wallace calling with an update, he grabbed the handset. "Hello?"

"Is Hal Geribaldi there?"

"Who?"

"Hal."

Virgil racked his brain, trying to figure out if he recognized the voice. He didn't, but that brought little relief. "How did you get this number?"

"Isn't this the Redwood Inn? Room fourteen?"

"No."

"Sorry, man."

Virgil disconnected, then sat staring at the phone.

Was it really a wrong number? Or had someone used it to confirm that he was in the room?

He pictured the caller standing next to Pointblank Thompson, a man who'd gotten his nickname by shooting a cop at close range, or Pretty Boy McCready, who'd gotten the name from his good looks. Imagined this stranger, whoever he was, holding the phone so they could hear his voice. Imagined Pretty Boy, a former cell mate, nodding once to signify that they'd found him. And wondered if someone from The Crew would be knocking on his door.

Were they coming for him? Already?

It was possible. He'd been out five days and hadn't made contact. They had to assume trouble, had to have started searching; they'd grown nervous way back when his exoneration was only a possibility. That was when they'd begun tailing Laurel, just in case he decided to break away. They were afraid a "lifeboat," as they called an exoneration, might lure him into a legal life. They were also afraid of what he knew and what he'd tell.

But they didn't need to worry about what he'd say. So far Virgil had refused to snitch on anyone. He understood all the arguments for ratting out those he'd once considered friends. Because of their criminal activities, he'd be doing society a favor, et cetera. He didn't care. The authorities would have to find someone else to inform on The Crew. Although his former brothers would do their damnedest to take him out, his personal code of ethics wouldn't allow him to turn traitor.

He'd soon be providing intel on the Hells Fury, but he didn't view that in the same light. He hadn't made them any promises. Perhaps the distinction was a bit blurry, but as crazy as his rationale sometimes sounded, even to him, this was the only way he could save Laurel, get out of The Crew and be able to live with himself when it was all over.

If The Crew hurt Laurel, however, he'd forget about the delicate balance he was trying to achieve. Redemption wouldn't matter. Starting over wouldn't matter. His future wouldn't matter. He'd scrap all his good intentions and make their destruction his final mission.

His life had been a tug-of-war from the beginning, hadn't it? Thanks to his mother and uncle. Maybe he was never meant to escape what they'd done. Maybe, in the end, he'd become what other people had, for all these years, believed him to be. And maybe his actions would lead him straight back to prison, if he didn't get killed along the way. But at least if he went to prison a second time, he'd deserve to be locked up.

Climbing off the bed, he went to his duffel bag, pulled a slip of paper from the zippered pouch on one side and studied the phone number scrawled across it. Pretty Boy's number since he'd gotten out of prison. Virgil was tempted to call him, to tell him that as long as Laurel was okay he wouldn't nark on anyone. He could get Pretty Boy to buy it. But even if Pretty Boy managed to convince Horse and Shady, the man who was really calling the shots, the gang couldn't allow him to disrespect them by walking off unscathed.

Just in case they were scrambling and hadn't yet decided how to react to his sudden disappearance, Virgil dared not call. Doing so might make them move on Laurel more quickly than they otherwise would. He wanted to give Wallace as much time as possible to get her to a safe place.

With a sigh, he tossed the number on the desk and stepped over to the window, where he held the drapes so he could peer out.

Fog made it difficult to see the parking lot, but a car idled in front of the lobby, its headlights boring holes in the mist. That car seemed suspect. But everything seemed suspect. He'd been living without trust for too long, had lost the ability to feel safe.

The phone rang again. Still leery, he stood to one side of the window as he answered. "'Lo?"

"Virgil?"

It was Peyton. Letting go of his breath, he sank onto the bed. "Yes?"

"You okay?"

He pictured that car, wondered if he had any reason to worry. "Fine, why?"

"I thought you'd be sleeping."

"You were trying to wake me up?"

"Since we've become friends, I knew you wouldn't care."

She was teasing, and now that she was at a safe distance, he welcomed the distraction. It relieved the tension inside him and gave him a chance to reassure himself that The Crew wasn't outside waiting. "Am I to assume you regret your earlier decision?" he asked.

"What earlier decision?"

"To take me back to the motel?"

"That was *your* decision. I would've been happy to feed you."

"I was more interested in dessert."

She ignored that comment. "I just spoke to Wallace."

His hand tightened on the phone. "Is Laurel okay?"

"He was getting on a plane and didn't mention Laurel. Should he have?"

"He's supposed to be taking care of her."

"Then that's where he's going. Trust me, he doesn't want to screw up. He has big plans for his future."

The comments Wallace had made about Peyton rose in his mind again. *Wait till you see her. She is* so *hot. What I wouldn't give for a piece of that.* "In more ways than one."

"What's that mean?"

"Nothing."

"You don't like Wallace?"

"Not particularly." He got up to check the window, saw the same car sitting in the parking lot. Surely it didn't take more than a few minutes to rent a room....

"Why not?"

"A lot of reasons. But I don't care who or what he is as long as he keeps his word. He *will* keep his word, won't he?"

She hesitated. "He...should."

"You don't sound too certain."

"I can't promise what's out of my control, Virgil."

"That's one of the reasons you're worried about this operation, isn't it? You know they don't expect me to come out of it alive."

No response.

"It's a pretty smart plan, really. If I get killed, they won't have to pay me the money they owe me. Easy way to save a large sum without risking one of their own people."

"I'm positive that's not true. No one's thinking any such thing. And even if they are, you'll get the money."

In other words, he'd live to see the day. He could tell she planned to ensure it. But he wasn't convinced she'd be able to make much of a difference. What went down in prison tended to happen very fast and not right under the nose of the warden or the chief deputy warden, either.

But he didn't say that. It felt good to have someone on his side. Somehow, he believed Peyton cared about his well-being, that she was sincere even though it would serve her better to look out for her own interests.

"I told Wallace, by the way," she said.

"Told him what?"

"That I'm aware of who you really are."

He checked the window again. Car still there. "Why'd you do that?"

"I wanted more information."

"On...?"

"You."

"Did you get it?"

"I think so."

"And now you know all my darkest secrets."

"I know the basics."

"Why are you telling me?"

"Because I initially said I'd keep it to myself. But I felt it was only fair to inform you that I'd changed my mind."

Footsteps sounded outside on the walkway—the footsteps of more than one person, moving fast. "We'll have to talk later," he said.

"Is something wrong?" She'd heard the tension in his voice, but he didn't explain. There was no time. Dropping the phone, he grabbed the knife he'd stolen from the restaurant. A steak knife wouldn't offer much protection, not from two men toting guns, but he could only use what he had.

Spine to the wall, he waited to see if whoever was coming would kick in the door.

9

What could've happened?

Peyton tried calling Skinner again—twice—only to get a busy signal. She wanted to keep calling until she could be reassured that all was well, but she was afraid Lena Stout, who was running the front desk, would recognize her voice and begin to wonder if something was wrong. In case she was worried for nothing, she didn't want to alert Lena or anyone else.

So…what should she do? She'd been concerned that Virgil might get hurt at Pelican Bay. She'd never seriously entertained the possibility that The Crew would find him *before* he could be incarcerated. *He'd* obviously been concerned about it, though. And he should know what they were capable of doing. He'd been one of them.

Is she in real danger? she'd asked Wallace about Virgil's sister.

As real as it gets. Because Skinner could help the authorities get convictions against most of The Crew.…

After putting on her tennis shoes, Peyton limped to her car on her injured ankle, which was improved but not perfect, and drove as fast as she could without causing an accident. She arrived at the motel in ten minutes instead of fifteen, but she knew it could already be too late.

Relying on the fog to cloak her identity from anyone looking out—fortunately, Lena was much less familiar with her than Michelle—she parked in the lot. Then she hurried to room fifteen.

The door was slightly ajar.

"Hello?" she breathed as she poked her head inside. The lights were on. So was the TV. A glance at the phone told her it was off the hook. It looked as if he'd aimed for the base but hadn't been watching to make sure the handset connected. Why? Clearly, he'd been distracted....

"Virgil?" Afraid she might find him crumpled on the floor between the beds, she crept forward. There was no body, no evidence of a scuffle. But she didn't think he'd planned on leaving, either. He'd gone through his bag—his clothes weren't as neatly folded as before—and tossed his sweatshirt over the chair.

It was cold and rainy out. Why hadn't he worn his sweatshirt? Also, some of the groceries from the sack Wallace had bought were spread out on the desk—peanut butter, jelly, a loaf of bread and some cookies. The files she'd given him lay on the bed.

Heart in her throat, she inched farther into the room. The bathroom door stood open. Would she find him murdered in the shower? That fear had her shaking by the time she reached it. Considering the company he'd kept in prison, nothing would be too gruesome to expect....

But the bathroom turned out to be empty. Did that mean he was safe? Or would his body be discovered in the forest or floating in the sea?

Hoping to catch Wallace before his plane could take off, she dug her phone out of her purse and was dashing from the room when someone came around the corner carrying an ice bucket and nearly knocked her to the floor.

When she realized it was Virgil and that he was fine, she threw her arms around his neck and pressed her forehead to his chest instead of stepping away, as she probably should have. "You're okay."

He didn't seem to know how to react, didn't put down the ice bucket and hold her, although she wanted him to. She could use the reassurance.

"You scared the shit out of me," she muttered into his clean-smelling T-shirt.

"Sorry." His lips grazed her temple as he spoke. She got the impression that was very much on purpose, although he wouldn't allow himself to actually put his arms around her.

Feeling awkward when he didn't make any other move, she let go. "Why'd you hang up on me?"

"I heard people approaching outside."

"And?"

He shrugged. "Two teenage boys and their mother hurrying through the rain so they could get to their room. That's all."

"You thought it was…someone else?"

"A guy called right before that, asking for Hal. It made me wonder."

Frowning, she took stock of his few belongings. She couldn't leave him here. No way would she be able to sleep. She didn't think he'd be able to sleep, either, not if he feared every footstep outside his door could be that of a man sent to shoot him. If she took him to her place, The Crew wouldn't have a prayer of finding him. Not unless her car was followed. But the drive to her house was a lonely one. She'd definitely notice any vehicle behind her.

"Get your stuff."

He'd just put down the ice bucket and was opening a Coke. "Am I going somewhere?"

"You're not staying here."

"Peyton, I appreciate this…mothering instinct of yours, but I don't need you to babysit me." He scowled as if she was being ridiculous, but she knew he was scared. If not for himself, then for his sister.

"I'm not *babysittting* you. I'm giving you a safe place to stay." What she felt was very different from what a mother would feel. As much as she knew she shouldn't let herself care about him, she couldn't help it. Probably because she was the only person who *did* seem to care.

He deserved more than that.…

"It's not wise for me to go home with you."

"I don't give a damn. Nothing is more important than your life. And I happen to feel you should get to enjoy the next two days without having to look over your shoulder all the time. We're talking about a short stint at my place. No big deal."

He poured the soda into a plastic cup with ice. "Wallace would never agree with this."

"You don't care what Wallace thinks, and neither do I."

"What if he decides it's irresponsible? What if he decides it's a good reason to go after your job?"

"He won't."

He offered her the Coke. When she refused, he took a drink himself. "He could."

"So we won't tell him," she said with a shrug.

"Peyton, no." Setting his soda aside, he retrieved the television remote.

Why wouldn't he let her do this for him? Couldn't he accept a good turn? Had it been so long since he'd received one? "Why not?" she demanded and took the remote away so he'd have to focus on her.

She'd expected him to enumerate the many practical reasons or at least grab for the remote, but he didn't. "I don't want to care about you," he murmured.

His honesty caused a flutter in her stomach the likes of which she hadn't felt since she was a teenager. They weren't touching, but the moment felt so intimate— because he'd just given her a glimpse of his soul.

Drawing a deep breath, she cleared her throat. Maybe they had no business sleeping in the same house, but she couldn't leave him here, *wouldn't* leave him here. And there wasn't another place she could take him, not where they'd go unnoticed. It was nearly midnight. "If caring about me is the worst thing that happens while you're here, I'll feel you got off easy," she said. "Are you going to get your duffel? Or shall I?"

He didn't move. "You'll be sorry. We'll *both* be sorry."

"No, we won't. I refuse to believe that."

A truck pulled up outside, one with a big diesel engine. When he glanced over his shoulder as if he wanted to check the window, she knew she had him. "See what I mean? You'll be able to sleep at my house. There will be good food, a beautiful view, serenity."

"What about you?" he asked.

"I'll be fine. I won't be on pins and needles wondering if it was a mistake to leave you here. I won't have to feel responsible if something happens because I didn't try hard enough to stop it. And, like I said, it's only for two days."

He blew out a sigh. "Your plan is to bring me back here before Wallace comes for me? To keep this little arrangement to ourselves?"

Doing so would risk her job, but she'd rather risk her job than a person's life. If working in a prison had taught her anything, it was the necessity of feeling valued by someone. She wanted to give Virgil that. "I'll drop you off at a safe distance on my way to work bright and early Tuesday morning. Transfers don't generally arrive until later in the day. We're a bit of a drive from anywhere else, in case you haven't noticed." She laughed to create the illusion that what she was doing was fine, that it wasn't a major breach of protocol. "You'll be on your own while you're waiting for him, but it'll be daytime and you'll only have to be on guard for hours instead of days."

She could see the exhaustion in his face. *Let go,* she silently urged. *Let me help you.*

"Fine. Go get in the car. We can't be seen leaving together."

"No, we should grab everything and go. It's so late and foggy, no one will see us. Michelle's not even working tonight."

"But someone else is. Do as I say. I'll meet you around the block."

Their eyes connected in a silent contest of wills, but she didn't keep arguing. He wouldn't relent on this. "I'll be waiting," she said, and ducked out into the rain.

"There's no way." Pretty Boy paced the length of the threadbare carpet in the dirtbag motel they'd rented not far from Laurel's house.

Neither Pointblank nor Ink, both of whom were with

him, appreciated his dissenting voice. Their expressions reflected that, as did Pointblank's tone. "What did you say?"

This wasn't a position Pretty Boy had ever wanted to find himself in. If it'd been anyone else, anyone besides Skin, he would've kept his damn mouth shut. He didn't like the politics of The Crew, just the drinking, the joyriding, the easy money and even easier women, the camaraderie. But they were talking about Virgil Skinner—*Skin*. There wasn't another man alive Pretty Boy respected more than his old cellie. If not for Skin, he would've been dead ages ago. The man could fight better than anyone and had never hesitated when it came to getting his back.

"I said there's no way." Now that he'd started this, he had to speak his mind, so he stopped in front of Ink with enough attitude to make it clear that he was ready to take this to blows, if necessary. He had no problem with a good brawl. Life in The Crew was filled with busted lips, black eyes, even knife wounds. Sometimes it felt like one glorious round of ultimate fighting. But he preferred to be facing a rival when he let loose, not a brother. "Skin would *never* flip."

At this, Pointblank propped the pillows behind his head with one hand while holding a beer in the other, and crossed his ankles. Obviously he didn't give a rat's ass that he had his boots on the bed. Pretty Boy didn't, either, but he noticed. And sometimes he noticed a few other things that made him feel just a little different from the men he'd joined.

"That's what you keep telling me, man," Pointblank said. "And I want to believe it. Skin's a tough dude. He's not someone I'd like to mess with. But if he's going to disrespect me, I don't have a choice. I'm responsible for keeping him in line. I got people to answer to."

"Skin wouldn't disrespect you." But if he disagreed with Pointblank's leadership, he might dispute it or simply walk away. *That* Pretty Boy wouldn't put past Skin because Skin lived life by his own rules and *he* didn't answer to anyone. His independence had created difficulties for him with The Crew before.

"So you've heard from him?" Pointblank taunted. "You can tell us where he is?"

Wearing his leather coat like a badge of honor, Pretty Boy shrugged to hide the discomfort in the pit of his stomach. Skin had already been gone a week, long enough to indicate that he didn't plan on coming back. But Pretty Boy couldn't give up hope. Not when it came to Virgil. "No. But…"

"What?" Pointblank demanded. "I'm supposed to cut this asshole extra slack just because he used to be your cellie and you know his mind and shit like that? Come on, the man got a lifeboat. That gives him a clean slate. And a clean slate can change the way you think about certain…affiliations." He tapped his skull before taking a pull of beer. "Skin knows too much. We can't let him forget who his friends are."

Pretty Boy ignored the sense of impending doom that'd crept over him the minute he'd been sent to Colorado to round up his old buddy. "I'm telling you he wouldn't rat us out. Maybe he'd disappear for good, but he wouldn't debrief."

"*Something's* going on," Ink piped up. "And we'd better get a handle on it. Watching his sister's place is a waste of time. He must think we're all pussies, that we won't really hurt her, because he hasn't even called the bitch. Hasn't even driven by to make sure she's okay.

What kind of asshole doesn't care about his own family, for chrissake?"

"He doesn't think *we're* pussies," Pretty Boy said. "He only thinks *you're* a pussy."

Pointblank nearly spewed beer across the bed, but Ink didn't take the joke quite so well. His face grew mottled, and he jammed a finger in Pretty Boy's direction. "I'll show him what a pussy I am when I gut his sister *and* her kids."

Pretty Boy had never hated Ink more. "You think that'll solve the problem? Killing the people he cares about?"

"It's better than sitting in front of her house for days on end, jacking off. That ain't gettin' us nowhere."

Ink was a bloodthirsty bastard who enjoyed abusing everyone and everything he touched. Pretty Boy had heard he maimed a couple of prostitutes before they left L.A. for Colorado. That was part of the reason upper management had given him this assignment. They wanted Ink out of the way until the flurry of interest surrounding that incident died down. His legendary cruelty gave him a degree of power in a group that prided itself on violence. But Ink had no loyalty, no honor, no *soul*. "You kill Skin's sister or harm those kids and you'll find him, all right. He'll come to you in the middle of the night and string you up by your balls. Then he'll pick off the rest of us." Pretty Boy stepped closer so he could make a point of staring down at the shorter man. "Starting World War III is hardly gonna improve our situation."

A flicker of fear danced in Ink's eyes, but he quickly masked it. Taking his gun from where he'd jammed it down his pants, he made a show of unloading and reloading the cartridge. "Just because you're scared of him don't mean I am."

Pretty Boy couldn't help wishing he'd blow his dick off. "I see him, I'll let him know how you feel."

"Enough with the bullshit," Pointblank said. "We're all going stir-crazy on this assignment. We want it to be over, and we want it to end well. But this…thing between you two—" he motioned to make it clear that he was talking about their mutual dislike "—it's not cool. We need to ignore our differences and finish the job so we can get the hell out of this dump." He tossed his beer bottle at the garbage can and hit the wall instead. When it shattered, a woman in the next room screamed that they should have some consideration, and Pretty Boy wondered what she'd think if she ever learned that Ink would probably kill a woman for less.

"Shut up, bitch!" Ink yelled back. Then there was silence.

Apparently she'd gotten the point. Or she was busy calling the manager. Either way, the interruption had been timely because it allowed them to refocus without either of them having to back down.

"So what do we do?" Pointblank asked. "Do we go back to Skin's sister's or not?"

Before they could answer, Pointblank's cell phone rang. "It's Horse," he said, checking the screen, and answered.

Pretty Boy walked to the window, parted the drapes and stared outside while listening to Pointblank's side of the conversation.

"She's there. She never goes anywhere but work.… She doesn't know anything, hasn't heard from him.…Ink went inside, confronted her. I don't think she's lying— he had a gun to her kid's head.…We'll do whatever you say, but…*What?* Who told you that?…*Shit!*" He threw down his phone.

They turned to look at him as he jumped to his feet, took his gun out of the drawer of the nightstand and began loading it.

"What's going on?" Ink asked.

"Skin's cut a deal with the feds."

Pretty Boy couldn't believe his ears. *"What?"*

"You heard me. Shady knows a woman inside the Federal Bureau of Prisons. He's had her doing some research. She says she doesn't know where Virgil Skinner is, but she heard his name mentioned in the hallway after a high-level meeting between the bureau and some guy called Rick Wallace from the California Department of Corrections. She claims a federal marshal attended one last week."

"That means someone's going into the Witness Protection Program." Ink's tone and his hatred stabbed at Pretty Boy.

"Skin?" Pretty Boy asked.

Pointblank shook his head. "No. A woman and two kids."

"Laurel." Virgil *was* trying to protect her. "But why didn't the feds act sooner?"

"Who knows? They're acting now. Word has it someone's coming for her."

"And?" Pretty Boy said.

Pointblank shoved his gun in his waistband and lowered his shirt. "We need to make sure she's dead before they can take her."

Pretty Boy's breath caught in his throat. "And the kids?"

"A rat's a rat," Ink muttered. "I say we kill them, too, and really make him pay."

Pretty Boy scrambled to find some way to stave off what was about to happen. "Wait! We kill them, Skin'll talk for sure. He'll tell 'em everything he knows. No one will be spared."

Ink started out of the room ahead of them. "He's talking, anyway, man. What don't you get about that?"

"But why would the CDC be involved? Something's up."

"Whatever it is, we don't have time to figure it out." Pointblank again.

Pretty Boy grabbed Pointblank's arm. "So you're going to kill three innocent people?"

Jerking away, Pointblank doubled his fist as though he was about to take a swing. "That's enough, do you hear? The feds don't spend the money to put people in the program unless they're getting something worth the expense. What does Skin have to offer except our heads?"

Pretty Boy had no answer to that, but he still couldn't believe it had come to this. Skin *wouldn't* rat them out.

Apparently willing to let their skirmish go, Pointblank stalked outside. "You coming or not?"

Was he? Pretty Boy wasn't sure he could go through with the slaughter. He'd killed other men, but never a defenseless woman. And he couldn't even imagine hurting a child.

But if he didn't fulfill orders, he'd soon be lying on the ground, bleeding out, himself.

"Yeah, I'm coming." He went outside and got in the car. But his heart was racing and his palms were sweat-

ing and he was deeply conscious of Ink's thirst for blood
as they tore out of the lot.

*What the hell, Skin? What am I supposed to do
now?*

10

Peyton didn't get it, Virgil thought. She had no idea that her kindness, her beauty, even the sanctuary of her house didn't help him. On the contrary, it gave him something fresh and memorable to miss when he went back inside come Tuesday. But he didn't expect her to understand. Someone who hadn't been through what he had couldn't grasp how necessary it was to remain aloof and detached. Having encounters like the ones they'd been having tempted him to soften. And he couldn't afford that. His first few days in prison would be rough—and make or break all the days after.

He should've refused to come here tonight, for that reason and others. But he hadn't. Instead of whiling away the hours at the motel, he was wandering around her house in the dark, hating the passage of every minute. Fatigue dragged at him, but he remained on his feet, studying what he could see of her pictures and furnishings—cataloging every detail while pretending he wasn't dying to slip inside her bedroom.

He'd have this night at her house and two others. Then his freedom would be stripped away from him yet again. But the memory of this place, of her, would fuel his dreams for days, weeks, months…who knew how long? Memories of the girl he'd known in high school had been a focal point for more than a decade, undoubtedly much longer than *she'd* been thinking about him.

The floor creaked behind him. Turning, he spotted a dark shadow—Peyton dressed in a T-shirt and sweat bottoms—at the entrance to the room. He'd left the lights off, been as quiet as possible. He wasn't sure what had awakened her.

"You realize it's three o'clock in the morning," she said.

His bare feet sank into the padded carpet of her office as he continued to walk around the room. He liked the feel of the heavy pile, the scent of lemon furniture polish that hung in the air. Her home was so warm and comfortable—the exact opposite of the concrete walls, floors and fixtures he'd become accustomed to. "Is it that late? I haven't been keeping track."

She came inside and snapped on a lamp. "Would you like a sleeping pill?"

Now that they could see each other clearly, he became ultraconscious of two facts. He wasn't wearing a shirt. And she wasn't wearing a bra.

Being constantly forced to strip for various searches had made him indifferent to his own nudity. But he would've liked to shield the scars and tattoos on his torso from her view. Prison tattoos weren't like other tattoos. For one, they didn't have the pretty colors. Securing the ink was too much of a problem. His had been done with various "rigs" constructed of tape recorder motors, a pen barrel and guitar string. The ink came from the carbon residue of burning plastic mixed with an aftershave solution. They were all blue or black and some of the symbols were standard jailhouse stuff. "No, thanks. I'll go grab a shirt—"

She raised a hand to stop him. "Don't bother. I've seen a man's chest before."

No doubt that was true. But he didn't want to be lumped in with the prison population and he couldn't imagine that she saw the proof of his history in a positive light.

"It might help you relax."

"What might help me relax?" Certainly not what he saw. That made it difficult to even *think*.

"A sleeping pill."

He forced himself to focus elsewhere—on her degree, which was framed and hanging on the wall, a wood carving of an owl that decorated a side table, the stack of work awaiting her attention on the desk. On anything except the soft mounds of flesh that acted like a high-powered magnet to his eyes and his hands. He cleared his throat. "I don't want to relax."

"Why not? Isn't that why I brought you here?"

"I'm not sure why you brought me here," he said. "I'm still trying to figure that out. But if I'm keeping you up…" He would've returned to the small guest room she'd outfitted for him, but she stood between him and his only escape route.

"You're not keeping me up. I was already awake." When her eyes ranged over him, he again wished for a shirt—but wouldn't insist on it. He was what he was and wouldn't hide from anyone, even a woman who made him wish he could be more.

Her breasts swayed slightly as she leaned on the back of a chair. "I'm surprised to find you in my office."

He examined a seashell paperweight. "Why's that?"

"Because there's nothing of interest in here."

"You're kidding, right?"

"Why would I be kidding?"

Returning the shell to her desk, he glanced up. "This room says so much about you."

"More than the rest of the house?"

"Of course. This is where you spend most of your time." He pointed to the books filling two separate cabinets. "You're well-read—psychology, forensic books, reference, self-help, classics and—" he bent closer to make out the titles of the paperbacks on the bottom shelf "—true crime."

"So…you're snooping," she said with a grin.

She was flirting with him. "Basically."

This made her laugh. "I guess that means you don't care if it bothers me."

He arched his eyebrows. "Does it?"

Raking her fingers through her tousled hair, she shoved it out of her face, and he decided she couldn't be more attractive than she was at this moment. Flashes of what she'd look like nude sent all the blood his heart could pump to his groin. "I don't plan to put a knife to your throat like you did mine, but—" she shrugged "—it's a little invasive."

"I'm sorry," he said. But he wasn't. Not really. She was the one who'd brought him here for a second visit. And she'd gone through his stuff at the motel, hadn't she? "I lost my sensibility to 'invasive' after my millionth body-cavity search."

"That's an indignity I wouldn't want to suffer."

"To get where you are today, you were once a C.O., right?"

"For ten years. I've performed more than my share of body searches, if that's where you're going."

"Did you ever proposition anyone you searched?"

She seemed appalled. *"Never."*

Pretending preoccupation with yet another pile of books, he tried to make his next question sound casual. "Ever have a relationship with an inmate?"

"No."

That told him what he wanted to know. He had less of a chance with Peyton Adams than he'd assumed—and he'd started out at zero. But he was still curious. Why was she being so nice to him? "What about C.O.s?"

"I had a brief fling with one—but he was quitting, had already given his notice. Today he owns a breakfast joint."

She was far more open about her background than he'd expected her to be. Maybe it was the late hour. Or maybe she didn't have a lot to hide. She'd lived a circumspect life, which made her even less likely to be interested in someone like him. "Have you ever been married?"

"No."

He thumbed through a *National Geographic* he found on the table, wondering why she'd brought this particular magazine in here at all. The cover showed a family of polygamists. "Engaged?"

"Twice."

Uninterested in learning about one man with ten wives and a zillion kids—too remote from his own experience—he abandoned the magazine. "What happened?"

"The first time I said yes to a marriage proposal

was in the eighth grade. We outgrew the infatuation by summer."

He had to smile at the thought of her making such a promise at that age. "And the other time?"

"I was in college and had fallen in love with a musician. He felt we were meant to be together, but wanted me to wait until he'd made his mark in the music industry. I wasn't too excited about becoming a roadie, always standing in the wings, hoping he'd have some energy left for me after everyone else took their piece of him. So I moved on."

The tips of her breasts had hardened. He could see the outline through the cotton material of her shirt. Was she as aroused as he was—or just cold? "Where is he now?"

"I've lost track."

"He must not have made it too big."

"I don't think he did. For all I know, he's still playing bars."

Had she slept with the musician? Made love to the C.O. with whom she'd had that brief fling? He wanted to ask, but wouldn't. He wasn't sure he could tolerate any more sexual tension. "Who is this?" He picked up one of the photographs standing on her desk.

"My mother. I took her to Napa Valley a year or two before she died. She said it was her favorite trip." Peyton walked around the chair she'd been leaning on and sat down. Pulling her legs up, she hugged them to her chest—thankfully concealing what he was having such a difficult time ignoring. "Was the C.O. who propositioned you, the woman you mentioned to me, someone who performed a strip search on you?" she asked.

He was staring at her mother. Peyton had the same smooth skin, the same chocolate-brown eyes. "Yes."

"Did it upset you?"

Confused, he looked up. "Why would it upset me?"

"Because it wasn't right. She was in a position of authority, which makes it a form of sexual harassment."

He couldn't help chuckling. "I don't know very many guys who worry about sexual harassment, at least from women. They can always say no, can't they?"

"Unless they feel it might adversely affect their situation."

Seemed like a small problem to him. If only that was all *he* had to worry about. "Maybe it's just a prison thing, but if a woman wants to get it on with me, I'm flattered."

She straightened her legs but folded her arms immediately after. "And yet you said no."

"Have you had sex with every guy who's paid you a compliment?"

"Of course not."

"There you go." Setting down the picture, he continued his exploration. "Anyway, she might've been a whore, but she wasn't all bad. She used to slip me extra paper, books she thought I might like, chocolate, stuff like that. And some of the other guys enjoyed more... personal favors from her. A woman wasn't an easy—" he was about to say *commodity,* but caught himself "—treat to come by."

She tilted her head as he fingered a stack of files. "If you think I have a file there on you, you're wrong."

"I know."

"Then why are you so interested?"

Because, as much as he wished otherwise, he was interested in *her*. She must realize that already. If not, he wasn't going to point it out. "These things…" He waved to indicate a cabinet that held a variety of handmade objects—baskets, pictures displayed on small easels, leather pieces, jewelry.

"What about them?"

"They're gifts?"

"Yes." She seemed proud.

"From inmates?"

"Mostly."

That wasn't difficult to guess. Many of the inmates he'd known made similar objects—weak attempts to make their lives matter when they didn't matter at all. "Why do you keep them?"

"Because they're special to me."

Jealousy stung him but he also experienced an emotion that went far deeper. "They're trophies of some kind?"

"Trophies?" she repeated.

"Tokens of the creators' admiration and devotion. Proof of how many men have wanted you."

She jumped to her feet. "Stop it!"

"Am I being too direct?" he asked, but he was glad she was angry. He wanted to make her angry because he was suddenly angry himself.

"It's the implication I'm having a problem with. That's the second time you've accused me of leading men on!"

"Isn't that what you do?" Why else was she being so kind to him? He could only imagine she liked the risk of "slumming." Or she enjoyed the thrill of bringing men like him—hardened, bitter men—to their knees.

She crossed over to him, coming close enough to jab a finger in his chest right below the medallion that hung from his neck—a Spanish eight-real coin from 1739, which was the only object of any value he owned. His father had left that behind. Not for *him,* exactly. He'd just forgotten it when he packed.

"You have no idea who I am, what I'm like. You know that?" she said.

Her touch sent an electric charge through him and nearly triggered the reaction he hoped to avoid. He almost dragged her up against him, but he knew that would scare the hell out of her, and fear wasn't what he had in mind.

He swatted her hand away instead. "Then why do you keep them?"

"Because they mean something to me, okay? And so do the men who created them. They're proof that beauty can be found where you'd least expect it. That most people have some good in them. That the amount of talent that goes to waste in prison is a tragedy."

She was too close. He couldn't think. He longed to take her in his arms and push her away at the same time, which made no sense. "That's bullshit! The men who created these things aren't significant to you. They're just a bunch of lost souls grasping for something, any- thing, to make them feel they have value. And you be- lieve you're a bigger person for patronizing them. But you'd never open your heart to one of them, not really, and you know it."

He was almost yelling when he finished. He could see the effect of his outburst, the way her face drained of color, and regretted it. But he was too far gone to change course, too torn by his own emotions to even apologize.

It was better this way, he told himself. Better if she hated him. Better if she took him back to the damn motel and left him there. Then there'd be no chance of becoming the next man to contribute to her "collection." The last thing he wanted was for some token representing him to be displayed here with all the others. Let her feel sorry for the poor bastards who'd made these arts and crafts. He wanted none of her pity.

What he wanted was her body, he told himself.

But, deep down, he knew he wanted much more than that.

What he really craved was her respect.

11

Her chest rising and falling much too fast, Peyton stood in the middle of her office long after Virgil had stalked out. She knew she needed to calm down. But she couldn't. She was caught in a web spun by her own emotions and desires—one that challenged every instinct she possessed regarding self-preservation, not to mention sense of duty. She'd hoped to achieve some sort of equilibrium with this new person in her life. But she couldn't. For one thing, he wasn't someone to whom she could simply explain how she felt—because he understood more than she wanted him to understand, looked far deeper, to the hard truth, blanching at nothing. For another, in all her years in corrections, she'd never encountered anyone so at war with himself. That made everything more complicated.

She didn't think of the inmates who'd given her these gifts the way he thought. She considered them friends, and there was nothing wrong with that. But she doubted she could convince him. What difference would it make, even if she could? Their argument hadn't been about other men. It'd been about the two of *them* and how they felt whenever they were together. He understood that she was attracted to him. She'd made that obvious

enough. He also understood that she was fighting it—
that she wouldn't, couldn't, take a chance on someone
like him—and he resented it.

She'd resent it, too, if she were him, wouldn't she?
Not only was he a victim of his mother's and uncle's actions, he was the product of an imperfect system. Her
hesitation to get involved with him further convinced
him that he didn't *deserve* to be considered by someone
like her, which wasn't true.

He'd said, *You know what I want from you. If you
want it, too, you don't have to make me dinner. You
don't have to view me as an equal. Hell, you don't have
to do anything at all. Just ask.* But now he acted as if
he'd accept nothing less than her soul.

Squeezing her eyes shut, she counted her own heartbeat. *Bu-bump. Bu-bump. Bu-bump.* It hammered away,
refusing to slow down.

Go back to your room, close the door and lock it.

She promised herself she would. But once in the hallway she turned to the guest room and, swallowing hard,
lifted her hand to knock.

Virgil's whole body tensed when Peyton came to his
door. "Go away," he snapped.

"That's it?" she said.

Yes.... No. God, he liked her *and* he hated her. Or
maybe it was what she stood for that he both liked and
hated. He barely knew her, and yet she represented everything he couldn't have and everything he wanted all
at once.

He should keep his hands to himself. That was the
one course of action where he couldn't go wrong. So he
gritted his teeth and clung to his control. "Yes."

He heard the weight of her footsteps as she left. Then

his stomach knotted and his hands curled into fists because he wanted to hit something, something that would send enough pain through him to crush the physical longing.

Pulling the pillow over his head, he ordered himself to let her go.

Fifteen minutes later he got out of bed and descended the narrow stairs leading to her room. "Peyton?" he called when he reached her door.

It took her a moment to answer. He got the impression that she couldn't decide whether or not she owed him that much. "What?"

"I'm sorry." He didn't know what else to say; he sure as hell couldn't explain his actions or his emotions.

She opened the door. The look on her face accused him of hurting her even though he had no idea how he'd managed to do that. Maybe it was her pride he'd damaged. He supposed a woman like her wasn't used to being turned down.

"I'm sorry," he repeated.

She must've believed he was sincere because her pained expression dissolved and she began toying nervously with the bottom of her T-shirt.

Once he allowed his gaze to fall lower than her face, he realized that the sweatpants she'd worn earlier were gone. Bare legs extended to bare feet, the sight of which sent a fresh charge of testosterone through him.

"I don't know how to help you," she whispered.

"Maybe I don't want you to help me."

"Then what do you want?"

For her to see him as an ordinary man. To desire him as an ordinary man.

"Take off your clothes." His voice sounded so raspy he almost didn't recognize it. He felt so much more than lust, but whatever else he craved was like an itch he could never scratch. He figured he could be happy with pure sex. Being able to make love to a woman, a woman like Peyton, was far more than he'd expected before returning to prison, wasn't it? So why had he tried so hard to resist?

She stood, seemingly transfixed. Would she refuse? He'd made his request a command because part of him hoped she *would*. That she'd save him, since he couldn't save himself. The other part felt as if he'd die a little if she shut him down.…

"Why do you have to tempt people, challenge them, into *not* giving you what you want?" she asked.

His chest burned; he wasn't sure why. "This isn't a psychoanalysis session. Are you going to fuck me or not?"

"No. Forget it. Just get out of here." She started to turn away, but she didn't close the door and he clasped her elbow.

"Don't say no," he murmured, but he didn't hold on to her very long. He didn't want her to feel forced.

She stared at him as if she understood why he'd been crude, as if she was just as lost as he was. Then she lifted her T-shirt over her head and let it drop to the floor.

The sight of her in nothing but a pair of sheer lace panties hit him harder than any physical blow he'd ever sustained. He stepped back and gulped for breath, dared not move toward her for fear she was just another dream that would dissipate into thin air if he tried to touch her.

"Virgil?" She sounded uncertain of his reaction, or lack of reaction.

His throat so dry he couldn't speak, he raised a hand to tentatively cup her breast. The weight and feel of her resting in his palm shot to his brain like a snort of heroin. It'd been at least ten years since he'd wasted any brain cells on drugs, but it was a feeling he'd never forgotten.

Half expecting her to stop him, he caught his breath. He'd had so much practice being disappointed in life he didn't truly believe she'd give him what he wanted. Bringing him here, teasing him with her nakedness, could be some sort of test, to see if he'd resort to force if she suddenly changed her mind. He'd heard of C.O.s who did that. Some got off on the danger of such games. But he had no desire to force Peyton or any other woman. It was her cooperation and participation he desired.

She didn't know that, of course. But she didn't refuse. Her lips parted and her eyes slid closed as his thumb brushed lightly over one tantalizing nipple.

When he began to shake, he tried to pull away so she wouldn't notice. His reaction embarrassed him. But she covered his hands and held them in place. "It's okay," she promised. "No matter what happens, it's okay."

He hadn't told her he'd been with only one girl, way back when he was a teenager, but he *had* told her he'd been eighteen when he went to prison and hadn't had sex since then. He wondered if Peyton found it ironic that a man who'd seen and done so much was almost completely uninitiated in physical pleasure. Maybe. Regardless, she didn't seem worried that he'd disappoint her.

Standing on tiptoe, she pressed her lips to his, kissing him softly, sweetly—and that was all it took. With a growl, he scooped her into his arms and carried her to the bed, where he bent over her so he could use his mouth as much as his hands.

Making love to Peyton made Virgil feel as if he'd

spent all those years in prison waiting for this one moment. He didn't want it to end, especially too soon, which was why he didn't remove his pajama bottoms when he removed her panties. It was Peyton who eventually peeled them off. Then there was nothing to stop them, and the drive to consummate became both frenzied and desperate.

"I want to feel you inside me," she whispered when he still held back.

He wanted the same thing. More than he'd ever wanted anything. But just in case all those tests they'd given him before releasing him from prison had somehow been wrong, and he'd picked up HIV or something else from all the fighting, he didn't want to expose her. Neither did he want to run the risk of getting her pregnant. That couldn't be good for her life or her career, for a lot of reasons, including the fact that it would provide proof, should Wallace care to make any accusations, that they'd been together.

Pulling ragged gulps of air into his lungs, he rested his forehead against hers. "Do you have a condom?"

"I thought you said you were clean."

"I am, but…what about pregnancy?"

"There's no need to worry about that. I've had endometriosis since I was thirteen. The doctor has me on the pill."

What, exactly, did that mean? "Endometriosis doesn't make this…painful for you, does it?" He knew that was probably a stupid question. She seemed eager enough. But one thing he hadn't come across in prison was any information on the various conditions that affect the female reproductive system.

"For me it's not usually painful. It just means I might have trouble getting pregnant if and when I want children. But there's a lot doctors can do these days, so…I'm hopeful."

"I'm sure they'll be able to help." He didn't know the first thing about it, but he would've said whatever she needed to hear. He felt too protective of her to do anything else. "So…we're good to go?"

"We're good." She whispered those words while tracing the rim of his ear with her tongue. He nearly melted into her right then and there, but he wanted one last look at her the way she was now, completely undone, her mouth swollen with his kisses, her hair tangled from his hands, her face slightly chafed from his beard growth. Pinning her hands lightly above her head, he stared at her, intent on memorizing every detail.

"What?" she said.

"Nothing." He traced the curve of one cheek, ran his finger along her lower lip and all the way down to her navel. Then he closed his eyes and gave himself over to the sensations that promised such sweet release: her satiny skin, her wet mouth, her musky smell on his fingers. He was trying to take it slow; he didn't want it to end too soon. But what they felt turned into such frantic need he could've more easily stopped a speeding train. Gripping his buttocks, she arched into him to let him know what she wanted, and he responded by pushing inside her as far as he could.

The tight warmth of her around him was almost too much. He tried, once again, to slow down, but it was a futile effort. The compulsion was too great, for both of them. She moaned her pleasure as the rhythm increased, and he began to shake again. This wasn't like those sloppy, careless sessions with Carrie. He'd lost enough since then to know that this was one of those moments he'd always treasure, regardless of what happened afterward.

"I think…maybe you'd better give me a minute," he gasped, "or I won't…be able to hang on until—"

"Don't worry about that." She wrapped her legs around his hips, drawing him even deeper. "Just let go."

And then the last of his defenses slipped away, along with his control, and the most exquisite pleasure broke over him, rocking him with a series of shuddering waves.

The soothing, metronome quality of Virgil's breathing suggested he was sleeping soundly. He lay on his back, one arm thrown over his head. Peyton wondered how long it'd been since he'd really relaxed like this. She was tired herself, but she didn't want to drift into unconsciousness. She preferred to relish the time she had with him. His warmth seemed to hold the fog's pervading dampness at bay and the size of his body offered a greater sense of security than she'd felt in ages. For the first time since she'd met him, except for when they were making love, he was unguarded. She liked that. More than liked it. And yet she had to ask herself: *What have I done?* She was the chief deputy warden of the facility where he'd be incarcerated on Tuesday. After *this,* how could they maintain any type of professionalism?

Playing their respective roles had been a battle from the start, hadn't it? He'd always defied her on one level or another. Because he wasn't really an inmate, she couldn't seem to employ the same defenses that normally kept her safe. Until she'd met him, she'd never dreamed anything like this could happen to her.

But if she'd been wrong to allow him into her bed, it

certainly didn't feel that way right now. Sharing what they'd shared seemed to ease his pain. It'd also left him exhausted and able to sleep, and that brought her a measure of relief, too. But she felt free to do as she wanted here, in her own home, especially in the dark of night. Would that perspective change come morning?

Shifting carefully, so she wouldn't wake him, she studied what she could see of his face, beautiful in its rawboned masculinity, illuminated by the moonlight slanting through her floor-to-ceiling windows. She had drapes, but almost always left them open. Living on towering ocean cliffs had certain benefits. Privacy was one. No one could see into her bedroom.

Lowering her eyes to his chest, she took particular note of the tattoos on his body and what they might represent. The grim reaper covered one shoulder as if daring death to take him. Or maybe it represented how often he'd stared death in the face? A medusa languished over his heart, the snakes of her hair detailed and real-looking as they slithered across his torso. She already knew he was familiar with Greek mythology. Had he chosen a medusa to represent his mother—someone once beautiful who'd become ugly because of her actions?

There were plenty of scars, too. He'd been shanked several times. How many fights had he been in? And what had the C.O.s done to him as a result? They'd probably vented their anger on a number of occasions, possibly with a few blows of their own. At the very least, they would've put him in isolation.

Peyton winced at what he must've gone through—a man falsely accused and erroneously imprisoned. It could've destroyed him. Maybe, in ways, it had. But it didn't seem like that. He was a gentle lover. A generous one, too. Surely that revealed as much about him as anything else.

Unable to resist, she pressed her lips to the most prominent scar she could see, two inches of puckered flesh that looked like a slash on the medusa's cheek.

She knew he'd felt it when he moved. His hand slid into her hair, holding her face above his so he could see her. "You okay?"

He appeared to be genuinely concerned. "Fine."

"What are you doing?"

"Just watching you sleep. You seem at peace."

His lips curved into a smile. "Come here." Guiding her down next to him, he curled around her and, feeling safe and oddly happy despite all the concerns that waited for her, Peyton let her eyelids grow heavy.

Two hours later, she was awakened by the warm, wet sensation of Virgil's mouth at her breast. He wanted to make love again. And she didn't mind being disturbed because the second time was even better than the first.

Reality intruded as rudely as Peyton had feared—and even sooner than she'd expected. The sun was barely burning off the morning mist when she heard the vibration of her cell phone. She'd left it charging on the counter in the kitchen, and if she hadn't known what that sound signaled, hadn't become so attuned to it after months of conditioning, she would've slept right through the soft buzz, just as Virgil was doing. But she could always hear it, almost anywhere in the house, and she knew that if someone was calling her at seven on a Sunday morning, it was important.

Had something gone wrong at the prison? Considering the rivalry that existed between the Nuestra Family and the Hells Fury, there was a constant threat of violence. Should that occur, whichever associate warden was in charge would call her. Warden Fischer lived in Brookings, Oregon, thirty minutes away. He couldn't respond as quickly as she could, especially on weekends, when he and his wife often traveled to Portland to see their grandkids.

It's time for him to retire....

Slipping out of bed, she yanked on the first article of clothing she came across on the floor—her T-shirt—and hurried out of the room to see who was trying to reach her. But when she saw caller ID she didn't want to answer.

The good news: it wasn't the prison.

The bad news: it was Wallace.

Afraid he'd insist on talking about Virgil, she was tempted to let his call transfer to voice mail. It might help her respond in a more detached manner if she learned what Wallace wanted *before* speaking to him directly. But the fear that he might be calling about Virgil's sister, to tell her something terrible had happened, made her hit the answer button despite her reluctance.

"We have a problem," Wallace announced as soon as she said hello.

The hair stood up on her arms. "Is it Virgil's sister?"

"No. Laurel and the kids are okay. For now. But I need to talk to Virgil, and he's not answering."

Because she'd brought him to her house and had sex with him. She'd compromised her authority, if not her integrity, which was why the department wouldn't approve. She'd told herself she was doing it for him, that sometimes human need trumped rules, but the fact remained that she'd wanted what they'd shared just as badly as he had. "Maybe he went for a walk."

"I've been trying his room for the past three hours. You think he got up at three or four o'clock to go out in the dark, foggy night and get some exercise?"

Guilt wasn't a burden Peyton was used to carrying. Chafing under the weight of it, she climbed onto one of the bar stools. "It's possible he couldn't sleep. Or that he's sleeping so deeply he can't hear the phone."

"No way. I've let it ring off the hook."

A noise from behind told her that Virgil had gotten up and come to investigate, but she didn't turn to face him. Now that she was back in her other world, the "real" world so managed by rules and restrictions, she wasn't sure how she felt about what they'd done. Or him.

"I'm afraid he's skipped," Wallace said. "And if that's the case, I'm screwed."

"He wouldn't skip."

"If he has—"

"He wouldn't," she repeated. "He cares too much about his sister."

"Oh, yeah? We'll see. Most inmates only care about themselves. Anyway, I need you to drive over there and find out what the hell is going on. I won't be some stupid-ass patsy he's using for his own purposes. My wife and I had a huge fight when I had to leave last night. She's sick of me traveling. But I left, anyway, because I'd made a promise."

That wasn't the only reason he'd braved his wife's displeasure. Feeling a measure of contempt for his self-deceit, Peyton couldn't let him forget his interest in what Operation Inside could do. "And you want to deliver a devastating blow to the Hells Fury, right?"

"Of course! Someone's got to do something before our whole society goes to hell."

This probably had more to do with boosting his career than saving society, but she'd said enough.

"I don't like being played for a fool," he muttered.

"Skinner isn't playing you for a fool."

"How can you be sure? You don't know him even as well as I do! So why are you defending him?"

God, it was already starting—her inability to hide that she had a personal interest in Virgil's well-being. She'd always been far too transparent.

Telling herself to at least *try* to be more subtle, she glanced over her shoulder and saw the man in question wearing nothing but his jeans, quickly donned and still unbuttoned, and an inscrutable expression. "I'm just saying he seemed committed. But I'll drive over and call you when I get there."

"You do that," he said.

Although Peyton was certain Wallace had disconnected, she pressed the end call button three times, even dialed her own voice mail to be sure. She couldn't take any chance that he might overhear her talking to Virgil.

"Laurel's okay?" Virgil asked.

She could tell he was worried. There was so much more at stake here than their attraction to each other. "From what Wallace tells me, she's fine. But there are some…complications. He wants to talk to you."

"Which means we have to go back to the motel."

"That would be best, yes." They could wait fifteen minutes and have him use her cell phone, as if she'd just arrived at his room. But she didn't suggest that because she knew she couldn't continue to spend time with him.

Last night scared her. It showed her how easily she could come to care about him—more than she already did.

When he made no move to get his shirt and shoes, she looked up.

"Just tell me one thing," he said.

"What's that?"

"Do you regret what happened last night?"

She hated having to lie to everyone about it. She hated thinking she might've made a terrible mistake, because she didn't typically make mistakes. Not like this one. And she knew seeing him go inside on Tuesday would be so much harder on her now than it would've been had she kept her distance. Did all of that add up to regret?

When she didn't answer right away, he said, "Forget it."

"Virgil—"

"Let's get out of here." He left the kitchen as she stood there, hovering indecisively about what to do next. The only way to recover and still be the same woman she'd always been was to pretend last night had never taken place, and to treat him in a strictly professional manner from here on out.

But that wouldn't be easy. She knew she'd never forget the way he'd touched her. For all his tattoos and scars and prison mentality, even his lack of experience with sex, he was the best lover she'd ever had. Just looking at him reminded her how lonely she'd been since coming to Crescent City. That loneliness would go deeper after such fulfilling intimacy. But another tumble in bed would only undermine what she wanted to believe about herself, would only postpone the inevitable.

They were better off trying to prepare for the future. He had a debt to pay society, one that could cost him his life. And she had to lock him up two days from now.

12

The drive to town seemed interminable. There was so much Peyton wanted to say—and yet she couldn't find the right words. She and Virgil both sat staring straight ahead, as if the attraction that had compelled them to be together now tore them apart with equal force.

Peyton hated the change. She didn't want what had happened between them to end this way. But she couldn't pretend she'd be willing to let the relationship progress, couldn't hold on to him for fear of where it might lead. He was the first man in a very long time to capture her interest, but she knew he wouldn't be flattered if she told him that. He'd expected her to balk at some point, to escape the risk associated with him, and now she'd done that. His anger made her feel rigid and judgmental and selfish—all the things she didn't want to be.

But she had the right to look out for herself, didn't she? She'd known from the beginning they couldn't have anything beyond a professional relationship.

She glanced over at him, his face an implacable mask. His defenses had snapped into place the moment he asked if she regretted being with him and she hadn't been able to answer. He'd withdrawn so completely she doubted she could reach him again even if she tried.

That caused an odd sense of loss, which added confusion to the already jumbled emotions churning in her gut.

"I know you're worried about Laurel, but you shouldn't be." She broke the silence with what she hoped would provide some reassurance. "Wallace isn't my favorite person, but I believe he'll try his best to keep her safe."

"He'll be sorry if he doesn't."

The steely determination behind those words frightened Peyton. She didn't want him to do anything that might land him in worse trouble—which proved she was making the right choice by backing away. He couldn't divorce himself from all the experiences that made him who he was or the responsibilities that forced his hand, and neither could she.

"You can't think like that," she said.

His eyes cut to her, and for the briefest moment she remembered the tenderness with which he'd touched her last night. Not that any of that tenderness showed now.

She adjusted the position of her hands on the wheel. *"What?"*

He didn't respond, but he didn't have to. That look was enough. He was telling her to mind her own business.

"Just because I'm not willing to ruin my life by getting any more...*involved* with you doesn't mean I don't care about you," she blurted out.

A muscle flexed in his cheek—evidence of some strong emotion. "I never asked you to care about me. Last night was nothing. We got off a few times. That was it."

His response felt like a slap in the face. She'd honestly wanted to be with *him,* not anyone else. That made it more than a purely physical encounter. "So I was just a piece of ass? Your last hurrah before going back inside?"

"First and last."

She shot him a dirty look. "Thanks for making me feel cheap."

"You're the one who did that."

"You know what our situation is. I don't have any choice."

He took a deep breath before hitting her with a penetrating stare. "That's true. So stay away from me in the future."

"Your gratitude astounds me."

"I didn't ask you for any favors."

"And I didn't do you one. I was…sincere, Virgil. I—"

"Stop it. We were never meant to be friends." He shifted his attention to the window until she pulled to the curb at the usual place. She thought he'd walk off without even a goodbye, but he turned back at the last second, removed the medallion that hung around his neck on a leather cord and handed it to her.

"What's this?" she asked in surprise.

"The strap it hangs on is the only thing I've ever made."

The pain in her chest grew more acute. After what he'd just said, after feeling his frustration and anger, she hadn't expected this and didn't know how to take it. "Why are you giving it to me?"

"Why not display a token of my admiration along with everyone else's?" he said. Then he shut the door and walked off.

The medallion was a Spanish coin from 1739. She had no idea where he'd gotten such a rare object, but she guessed it would've been worth quite a bit—which, once again, showed that he didn't think like most people, didn't value the same things.

The coin's monetary value meant nothing to her, either. What mattered was that it was still warm from the heat of his chest.

Because of that, she couldn't help pressing it to her own.

Laurel paced the living room of the old, two-bedroom house where Rick Wallace had taken her, pausing every few minutes to part the drapes and peer out at the street. As it approached eight, traffic increased, even though it was Sunday. The long night was over, but that didn't make her feel any better.

"Stop worrying," Wallace said for the umpteenth time, but he was one to talk. He'd just about worn a hole in the linoleum of the kitchen.

"They could've followed us," she responded. "We might not be any safer here than we were in Florence." They'd driven three hours to reach this 1920s brick house in the small ranching community of Gunnison, but that didn't feel far enough.

He scowled at her. "No one followed us because no one saw us leave. No one was around when I went to your door."

"You can't be sure of that."

"You said yourself that you'd just called the police, that they checked the house, the yard and the street."

"But it took a while to gather our belongings. I didn't know you were coming, so I wasn't prepared. The men in that Ford Fusion could've returned while we were pack-ing. They could've been hidden by trees or some other parked vehicle and watched us load up, then followed us when we drove away."

Rubbing a hand over his face, he cursed under his breath. "Quit spooking yourself."

"If you'd been around when that man showed up with a gun…when he pointed it at Mia…" Fighting tears of exhaustion and disappointment, Laurel swallowed hard. "He got into my house without making a sound. And he wouldn't have hesitated to pull that trigger if he'd thought we were worth more to him dead."

"Then it's a good thing I came when I did." Wallace wasn't any happier to be here than she was. He'd made it clear that he wasn't used to such duties, had no patience with them. It hadn't helped that her children had frayed his nerves by whining on the long drive. Amid all the chaos, Wallace had tried to explain who he was and why he was bringing her here. He'd said that a U.S. marshal would be taking over soon, but she wasn't sure what it all meant. Wallace had told her she'd never be able to take her kids back home—was that true?

She couldn't even conceive of it. What about her job as a janitor at the hospital? Her house? Her friends? She hadn't been in Florence long enough to put down many roots. She'd moved there just eleven months ago, shortly after they transferred Virgil from USB Tucson to ADX Florence, but she had more there than anywhere else. She couldn't imagine disappearing without saying a word to the people she'd met. Trinity Woods, the woman who babysat Mia and Jake while she worked had probably already arrived to find them gone. Although Laurel had wanted to call her, to tell her not to come, Trinity had shut off her cell phone service in order to save money.

"This can't be happening," she muttered.

"Oh, it's happening, all right," Wallace said. He claimed she was going into the Witness Protection Program, but until now WITSEC, as he called it, had had no relevance to her life beyond what she'd seen on TV. She'd never dreamed she'd be adopted into it herself. Her husband had been as physically abusive as the stepfather her mother had killed. She'd reported him and he'd spent a few months in jail, but the cops hadn't been able to do much more to help her. *Now,* after she'd worked through that problem mostly on her own, they were whisking her away, promising a new identity?

Wallace slumped into a chair. "Where are the kids?"

"In bed." He hadn't noticed? They'd been asleep more than an hour, but it hadn't been easy to get them settled down. They didn't understand why they'd been carted off in the middle of the night. Mia had had an earache—hence, the whining. Her complaints had upset Jake and made him cranky, as well.

"Maybe after a few years I can go back," she said.

"You'd be a fool to take that chance."

But she'd already started over and she liked Colorado.

The fact that her mother wouldn't be able to contact her was actually a relief. The same held true for her ex-husband, who'd threatened her numerous times even after his stint in jail and had only calmed down in the past few months, since he got a new girlfriend. But there were other people. People she'd miss. Melanie at work was one example. She'd been a good friend.

"Do you think they got to Virgil?" she asked. "Do you think he's dead?"

Wallace stared up at her. "You know what I think."

He'd explained Virgil's gang ties. She hadn't wanted to believe him, but she knew in her heart that what he said was true. Virgil had been so angry in the early years. He'd been determined to rail against the system any way he could.

None of that had helped his cause, of course. It'd only made things worse.

"He didn't run off." She'd said that before but Wallace didn't believe her. "He'd never abandon me."

"If he's returned to The Crew and made nice, he'd have no reason to fear for your safety."

"But *he* wouldn't be free. Not really. He must want to get out, away from them, like he told you, or he wouldn't be doing this."

Skepticism etched a deep frown in his face. "He's loyal, isn't he?"

"To a fault," she responded.

"Exactly my point. These guys, probably even the one with the firearm, are as much family to him as you are. Could be he's decided he can't live without them. It's a cold world with no friends."

She was lonely herself. They had only each other, which was why he *had* to be okay. "He's got me," she said, stubbornly refusing to doubt. "He'll always have me. And he's tired of fighting."

"Why would he be tired of it? That's all he's ever known."

"He never fought unless he was attacked."

Wallace didn't seem to care that he was upsetting her. He was just as worried, just as agitated. "When you're the man everyone else wants to knock off the top of the heap, you become a target. But he did more than protect himself. He made all comers pay."

She folded her arms to shield herself against his negativity as well as the cold. According to what Wallace had said on the way into town, Gunnison saw the sun almost every day of the year, yet it occasionally had some of the lowest temperatures in the nation. Today felt like one of those days. "Then that's what he had to do. Anyway, if he made a deal with you, he'll keep it."

Wallace checked his cell phone for messages before setting it on the table beside him. "We'll see, won't we? He's not in his motel room. There's got to be a reason."

Wringing her hands, she made another pass around the room. "The Crew must've found him."

"They *couldn't* find him, not unless he called them. It's not as if they have high-tech equipment like the FBI, for God's sake."

She pivoted to face him. "And yet the FBI can't stop The Crew."

He opened his mouth, apparently prepared to continue arguing, when his phone rang. Grabbing it off the table, he jumped to his feet. "Hello?...There you are! Where the hell have you been?...*In the middle of the night?*...No, she's fine. The Crew's been watching her, following her, but I got her and the kids out without being seen....I'm sure of it....Because she's been dying to talk to you....Just a minute." Looking relieved, he handed her the phone. "It's your brother."

Laurel's heart raced as she pressed Wallace's cell phone to her ear. She'd been so terrified that Virgil had been kidnapped or killed. A surge of gratitude swept through her; at the same time she tensed with the knowledge that the worst could still happen. "Virgil?"

"Laurel, you okay?"

The tears she'd been holding back streamed down her face. Reluctant to let Wallace see her fall apart, she took her usual place by the window and stared out at the street. "I'm alive. I guess that means I'm okay." She made an effort to control the trembling in her voice. "What's going on? I've been so worried about you!"

"I'm sorry."

The regret in those words made it difficult for her to blame him. He'd been through so much.

"I knew this would be hard on you," he went on. "But you have to trust me. There's no other way."

"When will I see you?"

"I don't know. As soon as I can fulfill my assignment."

What, exactly, *was* his "assignment"? Wallace had been vague about that. He'd said Virgil was helping the government take down a dangerous gang, a different gang than the one to which he'd belonged. But Laurel couldn't imagine one man being so instrumental in that kind of undertaking. Besides, the government couldn't need him more than she did. She'd waited so long. "Are we talking days or…"

"Most likely months."

"No, Virgil, please! Don't do this."

"Listen to me. There's no better alternative. And that means you have to soldier on. I need to know you're safe and well. Do you understand?"

She wiped her cheeks. "But…*months?*"

"Whatever it takes to set us free."

He was determined. She heard it in his voice. "Fine. Then where are you? We'll come there so we can at least visit you."

"They're putting me back in prison, Laurel, and you can't come anywhere close."

But that wasn't fair! He'd just been released.

For a moment, she was tempted to strike out at Wallace. He seemed the perfect person to blame, but he was also the man who was trying to keep her safe. She didn't know what to do. "The nightmare is supposed to be over," she said. "When will it be over?"

"Someday, okay? Be strong. It'll be easier on me if I know you're bearing up under the weight of all this."

Bearing up? She felt as if she was drowning in disappointment and fear and uncertainty. She'd been regularly beaten by the stepfather her uncle had shot. When her mother received the life insurance money and gave Gary almost half instead of hiring a better lawyer for Virgil, she'd run away. She'd been sixteen and survived on the streets for nearly two years, trying to scratch out a living. Then she'd married a man who'd turned out to be as abusive as her late stepfather. Through it all, she'd fought like crazy to save her brother, to hang on to her sanity and, later, to provide for the emotional and physical needs of her children. How could she continue to bear up when she was so tired?

And yet she couldn't put her brother through any more than he'd already suffered....

Sliding down the wall to sit against it, she covered her face and struggled to rein in her emotions. "I'll do what I can."

"That's it. I'm proud of you, Laurel."

"This man I'm with...Rick Wallace. Can I trust him?" She felt Wallace's eyes boring into the top of her bowed head, knew she wasn't being polite by talking about him while he was in the room. But she didn't care. She'd been pushed into survival mode, was well beyond observing common courtesies.

"He'll take care of you as long as I'm giving him the incentive to do so. If that changes...if something happens to me...you might need to take Mia and Jake and strike out on your own. In that case, go several states away or to the East Coast. If I'm out of the picture, I doubt The Crew will bother with you. But I've managed to piss off some very determined people. Don't take any chances."

Resting her forehead on her arms, she shut her eyes. How could she start over *again?* Where would she find the money? She'd never had the opportunity to go to college. Since following Virgil to Colorado, she'd barely eked out a living working at the hospital. When Tom didn't pay his child support, which seemed like every other month, she could hardly afford groceries. And now that he couldn't know where they were, even his contribution would be gone.

There were other issues, too. What about ID? She'd need a new identity if she planned to escape The Crew. Was the government going to provide that? Otherwise an everyday P.I. would be able to find her.

Survival had been a part of her life for so long, she knew what it required. But she didn't mention any of these details. Virgil had enough on his mind. "Wallace doesn't trust you," she said. "He believes you'll double-cross him."

"He was supposed to stay in his motel room. Anyone would've suspected him of taking off," Wallace said, but she kept her head down and didn't respond. Virgil was talking.

"If he didn't have me by the balls, maybe I would."

"So they're forcing you to do this?"

"In a way. In another way it's an opportunity. And it might be my last."

Scrambling for a sliver of hope to cling to, she tried *opportunity* on for size. But she'd waited so long for the truth to win out, for her brother to be exonerated, that facing such a big setback made it feel as if their lives would *never* be their own. "A man showed up at the house," she said. "With a gun."

"Mia and Jake—"

"Are fine. He grabbed Mia for a few seconds, put a gun to her head, but…that was it."

There was a silence, during which she felt his concern and his rage, before he asked, "What'd this man look like?"

"Short. Muscular. Lots of tattoos—maybe a full-body suit because even his face was tatted up. He'd shaved his head but had this little patch of hair growing from his chin—"

"Ink."

She wiped away the last of her tears. What good did it do to cry? Crying changed nothing. Hadn't she learned that by now? "That's what he called himself, yes."

"What'd he say?"

"He referred to you as Skin, wanted to know if you were getting the flag dirty."

"Dropping the flag. He was asking if I was bailing out."

"Of the gang?"

"That's right. What else?"

Her nose was running, but she was too dejected to head to the bathroom. She sniffed loudly. "He demanded that I tell him where you are."

"And you said…"

"What *could* I say? I didn't know. He gave me a message that you have until noon tomorrow to call someone named Pretty Boy. But that deadline passed yesterday. It's too late."

"I wouldn't have called him, anyway."

Conscious of Wallace, who was still watching her,

she got to her feet, turned her back to him and leaned into the window again. "What will they do?"

"If they find me, they'll kill me. They'll kill you, too, if they can. That's why I need you to do exactly as Wallace says. This isn't a game. It's for real. He'll put you in the Witness Protection Program, give you a fresh start. I know you don't feel good about that, but it's our only chance."

"What about Tom?" she asked.

"Your ex? What about him?"

"The kids will never see their father."

"He's no father. He takes them maybe twice a year, sends them a few bucks for Christmas."

"Still…"

"This is a matter of life and death, Laurel. That outweighs everything else. Everything."

"But are we talking *forever?* I don't want to tell them that."

"Then don't. Forever is a long time, baby sister. Let's get through now. Then we'll worry about later."

"Why?" she whispered. "Why is this happening?"

"It's my fault," he admitted. "I never realized how my decisions would affect you, never dreamed I'd ever see the day I got out of prison."

But the fact that he'd been put behind bars wasn't his fault. They had Ellen and Gary to blame for that. Maybe their mother and uncle hadn't murdered Martin with the intention of framing Virgil, but they didn't do anything to stop him from going to prison. Ellen had even testified about the many times Virgil had stood up for Laurel against their stepfather, said Virgil had hated his stepfather and had threatened him on a number of occasions. "This all goes back to Mom and Gary, and what they did."

A beep sounded, signifying another call. Afraid to let Wallace know someone else was trying to reach him for fear he'd rush her off the phone, she ignored it. "Will we get to talk, stay in touch?"

"Probably not. Don't write to me, either. If they manage to track me down, I don't want there to be any link between us."

That meant she was losing even more than she'd lost before. "But how will we connect when this is all over?"

"Wallace will tell me where you are. I'll find you. Don't worry."

A second beep sounded, and suddenly she wasn't sure she wanted to stay on the phone any longer. If she broke down again, she'd only make him feel worse. And she was on the verge of more tears. "Another call's coming in. I'd better go."

"Laurel?"

"What?"

"I love you," he said, but she was crying too hard to answer so she passed the phone to Wallace as if she hadn't heard him.

Wallace told Virgil to hang on and switched to the incoming call. No doubt he was hoping it was the U.S. marshal who was supposed to relieve him so he could return to his family and continue living his safe and predictable life. Laurel envied him that. She also resented his impatience with her and her brother when he had no idea what it was like to walk in their shoes.

"Hello?…This is Rick Wallace.…Say that again?… Damn it! How'd that happen? We told you to go over there.…I know, but it's so…unnecessary.…The bastards." He dropped his head, massaging his temples with one hand. "We're fine. Any witnesses?…What about

other evidence?…Whoever it was must have some con-
nection to The Crew….Of course….Thanks for letting
me know."

He stared at Laurel as he switched back to the other
line. "Virgil? I'm afraid I've got bad news."

Laurel's first instinct was to check on Mia and Jake.
But she could tell from Wallace's manner that it wasn't
the children. "What is it?" she murmured.

Reaching out, he took her hand. "It's Trinity Woods."

"My babysitter?" She had no idea how Virgil was
reacting. She couldn't hear him. But she assumed the
name didn't mean much to him. She'd never mentioned
Trinity. Or maybe she'd made some oblique reference
in one of her letters.

Wallace shifted from one foot to the other. "Yes."

And then she knew. The police hadn't stopped Trinity
from going to the house, didn't get to her in time. Why
not? Wallace had called them at least an hour before
Trinity was due to arrive, had explained who he was
and why it was important that someone intercept her.
But maybe he hadn't put enough urgency in the request.
They hadn't really believed she'd be hurt. No one had
any reason to hurt her, not even The Crew. "Don't tell
me…"

"I'm afraid so."

Laurel began to shake. "She's been shot?"

He couldn't quite meet her eyes. "Yes."

"How badly is she hurt?"

His hand gripped hers tighter, as if he'd warm the
blocks of ice that were her fingers, if he could. "She's
more than hurt, Laurel. She's dead. Someone gunned
her down while she was standing on your doorstep."

13

The woman who was shot could've been Virgil's sister. Only by the grace of God was it someone else. But that someone probably had a family who cared about her just as much as Virgil loved Laurel.

What a tragedy....

Bundled up in a coat and mittens, with her mother's old quilt draped across her lap, Peyton sat on her deck, letting the wind play havoc with her hair while she stared out to sea. She'd tried to work as a way to distract herself, but once she'd heard from Wallace and learned the news about Trinity Woods, she couldn't concentrate on anything except what Virgil must be feeling over at the motel—and whether or not he was really safe.

She wanted to go to him, reassure him if she could, maybe even bring him home. She felt she had a professional excuse to do just that. The CDCR wouldn't want him to renege on the deal.

But she knew in her heart that the real reason for her visit would have little to do with convincing him to keep the bargain he'd made. Whatever there was between them—this...*attraction*—wasn't something she seemed capable of conquering. She'd lost the fight yesterday and was in danger of losing again today; she dared not go to him. Once she saw him, all her good intentions could crumble, and if that happened they'd wind up in bed together for the second night in a row. She had to avoid that. It was already going to be difficult to face him on Tuesday, call him Simeon and pretend he meant nothing more to her than any of the other residents of Pelican Bay.

But the thought that he might need someone, might need *her,* kept chipping away at her resolve.

She was about to go inside out of the wind to call him and offer her condolences when a vehicle pulled into her drive. Living so far from town, she didn't get many visitors.

The sound of the engine drew her to the edge of the deck to see who'd arrived.

When she recognized the Ford truck, she nearly groaned aloud. It was Sergeant John Hutchinson, a recently divorced C.O. who'd been showing a bit too much interest in her. She liked him. He was nice, and not unhandsome with his sandy-colored hair, hazel eyes and lantern jaw. But he'd been hinting that he wanted to take her to dinner, to a movie, to Mendocino for a play—always something. Other than accepting an offer to grab a sandwich two weeks ago and permitting him to bring her dinner once last month, she'd politely refused his invitations. She'd already explained that she wouldn't date anyone who worked at the prison, but he didn't seem to hear her. And that edict now struck her as absurd. Was it worse to date someone who *worked* at the prison? Or someone who was going to be *incarcerated* there?

"Hey!" he called when he saw her leaning over the railing.

She forced a smile. "Hi. What's going on?"

"I brought you dinner."

Peyton sighed. She'd allowed him to cook for her once and here he was again.

Pushing down the irritation she felt at his persistence, she descended the stairs to tell him he couldn't stay. But by the time she reached his truck, he was taking out several foil-covered dishes.

"Wow, you really went to a lot of trouble," she said when she saw that he'd brought three side dishes, along with a couple of grilled steaks.

"Not too much. I can't wait for you to try my home-made marinade. It'll knock your socks off."

"John, I—"

He must've been able to tell by her tone that she was about to explain her position yet again, because he cut her off. "Hey, I know the rules. I'm not hitting on you. It's just dinner. Friends can bring friends dinner now and then, can't they?"

But this was the second time he'd done it in four weeks. And her mind was on Virgil, the woman who'd been killed, Laurel, Wallace and the Hells Fury. She wasn't in the mood for a social call—and yet she had to admit the distraction might be good for her. At least having John over would keep her home. "Of course, as long as you understand—"

"Relax, it's only dinner," he broke in. "What happened to your leg?"

"My leg?"

"You were favoring it."

"Oh, I twisted my ankle."

"How?"

She went with what she'd told Michelle. "I tripped on the stairs."

"See? It's a good thing I came over. You need a little TLC."

Telling herself he wouldn't stay long, she helped him carry the food into the kitchen.

"Pretty Boy called," Horse told Shady. "Ink iced a woman at Skin's sister's house this morning."

Shady was out in his garage, which he'd finished. The rest of his house was a dump. A weight set filled his living room. But this room was nice. He'd put in a bar along one side, bought a pool table, hung some beer signs and created a place of honor for his antique Harley over in the corner. He'd even poured a large cement pad outside for extra parking. But it was the gun cabinets along the back, and the weapons inside them, that were his pride and joy.

"What'd you say?" Setting aside the Taurus Millennium series PT145 he'd been cleaning, he swiveled from his worktable to face Horse. A giant of a man with a pockmarked face, bulbous nose and shaved head, Horse always made Shady feel like a kid by comparison. Shady had gotten his nickname from his resemblance to the white rapper Eminem; they had the same slight build and forever-young face. His appearance made it difficult for him to be taken seriously, but no amount of weight lifting seemed to change that. Horse, on the other hand, didn't need to lift. He had bulk in spades. According to Mona, the woman Shady was currently living with, Horse looked mean and stupid. She was right about the mean part. But he wasn't stupid. He made almost as much off pimping out whores as Shady did selling drugs.

"Ink busted a cap in a woman," Horse repeated.

Shady wiped his hands on a cloth before tossing it aside. "It'd better be Skin's sister."

"It's not. Laurel was gone by the time they arrived. They think she's in protective custody."

"Then what the hell? Why'd they kill someone?"

"Frustration and an itchy trigger finger. Ink said he wanted to let Skin know he's coming for him."

"We still don't have a clue where Skin is?"

"No."

That answered everyone's questions, then, didn't it? Made what Virgil Skinner was doing pretty damn obvious.

Cursing, he shoved the ammunition, gun parts and tools off his worktable as he stood.

Horse didn't flinch as they hit the floor, but the noise drew Mona, who poked her head into the garage. "Hey, what's going on?"

Shady could've said Martians had landed and she would've believed him. She was so stoned she had to hang on to the door frame so she wouldn't tumble headfirst into the pool table. "Did I ask you to come in here?"

He'd told her he wanted her to look like a Playboy bunny at all times—laughable considering the stretch marks on her stomach and the crooked teeth in her mouth. But he had to give her points for trying. She wore nothing but a black bra, a thong and a pair of high heels.

"What'd you say?" Her words slurred and her body swayed as if she might lose her grip and fall despite her efforts to remain upright.

What a worthless crack whore. She'd lost all five of her children to Childhood Protection Services, quite a feat even for a bad mother. He only kept her around because it was nice to have a piece of ass whenever he wanted. She didn't complain when it got too rough, and she let him pass her to the boys, which he did whenever he wanted to prove that he'd share everything he owned with his Crew brothers.

But he was tired of Mona's drug habit. "Go inside!" he snapped. "I don't want to see your ugly face!"

Glassy eyes smudged with mascara, lips stretched into a vacant smile, she stepped back and let the door close as if he'd asked her nicely.

"Any chance you want to take her off my hands?" he grumbled to Horse.

Horse considered the suggestion. "I can put her to work."

"Take her with you, man. I'm done with her."

"She got any clothes?"

"Does it matter? She won't need them where she's going."

"She'll need something to hide her worst features. But I can handle that. What do you want me to tell Pointblank?"

Shady pulled on his soul patch, the only hair he allowed on his body. "Anyone see Ink make the hit?"

"They don't know for sure. It was a drive-by. Someone might've spotted the rental car."

"They haven't been arrested, though?"

"Not yet."

"Have Ink come back as soon as possible."

Horse shoved his hands in his pockets. "The cops are looking for him around here. That's why you sent him away."

"And now they're looking for him there, too, so it doesn't improve things if he stays."

"I don't think he should be in either place."

Shady kicked a wrench off his seat. "What do you mean by that?"

"Ink's becoming too much of a liability. Attracting that kind of attention endangers everybody."

Horse wasn't the only one leery of Ink. Ink was crazy enough to frighten them all. "In some ways, he is a liability. In other ways, he's an asset."

Pursing his lips, Horse stared at the carpet. "They put the lot of us in prison, who's gonna take care of business on the outside?"

"It comes to that, we'll serve him up. We won't go down because he's too stupid to know when to keep his pistol in his pants."

Seemingly satisfied, Horse raised his eyes. "What about Pointblank and Pretty Boy?"

"They stay. Have Pretty Boy find a C.O. by the name of Eddie Glover who works at the prison in Florence."

Horse walked to the pool table and racked the balls into the plastic triangle. "You think Glover might know where Skin is?"

"If anyone knows what happened to him, it would be Glover. Word is they were pretty damn friendly."

Studying one cue and then another, Horse decided on a stick. "Skin was friends with a C.O.?"

"Part of his change of heart." Shady chafed at the fact that he hadn't been able to convince other members of The Crew that Virgil wasn't as great as they thought. Virgil was the kind of leader other men naturally followed. But he'd never been one to take orders. He was an independent son of a bitch and refused to back down even when it was in his best interests. That made him difficult to manage and as dangerous to the organization as he was to its enemies. Shady had been worried about Skin ever since he heard Skin might be cleared of his stepfather's murder. Who wouldn't be tempted by a clean break? Skin wasn't the gang type—not at heart.

Remembering how determined he'd been to walk his own path whether the rest of them liked it or not, Shady shook his head. There'd been times when he'd flat out refused a command. Anyone else who'd done that would've been killed. But everyone admired a man who could fight like Skin. They let him slide whenever he acted up because he was so damn good when he did get involved.

"How are they supposed to find Glover?"

"I just told you. He works at the prison."

"A lot of guys work at the prison. You don't have his address?"

"I can get it."

"What about a description?"

"He's five foot eleven, maybe one hundred and eighty pounds. Red hair cut short. Freckles everywhere. That tell you enough?"

"It should. I know someone on the inside who can get me his shift, which will also help," Horse said. "But what if Glover won't talk?"

Shady wasn't about to let Skin make him look like a fool. He had to prove he deserved the leadership role he'd fought so hard to obtain. "Everybody talks," he said. "You just have to give them enough incentive."

The pool balls broke with a loud clatter. "How far do I tell Pointblank to go?"

Wishing he could kill Skin himself, end the rivalry between them the right way, Shady eyed the guns in his cabinets. "Tell him to do whatever it takes."

"Then maybe Ink should stick around Colorado a while longer, don't you think?"

"Why?"

"He's already wanted. Might as well have him do the dirty work."

See? Horse was smarter than he looked. "Good idea. He can fly home when it's over."

"And Laurel?"

"Give me a few days. I'll find her."

Horse lined up for another shot. "How?"

"I'm gonna call a private investigator who's done some work for me in the past."

Closing one eye, he sent the thirteen rocketing into the left corner pocket. "A private investigator who can gain access to the police world?"

"She can gain access to *any* world," he said smugly.

"What's her secret?"

"She doesn't look like anyone who'd ever be connected to us, and she's willing to get creative."

Clearly intrigued, Horse forgot about his solitary game of pool. "Where'd you meet her?"

"She's a friend of a friend of a friend. Meeting her isn't the point. Money is. She'll do anything for the right price."

"You said she gets creative."

"She does."

"How?"

Shady started picking up the objects he'd tossed onto the floor. "You let me worry about that."

All during dinner Peyton wondered why she couldn't be more attracted to John. Or not John, exactly— someone *like* him. Someone without any rough edges, someone easygoing and civilized. Shelley, her assistant, thought he was a real heartthrob. The warden's assistant tittered about him, too. But Peyton felt none of what they seemed to feel, nothing that compared to the excitement of being with Virgil.

Was it danger that attracted her? Her way of rebelling against the strictures that governed her life? Or was it some kind of self-destructiveness, the tendency that drew some people toward the edge of a cliff?

Trying to make sense of it all, she kept asking herself those questions. But being self-destructive was too simple an explanation. She had no history of falling for bad boys. In fact, the opposite was true. She picked men who fit safe parameters, then tried to feel more than she did.

The problem was, she hadn't "picked" Virgil, didn't want to like him more than any other inmate. She just couldn't help herself. The decisions that had previously been controlled by cognitive function had been lost to instinct and hormones, a far less logical approach to selecting a lover.

After dinner, she went into the kitchen to rinse off the dishes and felt a measure of relief at being able to escape her guest, even for a short while. The time they'd spent together had dragged by. The clock on the wall indicated it hadn't been an hour. She wished John would leave, but she didn't ask him to go because having him around stopped her from visiting Virgil.

When he walked into the kitchen carrying their glasses, Peyton mustered yet another smile.

"I heard Wallace was in town on Friday." His tone suggested this was idle chitchat, but it made Peyton uncomfortable all the same. The associate director hadn't visited the prison. How had John learned he was in town?

"Who told you that?"

"Sandy saw him at Raliberto's."

"Sandy?"

"My sister."

Before quitting a year or so ago to be a stay-at-home mom, Sandy had worked as a nurse at the prison. Embarrassed that she'd been too preoccupied to recall his sister's name, Peyton ducked her head over the sink and kept washing dishes. "Oh, right. Of course."

"He had some guy with him she didn't recognize. Somebody in a baseball cap."

"Really?"

He scowled when she did nothing to further the conversation. "You didn't see Wallace while he was here?"

He knew there'd be some reason for Rick to visit Crescent City and that she'd most likely be aware of it. "Briefly."

"Oh, boy."

This made her turn. "What's that supposed to mean?"

"He usually doesn't show up unless something big's coming down. Or there's trouble brewing. I'm almost afraid to hear what it was this time."

"Nothing. He had a meeting with the warden. That's all."

"That's where it starts," he joked. "Any idea what it was about? Or will we hear at the weekly meeting?"

His interest struck her as too intrusive until she remembered that a couple of weeks ago, while breaking up a fight, he'd inflicted harm on one of the inmates. The case was under review to see if he'd acted appropriately or let himself get out of control, so he was probably worried about the outcome and whether he'd face disciplinary action.

She decided to tell him just enough to relieve his anxiety. "Thanks to the recent media reports that the

Hells Fury might be responsible for the murder of Judge Garcia in Santa Rosa, the CDCR wants us to step up our efforts to curtail gang activity. He didn't say but I'm pretty sure it had to do with that."

"How can we step up our efforts?" he asked. "To do that, we'd have to build a SHU big enough to accommodate everyone in gen pop. And then we'd have to answer to all the activists who are crying that isolation's cruel and unusual punishment." He shook his head in obvious disgust. "No one likes the problems we're dealing with, but they don't like the solutions, either. Not the ones that actually work."

Was he advocating more force? Or attempting to justify how he'd behaved when that fight broke out?

"There aren't any easy answers." She wasn't up for a debate tonight, not when she was so preoccupied.

"Wallace came to the prison, then?"

Unsure how to answer, she stayed as close to the truth as possible. "No. He met the warden for lunch."

"You weren't with them?"

"What?"

"I stopped by your office on my break. Your assistant said you'd gone into town with the warden."

She'd just acted like she *wasn't* at the meeting. Scrambling to cover her gaffe, she tried to clarify. "I was supposed to be there, but one of my friends called. She was in the middle of an emergency, so I had to beg off."

It wasn't a good excuse. Any meeting with Wallace, especially one in which they left the prison, would be important, making it unlikely that she'd accept outside calls. But she hoped he wouldn't think of that. For all he knew, she had a friend who was dying of cancer.

He stared at her for a few seconds, then shrugged and

seemed to accept her words. "So you have no idea who the other guy was?"

"Nope."

"Who do you *think* he could be?"

She wanted to blurt out that it had nothing to do with him but couldn't without revealing that she knew more than she was saying. Wishing she'd never let him stay for dinner, she finished loading the dishwasher. "No one special."

"He wasn't part of the meeting?"

Averting her face, she bent to fill the soap container. "Not that I heard of."

He leaned against the counter, considering.

"Why are you so worried about this?" she asked. "That meeting had nothing to do with the fight you broke up, if that's what's got you going. The warden specifically mentioned the gang problem."

"I just can't imagine who that person could be."

"It's no fun to eat alone. Maybe he was someone Wallace met at the restaurant and they ended up sharing a booth. For all your sister knows, the guy could've been another C.O. She hasn't met every officer. We've done some hiring since she left."

"She said he didn't act like a C.O."

Peyton laughed. "Not all C.O.s act the same."

"But there's a certain feel about them."

"I'm not convinced of that. Anyway, what else could he be?"

"A reporter."

No one who worked in corrections was ever happy about having a reporter around. Rarely did they heap praise on the system or those who ran it. Unless it was published in the local paper, which was generally supportive, prison articles were almost always steeped in criticism. That threatened change, and everyone feared change—the loss of jobs, the loss of tools necessary to do the job, a cut in funding, a court-ordered oversight. On top of this, John had been involved in an incident the media could easily use to "prove" the abuse so many inmates claimed. He didn't want to be named in a story like that. No one did.

"What makes you think it might be a reporter?"

"My sister said Wallace spoke in a low voice and kept leaning close. She tried to say hi to him, but he practically ignored her. When she approached, they hurried out."

"Wallace wouldn't try to wine and dine a reporter with *tacos*." She tried to make a joke of it, but John didn't even crack a smile.

"Since that judge was murdered, there've been a lot of media hanging around. Maybe he was trying to head off another scathing article condemning us."

If such an article condemned *him,* he'd probably receive harsher disciplinary action than he would otherwise. No doubt that played into his thoughts. "I'm sure it was nothing, John. Really. Investigative Services is still reviewing the incident. Lieutenant McCalley hasn't decided yet how he's going to react."

"How do you know?"

She faced him. "Because he would've told me."

His mouth rose up on one side. "You'll put in a good word for me, right?"

This was the reason she didn't fraternize with the C.O.s. She didn't want personal relationships to interfere with her ability to be fair. "I'll review the facts and make sure whatever action he takes is appropriate."

John didn't like her response. His smile faltered, but he covered it by acting as if he'd expect nothing more.

A few of the empty food containers were still on the table. More than eager to send him on his way, Peyton motioned toward them. "Get those, will you? I'll wash them so you don't have to take them home dirty."

"Sure." He walked out, but when he returned he brought only one dish—and her phone.

"Why—?" She didn't get the question out before he handed it to her.

"It buzzed. So I grabbed it for you," he explained.

She'd received a text message. From Wallace. Her iPhone gave a short hum by way of notification with every text and automatically displayed the message.

Anxiety pulled her nerves taut as she read what Wallace had sent. She'd just convinced John that nothing unusual was going on, and now he'd seen this:

Skinner's angry. See if you can settle him down. That woman's death was his fault, not mine. None of this would be happening if he hadn't joined up in the first place.

That was easy for Wallace to say. His safety and well-being had never been at risk. Neither had he experienced the same kind of fear, physical pain and pressure Virgil had known—as a mere teenager. But Wallace's reaction was beside the point. What concerned Peyton was the curiosity that lit John's eyes.

"Something wrong?" he asked, obviously trying to gauge her expression.

He'd read the text, all right. He also knew it came from Wallace. Her iPhone clearly identified the sender.

"A mutual friend was in a…car accident in which the other driver was killed," she said.

"That's tragic."

"Truly."

Her explanation wasn't enough. He must have a million unanswered questions. How could the—fictional—driver believe it was Wallace's fault? Why would he come to her to calm that person down? And what, exactly, had someone named Skinner joined?

John waited for her to elaborate, but she didn't. Thanks to his sister, he already knew far more than Peyton wanted him to. Slipping her phone into her purse so the same thing couldn't happen again, she finished the dishes, thanked him for dinner and walked him to his truck with the excuse that she'd brought home a lot of work tonight.

Then she reclaimed her phone and sat in the living room, reading and rereading that message. Skinner couldn't go inside Pelican Bay. This investigation was already starting to unravel.

14

A blanket of fog covered Highway 1, forcing Peyton to creep around the turns of the snakelike road hugging the rocky coastline. She couldn't see the ocean to the right, or the towering redwoods to the left. Even when she rode the bumper of the car in front of her, she could barely discern its taillights. But she'd made herself wait until it was late enough that she could approach the motel without fear of being spotted and was relieved to finally be on her way—until she arrived. Once she'd parked around the corner and hurried to Virgil's door on foot, she grew nervous because she had no idea how she'd be received.

"It's me," she murmured, following a brisk knock.

He opened the door, but he didn't speak. Setting his knife on top of the TV—he'd come prepared in case she was someone else—he stepped back so she could enter.

The warmth of the room embraced her as she closed the door. The television was on, but Virgil wasn't watching the kind of station most of the ex-cons she knew would pick. What with all the X-rated movies available on pay-per-view in this motel—she suspected that was part of the reason Rick Wallace preferred it—she thought a man in Virgil's shoes would be taking in as much skin as possible. Pornography was expressly forbidden on the inside in any form, so it wasn't as if he'd have another chance in the coming months. Instead, he was in the middle of a program about Egypt on the History Channel.

"I'm here to see if you'll change your mind," she said bluntly.

"About…"

Although he was dressed, she kept picturing him without his shirt as she'd seen him in her home last night. Her mind brought up other images, too, erotic images of them together, which made it strained and awkward to treat him as though he hadn't had his mouth on her less than twenty-four hours ago. "Going inside Pelican Bay."

He sank onto the bed and propped himself up on his elbows.

"No response?" she said.

"The fact that Laurel's babysitter was shot gives me more reason to go in, not less, Peyton."

She liked the way he said her name, the familiarity of it. "But you don't understand. The people here… There's not a lot going on this time of year. And thanks to the isolation, Crescent City's like the typical small town where everyone knows everyone else's business. Especially when that business has to do with the prison that supports us."

"So?"

Why was he making her spell it out? "That means there's less anonymity here than in some places. Folks notice the smallest details. Not only do they notice, they share every observation with others."

Sitting up, he found the remote and muted the TV. "Someone's said something to you?"

It was too warm in the room for the snug-fitting leather jacket she'd worn. She shrugged out of it as she explained what had happened with John. "His sister saw you at Raliberto's with Wallace, *and* he read a text Wallace sent me about you," she said when she came to the most significant part.

"I'm going in as Bennett, not Skinner," he told her. "He'll never connect me with that text. Chances are he'll never connect me with the man his sister saw at the taco place, either."

"Maybe not right away. But he can feel there's been a change. And he's asking questions. That makes me nervous."

"Why would he be so curious?"

"General boredom. Like everyone else. And he was reprimanded for being overly zealous in breaking up a fight two weeks ago. One of the inmates wound up with a cracked skull that might've had nothing to do with the original altercation. John's about to be disciplined for it, so he's looking over his shoulder."

"He's got an abusive streak and he's afraid it'll cost him his job?"

She'd been afraid he'd jump to that conclusion. The investigation wasn't complete, so she didn't know for sure, but she sincerely hoped that wasn't the case. "If I thought he was truly abusive, he wouldn't be working at Pelican Bay. He panicked and used more force than necessary. It won't happen again."

"There's a good chance you won't hear about it even if it does."

"How would he keep it from me?"

"There are ways to hurt people without cracking their skulls."

"Don't act like you know more about Pelican Bay or the people who work there than I do," she said. "You haven't even been inside. Not yet."

"Doesn't matter. One prison isn't that different from the next."

She shook her head. "I don't want to get into a pissing contest with you, okay? I'm against having you go in. That's all I'm here to say."

"You're spooked because of this guy. John. It'll be fine."

"You can't be sure it'll be fine."

He got off the bed. "It's not your decision, anyway."

The wait, the pressure and the fear for his sister, not to mention that he probably felt somewhat responsible for Trinity Woods's murder, had to be driving him crazy. He'd been on edge ever since she'd arrived. So had she. Add to that the tension between them—which they couldn't relieve in the same way they had last night— and the surfeit of emotion threatened to erupt into an argument.

An argument over nothing.

Taking a deep breath, Peyton focused on her purpose. "Why not leave, go and get Laurel, disappear?"

"Because it's not that easy—not without resources. And, in case you haven't noticed, a man doesn't build up a lot of resources in prison."

"You're sticking it out to get your compensation money?"

"No. Considering all the red tape, I don't have much chance of getting that money. I'm doing it because life on the run is not what I want for my sister or her children.

Someone who's always lived in an ivory tower wouldn't understand, but—"

"Excuse me?" she broke in. "I've never lived in an ivory tower."

"You've never lived the way I have, either."

"I work in the same kind of place."

"By choice. You get to leave at the end of each day and pick up a hefty paycheck for your trouble. I don't feel sorry for you."

"I don't want you to feel sorry for me. I'm only trying to help."

"And I don't need your help. I've told you that before. Quit treating me like some sort of…pity project. I'll make it on my own."

Feeling as if he'd just slapped her, she tensed. "You're an asshole, you know that?"

"I'm doing the best I can to protect the people I care about, okay? If it works, Laurel will have a new identity. She'll be able to remarry and live the rest of her life without fear and without running. I owe her that."

"You do? Why?" she challenged. "Did you ask for this?"

He hadn't expected that question. It took him off guard—she could tell—but he quickly rallied. "She's the only person who's ever been there for me."

"When are *you* going to be there for you?"

He scowled. "You're not making a damn bit of sense."

"Then let me be clearer. I don't want to see you hurt!"

He rolled his eyes. "Come off it. At least be honest. What happens to me has no bearing on you. We're not even friends."

Virgil had plenty of reason to be upset. But his

responses were more personal and much harsher than Peyton had foreseen, and she wasn't willing to put up with it any longer.

"Forget I ever came here." Grabbing her coat, she turned to go, but he moved up behind her and put a hand on the door, holding it closed.

"Let me out," she said, but only halfheartedly. She didn't really want to leave. She wished she could lean into him, that he'd be as tender with her as he'd been last night.

But what he was feeling didn't even resemble tenderness. She knew that when he spoke. His voice was low, grating. "I thought you didn't date anyone who worked at the prison."

Now he was looking for something else to fuel his anger. "I don't."

"Then what was John doing at your house?"

"I won't dignify that with an answer. You have no say over what I do or who I see."

"Did he bring a keepsake for your cabinet?" he asked, his lips brushing her ear.

She held the door handle in a death grip but didn't turn it. "He brought me dinner, okay? That's it. Now please let me go."

"You just told me you turn him down whenever he asks you out."

"I do."

"It doesn't sound as if you turned him down tonight." Taking her coat, he threw it on the chair, but she didn't face him. She wasn't sure how their clash of wills would play out if she did.

She rested her forehead against the wood panel. "He'd already brought dinner. I didn't have the heart to send him packing. He's recently divorced, lonely. I think he's looking for a friend."

He slid his hand up under her T-shirt, leaving a swath of gooseflesh as he skimmed his fingers along her bare skin. When she didn't resist, he changed direction and slipped his hand into her jeans, where his touch became far more intimate.

Get out of here before it's too late. He was no longer holding the door. She could go. He wasn't in the right frame of mind for this kind of contact, and neither was she. But knowing tonight was probably the last time she'd see him before he was incarcerated, she hoped for a better parting, one that would allow them to feel okay when they assumed their respective roles.

"Friendship isn't what he's trying to get from you," he murmured. "He wants this." His tongue plunged into her ear as two fingers claimed her with enough force to make her cry out. But it didn't hurt. Pleasure burned through her veins.

"How do you know?" she breathed.

"Because I want it, too."

Scarcely able to speak above the racket of her heart, Peyton squeezed her eyes shut. "We can't…make this mistake again." She wasn't sure who she was talking to. That comment hadn't really been directed at him. She was just grasping for a way to hold on to her resolve. But he answered.

"You've already given it to me once. What's one more time?"

"It's one more time."

"Good thing you're too nice to say no."

She wanted to correct him. She wasn't going along with this because she was "nice." Nice had nothing to do with it—or him. Especially right now. She could sense his anger, but she didn't complain, even when he peeled down her jeans and took her from behind without ceremony or foreplay.

Although she'd never been treated this roughly, feeling Virgil unleash his frustrations gave their coupling an eroticism that caused every nerve to quiver. He made sure she knew he was the one in control, but she felt safe with him at the same time. Physically, anyway. Emotionally, she hadn't felt safe from the beginning.

The rhythm of their lovemaking escalated so fast they were out of breath within seconds. Then it was over as suddenly as it had begun and he withdrew as if he didn't care any more about her than if he'd used a blow-up doll.

Stunned by such intensity followed by…nothing, she fixed her clothes while waiting to see if he'd say anything. Or kiss her. Or hold her. Or coax her to the bed.

He didn't. He went into the bathroom without so much as a "thanks for the quick piece of ass" and closed the door.

He'd done this on purpose, she realized. He wanted her to hate him. And, in that moment, she did.

What the hell had he just done?

Cringing as the outside door banged shut, Virgil stared at the haggard image looking back at him in the bathroom mirror. He wanted to go after Peyton, to apologize, even beg her forgiveness. But he wouldn't let himself. He deserved to have her go, would deserve it if she never spoke to him again. There wasn't any point in pursuing her, anyway. She couldn't possibly want him in her life, especially now. He'd acted no better than the other inmates he'd served time with—which, in a perverse way, was exactly what he'd been aiming for.

He didn't have anything to offer her. He needed to understand that and so did she.

He'd made his point. But he felt terrible about it.

"You're a complete asshole, like she said," he muttered, and splashed some water on his face before slumping against the wall. Did he really think that little power play could diminish her, make her any less than she was? That the harshness of his actions could obliterate how he'd begun to feel about her?

Not really. He didn't want Peyton to matter as much as she did, so he'd taken steps to ensure that she stayed out of his life. It wasn't fair to encounter someone like her when he was at such a loss, not after everything he'd been through. He wished he could relegate her to a different part of his brain or scare her away entirely. When he was bucking against her, telling himself he'd been using her from the start, it seemed to be working. He lost himself in lust and anger, had actually believed, for a few seconds, that he'd stamped out every other thought or feeling.

But in that final moment, he'd reached for her breast and felt something else, as well—something that let him know he hadn't won the battle he was waging. The regret that'd washed over him then had left him feeling worse than ever.

She hadn't put his medallion in a glass case with all her other keepsakes. She was wearing it.

15

John Hutchinson watched Peyton hustle away from the Redwood Inn Motel. He didn't have to worry that she'd notice him. She wasn't paying attention to anything except what was right in front of her.

Was she upset? Looked that way. She was jogging despite her sore ankle, even though he'd seen her favoring it an hour or so earlier. It could be the rain goading her on, of course. But he got the impression it was more than that.

What had happened at the motel? Who had she gone to see? And why hadn't she parked in the lot? There were plenty of spaces....

She didn't want anyone to know she'd been there. That had to be the reason. John couldn't think of any other explanation.

Trailing her at a distance, he saw her round the corner and get into her car, which sat in front of a dark house one street over. That she'd walk a block on a bad ankle in wet weather was weird and definitely confirmed what his sister had told him—something was up.

Good thing he'd dropped in at a friend's place before coming here or he never would've seen Peyton. Because he knew Wallace normally stayed at this motel, he'd stopped by to talk to Michelle. He thought she might be able to tell him about Wallace's mystery companion. But he hadn't expected Peyton to show up. When she'd sent him off, she'd used the excuse that she had a lot of work to catch up on. She hadn't said a word about going out.

Yet here she was....

Did her visit have anything to do with that strange text she'd received from Wallace? About someone named Skinner? What did it mean?

John clung to the shadows of a neighboring house until Peyton drove away. Then he returned to the motel.

As he walked into the lobby, the bell sounded over the door. Michelle glanced up with a "customer service" smile, a smile that became noticeably more personal when she recognized him. "Hey, handsome. What are you doing here?"

He didn't have any trouble getting Michelle—unlike Peyton—to respond to him. But he wasn't really flattered by her attention. People who were *that* obvious in their loneliness came off as desperate. "Came by to say hello. What've you been up to lately?"

"Not much. Working. Taking care of my kids."

Did she not realize that wasn't particularly interesting? "Busy, huh?"

She smoothed the smock she had to wear as if she felt a bit self-conscious about the stain on the front. "Always. What about you? Everything okay at the prison?"

"That's what I'm wondering."

"What do you mean? Are you worried about what happened a couple weeks ago?"

She was referring to that fight he broke up. As much as he hated the fact that everyone knew, it'd been the talk of the town. Most casual acquaintances would be careful not to mention it, but she wasn't very tactful.

"No. There's nothing to worry about because I didn't do anything wrong."

"And everyone knows that," she hurried to assure him.

The investigative lieutenant of ISU didn't seem too convinced or the issue would've been resolved by now, but he didn't want to discuss it, especially with someone like Michelle who said whatever came into her head. So he guided the conversation where he'd wanted it to go in the first place. "My sister told me Wallace was in town this week."

"Only for one night."

"What about the guy who was with him?"

"He hasn't gone anywhere. He's in room fifteen, if you want to talk to him."

John had taken a risk assuming his sister was right and it had paid off. Wallace hadn't asked someone to join him once he was at Raliberto's. He'd had a companion to begin with, someone he'd brought to Crescent City. And Peyton knew that. Although he hadn't noticed her in time to see which room she'd been in, he now felt quite confident it was room fifteen.

Why had she lied to him? And was this person associated with that odd text about someone dying? *See if you can settle him down...* Who—this guy?

"What's his name?" he asked Michelle.

"Don't know," she replied with a shrug. "Room's booked under the department, and I haven't met him. I haven't even *seen* him, to tell you the truth."

"He hasn't come out?"

She frowned as she shook her head. "Not on my shift."

"What about the maids? Have they seen him?"

"I haven't asked." She got a funny look on her face. "Why are you so interested in this guy? Wallace will be back next week, if that helps. He reserved a room for Tuesday."

This was news, too. Wallace wouldn't return so soon unless he had important business. And whatever it was, Peyton wouldn't talk about it. She'd even lied to cover it up.

This wasn't about that scumbag pedophile he'd bashed in the head. It was bigger. A lot bigger.

As soon as she got home, Peyton threw her keys on the counter without bothering to see where they landed, pulled her cell phone from her purse and plopped onto the couch.

Allowing Virgil to use her proved she was in over her head. Where was her self-respect? She'd never had an illicit relationship with anyone before, hadn't even slept with the C.O. she'd briefly dated *after* he'd given his notice. But she couldn't seem to maintain any distance when it came to Virgil and that scared her. She had to change that, do whatever was necessary to get a grip on her behavior. And the only way she figured she'd be successful was to confess.

She needed to tell the truth, anyway. She couldn't be hypocritical enough to hide such a secret while acting as if she'd done nothing wrong. A liar wasn't the kind of person she aspired to be.

But would opening her mouth mean the loss of her job?

Possibly. The CDCR could call it malfeasance of office and put her on probation. They could transfer her somewhere else, maybe demote her. They could even dismiss her. It depended on how flagrantly, in their opinion, her actions had crossed the line. Virgil wasn't on the state's payroll. She had that going for her. He wasn't a ward of the state, either. At least, not yet. Even after he went in, he wouldn't be exactly like the other inmates because he'd be there voluntarily.

He fell into a gray area; and the gray aspects of the situation were what had gotten her in trouble. Maybe they'd save her, too. But her lack of professionalism had complicated an investigation on which the CDCR, even the governor, had pinned high hopes. She'd been told that she and Virgil would be working together—yet she'd slept with him.

That wasn't right.

So who should she tell?

Determined to recover some dignity, she blinked rapidly to avoid the tears that threatened and scrolled through her electronic address book until she reached the warden's number. Based on the chain of command, she should tell *him*. But it was almost midnight. She couldn't disturb him this late.

Afraid she'd lose her nerve or attempt to justify her behavior if she waited, she thought about telling Rick instead. She was pretty sure he'd be awake. Last she heard from him, the marshal had arrived at the safe house to guard Laurel and he was boarding a plane to Sacramento. He'd said it was a direct flight, so he should've landed by now—or would be landing any minute.

"I really don't want to do this," she moaned. Rick wouldn't be happy to hear she'd undermined their chances of success. But he was younger than the warden, more flexible about this type of thing, and she had a feeling he'd made his share of mistakes. Maybe that would inspire him to be at least a little understanding.

Her finger shook as it hovered over the keypad, but she forced herself to place the call and ignored the jittery feeling that came over her once the phone began to ring. That feeling only grew more intense when her call transferred to voice mail, because it meant she had to stew a bit longer.

Thirty minutes later, she was still stalking her living room, chewing her nails, when Rick finally returned her call.

"What's going on?" he asked. "Did you speak with Skinner?"

"Where are you?"

"Walking to my car. Why?"

"Just curious." She didn't want him to be with anyone else when she told him *this* news.

"Have you heard from Skinner or not?" he asked again.

Slumping onto the couch, she groped for the words to tell him what she needed to say. "I did."

"And?"

"He's...fine."

"He's still going through with it?"

"Definitely."

Wallace sighed loudly enough for her to hear. "Good. I was afraid we were in a bit of a mess."

"Mess" was the perfect segue. Taking hold of Virgil's medallion, which hung around her neck, she gathered her nerve and confronted her guilt. "There's just one... problem."

"What's that?"

"I'm afraid I have...something to tell you. Something you won't like."

"About...?"

A tear escaped. She wasn't used to being in this

position, had always been so cautious to avoid censure. Terrified that she'd lose everything she'd worked so hard for, she clutched the medallion more tightly. She had only herself to blame.... "Virgil Skinner."

"You said he was fine."

"He is, but...I've had an inappropriate relationship with him," she blurted out.

Stunned silence.

"Rick?" she ventured.

"Does inappropriate mean what I think it means?" he asked.

Leaping to her feet, she began to pace. She considered trying to explain how deeply Virgil affected her, but she refused to offer excuses, especially that one. She didn't want to acknowledge that he held *any* power over her. Wallace wouldn't care to hear it, anyway, and probably wouldn't understand the compelling nature of what she felt for Virgil. *She* didn't even understand it. "Yes."

"You slept with him?"

Her stomach muscles cramped. "Yes." *More than once.*

"Why? My God, you're so uptight about rules and doing what's right, I never dreamed you'd do something like this. You barely met him!"

She flinched. "I know."

He covered the phone and hollered, "Mind your own business," and she imagined the shock of those who must've overheard his part of the conversation. She almost asked him to wait until he was in his car before they finished discussing this, but he was already railing at her, as if he didn't care whether or not he made a spectacle of himself. "I can't believe this! Maybe if you were someone else I could see it. Your friend Michelle is so hungry for a good screw she nearly salivates when she meets a prospective—"

"Leave Michelle out of this," Peyton broke in. "She's had it rough the past year."

He continued as though she hadn't interrupted. "But not you. *Nothing* shakes you."

"Unlike Michelle, I haven't just been through a painful divorce."

It didn't seem to matter what she said. "While we were at the library, you and Skinner didn't even seem to *like* each other."

She fingered Virgil's medallion again, felt the heat of it. "I'm sorry."

The tenor of his voice changed, suddenly dropped. "He didn't force you, did he?"

She wondered if he'd be willing to forgo this investigation if she answered in the affirmative but she wasn't going to make Virgil look bad just to test Rick. "No."

"Not at all?"

"Not at all."

The protracted silence became almost unbearable. "I haven't told the warden yet," she said. "I didn't want to wake him. But…I'll talk to him in the morning."

"No, you won't."

She stopped pacing. "What?"

"He doesn't even know Skinner's—Bennett's—an ex-con. And keeping it from him was your idea, remember?"

"It was *your* idea first. You lied to all of us."

"But I was willing to bring Fischer in on the secret once you found out."

"I realize that. It's not too late. Maybe it's time for full disclosure."

"No. Don't tell Fischer or anyone else *anything,* do you understand?"

"I don't think so. I'm not proud of what I've done but I feel I should accept the consequences."

"Consequences…" He laughed bitterly. "Let me tell you what the consequences will be. They'll begin with several uncomfortable meetings where you'll have to explain your conduct in detail."

She winced. "I'm prepared to be honest."

"Even if it puts an end to any career advancement for the next decade or two?"

Refusing to let him undermine her courage, she squared her shoulders. "I can't base the truth on what the punishment will be."

"Shit!"

"What?"

"You're not the only one it'll affect."

"Excuse me?"

"Even if this narrows *future* opportunities, your reputation will work in your favor. That means you'll probably retain your post, at least for the time being. Instead of canning you, they'll yank Virgil."

She experienced a flash of relief. This was what she'd been hoping to achieve when she called him. Virgil wouldn't be incarcerated, and she wouldn't be tempted anymore. "Then they'll yank Virgil."

"I won't let it go that way. We have it all set up. Everything's ready."

He was already writing his acceptance speech for his next promotion. "Maybe putting a stop to the investigation as it stands would be the right thing. I'm not sure Virgil will be safe at Pelican Bay."

His voice rose. "You did this to get what you wanted from the start!"

"That's not true!"

"Isn't it? You never liked the idea."

"That doesn't mean I'd sabotage it!"

"Then listen. You've reported your behavior. I've reprimanded you, you've promised you'll never make that mistake again and now it's over. Forget it."

She nearly dropped the phone. "*Forget it?* That's it?"

"Yeah. Consider your conscience clear. Who cares whether or not you were together? It doesn't affect anything. You think I'm going to toss this whole investigation because you wanted to get laid by a piece of prison trash?"

Peyton ground her teeth. "He's not prison trash, Rick. He didn't kill his stepfather. He's no different than you or me."

"Yes, he is, Peyton. He's killed. That makes him a whole lot different. If you don't think he's dangerous you're wrong."

"You don't know him."

"Neither do you! One cheap lay and you're an expert on this guy? Are you really that infatuated with him?"

She remembered how Virgil had treated her at the motel. "No," she said, but then she tried to be more honest, since that had been her intent in the first place. "I don't think so. It's all a bit confusing. I...I don't want anyone to be hurt."

"It's the Hells Fury who'll be hurt. Irreparably, I hope."

He could imagine the headlines. But she feared those headlines would say something different than he hoped. "You don't know that the damage will stop there."

"I've got too much riding on this investigation to

flush it down the toilet over a little bump and grind. So you gave him a ride. What does it really matter? You're two consenting adults, right? Hell, I was thinking I should hire the poor guy a hooker considering how long he's been behind bars. Now I won't have to."

Peyton straightened her spine. "Thanks for treating me with respect despite my mistake," she said in a withering voice. "It means a lot to me."

"Hey, you can thank me when I come back to town."

"What do you mean?"

"As long as you're giving it away for free, I'm next in line," he said, and hung up.

Surely he was joking. Wallace was married; she wouldn't let him near her. She hoped he understood that, but it didn't matter whether he did or not. He'd learn. She just needed to keep her distance from Virgil, and she'd soon be in control of her life again.

Dropping her phone on the couch to free her hands, she removed his medallion and went to hide it in a drawer.

16

Eddie Glover felt like the walking dead. Because his wife had recently taken a job working afternoons and evenings at a craft store, he'd switched to nights at ADX Florence. Someone had to be available for the kids after school. But a week into the change, his body hadn't made the adjustment yet. Eight hours on his feet during the time he normally slept left him dragging, feeling punchy, dim-witted, slow to react.

Apparently he *was* slow to react, and none too observant. He didn't notice the car that turned down his street until it drove up onto his lawn and three white men, all of them wearing beanies and overlarge sweatshirts, jumped out. Once he understood what was happening, he stood slack-jawed as the tallest of the three waved a pistol in his face.

"Glover?"

Eddie didn't bother denying his identity. Although he was wearing a heavy coat, his uniform bore a tag and would be easy enough to check. "What's going on?"

With the help of the others, the man who'd verified his name started dragging him to the front porch. But Eddie couldn't let these men in the house. His wife and two little girls were there.

Adrenaline blasted away the cobwebs in his mind, but there wasn't much he could do to gain the upper hand, not when he was surrounded by three thugs toting guns. His cell phone was in his shirt pocket, but he knew they'd shoot him the minute he tried to get it out. He had only the lock on the front door and his ability to reason with them.

As soon as they realized the house was locked up, the tall man with a thin line of hair along his jaw—and a pointy chin reminiscent of pictures representing the devil—nudged him. "Get your keys."

They were in his pants pocket, but he made no move to retrieve them. "No."

"You're joking, right?" Devil said.

"Not at all. I won't let you in my house."

They stiffened as if he'd surprised them. But he couldn't imagine why. If these men thought he'd give them access to his house under *any* conditions, they had no idea how much he loved his family.

"What did you say?" Devil demanded.

He eyed the storm drain, judging the distance. If they tried to get his keys, he'd throw them in there, he decided. "I can't let you in the house. You can do what you want with me, but that won't change."

"Are you stupid?" This came from a much shorter man with tattoos covering every inch of visible skin, including his face. His wild eyes made Eddie nervous. He'd seen that look before, plenty of times. It usually indicated drug use and often preceded violence.

Struggling to remain calm, he drew measured breaths. Panic would get him nowhere. But it would be easier to figure out how to defuse this situation if only he understood why it was happening. He'd worked at the prison for ten years and never had an incident. "Not stupid enough to let you in my house."

"Then we'll shoot you here." Wild Eyes shoved the muzzle of his gun between Eddie's ribs. Eddie wished his neighbors were early risers, but it wasn't even light yet. The ones who were up were probably getting into a hot shower, not peering out their windows to see if he'd made it home safe. Even *his* house was dark.

"If you'd just tell me what you want, maybe I could help you instead," he said, hoping to calm them. "I've got my wallet. It's right here. We could go down to the ATM." He'd seen enough gang members to know these guys were affiliated. Their tattoos told him that much. The third man—dark hair and eyes, average height, average build—had a clover tattoo with AB on the back of his hand. Eddie recognized it as an Aryan Brotherhood tattoo and guessed they were after money. That had to be it. There wasn't any other reason for the AB to come after him. He had good relationships with the convicts at Florence. That didn't mean he condoned their actions; it just meant that, in his opinion, anyone who expected to be treated like a decent human being should treat others the same way.

Devil nudged his compatriot aside. "If he doesn't want to go in the house, we'll put him in the car."

The car wasn't any less dangerous for Eddie, but he was willing to go with them to draw any threat away from the house.

Devil jumped behind the wheel and fired up the engine. The more aggressive Wild Eyes shoved Eddie in the passenger seat before getting in behind him, and Clover Tattoo, who hadn't said a word and didn't seem all that thrilled to be there, took the other seat.

"Are we going to the bank?" Eddie asked as they

ran up over the sidewalk and spun out, tearing up his lawn.

No one responded. They lurched into the street and careered around several turns, but when they headed away from the city, Eddie knew this wasn't a robbery.

Eventually they found a dirt road leading into the countryside. Judging by the way they hurtled over grooves and potholes without any consideration for the vehicle, Eddie wondered if they were driving a stolen car. But it had very little wear and tear.

It smelled like a rental....

These boys were from out of town.

But that only added to his confusion. What was going on?

Spotting a rental agreement lying on the floor with several fast-food wrappers, he tried to get a glimpse of the name. But it wasn't easy. The agreement had been stepped on and torn, and he was trying not to be obvious.

Something Thompson. That was what it looked like.

Eddie didn't know anyone by the name of Thompson.

At last they came upon a wooded area, stopped and piled out. As they marched him into the woods, he thought they must have him confused with someone else. Except that they'd clarified his name. Were they trying to learn how ADX worked so they could break friends out of prison? Did they want his uniform to help with the attempt?

Once they were well-concealed by foliage, they shoved him up against the trunk of a tree and raised their guns.

His heartbeat crashed like cymbals in his ears as he

studied his captors, all of them strangers. *This is how my life is going to end?* They gave him the impression that they were going to kill him without so much as an explanation.

But then the tall guy stepped forward. "You see how serious this is?"

"Yes, sir, I do," he responded.

"You'd better call him sir!" Wild Eyes exclaimed, but Eddie ignored him. He addressed all inmates as "sir" and had done so for his entire tenure. It was a commitment he'd made when he'd started working at the prison. He'd decided he could judge and hate the men he guarded, or he could learn to treat them kindly, as his church taught.

"We pull the trigger and walk away, no one'll even know where to find you, Mr. Glover." That was Devil, who afforded him a bit of the courtesy Glover had first extended to him.

"You could be right about that," he agreed.

"So why don't you help us out?"

His eyes shifted from face to face. "If you'll tell me what's going on, I'll see what I can do."

"What do you know about Virgil Skinner?"

Oh, God…he didn't have a chance. This didn't involve an escape plot—it involved the life of a friend.

His thoughts splintered, slammed together. "After serving a number of years in USP Tucson, Skinner was transferred to ADX as a behavioral problem. We had him for almost a year but he gave us no trouble. The months he spent in Florence proved uneventful until he was exonerated and released last week." He hoped that sounded cooperative *and* professional.

"You're doing great so far," Devil said. "Now, tell me where we can find him and we'll let you go."

Perspiration caused Eddie's uniform to stick to him. "I don't know where he is."

Devil stepped closer. "I don't consider a lie to be very polite. And you're a polite guy. So why don't we try that again?"

Clover Tattoo intervened. "He's a C.O., man. How much can he know? Skin wouldn't hang with no stinkin' C.O."

Hocking up some phlegm, Devil spat on the ground. "That was before he knew he was going to be exonerated." Waving his gun, he drew Eddie's attention again. "Word has it the two of you were tight. That true?"

Skinner was the brother he'd always wanted and never had. Eddie had never admired anyone more. But they made an unlikely pair, and that was all he had to hang his hopes on. "I'm not sure you'd call it tight. But I liked him. I feel terrible that he got such an unfair shake. Still…he was just another inmate, you know? You can't get attached to them all."

The first glimmer of sunrise lit the horizon with a pinkish hue. Eddie wished that meant someone would see what was happening and put a stop to it, but there wasn't another soul in sight.

"You're saying you don't keep in touch with him?" Devil asked.

"No, sir." Eddie thought about Virgil a lot, missed their discussions, but hadn't tried to contact him. He knew he couldn't.

Wild Eyes kicked dirt onto Eddie's boots. "Who picked him up when he was released?"

Once again, Eddie felt the weight of his cell phone in his shirt pocket and wished for the opportunity to use it. "I'm guessing his sister. I think that's all he has, one sister. I wasn't there." This was a blatant lie, one that could easily blow up in his face if they knew differently. They had to have selected him for a reason. But Eddie couldn't give them any information. If they found Virgil, they'd kill him. And Virgil had already been through more than any man should have to endure. He deserved a shot at starting over, at building a better life. He also deserved to be able to count on someone who wouldn't let him down.

"It wasn't his sister," Devil said.

"No? Then I can't imagine."

Devil wasn't pleased. "I'm not buying it. You knew him too well not to show up for the big day."

Eddie had been there. But he had to deny it—and pray his body language didn't betray him. "I wanted to go. I couldn't. I had the kids and my wife won't let me take them anywhere near the prison."

"Wife wears the pants in your family, does she?" Wild Eyes jeered.

"What kind of piece of shit friend are you?" Devil chimed in.

"I do my job, then I go home. I don't carry it with me." There was some truth to that. Treating the inmates with respect was one thing. Making them part of his personal life was another. Eddie had made an exception for Virgil because Virgil was an exceptional man.

Devil spat again. "You're not gettin' the point. We know where you *live,* man."

Eddie's knees nearly gave out. They *had* to believe him. He had to say something to *make* them believe. "I'd help you if I could, but I can't. I swear."

"You're forcing my hand. Look at this guy." Devil motioned to Wild Eyes. "See him?"

Eddie glanced at the crazy man who wanted to shoot him with or without cause. "Yes, sir."

"He's nuts. He'll kill anybody. Women, children. Don't matter to him. You know the type. You've met 'em, working where you do."

"I've never had any serious problems with an inmate," Eddie said.

"You're going to have problems with my friend here, because we gotta have some info to take to our boss. We gotta find out where Virgil went. He's not a magician. He had to go *somewhere*. And someone at that prison knows. I'm guessin' it's you."

Eddie's mind flashed to the day Virgil had told him about the Federal Bureau of Prisons coming hand in hand with the California Department of Corrections to offer him a deal.

They want me to help them bring down a gang in Pelican Bay.

You gonna do it?

I don't know.

You've been through enough.

What do they care about that?

That's a tough place to do time.

Every prison is a tough place to do time.

In the end he'd agreed to their terms, for the sake of his sister. Eddie respected that, respected *him*. "Why do you think he'd tell *me?*"

"You aren't the only one who has friends in Florence. We know you two were pals. C.O. or not, you and Virgil hung out as much as possible."

He hadn't kept his friendship with Virgil a secret. He'd never dreamed there'd be any reason to. So now all he could do was try to downplay it. "We got along. But I haven't seen or talked to him since they let him go."

"That doesn't solve our problem."

"I can't help you. I'm just a C.O. who once knew Virgil Skinner. It's not like we're family."

Devil made a noise with his tongue. "I was hoping it wouldn't come to this," he said and, just like that, he waved for Wild Eyes to shoot.

Squeezing his eyes shut, Eddie began reciting the Lord's Prayer.

Clover Tattoo interrupted. "You kill him, we won't get anything."

"He's not talking, anyway," Devil responded. "What good is he?"

Eddie went on with the Lord's Prayer. He didn't want to be the kind of person who'd betray a friend. He wanted to be better than that, better than these men who felt they could tempt him to do anything to save his own neck. If their roles were reversed, Virgil would die before giving *him* up. He was sure of it.

"Last chance," Devil warned. "You gonna tell me about Virgil or not?"

Some things were worse than death. Losing his honor was one of them. Virgil had taught him that. And Eddie believed it. "He's gone. They let him go."

"You know more than that!" Out of nowhere, Devil kicked him so hard he doubled over but, strangely enough, he couldn't feel the pain. He was already numb with terror.

"This isn't working," Clover Tattoo complained. "Let's leave this dude alone and get the hell out of here."

Wild Eyes swung around as if he'd shoot Clover Tattoo instead, but then he halted. "I'll get this bastard to talk."

"You're about to blow his head off," Devil responded. "What more can you do?"

"This." Coming right up into Eddie's face, he lowered his voice. "Tell us where Virgil Skinner is, or I'll drag you back to your house and make you watch as I rape and kill whoever I find there. Boys, girls, it don't matter to me. You understand? No one'll be spared.

A bead of sweat rolled from Eddie's temple.

"Is Virgil worth your family, *sir?*" Wild Eyes whispered.

Tears streamed down Eddie's cheeks. No. As much as he loved Virgil, he loved his wife and children more. And that was why he finally told them.

17

Rick sat in his car on the shoulder of Interstate 5 near the Sacramento airport. Farmland stretched for miles on either side, but he could see the cityscape in the distance with its handful of high rises. It probably wasn't safe to remain where he was, not with the Monday morning commuters whizzing past, but he wasn't in the mood to return home *or* go to work. He'd gone home after he got off the plane, but fled the house when he and Mercedes got into a fight. From there, he'd driven almost to Redding before turning around. And now this. He'd just received a call from a detective in Colorado who said he'd been assigned to a shooting. The victim of that shooting, a corrections officer from ADX by the name of Eddie Glover, wanted to speak with him.

The conversation hadn't been easy to understand, which was why Rick had pulled over—so he could concentrate without having to worry about navigating. Glover had been shot in the chest an hour ago. The bullet had punctured his lung, but he'd managed to use his cell phone to call for help. Now he was in a hospital, ready to be sedated for surgery, but he'd refused to let the doctors treat him until he spoke to Rick.

How Glover knew him, Rick couldn't figure out, until

the detective put him on the line. Then Glover had mumbled that someone named Thompson and The Crew had found out Virgil was working for the CDCR.

Why Skinner had confided in Glover, Rick didn't know. Glover couldn't say much so he didn't ask him. It didn't matter, anyway. What did matter was that the whole operation had been compromised.

What the hell was he going to do? Twisting the rearview mirror so he could look into his own eyes, Rick glared at himself. He'd had such big plans for this investigation, such high expectations.

Hard to believe it was over before it had even begun....

Or was it? Did he have to pull Skinner and turn him back over to the feds?

It wasn't hard to guess what Peyton would say. She'd never liked the idea of putting Skinner in Pelican Bay, had harped on about the danger from the first. She'd think this latest news was the proverbial last straw. But Rick wasn't so sure. Just because The Crew realized Virgil was working for the department didn't mean they knew he was going to Pelican Bay. Rick had asked Glover that exact question several times.

Did you mention Pelican Bay?

A rattle, a gasp and then, "No."

You're sure? Mr. Glover, you're sure?

Another gasp. "Yes."

A man who'd gone to that much trouble to reach him wouldn't get the answer to such an important question wrong.

The detective who came on the phone after had explained a bit more fully. He'd said that from the moment he reached Glover, Glover had been trying to tell him that The Crew knew Virgil was doing some informant work in California. He claimed he hadn't mentioned where, that he'd convinced the men who'd shot him that he didn't know, which was why they'd pulled the trigger. They were frustrated about not getting more.

The detective also told him that Glover insisted The Crew had a very strong network in California, and that it wouldn't take them long to track Virgil down, but Rick wasn't confident of that. Virgil wasn't using his real name. And there were a lot of prisons in California. It could take The Crew a long time to find their buddy. Perhaps they'd *never* find him. It wasn't as if they were well-educated or sophisticated. They were a bunch of two-bit losers who'd rape their own mothers for a six-pack of beer.

So why panic? He didn't want to give up too soon. There'd been an element of risk involved in this investigation from the beginning, and everyone understood that. As far as Rick was concerned, the level of risk hadn't changed all that much. Skinner could handle himself. He wouldn't get hurt. Cons like him, they were survivors.

And if Skinner *did* get hurt…well, Rick couldn't say he'd be too upset. Not after Peyton's call.

I've had an inappropriate relationship with him….
Does inappropriate mean what I think it means?
Yes.

Just the thought of the two of them together made him shake his head in disbelief. Where did Virgil get off thinking he could show up with all his tats and prison swagger and jump into bed with the woman Rick had been dreaming about for months? Virgil was a lowlife. Rick couldn't figure out how he'd managed to overcome Peyton's resistance. There had to be something about him, something she liked. She'd never shown any interest in Rick.

But she might have. If he wasn't married…

Leaning back against the headrest, he thought about the promises he'd given his wife to get counseling. After the argument this morning, which had nearly turned to blows, he knew that was never going to work. Not in a million years. It was too late. He didn't dream about Mercedes anymore. He didn't think of her at all, at least not when he was away from her. And if they made love? She became Peyton.…

Maybe he'd needed a shocking event like this to wake him up and make him realize his marriage was over. If not for Mercedes, he could move on and be with someone who *did* turn him on, someone like Peyton.

The flash of lights reflecting off his mirror startled him. Sitting up, he checked to see where those lights were coming from and found a black-and-white tucked behind his vehicle. A highway patrolman was running his license plate. A few seconds later, he used a loud-speaker to ask Rick to get out of the car.

Feeling a little self-conscious about his appearance, Rick located his driver's license and registration and stepped outside. He'd thrown on some sweats when he stormed out of the house and hadn't shaved or combed his hair. That plus having minimal sleep in the past twenty-four hours, and he knew he looked like hell.

"Why are you here?" the officer demanded.

Had Rick been wearing his suit, ready for the day, he might've played on his position within the CDCR. But, as it was, he didn't want to mention where he worked, so he simply handed over his license. "Drowsy driving kills, right? I was sleepy so I pulled over."

"You been drinking?"

God, he must look worse than he'd thought. "At nine o'clock on a Monday morning? Do I act like I'm drunk? Do you smell alcohol?"

Apparently his irritation was convincing because the cop didn't ask for a sobriety test. He angled his head to peer inside the car and, when he didn't spot anything suspicious, said, "This isn't a good place to rest, Mr. Wallace. The cars that come past here are going too fast. One swerve and it could all be over."

So it was safer having him get out of the car to stand on the shoulder?

"I suggest you pull off at the next exit." He studied Rick's license. "You only live five or ten minutes away."

Rick's proximity to the airport and his comment about being too tired to drive had obviously led the officer to believe he'd been traveling all night. "I didn't say I was from out of town. I said I was tired. I was resting my eyes for a few seconds, that's all."

"Right. I see that all the time."

Rick didn't appreciate the sarcasm, but said nothing as the officer returned his license.

"Tired or not, like I said, this isn't an appropriate place to stop. You'd better move on."

Or he'd cite him for endangering other motorists or some such infraction. Rick was sure the cop could come up with a reason if he really wanted to. "Will do."

The crunch of the patrolman's boots receded as he walked to his car. Then a semi passed, blasting them both with damp, cold air. "What a crappy day," Rick grumbled, but he got in and started the engine, clicked on his turn signal and merged into traffic at the first opportunity. There was no reason to linger. He'd already made his decision.

He wouldn't dismantle the investigation.

He wouldn't tell Peyton about Eddie Glover, either.

It was a hell of a night. Peyton tossed and turned, drifted into unfriendly dreams and startled into wakefulness again and again. And when it was time to get up, a hot shower couldn't ease the tension that'd ruined her sleep. She stood beneath the spray longer than she should have, allowing her mind to wander back to her last encounter with Virgil at the motel.

She had such mixed emotions about that incident, and him. He'd been more forceful than anyone she'd ever been with, but she'd encouraged his aggression. The thrill of being able to evoke such a visceral response in a man who thought he was too jaded to need anyone had been very stimulating.

So she wasn't upset about the sex. It was his rejection afterward.

But what did she expect from him? She hoped to marry someday and start a family, but a man in Virgil's situation wasn't husband material, especially for a chief deputy warden.

Virgil wasn't her only concern. Her confession to Rick Wallace weighed just as heavy. Now that she had some distance on it and wasn't quite as desperate to drive a permanent wedge between her and Virgil, she felt remorse for telling him what she had. But if she wanted to be different from the men she locked up, she needed to be honest. And the warden probably would've written her up or relieved her of duty, so…it could've been worse.

Based on your conduct I'm issuing you a letter of reprimand….

With such a large staff, all working in a high-stress

environment, she'd signed her share of letters like that since becoming chief deputy. She might have to sign another one today. When she got out of the shower, she checked her day planner and realized that she had a meeting with Lieutenant McCalley of the Investigative Services Unit this morning. They were supposed to come to a decision regarding John's conduct.

A glance at the clock told her she should quit dawdling and get ready.

She put on her suit and chose a pair of flats—her ankle wasn't quite healed—but by then she was afraid she'd be late. If she was, it would be the first time since starting at Pelican Bay. Somehow meeting Virgil had thrown her whole world off-kilter.…

She needed to get back in control. Besides her usual workload, she had to make arrangements for his arrival at the prison tomorrow.

After rushing through a cup of coffee and a bagel, she flew out the door in such a hurry she almost didn't see the flower lying on her picnic table. As it was, she caught barely a glimpse of pink petals and was halfway down the stairs before realizing it didn't belong. Turning back despite the pressure she felt to keep going, she crossed the deck and was soon staring down at a perfect long-stemmed rose.

Where could this have come from? she wondered. It wasn't even summer. Someone had purchased it from a florist, a grocery store or maybe a gas station, and that person had brought it here. There weren't any roses growing in the forest surrounding her house.

She looked over the railing to see if she could spot anyone leaving. But she appeared to be alone. Whoever had brought this had done so earlier.

She thought that was it—all she was going to find—

until she noticed a white card that'd blown off the table.
Hoping it would explain what the flower was for, she
bent to retrieve it from the floor of the deck.

The sender hadn't signed his name. But he didn't
need to. There were only two words written in a man's
blocky print: *I'm sorry.*

Peyton hadn't been nervous about meeting with an
inmate in years. She'd grown too accustomed to working
in a prison for that. Even the most dangerous convicts
typically treated her with respect. She got the impression the majority of the men liked her. Or maybe it was
simpler than that. Maybe they enjoyed seeing a woman
dressed in something besides a uniform.

According to one study on the impact of females
working in all-male prisons, the inmates behaved better
when women were present. Women symbolized gentle-
ness and caring, providing a counterbalance to the harsh
realities of prison life. And that was how it'd worked
since she'd come to Pelican Bay. To some degree she
helped offset Warden Fischer's hard-ass image. It was
the "good cop, bad cop" routine, and it worked quite
well. She gave the men hope that their difficulties,
fears and complaints might reach a sympathetic ear.
And often they did. She was certainly more sympathetic
than Fischer.

But this was no normal meeting. She'd sent for Buzz
Criven. She knew it would take a while for Sergeant
Hostetler to bring him to the conference room she was
using—unlike her office, it was inside the prison—but
she couldn't sit still while she waited. Lieutenant McCalley of the ISU had just left. After reviewing the medical
report and the testimony of the men involved, as well as
various witnesses, they'd arrived at a conclusion on the

incident with Sergeant Hutchinson. She wasn't looking forward to sharing that conclusion with anyone, least of all him. Based on what he'd said after dinner last night, she knew he didn't feel he'd done anything wrong. But he'd overstepped his bounds and had to be disciplined, or she wouldn't be doing her job.

She'd deal with that later, once she'd talked to Buzz. It was only eleven; she'd have time.

Getting to her feet, Peyton walked over to pour herself a fresh cup of coffee. She didn't need any more caffeine, but holding the cup would keep her hands busy and camouflage her anxiety. The last thing she wanted was to let on—to Buzz or Sergeant Hostetler—that this interview was a test.

The knock, which came sooner than she'd expected, startled her. "Peyton?"

It wasn't Buzz; it was the warden. Somehow, he'd tracked her down. "Come in," she called.

Fischer stepped into the room. Careful to close the door behind him, he lowered his voice. "I wanted to confirm that everything's going as planned for…Wallace's project."

Obviously he was being cautious in case anyone was within earshot.

"I'm still working on it," she said. "But don't worry. We'll be ready." Hopefully Buzz would be the right man. If not, she'd have to find someone else.

Pivoting, she returned to the head of the table. "Why, have you spoken to Wallace?"

"He called this morning to say he's taken care of that other business he had to attend to. He'll be here tomorrow."

She hoped that nothing on her face revealed her personal interest in this situation. "Great. Glad to hear it," she said, but as far as she was concerned, Wallace hadn't taken care of that other business at all. A woman had been shot and killed. Trinity Woods was dead because he hadn't taken Virgil's warnings seriously enough— although she had to concede that maybe it wasn't *entirely* fair to blame Wallace. The Crew had no reason to murder the babysitter. They'd done it to make a statement, which was taking the situation further than *she'd* expected it to go, too. She was just angry at Rick because she'd called him herself this morning, twice, and he hadn't bothered to respond. He knew it would leave her worrying about what she'd revealed, yet he'd contacted Fischer instead.

Did that mean he was more upset with her than she thought? It was a pretty safe guess. But there wasn't anything she could do about it. She considered telling the warden what she'd told Rick, but decided it was too late. Since she couldn't convince the associate director to call off the investigation, it wouldn't be wise to make any more of an issue of it. That would only leave Virgil friendless in an environment she could help him navigate.

For better or worse, she was suddenly committed to secrecy. And celibacy.

"There's just one thing," Fischer said.

Setting her cup on the table, she waited for the warden to continue.

"You haven't said anything about this to anyone, have you?"

The gravity of his tone caused a trickle of fear. "You mean what we discussed at the library?"

"Yes."

"Of course not, why?"

He thought for a minute, then shook his head. "It's nothing."

"You think word of it has gotten out?"

"A couple of the C.O.s have mentioned that there's added tension in gen pop. I'm wondering why."

It could be anything; it didn't have to be word that the CDCR was trying to infiltrate the Hells Fury. So why had Fischer's mind gone in that direction? What *wasn't* he saying? "That's *all* you heard?"

"That's it." He shrugged. But he'd gone to the trouble of finding her to verify that she'd kept her mouth shut. He could've called her later, at her office. Was it because he wanted to see her face when she answered?

"Did you check with Frank Rosenburg and Joseph Perry?" she asked.

"I did."

"And?"

"They claim they haven't breathed a word to anyone."

Was that true? *Shit!* This was exactly what she'd been afraid of. "And you believe them?"

"Of course. Just like I believe you."

She didn't have the chance to say more. Sergeant Hostetler had arrived with Buzz.

Nodding a quick goodbye, Fischer opened the door for them and slipped out as they came in.

Peyton was tempted to tell Hostetler that she could handle the interview alone. She was interested in more than a few cursory answers on top of what she could read in Buzz's C-file, and she figured he'd be more likely to open up if Hostetler wasn't standing guard at the back of the room. But she couldn't act out of the ordinary. He'd be able to tell something was different and so would the staff.

"I have a problem," she announced.

Buzz glanced over his shoulder as if he thought she had to be talking to Hostetler.

Peyton walked around the large table. "That was meant for you."

Because of food allergies and irritable bowel syndrome, Buzz had trouble gaining weight. His hollow eyes indicated that today wasn't one of his better days. But his illness didn't make him safe. He had a restless nature that made her fear he might be too unpredictable for her purposes. With tattoos covering his bald head, even part of his face, he looked as hardened as he probably was.

How would he react if she put Virgil in his cell?

He was smaller than Virgil. That, she liked. She wanted Virgil to be able to win if his cell mate ever attacked him. Of course, she thought Virgil could handle most men, as long as he knew what was coming. But there wasn't much anyone could do to avoid getting shanked while sleeping.

"I'm sorry to hear you have a problem, Chief Deputy," he said. "I really am, but there's nothin' I can do to help you."

She arched her eyebrows. "You don't even know what's wrong. Why don't you sit down so I can explain it to you?"

He did as she asked but bounced his knee as if he could hardly stand to be in the same room with her. "No offense, but I'd rather not get involved. I can't do you any favors, you hear what I'm sayin'? I'm gettin' out soon. I wanna serve my time and go. You understand."

Despite his gang ties, he hadn't been much of a behavioral concern in the past several years. His desire to sidestep her and stay out of trouble made her think he might actually work. It wasn't like she had a lot of men to choose from that she considered safe. Everyone in Pelican Bay was there for a reason.

"Of course I understand."

He relaxed slightly—until she continued to speak and he realized she wasn't about to back off.

"But that still leaves me with a problem."

Adjusting his position, he squinted at her. "What do you want from me?"

Peyton sat on the edge of the table. "There's some sort of unrest in gen pop. It's subtle, but…you know why I'd be concerned about that, right?"

"Of course. It's your job to keep things under control."

"That's one way to put it. Another is that I don't like it when people get hurt. So I'm hoping you can tell me what's making everyone so…uptight." This wasn't the approach she'd planned to use. She'd been thinking of telling him that someone claimed he was making threats of bodily harm. But the warden's visit, and what he'd said during that visit, had created an opportunity to put Virgil in Buzz's cell, and make Buzz believe it was *his* fault.

"I don't know what you're talkin' 'bout," he complained. "There's nothin' happenin' in gen pop. If there was, I'd know about it."

"That's why you're here."

Realizing that he hadn't made it any easier to maintain a low profile with that comment, he flushed. "There's nothin' to tell."

"So why are you nervous?"

He wiped his palms on his jeans. "If you were me, you'd be nervous, too. Meeting with you isn't good. I don't want trouble."

"I don't want trouble, either. That's why I'm asking for your help."

"But helpin' you *is* trouble. I ain't no rat, Chief Deputy. If you think that, you got me mixed up with someone else. You hear what I'm sayin'?"

"Letting me know what's going on in gen pop is ratting someone out?" She rose to her feet. "Now I'm really worried."

The teardrop tattoo on his cheek stretched and shrank as he clenched and unclenched his jaw. Only twenty-eight, he was too young to have spent as many years in prison as he had. "I didn't say that."

"What are you saying?"

"The guys are jittery, that's all. You know…it's the fog, the cold. Winter ain't the best time to be in the joint."

"So you won't tell me what's going on?"

"I *can't* tell you anything. One wrong word and they'll call me a snitch. That's a death sentence. You know it as well as I do."

"Fine. If you won't do me one small favor, I won't do you any favors, either."

The knee that'd been bouncing stopped, and his eyes sharpened. "What?"

"Transfers are coming in tomorrow afternoon."

He shook his head vigorously. "That's got nothin' to do with me."

"Now it does. There's a man who'll be joining us, someone the good folks at Corcoran are tired of dealing with."

"Behavioral?"

"Yes."

Buzz jumped up. "Don't tell me—"

"He'll be your new cellie."

"Ah, man, no! I don't want a new cellie. I'm good the way I am. I have one month left, one month! What am I gonna do with some badass causin' me grief?"

Hostetler growled for Buzz to calm down, but Peyton waved the sergeant back.

"He'll need someone who's capable of setting a good example, someone who can show him how to stay out of trouble. You're the perfect candidate."

"Just put him in the SHU."

"If he doesn't behave, that's exactly where he'll go. But we're going to give him a chance to be a stand-up guy. You know how it works in here."

"That's the problem," he grumbled. "I know how it works."

"We could make a deal, if you'd like...." She let her voice trail off, and he shook his head again.

"No way."

"Fine. Then you'll meet your new cell mate tomorrow."

He muttered some profanity under his breath, but Peyton didn't react because she couldn't really hear it. Then Sergeant Hostetler came forward to lead him out.

Once they were gone, Peyton returned to her seat, cautiously hopeful. She'd found Virgil a Hells Fury cell mate she felt somewhat comfortable with, and she'd set up a context for his insertion into the prison. If she'd pegged Buzz accurately, he'd complain to high heaven—everyone would be expecting Virgil when he showed up.

A moment later, a C.O. by the name of Gibbs appeared in the doorway. "We got a challenge coming in, huh?"

How had he heard? The door had been shut. He'd

probably tried to listen in. But…maybe not. Life at the prison had a certain rhythm and the slightest change put everyone on notice.

"That's the latest." She smiled as if it was business as usual. But she had no idea how they'd pull off what they were attempting to do. Especially now. The warden had spooked her with his talk of changes in gen pop. If the inmates had been tipped off, they'd be more watchful than ever. And that kind of tension could lead to anything.…

18

John Hutchinson was the last person Peyton wanted to see, especially now, just before she left the prison. Today she'd worked fewer hours than she normally did, but her long nights over the weekend and the stress of what was going on in both her personal and professional lives seemed to be taking a toll. She couldn't remember the last time she'd been this exhausted. Shelley had gone home an hour ago. She wanted to follow her assistant's example and head out—preferably without speaking to anyone.

But she could tell by the look on John's face that there was no way to avoid this encounter. ISU had delivered the bad news.

"Can I talk to you?" he said, his voice clipped.

She'd stood the moment he poked his head into her office. Reluctant to deal with the high emotion inherent in this particular situation, she almost said it would have to wait until tomorrow and reached for her purse. But she felt too obligated to everyone who worked at the prison to walk out on a C.O. who was this upset. The time she and John had spent at dinner last night, and the other two meals they'd shared, only heightened that feeling.

Resigning herself to staying another few minutes, she drew in a deep breath. "Of course. Come in."

As he entered, his jaw jutted forward, telling her just how upset he was—as if his taut posture and tone hadn't already communicated that.

"Lieutenant McCalley has spoken to you?" she said.

"He has."

Assuming he'd take the seat opposite her, she sank into her chair. "I'm sorry, John."

Obviously agitated, he remained on his feet. "He came to you, then? You know about this?"

"Of course. We met this morning. After a careful review of the details, I had to agree. You deserve to be suspended. You made a mistake, a serious mistake."

"But I didn't mean to hurt anyone!"

Was that true? The testimony of the witnesses contradicted him, which had come as a surprise to Peyton. She knew some of the C.O.s pushed the limits sometimes. She wasn't naive about what went on here. But she'd never expected such behavior from John. "You went too far. What if Bentley Riggs had died as a result of that kick?"

"He didn't. He's fine—fine enough to be talking smack to everyone around him about how he's going to come after me someday."

She refused to let him cloud the issue. Riggs wasn't on trial here. "He fell and cracked his skull when you kicked him. And there are… Never mind."

"There are what?"

She wasn't sure she wanted to get into this part. But she felt she owed it to him to back up her decision. So she finished her statement. "People who claim you used the fight as an excuse to unleash your aggression."

He threw up his hands. "Are you kidding me? *Who* said that? Other inmates? Like they'd ever come to *my* defense."

"Not just inmates." That was the shocking part....

His eyes turned so cold she nearly shivered. She'd never seen him like this. "So...Rathman? Ulnig? My fellow *officers*—they claim I was out of line?"

"I'd rather not go into who said what. No one likes what has to be done, least of all Rathman and Ulnig. But we talked to everyone, those most likely to defend you and those most likely to accuse you. You got a fair shake."

"How can it be a fair shake when you think I 'unleashed aggression' and *tried* to hurt an inmate?"

There were times when they all wanted to hurt an inmate. They wouldn't be human if they didn't get angry when they were physically or verbally abused. It was not being able to overcome that reaction that became the problem. "If I truly believed that, I would've insisted on dismissal. You know I've done it with others. So you're still getting the benefit of the doubt."

His knuckles whitened on the back of the chair. "They were fighting, Chief Deputy. I had to stop it and stop it fast."

"The fight was over, John. Almost everyone agrees you'd already split them up. It's your intent we couldn't quite figure out, and that's why we decided on suspension instead of termination."

"If I hadn't acted, those two would've gone at it again."

"But you had help by then. And someone heard you say you were going to teach 'this bastard' a lesson."

"I didn't say that."

"There were two witnesses."

"Oh, come on," he said with a groan. "You've been a C.O. You know how it is. Once your adrenaline starts pumping you simply...act."

"I have been a C.O. so I sympathize with the difficulty of the job. But that doesn't change what happened. You can't let your temper, or adrenaline or anything else, get the better of you."

He scratched his head in apparent frustration. "Think about what you're doing. If the papers get hold of this they won't just vilify me. They'll go after the institution."

Peyton was very aware of that. She'd seen it before. In 1992, a mentally ill prisoner smeared himself with fecal matter and refused to bathe, so the guards dragged him from his cell and forced him into a tub of hot water that left him with third-degree burns on the lower half of his body. And that wasn't the only incident in Pelican Bay history of which she wasn't proud. There'd been other allegations of torture, other lawsuits through the years. But since she'd begun working here, she'd been doing her best to improve the reputation of the prison, and she did that by keeping the guards as honest as she could. She didn't want Pelican Bay to face another dark moment like the one in 1992, not after all her hard work. And not because John couldn't control his temper.

"ISU and I had to take that into consideration, too," she said. "What you did could cast us all in the same bad light."

He glared at her. "Wait—you're punishing me as some sort of insurance, so if it does become public you're in the clear?"

Growing impatient, she got to her feet. "I'm punishing you because you deserve it."

"No. What happened in those few seconds could've happened to you or anyone else."

She didn't think so, but there was no point in arguing. The next time he acted up, if he did, he'd be fired. He needed to understand that. "You've got a second chance, John. You should be grateful."

"Grateful…" he repeated with a bitter laugh.

"The suspension is only two weeks. My advice is to enjoy the days off and come back refreshed and ready to do a better job."

"That's easy for you to say. You're not paying child support or trying to support two households on what a guard makes."

"You'll have some time to prepare for the financial loss. Your suspension won't start until next month. Other than that, there's nothing more I can do for you. I'm sorry."

For a few seconds, she thought he'd mock her by saying, *I'll bet you are,* or something similar. But then he made an attempt to improve his tone and demeanor. "I'm sure you did what you could for me."

Peyton didn't like this response any more than she liked his accusations. He kept trying to create a bond between them she couldn't allow. "I did what I'd do with anyone else under the same circumstances."

"Of course." He managed a wry smile, the kind that was intended to hide the emotion behind it but was quite obvious in revealing his self-pity. "You'd never pick favorites. You're always so…*careful.*"

"I'm fair," she clarified.

"Right."

She thought he'd go. What more was there to say? This event had strained their relationship. She doubted he'd be bringing her any more dinners. But he continued

to stand there, tapping his long fingers on the back of
the visitor's chair. Then his attention shifted to the pink
rose Virgil had given her, which she'd put in a tall cup
of water on her desk.

"Secret admirer?"

Peyton didn't know why she'd brought that flower
to work. She'd kept the card, too. She certainly wasn't
doing a very good job of forgetting about Virgil in a
romantic sense. But his apology was important to her.
Probably because her house wasn't anywhere close to
the motel, which meant he'd had to walk for hours. "No.
Just a spot of color."

"From where?"

"I bought it on my way to work."

"Nice." He adjusted his utility belt. "So how'd things
go last night?"

"Things?"

"After I left. You said you had a lot of work to do."

Where was he going with this? "I made some progress. Why?"

"It's difficult to be under so much stress all the time,"
he said.

What he'd done to Bentley Riggs didn't make her job
any easier. "I'm coping with it."

"Good to hear."

Finally he headed for the door, even waved as he left,
but Peyton could tell it was a front.

They were no longer friends.

Virgil had no idea how he'd be received. In some
ways, this was the last place he should've come. And
yet…it was the only place he wanted to be. He couldn't
go back to the motel. Not before dark. Subtle though it'd
been, he'd sensed a heightened interest in him from the

people in the front office. It'd started when he'd turned the maid away and the manager had called to see if he was okay.

Why wouldn't he be okay? There shouldn't have been anything to indicate otherwise, nothing to trigger her concern. Other people refused maid service if they had enough towels. So why had Michelle Whatever-her-name-was become so damn inquisitive? She'd even made a joke that people were starting to question her about the mystery man from the CDCR.

Drawing that kind of attention was *not* something he needed. With less than twenty-four hours to go before he was incarcerated at Pelican Bay, it was smarter to stay out of town entirely. He'd had a long walk here, his second trip in one day, and he'd already been waiting on Peyton's deck for two hours, but in the forest, there was no one to see him or question him.

After what had happened between him and Peyton last night, however, he doubted she'd be pleased to find him on her property. The flower and the card he'd bought were gone, suggesting she'd found them, but that didn't mean she'd forgiven him. Chances were she wouldn't want to see him. He'd been too callous yesterday. Sheer frustration had welled up and taken over, frustration and other emotions, but his inability to cope wasn't her problem. She probably thought he was some kind of monster with no feelings.

He wondered what she'd think if she knew it was just the opposite. She tore him up inside, made him feel *too* much. The sudden influx of everything he'd been missing had knocked him off balance, and because he hadn't adjusted to the real world yet, his behavior was out of whack.

For the millionth time, he remembered the moment

he'd felt his medallion hanging between her breasts. There'd been a brief exultation that coincided with his body's release, quickly followed by such a wave of self-recrimination he'd hardly been able to stand himself.

The sound of an engine brought him to his feet. Peyton was home. He walked to the stairs to make his presence known so he wouldn't frighten her, but it wasn't Peyton. It was Rick Wallace. Even in the dwindling sunlight, Virgil could tell the difference between Rick's state-issued Chevrolet Impala and Peyton's SUV.

After parking to one side of the drive, Wallace got out and retrieved his briefcase from the backseat. Virgil nearly called out to him. But he was a little annoyed with Wallace. He'd tried to reach him half a dozen times today, but Wallace hadn't bothered to return one call. Was it too much to ask for an update on his sister?

Wallace didn't care—about him *or* Laurel. He was using Virgil to advance his career. Nothing more.

Wallace got halfway up the stairs before noticing him. Then he startled so badly he nearly fell.

"What the hell?" he growled, clinging to the handrail.

Virgil stepped aside so that, once he recovered, Wallace could climb onto the deck. "You couldn't return my calls? Let me know Laurel's okay?"

"I've been busy."

Virgil had a feeling it was more than that. Wallace wouldn't even look at him. The guy had gone to ridiculous lengths to impress him on Friday. Virgil wanted to laugh when he remembered how he'd bragged about his life, his job, the money he was making. Today Wallace seemed like a completely different person, almost… morose.

Why was he so upset? *Had something happened to Laurel?*

"You wouldn't lie to me, would you?" he asked. "Laurel's safe? She's okay, right?"

"Of course. She's miles away from Florence in a safe house with a U.S. marshal. Her and the kids. No one'll find them, let alone hurt them."

"Can I talk to her?"

"No."

Anger tugged at his restraint. "Why not?"

"It's better to have no contact until this thing's over."

Better for whom? Not for him. Or Laurel. Not if they could communicate safely. And Virgil believed they could—at least until he went inside. "I could use a pay phone."

Wallace held up his hands. "Listen, I'm exhausted, okay? So just…back off."

Virgil folded his arms. He'd expected Wallace to ask how he knew where Peyton lived and had planned to explain that she'd brought him out here to go over some information on the Hells Fury. That was true. His first visit had been very innocent, although the situation had changed since. But Wallace didn't ask. And that made Virgil even more uncomfortable. "What's going on?"

"Nothing." Wallace acted beleaguered, as if he'd had a bad day.

"Travel too stressful for you?"

The associate director glared at him. "Among other things."

Virgil felt no sympathy. From his perspective, Wallace had a damn good life. He'd certainly portrayed it as ideal on Friday. Even if he knew Virgil had been with Peyton, he had no right to be upset. He was married.

He should be thinking about his wife, not Peyton. "You haven't asked me what I'm doing here," he pointed out. *Or how I found the place....*

The malevolence that came over Wallace's face surprised Virgil. What the hell was wrong with the guy? Virgil hadn't liked him much, but he hadn't felt any animosity between them, either. Now, suddenly, they were enemies?

Wallace knew about Peyton. He had to know. But how?

Trying to get a better look at his expression, Virgil stepped forward, but Wallace turned away. "That's a good question," he said. "What *are* you doing here?"

"This morning the manager of the motel called to ask if I was all right."

"So?"

"I got the impression she was more curious than concerned. So I left."

"You're being paranoid."

Had he forgotten Trinity Woods? "That's what you thought when I told you my sister was in danger. I had to push you to go to Florence to get her. If you'd waited until Monday, like you planned, she'd be dead instead of the babysitter."

"This is different."

"How?"

"Why would the manager of the Redwood Inn be curious about you? You're just some guy who rented a room."

"Not quite. The room's on your tab, so that connects us. And there are a lot of people in this town who keep an eye on whatever you do, since their livelihoods depend on the prison."

"So what? I stay at that motel all the time, and I often

bring people to town, to tour the prison or for meetings. What did the manager do that made you think she was acting suspicious?"

"She gave me a funny feeling, so I decided to get out of there. Why take chances?"

With a sigh that signaled a small concession, Wallace put his briefcase on the picnic table. "Did she get a good look at you?"

"I don't see how she could have. I slipped out while she was handling a delivery."

"And that's when you called Peyton to come to your rescue." The steely note was back in his voice.

"I haven't called Peyton for anything. I don't even have her number. It's not like the phone at the motel has caller ID."

"If she didn't drive you, how'd you get here?"

"I walked."

"Ten miles?"

"I'm not helpless." Virgil had made the same trek last night to leave her the rose. It took him a little over two hours each way. But he didn't mind the exercise. After being locked up, it was empowering just to be *able* to go where he pleased.

How would he handle being locked up again? It wouldn't be easy; he understood that. The freedom he'd enjoyed these past few days had been intoxicating.

Knowing Peyton would be there, at the prison, was the only thing that made it tolerable. He didn't want to acknowledge why.

Wallace glanced around. "So where is she?"

"Haven't seen her."

He checked his watch. "She's probably not home from the prison yet. You ready for tomorrow?"

"I am."

"Peyton briefed you on who's who in the Hells Fury?"

"She did. She brought me here on Friday, showed me photos, told me everything she knows about them."

They both heard a car coming up the drive. Rick was closer to the edge of the deck and walked over first, so Virgil hung back. Neither of them spoke as she climbed the stairs. Wallace's car would've alerted her to the fact that she had company.

"What are you doing here?" she asked Rick.

Maybe he hadn't communicated with her, either....

"I figured I'd better come back to...protect my interests."

"Which are...?"

"A successful operation, of course."

"Coming today instead of tomorrow is somehow going to help?"

"I'm needed here." He motioned to Virgil. "Our *friend* is afraid to stay at the motel. I guess Michelle's been showing some interest. And I wouldn't want him becoming an imposition on you."

When her gaze swung his way, Virgil could tell she hadn't realized he was there. Her lips parted, but she didn't reveal any more surprise than that.

Thanks to Wallace, Virgil felt completely exposed. He could've lain low without showing up here as Wallace had just pointed out. He'd come because he wanted to see her. And that had to be apparent. "It's dark now, so I can go back," he said, and skirted past them.

He wished she'd do something to show she'd forgiven him. But she didn't. She averted her eyes as if she couldn't bear to look at him and let him go.

19

Wallace studied Peyton as Virgil left. He thought she might run after him. The way her eyes followed him suggested she wanted to. That bothered Rick, but she held back and, to be sure she didn't surrender to the impulse, he moved in front of her and indicated the door. "Shall we go in?"

She lowered her voice even though Virgil's footsteps had faded. "What are you doing? You can't let him go back to that motel."

"Why not?"

"Because it's not safe! If he's really on Michelle's radar, she won't forget it. You don't want *her* to start talking. All of Crescent City will wonder about Virgil if she does."

"Virgil."

"That's his name."

It was her familiarity with it that drove him crazy. "So what do you want me to do? Rent a room for him somewhere else? How do we know that won't make matters worse?"

She bit her lip. "There's no need to do that. You can both stay here. It might be a bit cramped and...odd, considering—well, everything—but it's only for one night and at least we know it'll be safe. That's the most important thing, the one thing we can't lose sight of."

"Is that *really* why you want him here? To keep him safe?" He shouldn't have said it but couldn't refrain.

"You're being ridiculous! My offer protects your plan. Isn't that what you want? For this investigation to be successful? Because if he goes back to that motel, I'll go to the media if I have to but I'll stop him from entering the prison tomorrow or any other day. Either we do everything we can to keep him safe or we release him from the obligation and turn him loose."

Rick didn't want Virgil Skinner anywhere near Peyton, not after what had happened while he was gone. He needed some time alone with her to let her know he was available now. Surely, once she realized that, Virgil would hold no interest for her. But she could be so stubborn. And it made sense to hunker down here, all three of them. "I'll get him."

She looked so pretty standing in the moonlight. He'd fantasized about her for months, maybe even a couple of years. So why hadn't he pursued the possibilities between them? Why hadn't he prepared for what he now wanted by at least flirting with her?

Because he was too damn practical. A cheap one-nighter with a stripper once in a while kept his sex life interesting without endangering his job. But now that he was divorcing Mercedes, it was time to figure out who would replace her.

"If I bring him back, will you be grateful?" he teased.

"Grateful?" she echoed.

"You know, make me glad I did?"

Instead of smiling in return, she studied him as if

she'd never seen him before. "I'm not sure what you mean."

It was too big a reversal, too soon. He decided not to push it. "I'm just messing around."

"No, you're not. You're treating me differently after what I told you last night."

So that was what she was worried about. "But not because I hold it against you. I know you're under a lot of pressure, and you've been without a romantic relationship almost as long as I've known you. I can't blame you for taking what's right there, what's easy." Especially because he hadn't been available to give her a better option—until now.

He thought she'd be relieved to hear this. It was a pretty generous response, in his opinion, but she didn't seem to appreciate it. "That's not how it was."

He stepped closer. Knowing she'd been with Virgil made him jealous on one level, but it also turned him on because it convinced him there was a sexual side to Peyton he hadn't seen. Maybe he'd never wanted to acknowledge this before, but she was everything Mercedes was not—attractive, successful in her own right, a woman he could respect and someone who could create a little more excitement in the bedroom. "Then how was it?"

"I don't want to talk about it." She tucked a strand of hair behind her ear. "I should never have told you."

"I'm glad you did."

"Why would you be *glad?*" She seemed appalled by his reaction, but she didn't understand that *everything* had changed.

"Because it shows that you trust me. And that prodded me into making a decision I should've made when I first met you."

When he took her arm, she glanced at his hand as if ready to bolt. "What decision?"

"I split with my wife today."

He couldn't help hoping she'd act excited about the news. But she didn't. She pulled away, looking shocked, upset. He had to admit the breakup of his marriage had been sudden. He'd never indicated to anyone that he might take such drastic action, almost couldn't believe it himself. If Peyton hadn't told him about her and Virgil, he might've struggled along with Mercedes indefinitely, but the knowledge that she'd slept with another man, especially a man so unworthy of her, had galvanized him into action. If he couldn't fix his marriage, why was he hanging on? It was better to toss out what was already ruined and start fresh with someone who wasn't angry and bitter and run-down. Someone who understood his work—who was part of it. With his support, her star could continue to rise, too. Getting together would be perfect for both of them.

"What did you say?" she whispered.

"I left my wife."

"Why?"

"Because it wasn't working. I didn't even realize how miserable I'd become until this morning, when I suddenly understood how...different my life could be." Peyton's, too, but he didn't say that.

"What about your kids?"

"We'll share custody, like millions of other divorced parents. It's not what I wanted for them, but they'll survive. Hell, I survived, didn't I? And no divorce could've been more acrimonious than my parents'. Mercedes and I won't make it that hard."

Fortunately, she didn't point out that he couldn't control Mercedes, that he might not have a choice about the level of difficulty. He was counting on his wife's love for their children, but she'd grown so depressed in recent years he wasn't entirely sure *what* she might do. He didn't like the financial repercussions of divorce, either, but he figured it was preferable to get that over with and start rebuilding rather than let the marriage drag on until he had even more to lose. Peyton made a nice living. If they got together, her income would help compensate for the money he'd have to forfeit.

"But..." She seemed at a loss. "I didn't even know you were having problems."

"It's not something I wanted to face. But now that I've made the break, I feel like a new man."

She said nothing.

"And it's been coming for a long time," he added. When he'd gone home and broken the news to Mercedes she didn't even cry. She'd acted relieved, and that was how he felt, too.

Peyton set her purse and briefcase on the picnic table as if they'd become too heavy. "Rick, I'm getting some weird vibes here. Please tell me this has nothing to do with me."

"You didn't cause it. You just showed me it doesn't have to be the way it is."

When she hugged herself, he nearly repeated his suggestion that they go inside. She was cold. And if he could have a few minutes to explain everything in the warmth and quiet of her house, he felt confident she'd understand.

But if he pushed her to go in she'd just tell him to find Skinner. She was set on making that happen, and she was right to be anxious about it. Today he'd let his personal problems intrude, but that wasn't like him, not when he had so much riding on this investigation. He was counting on the goodwill and gratitude that would be generated among his superiors when he made it possible to curtail the criminal activities of the Hells Fury.

"How?" she said. "I don't understand the sudden switch."

"Like I said, it's not as sudden as it seems."

"I'm not only talking about your divorce. It's…your attitude toward me. Where is this coming from?"

"I'm attracted to you, Peyton. I have been for a few years."

"But…"

"I just never let myself consider it. Thinking about it scared me because I knew I'd feel too unsatisfied with Mercedes."

"Rick, don't do this—"

He had to stop her before she made up her mind. She was exhausted, stressed, preoccupied, wasn't really taking in what he was telling her. "I realize it's a lot to grasp with everything else that's going on. Just…know that I'm interested, okay? You don't have to settle for someone like Virgil. You have options."

"Options? You're my boss!"

"I don't work at the prison. That should alleviate the department's potential concerns. It's not as if the director would ever *encourage* a relationship, but you and I both know it happens and it doesn't necessarily mean a loss of employment. I think we can get Tillamont's blessing to at least start dating. After that, we'll take it one day at a time."

She covered her face. "This can't be happening."

"Just think about it."

"Fine." She dropped her hands. "I'll think about it if you'll make me a promise."

"What's that?"

"You'll keep what I told you to yourself and wait until this investigation is over before we deal with anything between us. Operation Inside is all I can focus on right now. It scares me, as you know. So will you go get Virgil?"

That she kept going back to Virgil brought a fresh twinge of jealousy. She could act a *little* grateful that he was willing to speak to the director so they could see each other, couldn't she?

But maybe he was expecting too much. She was as ragged as he was. So he tamped down the negative emotion. "If it'll make you happy, I'll go and grab him."

"You might want to drop him off here, then go to the motel for his bag. I don't think he should show up there at all, do you?"

He'd be leaving them alone together; that registered immediately. But he was crazy to worry. Peyton wouldn't want someone like Virgil now that he'd let her know she could hope for so much better. "You're probably right," he said, and strode off.

"God, if I hang on to my job, it'll be a miracle," Peyton muttered as she stood on the deck listening to the sound of Wallace's car growing fainter. She was so shocked by what he'd told her she hadn't known how to respond. She wasn't interested in him. She'd *never* be interested in him. But there was no reason to make that as clear as she wanted to. Not right now. They were all in a very tenuous position. She needed to keep Rick on her side for Virgil's sake, if for no other reason. It would be smarter to get through the coming weeks without defining anything that might upset the delicate balance of ego, desire, jealousy, pride, ambition—even survival instinct—ebbing and flowing between the three of them.

If she kept Rick mollified, she'd have a greater chance of retaining control of the situation at Pelican Bay, and that meant Virgil would have a greater chance of surviving his experience there.

Telling herself that Rick would soon go back to Sacramento, which would make it easier to ignore everything he'd just said, she went inside to change and make dinner. Never would she have guessed that she'd have both Virgil and Rick Wallace over for a meal, let alone staying the night.

But without knowing what was causing the unrest in gen pop, she wanted to be as cautious about Virgil's safety as possible.

"You told him, didn't you."

Peyton jerked around to find Virgil standing in the kitchen doorway. She'd been so focused on preparing the fish she'd taken from the freezer she hadn't heard him come in. She hadn't even heard Rick's car, but in this part of the house, she didn't always know when a vehicle pulled up. "Is he here?" she whispered, angling her head to look past him.

"No. He went to get my things from the motel."

Pretending not to notice the spark she felt at his proximity, Peyton slipped past him and went into the living room so she could check a side window, just to be sure. Her driveway was empty.

Virgil didn't leave his post in the kitchen doorway, but he turned to face her. "Well?"

"I did," she admitted.

Muttering a curse, he took his hand from his pocket long enough to scrub his face. "What were you thinking?"

"I was putting a stop to our…affair or whatever you want to call it."

"By trying to get me killed?"

His words scraped her nerves like sandpaper. "No. Of course not."

"You've given him the perfect excuse to make my life miserable. You know that, right? Don't you understand how much he wants you? How much it'll bother him to think I got there first?"

She did now. Rick had just explained it to her. But she didn't want to dwell on that uncomfortable conversation. It distressed her that she had to deal with unwanted interest from one man while trying to control her desire for another. "He's not like that. Maybe he's not particularly deep. Or much of a humanitarian. But… he wouldn't purposely put you in harm's way."

When Virgil chuckled without mirth, she knew he had to be thinking that Pelican Bay was practically a synonym for being "in harm's way."

"Look, if you want to know the truth, I regret telling him, okay?" she said. "I should've waited, thought it out. Maybe then I would've realized the pitfalls of going in that direction. But it was late last night when I got back from your motel room and…and I wasn't feeling too great about what we did. I would've called the warden instead, but I knew he wouldn't be up. I went to Rick because he was available, and I wanted to be honest."

He lowered his voice. "You could've called me if you needed to talk."

"You caused the problem in the first place, remember?"

She saw a pained expression on his face. He thought she was blaming him for more than she really was. "I didn't mean to be rough with you. I feel…bad about that."

"I got over it," she said, but that was an understatement. If she was being completely honest, she would've said she *enjoyed* it.

"Apparently not as well as I'd hoped."

"I would've confessed anyway," she told him. "It's the way I live my life."

He shoved away from the wall but didn't approach her. He circled the coffee table going toward the living room instead and checked the drive himself. "What, exactly, did you say to him?"

"I was vague but truthful. I said we'd had an inappropriate relationship."

"How did he react?"

"He wasn't pleased."

He chuckled again but didn't comment.

"When I said I was going to tell the warden, too, he told me not to."

This seemed to surprise him. "Why?"

"He was afraid it would interfere with our little… operation."

"Taking down the Hells Fury means a lot to him."

"He wants the glory of doing what no one else has been able to do. If this works out, he'll be a hero, and being a hero can really boost a man's career." Remembering the fish, she headed back to the kitchen. "What did he say to you about…us?"

"Nothing."

She paused at the entrance. "Then how did you know?"

"I could tell by the way he was treating me."

"Which was…?"

"Like a rival."

"I'm sorry. I didn't expect to create a jealous monster. I was feeling guilty for not being more responsible and…removing temptation seemed like the right thing to do."

She went into the kitchen, but he followed her. "There's a law that says you can't sleep with an informant?" he asked.

"Maybe not a law, but definitely a rule. If my behavior threatens everything the CDCR has put together in order to bring down the Hells Fury, I'm wrong for doing it. That could be considered malfeasance of office and might get me fired." And yet the possibility hadn't stopped her. That was why she'd resorted to such desperate measures. But telling on herself, however well-intentioned, had only made matters more tenuous and frightening—and done nothing to diminish the desire she'd hoped to eliminate.

"You knew you could be fired, but you told him, anyway?"

What astonished her was that she'd risked her job in the first place. Didn't he get that? Probably not. Why would he? He didn't understand how important her career was to her, how much she wanted to change the system because of her father. "I won't pretend to be one thing while being another. I hate hypocrites. I felt if I confessed it would put an end to the conflict I was feeling."

"How?"

"By raising the stakes so I wouldn't dare take that risk again, I guess."

"Did it solve the problem?" he challenged, obviously not pleased.

No. The same raw magnetism that had drawn her to him before was still at work. But no way would she make the mess she'd created any worse. Not after last night. The few minutes she'd spent in Virgil's motel room had shown her just how much power she was willing to give him. And that wasn't in keeping with who she was, or at least who she wanted to be. It was frightening to lose control of any relationship, but especially one with someone like Virgil. "Yes."

He came into the kitchen. "Look at me when you say that."

She forced her eyes to meet his. "Yes," she said again, but when she glanced away she knew her body language called her a liar.

Taking her by the shoulders, he gently turned her toward him and parted the opening of her blouse.

Preparing to slip out of his grasp if he tried to unfasten her buttons or touch her intimately, she tensed, but soon realized that wasn't his intent. He was looking for his medallion. He wanted to know if she was still wearing it.

When he saw that she wasn't, his gaze dropped to the floor and he stepped back. "Can you ever forgive me for last night?" he asked.

His remorse troubled her. She knew he'd been dealing with a lot and still was. "Don't be sweet," she whispered. She didn't need anything to undermine her sagging resistance.

That wasn't a yes, but it was the best she could do. Assuming she was rejecting his apology since she hadn't really accepted it, he started to walk away, but she caught his arm. Removing his medallion had been a symbolic gesture meant to signify that she was also removing him from the areas of her life where he didn't belong. But now she regretted doing it as much as she regretted telling Rick about them, and she couldn't even say why.

"We'll get through this somehow," she promised.

"Sure, piece of cake," he responded, but she could tell his mood was nowhere near as light as his tone. She also knew it was far easier for her to be optimistic; over the next weeks or months he'd be coping with much more than she would.

That was Rick Wallace!

Sitting in his truck, John put down his laptop and twisted around to get a better look at the associate director, who'd parked his blue Impala at the perimeter of the lot and walked to room fifteen.

"What do you know," he muttered, slapping the steering wheel. Coming to the Redwood Inn was going to pay off, after all. When he'd decided to watch the place to see if he could figure out what was going on with the CDCR, he'd never dreamed he'd see action quite this early. He'd thought Peyton might return later and had wanted to see what she might do, or try to catch a glimpse of the person she'd come to visit last night.

But this was the next best thing. Especially since the wait hadn't been that long, barely an hour, and he'd been surfing the internet for much of that time.

Hoping to strike up a conversation with Wallace—and get a look inside the room—he climbed out and hurried down the walk.

The blinds were drawn, as they'd been since John had become aware of this particular room, but he knew Wallace was in there. Pasting a friendly smile on his face, one he hoped conveyed enough awe and respect, he ignored the do not disturb sign dangling from the knob and knocked.

"Who is it?"

Wallace sounded nervous, suspicious, as if he was reluctant to open the door.

John found that strange, too, especially here in Crescent City. For all the hardened criminals housed seven miles away, this had to be one of the safest cities in America. There was probably more law enforcement per capita than anywhere else.

"It's Sergeant John Hutchinson, sir."

"Sergeant John *who?*"

Had Wallace heard about the Bentley Riggs incident? John didn't see how he could, not so soon. It looked as if Wallace had just gotten into town. He certainly hadn't been at the prison earlier when John had received the bad news.

But *something* was making Wallace act suspicious....

Clearing his throat, John spoke louder. "Hutchinson, sir. I'm a C.O. at the prison. We met once, almost a year ago?"

The delay was so long, John believed Wallace wasn't going to respond. He stood there, feeling awkward and uncertain, and wondering if he dared knock again, when he noticed a curtain fluttering in his peripheral vision. The associate director had come to the window.

What was wrong with him? Was he afraid to answer?

Waving to reassure him, John waited another second—and then the door opened.

"What can I do for you, Sergeant?"

Brisk and to the point—the associate director didn't seem pleased to be interrupted. So John upped the wattage of his smile and changed the excuse he'd prepared. Instead of saying he'd stopped to let Wallace know what a difference his leadership was making, he decided to ask for his understanding and support over the Riggs debacle, because even if he hadn't heard about it yet, John had no doubt he would eventually, in a report if nothing else. If he broached the subject himself, he'd at least have the chance to convince the associate director that he'd acted without malice.

"I was driving by when I saw you turn in." He motioned to the street and the traffic streaming along it.

"And?" Grooves of impatience were etched in Wallace's forehead. Obviously the man was in a hurry.

John swayed to the side, trying to see if there was another person in the room, but it appeared to be empty. An army-green duffel bag sat on the bed, stuffed to capacity and zipped shut. It didn't look as if it belonged to someone who dressed in expensive, tailored suits like Wallace did, but John couldn't imagine why Wallace would be packing up another person's belongings.

A sack on the counter contained groceries, a jar of peanut butter and a loaf of bread, judging by what he could see from the door. That explained how someone might be able to stay locked up in a motel room for several days. "I was hoping you'd have a minute to talk about an unfortunate incident that occurred a couple weeks ago," he said.

"What incident is that?"

The gravity of John's tone had piqued his interest, so John took great care to describe what had transpired in a more favorable light than Wallace would probably hear from anyone else. "I feel terrible about it," he finished, "but I really don't believe my actions were out of line, sir. I was just doing my job."

"And there are witnesses to corroborate your story?"

There were witnesses who should've supported him

and didn't, which angered him. He would've lied for any one of *them*. "There should be. Two other C.O.s came over to help once the fight broke out, but everyone seems to have a different version of it."

"Then I'm not sure what you think I can do."

"I was hoping you could convince the chief deputy warden to revisit the issue. I don't deserve to have this on my record, sir. I'm a damn good C.O. And I can't afford the loss of two weeks' pay. I'd never use more force than necessary. If I hadn't kicked Bentley Riggs he wouldn't have stopped fighting."

"Punishing a man for doing his job doesn't send the right message," Wallace muttered.

"Exactly. Next time there's a fight, I'll be so afraid of getting into trouble I might end up on the floor with a cracked skull myself. Or worse."

"We can't tie the hands of our guards," he agreed. "I'll see what I can do."

"Thank you, sir. I appreciate it. I'm so glad I spotted you turning in here. Any chance you'd let me take you to dinner?"

"Sorry, I've got other plans."

John wondered what those plans might be. "No problem." He nodded toward the duffel on the bed. "Can I help you carry any of your stuff?"

"I've got it."

"You sure?"

"Positive."

"Okay. Have a good night." He returned to his truck, even drove out of the lot so it would look as if he'd moved on. But he waited down the street to see what would happen next. Then he followed the associate director all the way to Peyton's house, where Wallace, carrying that duffel bag from the motel and a nice piece of rolling luggage, went in but, oddly enough, didn't come out.

John watched until all the lights in the house went off before realizing that Wallace must be staying the night.

At least now he knew how Peyton had been getting her promotions. And she thought she could fault *his* behavior? She was a whore at heart, just like his ex. Women were so full of shit. They only did what benefited them.

But he still wasn't sure what the man who'd been staying in room fifteen had been doing in town, how he was connected to Wallace and Peyton, or where he'd gone.

Skinner's angry. See if you can settle him down. That woman's death was his fault, not mine. None of this would be happening if he hadn't joined up in the first place.

None of this would be happening…

None of *what?*

20

It was difficult to sleep in Peyton's house without remembering what had happened the last time he'd been under her roof. Virgil told himself he shouldn't think about it. He had to put the past few days behind him and prepare for what lay ahead. But he couldn't seem to get the memory of making love to her out of his mind. And with this being his last night of freedom, he wanted to spend it with her, cancel out what he'd done at the motel.

If only he could convince her that he wasn't really the prick he'd made himself out to be. But he couldn't talk to her in private. Wallace was keeping a close eye on them both. From where the associate director was sleeping on the couch, he'd be able to tell if either of them came out.

Let it go. She doesn't need someone like you. She had too many better options. Hell, even Wallace was a better option. Maybe he was arrogant, self-absorbed and married, and maybe he irritated Virgil, but he'd never killed anyone, even in self-defense. No one was trying to kill him or his family. And he had a successful career, a place in life, a future. That was a lot to offer a woman—a lot more than Virgil had.

A creak in the hallway made him catch his breath. Someone was up. He hoped it was Peyton, that she'd come to him.

"Virgil?"

It wasn't her. Wallace knocked softly at his door.

"What?" Why the hell would *Rick* bother him in the middle of the night?

"Can I come in for a second?"

"As long as you have a good reason."

The door creaked as he opened it, but he walked quietly as if he didn't want to wake Peyton, and closed the door behind him.

Virgil sat up. The fog that had been so prevalent the past few days had dissipated. A full moon hung in the sky, as round as a silver dollar. After being denied any sight of the outside world for so long, Virgil refused to lower the blinds and block out such beauty. The light that streamed in didn't disturb him. He was conditioned to it. He'd spent fourteen years living in places that never went completely dark.

Rick looked as if he owed his build to a carefully monitored diet as opposed to any physical activity. Wearing a deep V-neck T-shirt that revealed a hairless chest and designer pajama bottoms, he seemed a little too conscious of his own assets.

For a second, Virgil envied him the ease of his life. He could've become a polished professional, given half a chance. But why waste time lamenting what could have been? He was what he was.

Rick cleared his throat. "I wanted to let you know...I'm aware of what happened between you and Peyton."

Unwilling to confirm or deny what Peyton had told

him, Virgil held his tongue and waited for Wallace to disclose why he'd confronted him on this subject.

"I guess I can't blame you for taking what you can get. A man in your shoes would have to be desperate for a woman. And Peyton's beautiful. What ex-con wouldn't climb on if he could? But I split up with my wife today so…things are going to change. I thought you should know."

"Things?" Virgil prompted.

"Between Peyton and me."

Virgil warned himself to keep his mouth shut. He had enough to worry about with Laurel and the kids and whether or not he'd get out of Pelican Bay alive. Why did it matter what Wallace had to say?

And yet…it bothered him that Rick felt he had the right to do this, that he could clear the field with a few simple words. "I don't think she's interested in you, Rick."

His mouth dropped open. "What'd you say?"

"You heard me."

"You think she's interested in *you?* Because you caught her at a weak moment? The way she lives, she was probably as sex-starved as you. Peyton's not the type to sleep around. But that doesn't mean she'd ever go for a man who has little or no chance of even getting a *job.*"

Leave it to Wallace to hit him where he was most vulnerable. "I wouldn't expect her to," he responded. "Unlike you, I have no false hope."

"False hope?" he scoffed. "You don't know any-thing."

"I know a fool when I see one. Now get out of my room."

Virgil dismissed him by lying back down, but Wallace didn't leave. His voice lowered to a whisper as menacing as any Virgil had ever heard in prison. "I'm going to credit that response to your uneducated and uncouth background—further proof of the many reasons you wouldn't be right for a woman like Peyton."

"Credit it to whatever you want. It's the truth."

"Just consider yourself warned."

Virgil rose onto one elbow. He'd been threatened by a lot of men, but no one who'd be easier to take than Wallace. *"Warned?"*

"To stay away from her."

"Or what?" he said with a laugh. "You'll kick my ass?"

"*I* wouldn't have to touch you," he said, and left.

Virgil stared at the door long after Wallace had closed it. He hadn't liked the associate director to begin with, but he especially didn't like him now. Apparently it didn't matter that he was on the outside dealing with someone who was supposed to live according to the law. Men were the same everywhere. If it served their purposes, they'd do whatever they felt they could get away with.

Tempted to march out and grab Wallace by the throat, to teach him a lesson he'd never forget, Virgil got up and started for the door. But he stopped himself before leaving the room. He couldn't touch Wallace, not if he cared about Laurel and the kids. He had to keep the agreement he'd made. Peyton didn't nullify that.

Soon this would all be over; Laurel and his niece and nephew would be safe, and they'd build new lives. Whatever happened here wouldn't matter; Wallace would have no hold over him.

But in the meantime, he'd have to watch his back more carefully than ever.

Because it was now clear that he had more than just The Crew out to get him.

＊

The tension at breakfast was palpable. Peyton wasn't sure why. Everything had seemed fine—or as fine as could be expected—when she went to bed last night. She'd been so exhausted she'd fallen asleep almost as soon as her head hit the pillow and for that she was grateful. At least she hadn't tossed and turned for hours as she feared she might when she knew she'd have these two men as houseguests.

But this morning she felt certain there'd been some exchange she'd missed between Wallace and Virgil—and wondered about the nature of it.

"You two okay?" she murmured as she put a plate of scrambled eggs in front of each.

Rick sat closest to the stove. He'd been reading the paper and drinking coffee while she prepared breakfast. "Fine, why?"

Virgil didn't answer her. After selecting a seat two empty chairs away from Rick and across the table from her, he kept staring out the window at his elbow as if he wasn't sure he'd ever see the outdoors again, which made her hyperaware of the possibility that he might not.

"Because it's colder in here than it is outside, if you get my meaning," she said, answering Rick. "What's going on?"

Setting the paper aside, he reached for his coffee. "Nothing."

That assurance meant little to her, since he wasn't the one she was concerned about. "Virgil?"

He glanced at her. "Don't worry about it."

She hesitated in the middle of the kitchen, still holding the frying pan. "Look, if there's a problem—"

"There's *not* a problem." Rick gestured to the empty seat next to him. "Quit worrying and sit down so you can eat. This is our big day."

When he punctuated that comment with an arrogant smile directed at Virgil, Virgil shot him a look that told Peyton he was no longer pretending to like Rick. Not that he'd gone to any great lengths before....

Afraid she was at the root of the conflict, she turned back to the stove, left the rest of the eggs in the pan and poured herself a cup of coffee. It'd been a mistake to get involved with Virgil, but it'd been an even bigger mistake to try and fix what she'd done by going to Rick.

Her misgivings about the investigation edged up another notch as she waited for them to finish eating, but she'd always felt nervous about it, so she was growing used to the sense of unease. It wouldn't do any good to speak out again, anyway. She'd been trying to get Rick to listen to her from the beginning. Virgil, too. They wouldn't.

She carried her cup to the table, where she sat down in a chair other than the one Rick had indicated. It felt like the only neutral choice because it wasn't any closer to Virgil than it was Wallace. "How will you manage the transfer?"

Rick stopped chewing long enough to answer. "I've got a couple officers from Santa Rosa coming to transport him."

She could tell that Virgil was paying attention to the conversation, but he wouldn't look at her. He finished his breakfast, then stared out the window some more, brooding.

"Those officers know he's not at the motel anymore?" she asked Rick.

"They do." He washed down his last bite with a swallow of coffee. "I spoke to them while you were in the shower and explained that he was generating too much interest, so we moved him."

Having Virgil picked up at the house would be so much safer than smuggling him out of the Redwood Inn. As awkward as last night had been, it was well worth the discomfort if only for this one reason. "So you won't be coming to the prison yourself?"

"There's no need. I want this to look very routine. So I'll wait here until he's been picked up. Then I'll head back to Sacramento." He set his fork on his plate and shoved it away. "Unless you'd be more comfortable if I stayed a day or two—to be sure he settles in okay."

The way he glanced at her said he wanted her to act as if his presence would be welcome. But she knew it was highly unlikely that he'd really take the time, not unless there was a need greater than making her feel "comfortable." He was showing off for Virgil's benefit. He'd behaved in a proprietary fashion ever since he'd arrived, touching her now and then and showing more familiarity when he spoke to her. But she didn't even want him around. At this point, she could barely stand the sight of him.

"No. I'm fine." She added a smile so she wouldn't be too obvious about wanting him to go. Maybe he and Mercedes would reconcile. She hoped so. She didn't want the problem of Rick being single and available, which complicated *everything*. Only if he decided to put his marriage back together would he be able to forget her little faux pas with Virgil, because then he'd be focusing elsewhere, no longer looking to her as the next woman in his life.

Checking the clock, she got up. "I have to go or I'll be late."

"But you didn't eat," he said.

She *couldn't* eat. She was too nervous, too aware of Virgil sitting at her kitchen table. "I've got some granola bars in my desk if…"

Virgil was finally looking at her. She could feel his gaze. But when their eyes met, the strangest bittersweet sensation swept over her. In another time, another place, she could've fallen in love with this man. She felt quite certain of that, even though it didn't make a lot of sense. They hadn't spent more than a few hours together. And they came from very different worlds. There was just… *something* about him.

Belatedly she realized that she'd stopped talking. She returned her attention to Rick. "If I get hungry," she finished, but that brief interruption must've given her away because, in the same split second, Rick had clenched his jaw. "Just make sure everything goes smoothly on this end, okay?" she said to fill the sudden silence.

Rick smiled blandly. "Don't worry about Virgil. He's already killed…what, two men?" He turned to Virgil, who glared at him as if those blue irises were laser beams. Rick knew the answer to his own question. Peyton knew it, too; by Rick's own admission, four men had jumped Virgil, but he didn't add that. He wanted to emphasize Virgil's background, to taunt him with it in front of her, not justify his actions. "He gets in trouble, he'll just kill again."

Peyton didn't appreciate the reminder. But…maybe it was necessary. She was having trouble seeing the man she'd come to know as a murderer. Probably because she felt she'd never really *lived* until he'd come into her life.

"There won't be any need for violence," she said, and purposely dropped her purse as she picked it up off the counter.

The clatter of the contents that spilled drew Rick's attention to the floor. He bent to gather everything up, and that gave her the opportunity she'd been hoping for. Quickly shoving one hand behind her back, she held out a note to Virgil—and felt him take it.

Cooley had arrived. At last.

John climbed out of his truck while waiting for the man in the old Corvette rolling down the narrow dirt road. He'd met the same guy here in the forest twice before, and he hoped this meeting would be as financially rewarding. He was overdrawn on his checking account, needed to cover the drafts he'd written before the bank manager called him.

The bass of Cooley's stereo pounded against the windows as he slammed on his brakes and slid to a stop, nearly hitting John.

Scrambling to get out of the way, John cursed. Each time he dealt with this punk, John swore it would be the last, but with spousal support and child support and his new truck, which he'd bought when his marriage fell apart, he couldn't get ahead.

Heavy metal blasted into the small clearing as Cooley, a kid of maybe eighteen, left the motor running and got out. The little prick knew better than to come charging in here with his stereo turned up so loud. John had asked him a number of times to be more discreet, but Cooley wanted to come off as too much of a badass to care whether or not he attracted attention. His cockiness was reflected even in the car he drove. That old Corvette wasn't worth more than a few thousand dollars, not these days, but he raced around in it as proudly as though it were fresh off the lot.

"What's up, man?" Tall and skinny, with long greasy hair, Cooley wore an MMA T-shirt with tight rocker jeans and Vans on his feet. He looked more like a skater dude than a gangbanger. He had the usual tats, of course, but tats were so common these days they no longer signified anything. Too many wannabes inked up. Cooley strove for a tough image, talked like he'd spent a few years in prison, but John knew the truth. He was just a foot soldier, recruited by Weston Jager, his older brother.

"What the hell took you so long?" John growled, relieved when the car door slammed, muting the discordant music.

Cooley shot him a dark look. "That's the first thing you say to me? What's your problem, dude?"

What did he think? John risked a lot coming out here. If he was caught doing business with the Hells Fury he'd go to prison himself. "Nothing. Just give me what you owe me so I can be on my way."

Cooley dangled a thick envelope in front of him, but when John tried to take it, he yanked it out of reach. "My brother's got another job for you. If you're man enough to handle it."

"I was man enough to handle the last one, wasn't I?" They'd wanted Bentley Riggs and he'd delivered him. He'd even kicked the bastard when the presence of other C.O.s forced him to break off the attack before Weston was finished.

Cooley made a *tsking* sound. "I heard you got yourself in trouble with that one."

"See the risks I take?"

"That shouldn't have been a risk. You didn't sell it right. Westy said you came in late."

Because he'd almost chickened out. "All's well that ends well," he said to cover his embarrassment.

"That's a *happy* ending?" Cooley cracked a smile.

"He was sent to the infirmary with a broken skull, wasn't he?"

"I'm talking about what's happening to *you,* man."

John didn't want to go into it. It was too upsetting. But curiosity compelled him to find out what the Hells Fury had to say about him. They thought they were so tough, but *he* was the one who'd done the bulk of the damage that day. "How do you know what's happening to me?"

"Word has it you're gonna be suspended."

News traveled fast in prison, especially bad news.

"And that's just for jumping in at the end," Cooley added. "If they knew it was because of you Westy got to that faggot in the first place, they'd fire your ass."

"They're not going to fire me. I'll get through this."

"Too bad you have to worry about it. That's what's wrong with the system. We're only trying to take out the trash, you know? Cleanse the world. Creeps like Bentley Riggs don't deserve to live."

John heard that all day, every day. If the Hells Fury weren't pressuring him to smuggle cell phones, cigarettes or crank into the prison, or to provide privileges they didn't deserve, they were asking him to serve up chomos—or child molesters—so they could exact retribution on behalf of the innocent victims who'd been harmed. Which was pretty damn ironic considering all the innocent victims *they'd* harmed. But John didn't mind the irony. He hated chomos as much as they did.

"We can't snuff them all out. And I'm done doing favors for your brother. At least for a while."

Cooley pulled out a pack of cigarettes and lit up. "What do you mean by that?"

"Isn't it obvious? I've been written up. I need to lie low."

With a wave of his hand he suggested John was too concerned. "Stop worrying. My brother's got your back."

John wasn't sure whether to take him seriously. "There's nothing Weston can do. ISU has already given me notice. My suspension got the rubber stamp from everyone, all the way up to the chief deputy warden." Who should've shown more loyalty...

"That chief deputy...shee-it." Drawing out the word, he punctuated it with a whistle. "She's a mighty fine piece of ass, isn't she?"

Peyton *was* attractive. No denying that. In the beginning John had liked her. When he'd first started having problems in his marriage, he'd even harbored some hope that Peyton might like him in return. That if he lost Marguerite, he'd take a step up. But he didn't care for her anymore. He preferred women who acted like women, not some ballbuster ice queen like Adams. She made him feel...inadequate. "She's okay, I guess."

"She's more than okay, dude. She's *hot!* What my brother wouldn't pay for five minutes alone with her..." He made a thrusting motion with his hips. "I might even be willing to serve a nickel for some of that action, you hear what I'm sayin'?"

John backed away. "Listen, if that's what Weston has in mind, tell him to forget it. I might need a few aces here and there to cover expenses, but I'm not crazy."

"Chill out. You think we're stupid? That would bring

down the whole place, which would interfere with business. There's no need for that."

Detric Whitehead, the leader of the Hells Fury, would probably kill them both if they did.

"Westy has a message he wants you to deliver, that's all," Cooley said as he exhaled a fresh stream of smoke.

Communication work paid well and was the safest way to augment his income. Even if he was caught passing a written message, what convicts called a "kite," he could claim he'd confiscated it. But right now…he was too concerned about the added scrutiny he was under.

"I'd do it, but I'm already in enough shit. I need to stay aboveboard for a while."

"I told you, my bro's handling your problem."

"There's nothing he can do."

"Where's your faith, man? We *run* the place. You know that."

His arrogance annoyed John. The war wasn't over yet. Peyton and the warden were doing all they could to weed out dirty C.O.s. They had Rosenburg working overtime, investigating anything that smelled remotely suspicious. But with so many inmates wanting so many things, there were simply too many ways to earn a buck and too many ways to spend the extra dough. He wasn't the only one to sell out.

"Yeah, well, I'll believe it when I see it." John was pretty sure the administration had won this battle. It was too late for anyone to fix, even Weston Jager. Or Detric Whitehead himself. "You going to give me the money or not?"

As soon as Cooley handed over the envelope, John counted through the stack of money. It was all there— two thousand bucks for making sure Bentley got his ass kicked and for smuggling in a cell phone. It would've been a nice financial boost if he hadn't gotten busted. As it was, he'd lose more than that due to the suspension.

"We're even," he muttered, and turned away.

Cooley remained where he was. "That's it, then?" he called after him. "I should tell Westy it's a no? Deech won't like that."

"Deech" was Detric Whitehead's nickname. They all had one. Even the general. "I can't," John said, but he was already calculating up his financial obligations, knew he'd be broke again in a few days. How would he survive the coming weeks?

He'd figure out what was going on with Rick Wallace and that stranger, that was how. News of what they were doing had to be worth more than the petty amounts he'd earned in the past—maybe even enough to finally get him out of the red.

He'd climbed into his truck when he waved to let Cooley know he had more to say. It might take a while to learn Wallace and Peyton's secret; he could use a few bucks to keep him going in the meantime.

Driving forward, John lowered his window.

Cooley took a final puff on his cigarette and ground it into the dirt. "Change your mind already? You are *so* predictable."

"Shut up," John snapped. "Just tell me what Weston wants me to do and how much he's offering."

21

Eleven guard towers surrounded the maximum-security facility erected on land carved out of the surrounding forest. Shifting, Virgil tried to take in as much as he could while the two officers who'd picked him up at Peyton's house—Nance and Parquet—turned into the main entrance. Pelican Bay sprawled over two hundred and seventy-five acres, ten miles south of the Oregon border. If it wasn't for the three fences that established the perimeter, two topped with razor wire, the middle one electrified, the white two-story concrete buildings would've looked as innocuous as an industrial park.

Another of the many ironies he'd noted since coming here, Virgil thought. Half the men living at this "industrial park" were lifers, which gave them little to lose. And thanks to the overcrowding in California prisons, as many as three hundred inmates were, at times, supervised by only two guards.

Surviving here wasn't going to be easy, even if he managed to keep his purpose a secret....

"Big mother, isn't it?" Dangling one hand over the wheel, Nance paused in the parking lot of the administration building located out front, turning around to gauge Virgil's reaction.

Virgil didn't answer, but he arched his eyebrows, awed in spite of himself.

"It's a freakin' city," Parquet chimed in from the passenger seat. "Has its own fire department, water treatment facility, boiler plants and electrical generators. It even has a full medical department with hundreds of medical staff, and an education department with teachers and a school district superintendent."

Nance gave the car some gas. "No wonder it takes one hundred and eighty million dollars a year just to keep it running."

"With that kind of cash outlay, conditions here must be pretty good, right?" Virgil said.

Nance and Parquet both chuckled at his sarcasm. From the outside, the institution seemed clean and quiet, but it was a bit too sterile. Pelican Bay's reputation, one of efficient brutality, was well-known. But there was no time for the police officers to respond to his remark. They'd reached the vehicle sallyport, which was surrounded by carefully groomed gardens.

More irony....

Lowering his window, Nance showed the proper paperwork and signed in.

Twenty-three if he was a day, the chubby, baby-faced sallyport officer squatted to positively identify everyone and get a better look at Virgil. "Heard this guy was comin' in. You like to cause trouble, huh, buddy?"

Virgil didn't dignify his question with a response. Obviously this guy was another "HACK"—horse's ass carrying keys—like so many of the C.O.s he'd met over the years. Since the job didn't require much more than a high school diploma, C.O.s weren't always the brightest individuals society had to offer. Pelican Bay C.O.s had often been accused of being racist and cruel. They denied that, of course. And in recent years administration had worked hard to clean up the image. But Virgil had a difficult time believing those rumors were completely unfounded. *Where there's smoke…*

Nance answered. "Trouble of the worst kind."

"He'd better watch himself," the guy said. "This is the end of the line for guys like him. We don't put up with any shit."

Officer Nance had been teasing—Virgil could tell by his tone—but the young man in the green uniform was dead serious. He sounded eager for the opportunity to conquer, to punish, and that tempted Virgil to prove the guy wasn't half as strong, mentally or physically, as he pretended to be.

But a response like that didn't make sense. Virgil was on the other side for a change. On the same side as this officer. Not that it sat well with him. There were moments, a lot of them, when he didn't want to join forces with the law. He'd spent too many years hating those who'd oppressed him. Maybe the cons he'd associated with in prison weren't pillars of the community, but they had a code and they adhered to it. That was something.

"You don't have anything to say?" the guard prompted.

Eat shit and die came to mind, but that was his anger talking.

Closing his eyes, Virgil relegated this gatehouse asshole to the list of people not worth hassling. It wasn't difficult to tell the kid was all talk. He'd run if Virgil ever confronted him one-on-one. Virgil had received similar comments from other C.O.s dozens of times. They acted tough when they had every advantage. But they were merely attempting to cover their own inadequacies.

"It's probably better not to provoke some people," Nance told him.

"He doesn't scare me. We've got fourteen hundred of these hard-asses." Wearing a self-satisfied grin, he searched the inside compartments and undercarriage of the car.

"What an idiot," Nance grumbled as the kid waved them through the second gate.

Virgil ducked his head to gaze out at the prison ahead of them. Shaped like a giant X, the Security Housing Unit took up one side of the property. The regular maximum-security prison took up the other. It consisted of eight cell blocks radiating, like the spokes of a wheel, from a yard of at least three acres.

They parked next to a bus that had held other prisoners, judging by the crowded intake area and the C.O.s waiting there.

Parquet got out and opened Virgil's door. "Welcome to twenty-first-century hell."

The belly chain connecting his handcuffs to the shackles on his ankles rattled as Virgil climbed out of the backseat and stood in the dwindling afternoon sunlight, squinting up at the edifice he'd call home. The chill wind whipping over the treeless grounds reminded him of how cold and sterile it could be in prison.

But he'd been to hell before. It didn't scare him. At least Laurel and the children were safe. Besides, he was taking something with him this time that they couldn't strip away—his memories of that night with Peyton, the hope of seeing her inside these concrete walls and the phone number she'd slipped him at breakfast.

Peyton stared out her office window at the empty yard and a section of blacktop where the inmates played basketball. She couldn't see R & R—Receiving and Release—from the administration building, but she knew Virgil had arrived on the heels of the bus transporting thirty men from other prisons in the state. The C.O.s down there had called her, as requested.

Normally, new arrivals were given a Fish kit—underwear, sheets, a blanket and one change of clothes—and housed in a separate unit called the gym until staff could observe their behavior and determine where they should be placed. But the gym provided a home for those with a "bit" or short prison sentence, too, and was severely overcrowded at the moment. The whole prison was. Originally built for 2,280 inmates, it held a thousand more, and that gave her a good excuse to drop Virgil into gen pop. It was important to get him into regular circulation as soon as possible. She wouldn't rest easy until he was out of this place and safely away. The 2002 riot, when blacks and Hispanics started stabbing one another in the exercise yard known as Facility B, had taken one hundred and twenty guards and thirty minutes to stop, and that was using everything from pepper spray, to tear gas, to rubber bullets, to wooden bullets, to two dozen .223-caliber rounds from Ruger Mini-14 rifles. The inmates wouldn't quit fighting until someone was killed.

Although there was only one death, due to a rifle shot, many convicts were injured, mostly by other prisoners. Once it was all over, the staff found fifty makeshift weapons in the yard.

"Hey, you got a minute?"

Surprised that she had company, Peyton turned to find Lieutenant McCalley standing in the doorway. Shelley wasn't at her desk—probably out having a smoke—and Peyton had left the door open. She'd been

too anxious to shut herself in, had wanted to hear and
see everything going on around her, even though the
administration building was beyond the electrified perimeter that enclosed all the level-four inmates. She'd
never see or hear a disturbance involving Virgil from
where she worked.

"Sure." Concerned by the serious expression on Mc-
Calley's face, she gestured that he should take a seat.
"What's wrong?"

He walked into the room and sat down but got right
up again. "The disciplinary action we're taking against
John Hutchinson?"

John *again?* "Yes? What about it?"

"A few more details have come to light."

Finally able to forget, for a moment, that Virgil was
entering the prison at this very moment, Peyton came
around to sit on the edge of her desk. "What kind of
details?"

"One of the C.O.s who helped break up the fight came
to see me this morning."

"Who—Ulnig?"

"No, Rathman."

"And?"

"He's changing his story."

"Why do you think he's doing that?"

McCalley began to circle the room but paused at the
picture of her father, even though she knew he'd seen
it many times before. "No clue. He says I misunder-
stood him. That he doesn't believe Hutchinson over-
reacted. He's now claiming Riggs was trying to come
after Hutchinson with a sharpened toothbrush. He said
if Hutchinson hadn't kicked Riggs, he would've been
shanked."

"But Riggs had no weapon. We already established that."

The lieutenant ran a hand through his hair, mussing the only long part—the bangs he usually combed off his forehead. "Rathman produced the toothbrush Riggs supposedly had."

"But it was Riggs who was jumped by Weston Jager. It's also Weston who has a history of violence, both inside and outside the prison. Why would Riggs have a shank?"

"Rathman says he knew what was coming and wanted to be prepared. When it finally happened, he decided it was time to get himself out of gen pop and into the SHU, where he wouldn't have to watch his back anymore. If that meant he had to stab a C.O., he was willing to stab a C.O."

Peyton scowled as she tried to assimilate this information. "Why didn't Rathman explain this before?"

"He said he told me what he *thought* had happened but has since realized he made a mistake. He said Riggs must've dropped the weapon after he hit his head. Weston Jager picked it up, and once Rathman saw Weston with it, he didn't believe it had belonged to Riggs."

"That part I can understand."

"And Rathman's been able to prove it was Riggs's weapon, not Jager's."

"How?"

"Riggs no longer has a toothbrush in his cell, for one. And his cell mate insists he spent hours and hours at night sharpening something he wouldn't show him."

"Oh, jeez." Rubbing her temples, Peyton scrambled to figure out what should be done. "Have you talked to Hutchinson about the toothbrush? I mean…if he saw it in Riggs's hand and felt threatened by it—if that's why he lashed out—why didn't he say so?" Instead of all that garbage about adrenaline and the heat of the moment…

"I don't know. I haven't gone back to him yet. I wanted to speak with you first, inform you that we might need to reevaluate."

"Reevaluate what?" It was the warden. He'd come to her door. Peyton had met with him earlier to assure him she was prepared for "Simeon's" arrival. They'd also gone over the Hutchinson situation but, apparently, everything wasn't as it seemed.

"The suspension of John Hutchinson," she said.

His forehead rumpled as he walked into the room. "What's going on?"

Hearing Shelley's voice out in the hall, Peyton closed the door to give them some privacy while she explained. When she'd finished, the warden cursed in disgust.

"Sounds to me as if you didn't do enough research," he said to McCalley. Then he turned to her. "And *you* didn't make sure he did enough research. Which means you were both derelict in your duty."

"This is the first we've heard about Riggs having a weapon," Peyton said.

"You should've known before, should've kept digging until you had all the facts before you handed down a decision."

At the time, they'd believed they *had* all the facts. They'd interviewed everyone, spoken to John repeatedly, held off on making a decision until they felt confident they'd chosen the right course of action.

"Hutchinson is one of *us*," Fischer said. "That means he deserves the benefit of the doubt."

But just this morning, the warden had said they

needed to make an example out of him, emphasizing that abuse would not be tolerated. He'd reacted the same way they'd reacted to the information available, which made him just as "derelict" in his duty.

Not that he'd ever admit it. He always acted as if he never would've made a particular mistake—after it was proven to be a mistake.

"Yes, sir," she said. "So…now that the situation's changed, how do you suggest we handle it?" Peyton wanted him to take full responsibility for the decision, so he'd have no room to blame her later if it was wrong.

"That's obvious, isn't it?"

She kept her mouth shut and waited for him to explain.

"Call Hutchinson in, apologize to him and make sure he understands that there'll be no disciplinary action. And while you're at it, try thanking him for risking his life to keep order."

McCalley shot her a glance before focusing on the warden. "But there are still a lot of unanswered questions, sir. Shouldn't we continue to investigate?"

"And draw even more attention to the fact that you suspended a man without sufficient cause? Hell, no! I don't want our officers to think we won't stand behind them when they need us most. What'll that do for morale around here? We're a family. Riggs had a weapon. Hutchinson acted to disarm him. That's all we, or anyone else, need to know."

Protect the family.… Peyton wondered if the C.O.s who'd scalded that mentally ill prisoner back in '92 had relied on getting "the benefit of the doubt" when they'd been scrubbing the skin off his legs. She preferred to believe staff over prisoners, too, but checks and balances were an essential part of the system. "John didn't say anything about a shank, sir," she said. "I'm sure he would've mentioned it if it had been a real threat."

"We have enough to worry about without going after our own," Fischer retorted. "As long as no one can prove John acted out, we're fine to assume he didn't." He turned to leave her office, but she called after him.

"Sir—"

He turned back. "Have I not made myself clear, Chief Deputy?"

"Yes, you have, but—"

"Just do as I say and quit arguing for a change," he snapped and left.

Apparently the brutality issue had sidelined whatever he'd come to say. Or he wasn't willing to discuss it in front of McCalley. Maybe he was so disappointed in how she'd handled the Hutchinson problem, he didn't want to talk to her about it at all anymore. Lately, they seemed to disagree far too often. Only by sheer will was she able to implement some of his directives.

"You heard him," she told McCalley. "Give Hutchinson a call."

"I think he's making a mistake," he murmured.

She remembered John's demeanor when he'd been in her office yesterday. If Riggs had had a shank, and John knew it, he definitely would've used that as part of his defense. "So do I."

Ink wouldn't leave Colorado, even though Shady had ordered him back to L.A. He was too pissed that Eddie Glover had lived. They'd gotten all the information they were going to get out of Eddie, so it shouldn't have mattered, but to Ink killing Eddie had become an obsession. He talked about it constantly, said he wanted to add another tattoo to his body depicting him shooting "that miserable son of a bitch C.O." All he ever craved was blood. As far as Pretty Boy was concerned he was a fucking psychopath. But no one else seemed to care.

Fortunately, there'd been too much activity at the hospital to finish Eddie off, especially when it served no better purpose than to appease Ink's twisted desire for revenge. Pointblank had flat-out told Ink that every single Crew member would be lying in wait for him if he risked that kind of heat. So he'd finally quit raving about killing Eddie and fixated on going after Laurel again. They'd been arguing about how he was going to accomplish that all day.

"We won't find her." Pretty Boy lounged on a bed in the cheap motel where they'd holed up since the shooting. "There's no reason for her to stay in Colorado. For all we know, she could be halfway across the country."

Pointblank, who was on the other bed, had been watching television. At this, he finally deigned to enter the conversation. "We stay until we're told to leave."

"Ink *has* been told to leave," Pretty Boy reminded him.

Pointblank motioned to Ink, who was fiddling with his gun at the desk. "That's his problem. He'll have to answer to Shady. You won't. So don't worry about it."

"Shady won't be pissed at me, not once I get the job done," Ink said.

"And how do you plan to get the job done when we don't even know where she is?" Desperate to be rid of him, Pretty Boy fantasized about waking up in the middle of the night and putting a bullet through his brain while he slept. Killing Ink might cause a backlash inside The Crew. The hit wouldn't be sanctioned by the gang's leaders. But Pretty Boy felt he'd be doing the world a service. He'd be doing Skin a great service, too. Except he wasn't sure if he should be motivated by the loyalty that still lingered in his heart. How should he feel about his old cellie? Was Skin debriefing as the others claimed?

If not, why hadn't he made contact?

Maybe he couldn't. Maybe something else was going on....

"Shady'll find her," Pointblank—Thompson—said. "You heard what he told us when he called. He's got some contacts in the CDC."

But would they go crazy cooped up together before those contacts came through? At this point, Pretty Boy was having fantasies about putting a bullet through his *own* brain just to escape the monotony. "We'll see."

He got up to go outside for a cigarette. He never used to smoke. He'd taken it up a few days ago. The nicotine calmed his nerves, and the act of bringing the cigarette to his mouth kept his hands busy. Besides, it provided a good excuse to take a walk every couple of hours.

Thompson's phone vibrated on the table as Pretty Boy passed by. When he glanced down, he saw that the caller was Shady and froze. Shady's contact had delivered what they'd asked for. Shady wouldn't be contacting them again otherwise. They'd already talked to him today.

"Hand me that," Thompson said.

Pretty Boy hesitated. The last time they'd received orders from Shady, Ink had shot Glover, a corrections officer, and it'd been all they could do to keep him from going back and killing Glover's whole family. Pretty Boy didn't want to see anyone else hurt, especially Laurel.

"What's up with you?" Pointblank snapped at his lack of response.

Ink grabbed the phone before Pretty Boy could reach for it and tossed it over to Thompson, who answered.

"'Lo?...No kidding?...Never heard of it....Where?... Got it....'Course....This is a step in the right direction, anyway....If it's not a big place, maybe we can find her on our own....Sure....Will do."

When he hung up, he scooted off the bed and began stuffing his clothes into his duffel bag. "Get your asses moving," he said. "We're out of here."

Pretty Boy remained rooted to the spot. "Where we goin'?"

"Town called Gunnison."

"Never heard of it," Ink said. "Is it close?"

"Not far, maybe two, three hours."

Pretty Boy's mind raced. That was as far as the feds had taken Skin's sister? What had they been thinking?

They'd underestimated the network that served The Crew, didn't realize that gang members had loyal girlfriends and wives who held regular jobs and could be privy to sensitive information. "Laurel's there?" he asked, but he already knew the answer.

"'Cording to Shady."

"So his contact came through," Ink said, obviously impressed.

Pointblank headed into the bathroom. "Damn right. Just like I told you. Shady means business. He does his part."

Ink shoved his gun in the waistband of his jeans. "Does that mean we have an address?"

"Not yet," Pointblank called back.

Pretty Boy could hear him packing up his shampoo

and razor and whatever else he had in there. "When's that coming through?"

"Shady's not sure he can get any more than we got now. He's hoping we'll be able to find her ourselves."

Hope buoyed Pretty Boy's flagging spirits. "That won't be easy."

Sticking his head out of the bathroom, Pointblank grinned. "Shouldn't be too hard. Gunnison's only got five thousand people."

Stubbornly clinging to that brief flash of hope, Pretty Boy said, "But if she's hidden away, there's no—"

"She won't stay hidden forever, man." Pointblank had disappeared into the bathroom again. "Most people can't take that shit for long. When nothing happens, she'll start to feel safe, get bored, and then she'll go out to the grocery store, to church, take the kids to the park."

"And she'll be new in town," Ink added with an eager gleam in his eye. "That means she'll stand out."

"So will we," Pretty Boy said.

The toilet flushed and Pointblank walked out zipping his fly. "We'll be lookin' for her. She won't be lookin' for us. That'll give us an advantage. And Gunnison's only a temporary stop until the government can decide where to put her, so she's in a rental."

Pretty Boy's hope died on the spot. "That's what Shady's contact said? Gunnison's temporary?"

"That's what she said."

"What are we supposed to do once we find her?"

Ink, who was packing his own bag, looked up. "What do you think, stupid?"

Trying to avoid another confrontation with the psycho asshole, Pretty Boy kept his attention on Pointblank. "I'm talking about the kids. I don't want to kill kids. Or a U.S. marshal. That shit's asking for war."

Pointblank slung his duffel over his shoulder. "We'll figure it out when we get there. First, we gotta find her."

But Pretty Boy imagined that wouldn't take too long. They'd be in Gunnison before nightfall. How many rental houses could there be in such a small community?

22

"Maybe we should lay down a few ground rules," Buzz said.

Virgil stretched out on his bunk. There wasn't a lot to unpack when you were allowed only six cubic feet of personal belongings. "Like…?" He shifted his gaze to his cell mate, who was standing up and staring morosely out onto the tier.

"Just one rule, really. You leave me alone, I'll leave you alone. It's that simple."

Despite an abundance of tattoos, a series of devils with their tongues sticking out KISS-style, Buzz wasn't particularly frightening. He wasn't big and didn't look very strong. But that didn't mean he wasn't dangerous. Virgil had learned long ago not to discount anyone, not until he knew what the guy was like on the inside. Vanquishing an enemy was largely a matter of determination and often depended on how far you were willing to go—whether or not you'd risk your own life to accomplish what you wanted. Some of the meanest men Virgil had ever fought were less than a hundred and eighty pounds. And some of the other guys, the bigger ones, weren't worth a damn when it came to throwing punches.

"Let's make it even simpler than that," Virgil said. "You leave me alone or I'll make you sorry you didn't." He wanted to start gathering information. Now that he was here, all he could think about was getting out, and he couldn't get out until he had something for Wallace. The smell of this place, different and yet so similar to the other institutions he'd known, threatened to suffocate him. But until he built up some credibility with Buzz, any attempt to befriend him would be wasted. Worse than wasted. It would have the opposite effect.

First, he had to play his role, sell his image and do it well. In order to infiltrate the Hells Fury, he'd need a sponsor. He hoped his cell mate would take that on, but Buzz had to have some reason to trust him or admire him. Otherwise, he wouldn't be willing to stick his neck out. Virgil had been part of the criminal world long enough to understand that.

"So you're a tough guy?" Buzz said.

Obviously he accepted nothing on faith. They had that in common.

"No need to take my word for it." Virgil sat up to see if his cellie wanted to test him, but Buzz glanced away. He wasn't going to be issuing any challenges. At least, not right now.

"I don't want trouble," he muttered. "I get out in less than a month. You screw that up and you'll end up dancin' on the blacktop no matter how tough you are. And that's a promise."

Dancing on the blacktop... Virgil hadn't heard that phrase before, but it wasn't difficult to figure out. Buzz was saying he'd be shanked in the yard.

"You're the one getting in my face," he said. "If you don't want trouble, stop asking for it."

"I'm just pissed," he grumbled. "I shouldn't have to deal with this."

Virgil propped his hands behind his head and spoke through a yawn. "With what?"

"With *you,* man."

"Then *don't* deal with me. I thought we just went over that."

Shifting from one foot to the other, Buzz went back to staring into the tier, which held some concrete tables and a couple of telephones. Nineteen other cells opened onto it. They were allowed to play cards and socialize there when they weren't on lockdown.

Virgil assumed their conversation was over, so he lay back and closed his eyes. After the week he'd spent in the real world, he was beyond tired. But Buzz was too agitated to shut up.

"What'd you do?" he asked. "What you in for?"

Virgil cracked open his eyelids. Where he came from it wasn't polite to ask. "None of your damn business."

"Let me see your papers."

Buzz wanted to know if he had any gang affiliations. That was pretty standard.

"No."

"Fine. Tell me this much, then. Where'd you do time before here?"

"That's none of your business, either." Virgil knew that the less he said about himself, the less he'd have to remember and the harder it would be for anyone to prove he was lying.

"It's gonna be a *long* month," Buzz breathed.

Virgil couldn't help laughing.

The way Buzz whirled on him told Virgil the man had a weapon hidden somewhere. Otherwise, considering their difference in size, he'd move with more caution. "What? What's so damn funny?"

"Quit whining. At least you're getting out." In a show of contempt for any threat Buzz might pose, Virgil rolled over and presented his cell mate with his back.

"I could kill you in two seconds," Buzz growled, obviously offended by Virgil's lack of fear.

"You could try." Virgil knew he was extending a challenge Buzz might not be able to resist. Parole pending or not, Buzz could lash out to save face, vent his anger and hatred or impress his Hells Fury pals. But Virgil *had* to establish superiority. And forcing him to fight or stand down from the very beginning was the fastest way to do it. That approach would also reveal certain aspects of Buzz's personality—how volatile he was, whether he'd act with more than his mouth when cornered and exactly how far he was prepared to go to salvage his pride.

Hoping he'd have the chance to retaliate if he was shanked, Virgil listened for any movement that might alert him. But Buzz defused the tension instead.

"Those tattoos you got," he said.

Virgil faced him again. "What about them?"

"You part of the Brand?"

"No." Buzz was referring to the Aryan Brotherhood, the most dangerous of all prison gangs. Small but ruthless, they didn't accept many new members. Virgil had heard that Tom Mills and Tyler Bingham—two of their most powerful leaders—were incarcerated at Pelican Bay. Probably in the SHU.

"You belong to another gang, then. I can tell."

Virgil hadn't tattooed any obvious Crew insignia on his body. He hadn't been that indoctrinated. The gang was the best social network USP Tucson had to offer, and once Pretty Boy, Shady and a guy they called

Tucker, who'd since died in a police shootout, became his brothers it was tough to let go. He still missed Pretty Boy and a couple of the others. But his tats weren't the same quality you could get on the outside. Anyone who knew that would realize they signified some type of affiliation.

"What's your point?" Virgil said.

"My point is you better clique up in here right quick."

Virgil shrugged as if he'd heard it all before. Truth was, he had. "Why?"

"Something's gonna come down." He scowled. "I was hopin' to get out of here first, but…I think it's gonna happen sooner rather than later."

So that was what had Buzz on edge. It wasn't just getting a new cellie. "What is it? Trouble with the Nuestra Family?"

"What do you know about the NF?"

"They're in charge here, right?"

"Hell, no! Who's been telling you that shit? They're afraid of *us*."

"And who's us? Public Enemy Number 1?"

Buzz bared his arm to show off a pitchfork tattoo. "The Hells Fury, that's who. *We're* the ones runnin' this place."

"So what's going down?"

He shook his head. "Ain't sayin'."

Virgil gave Buzz a few seconds to think before speaking again. "Who should I clique up with?"

"Someone you can trust, man."

"What if I can't trust anybody?"

"That's your problem."

There was no time to say more. A loud buzz sounded as the locks retracted and the doors slid open. It was mealtime.

* * *

Virgil sat alone at a table in the dining hall, his back to the wall so he could protect himself if need be, and watched the other inmates. It was important to note who hung out with whom, where each group sat, how they interacted. The next few days would be the most dangerous of his life, even more dangerous than when he'd gone to prison the first time. He was better able to defend himself now, but that could convince him to take risks that might not be wise. Or, because he hoped to change his life and had plans for the future, he could have the opposite problem. He might hesitate when he shouldn't, reveal his reluctance to fight or kill, and destroy any chance he had of gaining the respect he needed. Although he couldn't be too reckless, he couldn't be too cautious, either, couldn't lose the edge his anger had always given him. Those who held power, on both sides of the law, would want to establish where he belonged in the pecking order. And the only way they could determine who he was and what he might do was to test him.

Virgil wasn't looking forward to proving himself. Even if he managed to survive and convinced Buzz to sponsor him, he'd have to assault an HF enemy for initiation purposes and make it brutal enough to be decisive and believable. That would be tricky to orchestrate without actually hurting someone. He'd have to work out the details with Peyton if he hoped to make a fake stabbing look real; he wasn't sure that *could* be faked. Coordinating with her wouldn't be easy. The more often he contacted her, the more often he risked exposure. He couldn't call her unless they were allowed on the tier. If there was really as much unrest here as Buzz had intimated—and Virgil saw no reason to doubt him—he might not have the opportunity to use the phone. Pelican Bay could go into lockdown and stay that way for months. The prison had a long history of resorting to those measures. Wallace had said as much while they were driving to Crescent City from Sacramento. All conversations from pay phones were taped, anyway. Virgil had known they would be, of course, but the associate director had warned him of that, too. Wallace had filled him in on a lot of things…including how badly he wanted to get into Peyton's pants.

Catching himself, Virgil tried to put Peyton out of his mind. It required constant effort, but thinking of her made him more anxious than he already was. Especially when he acknowledged that Wallace was set on making his desires real, and he wouldn't be around to do anything about it.

While drinking some milk, he let his gaze circle the room again. Blacks ate in one corner, Mexicans in another. There were some stragglers in between—fags, misfits, even a couple of transvestites.

Buzz ate with a group of whites across the room. Not all of them were tatted up to the degree Buzz was, but the amount of ink extending beneath the sleeves of their prison-issue blue shirts and on their necks and heads added to the intimidation factor. They counted on that; it was part of the reason they got so many tattoos.

As Buzz spoke to those around him, he nodded toward Virgil. When the group realized he was paying attention, they rose to their feet and openly glared at him. One even called out, "You think you're a badass, huh?"

Virgil wanted to ignore them and eat his dinner, but he couldn't. Such aggressive behavior was the equivalent of throwing the first punch. They were disrespecting him to see if he'd take it. If he didn't retaliate, it would be that much harder to win their respect later. Maybe it would be impossible. And if he couldn't gain any power in here, there'd be no purpose in staying. It would all be over. For him. For Laurel. For Laurel's kids.

So instead of finishing his meal, he shoved the tray aside and, with a grin, gave them the finger.

Fortunately, Peyton hadn't been in any hurry to leave the prison. She'd worked late, then lingered in her office, trying to figure out a way to see Virgil before she went home. She thought it might put her mind at ease to know he was okay and in good spirits. But before she could make any arrangements, she received a call from an officer named George Robinson in Facility A letting her know there'd been an altercation in the dining hall.

Four men had attacked one. "Simeon Bennett" had been involved and was injured. Robinson gave her the names of the others, too—names she recognized as members of the Hells Fury. Virgil had jumped into the thick of prison politics and created a disruption, because that was what he had to do.

Either he'd get what he wanted or he'd die trying.

She feared it would be the latter.

"How badly is he hurt?" she asked.

"Which one?" Robinson wanted to know.

Aware that she was pressing the phone too tightly to her ear, she eased up. "The new transfer, Simeon Bennett." She knew it might seem strange that she'd ask about one convict specifically, but she didn't care. She had to know if he was okay.

"Hard to tell," he responded. "He's covered in blood. We'll know more once we get him cleaned up."

Oh, God, it's happening, she thought. But that wasn't

what she said. She kept her voice as cool and imper-
sonal as she could, given that her heart was beating in
her throat. "I'll be right there."

He didn't bother to respond. The phone clicked and
she jumped to her feet.

She was rushing down the hall when the warden
hailed her from behind. "Peyton?"

Reluctant to stop, she considered ignoring him but
couldn't bring herself to do it. It was far too apparent
that she must've heard him. "Yes?" she said, turning
back.

"May I have a word with you?"

He wanted to tell her what he'd come to her office to
discuss earlier, no doubt. But she didn't have time for
it. "I'm afraid I'm in a hurry, sir. Could we discuss it
tomorrow?"

His expression told her he didn't appreciate her response. "Where are you going?"

Most of the administrative staff was already gone, but
she still hesitated to discuss Virgil in the open, where
someone might overhear. "To the infirmary."

His eyes widened. "Why? Is everything okay?"

"There's been a fight in Facility A." She couldn't
prevent the accusation that crept into her voice. She'd
tried to warn the warden that Virgil wouldn't be safe at
Pelican Bay; she'd tried to warn them all.

"How many were involved?"

"Five, from what I've been able to gather."

He shook his head but his sympathy didn't seem gen-
uine. "How bad is it?"

"Don't know. The C.O.s have it under control, but several men are injured. Simeon Bennett is one of them."

She thought he might show some concern by going
to the infirmary with her. Virgil didn't even deserve to

be in prison. He was risking his life to save his sister and her kids and bring down the Hells Fury. But Fischer didn't care about that. No one did. "If it's under control, there's nothing you can do."

"I just…I wanted to check on…them."

"Give the doctor a chance to do his job. Anyway, this won't take long. Do you mind?"

She *did* mind, but she knew she had no choice. Curving her fingernails into her palms, she followed him to his office. "Yes, sir?" she said as soon as he closed the door.

"Rick Wallace called me today."

"He did?"

"He did. He mentioned that he and his wife are splitting up."

She didn't care about Rick's marriage. It was all she could do not to tap her foot. "He told me that, too. Unfortunate, isn't it?"

"That depends on how you look at it."

"Excuse me?"

"You don't know that he's interested in you?"

Oh, hell. Rick had already spoken to the warden? She'd said she wanted to wait until they were finished with Operation Inside to address any personal issues! "I had some idea, of course, but I told him it'll never work, that the department would never allow it."

"Actually, I'm not so sure about that. I'm in full support of it. You work too much. You've let your job become everything when there's so much more. I think the two of you would make a perfect couple."

She wondered if he'd give her his blessing to see Virgil instead, but she wasn't about to ask. She wasn't about to discuss Rick with him, either. "I doubt it'll come to anything," she said. "But thank you, anyway."

"Don't be too hasty to turn him down. That boy's going places."

And had probably asked Fischer to reassure her, which only irritated her more. As she'd told Rick, now was not the time to deal with this. "I'll keep that in mind." She glanced at her watch as a way to remind him that she was in a hurry. "Are we done?"

"For now."

"I'd better get to the infirmary." She started out, then quickly turned back. "Warden?"

"Yes?"

"If Simeon Bennett lives through this, can I have your permission to transfer him out of here?"

"That's the CDC's call, not mine."

But Wallace would never agree. "*We* should take a stand."

Fischer didn't like the tone of her voice, and he let her know it by the tone of his. "I told you, that's the CDC's call," he said. Then, strained though it was, he produced a smile. "Have a nice evening."

Virgil didn't look good. Eyes closed, he lay perfectly still while a nurse, who'd already removed his shirt, cleaned away the blood that covered so much of his torso. She was working too fast to be gentle, which bothered Peyton. But Virgil didn't react to her pushing and probing.

Peyton hoped he wasn't as badly hurt as it appeared from out in the hall. He'd been stabbed at least once—in the stomach. That was obvious from the blood that poured out. And he cradled his left hand close to his body as if it hurt.

At the sound of the door opening, the nurse turned toward her.

Cute, petite, dark-haired Belinda, a young mother of two, must've been expecting the doctor or someone else. When she saw Peyton she straightened in surprise. "Chief Deputy Warden. I, um… Is there something I can help you with?"

Virgil's eyes opened and riveted on hers. Hardly able to keep from rushing over to him, she stood against the wall.

"Don't stop," she said. "I won't get in the way."

"We're a bit short-staffed tonight," the nurse explained as if she thought Peyton had come to observe how well she was handling the emergency. "But the doctor will be here as soon as he's available."

As soon as he's available? Virgil had been stabbed. Why wasn't the doctor here *now?* "Where is he?"

Belinda jerked her head toward the examination room next door. "With another inmate."

"Who?"

"Weston Jager. And there are two more across the hall. They were all in the fight that caused this."

"Are Weston's injuries more life-threatening than what you have here?"

At the anger in her voice, the nurse blinked several times. "No…"

"Then why is the doctor with him?"

"He, um, he demanded to be first. And it was easier than putting up with his abuse," she admitted sheepishly.

Peyton wasn't willing to reward Weston's sense of entitlement. "He can wait," she snapped. "And so can his buddies. Get the doctor in here."

The nurse hesitated. "You want this guy seen first?"

"His name's Simeon Bennett, and that's exactly what

I want." Peyton groped for an excuse to explain why she cared so much. "He's the brother of a friend of mine."

"Oh! You *know* him?" She seemed relieved to finally understand.

"Not personally," Peyton hedged. "But I've promised my friend he'll be okay while he's in here. I feel responsible for keeping that promise. You understand."

"Of course. I'll tell Dr. Pendergast."

After giving Virgil a piece of gauze to hold against the knife wound near his navel, the nurse left and Peyton allowed herself to move closer.

"Good line," Virgil mumbled.

"Line?" She wasn't sure what he meant. Her thoughts were too busy vacillating between self-recrimination for letting this happen and prayers that Virgil would be all right.

"About me being...related to a friend...of yours. Good...cover for our association."

Association? The panic she felt went way beyond that. "Yeah, well, hopefully she bought it." She had no reason to believe otherwise; she was just wound up.

He managed a smile. "Quit worrying, okay? Everything's fine."

"This is *fine?*" She motioned to his injuries. "You look like hell."

"I've seen better days. But I've seen worse, too." His smile turned into a grimace as he repositioned himself on the table. "What about the other guys? I hope they're in worse shape than I am."

"I haven't checked. It's you I'm concerned about."

His bandage was already soaked with blood. She got him a new one and tried to help stanch the flow, but he knocked her hand away before she could touch it. "You're not wearing gloves."

"You think you might give me a disease?"

"Why take the chance?"

"It's a bit late for that, isn't it?"

Another wince told her he was in significant pain. "It's not *my* blood I'm worried about."

"What happened?" she asked.

He let his head fall back. "Isn't it obvious?"

"You've been in a fight. *That's* obvious. But you were only inside for a few hours!"

"I had to clear the first hurdle." His chest rose as he drew a breath. "Once I settle in, we'll have a better chance of not meeting up in here."

The new gauze was as saturated as the old one. Since he had to struggle to do even simple things, she jerked the bandage away from him and held it in place herself.

"I told you not to touch—"

She blocked him so he couldn't stop her. "I've got it. Just relax."

When his eyes closed, she was afraid he was in worse shape than he wanted her to know. Talking cost him a great deal of energy, but as long as he was alert, she felt reassured—and that prompted her to keep the conversation going. "You jumped them?" she asked.

"Four men?" He tried to laugh, but couldn't. "They… jumped me. I just…issued the invitation."

"Big of you to get things started."

"Calm down. I'm fine."

"You're fine, huh? For how long?"

"For now."

Had he done enough to impress the Hells Fury? Or would the job require more? "Please tell me you did what you were hoping to do."

"Too early to tell."

"So this could happen again. And again."

"Maybe. Depends."

She examined his wound and frowned at the blood that continued to pour from the jagged opening. What had they knifed him with? A sharpened toothbrush? A piece of metal they'd brought from the industry yard and sharpened for days on end? She twisted around to stare into the hall. Where was the damn doctor? "God, tell me this isn't deep."

"I have no idea. I didn't…expect anyone to have a… weapon. No one did…at first. Buzz must've…slipped one to his friends."

"*Buzz* was involved in this?" The man she'd carefully vetted as his cell mate?

"He backed off once the fighting got serious. He's dead set…on getting out of here…didn't want to screw that…up. But, yeah…he was the instigator…and the only one who…didn't get hurt."

"Then we'll move you to a different cell."

Virgil shook his head.

"It's the only way to keep you safe."

"No."

"If you won't move, then I want you out."

"Absolutely not."

"But—"

"Peyton, stop."

She glanced behind her to make sure they were still alone. "I *can't* stop."

His hand covered hers. "Yes, you can. This…is my only shot."

Tears stung her eyes. "We'll figure out something else."

"It's too late. Wallace won't let me off the hook. He'll

leave Laurel unprotected if I do anything except what I agreed to. He's looking for any excuse."

She sniffed. "I shouldn't have told him. I don't want you to be here."

His fingers slid between hers as he tried to comfort her. "But I can't leave."

She wiped her tears with her free hand. "You think Wallace would let Laurel get hurt? He's that vengeful?"

"I know he is. Any man is vengeful, given enough motivation."

"I'm not enough motivation for Wallace. I don't even understand why he's suddenly so interested."

"Because he knows I want you, too. It's the competition, the fact that he feels he should have first dibs."

"So get out of here and protect Laurel yourself!"

The pain seemed to be getting to him. "How can I do that if they…charge me with another crime? If they…put me away for good?"

"Could they really do that?"

"They could try."

She knew a little about it but had to ask, had to hear his version. "What happened when you killed those men, Virgil?"

His Adam's apple bobbed as he swallowed. "Pretty much…what happened here."

"They jumped you when you were in USP Tucson?"

He nodded. "That's why they moved me…to Florence, because of…what happened. But…they weren't just looking for a fight. It all happened so fast. I…did what I could to survive."

She believed him. "That's self-defense."

His mouth twisted in a wry grin. "It's only self-defense if you can prove it."

"Why can't you prove it?"

"The two other men involved…tell a different story."

"So? It's your word against theirs. They'll never get the charges to stick."

"If I could be sure I'd get a fair trial, maybe I'd risk it. But…I don't have much faith in the system. Besides, they have my reputation for fighting and my gang affiliation. I don't even want…to go that route. We've come this far. I have…to finish. Let me finish."

"You're not giving me any choice."

His fingers tightened on hers. "I need you, your support."

"What if this kills you?" she whispered.

"Then it kills me. I have to…do it."

"You're kidding, right? That's reckless! I was afraid of this."

"And you…made your reservations plain to…everyone. Your conscience…is clear."

"It's not my conscience that's bothering me!"

He raised his eyelids and those blue eyes drilled into hers. "Careful…"

More tears welled up. She'd known she was rattled, but she hadn't realized just *how* rattled until this moment. Frustrated by her own reaction, she snapped, "Careful of what?"

He grinned at her. "You're acting like you care."

"I do!"

"About *me*," he clarified, sobering.

Those two words were more of a question than anything else. He was asking her about her concern, wanting to know if it went any deeper than what she might feel for anyone else in this situation. Did it? She was fairly sure it did. But how much deeper? And how should she respond?

"All I know is that I can't stop thinking about you," she said. "Every time I close my eyes you're there."

She hadn't expected to make this admission. But now that she had, she thought he'd be pleased. Instead, he frowned as if he'd just changed his mind. "We can't do this. It'll only make everything harder on both of us." The nurse must've given him some painkiller because speaking suddenly seemed less difficult, but he was beginning to slur his words. "I have to do what I have to do, Peyton. I can't change that. And even if I could, even if I already had a fresh start, I don't have anything to offer a woman like you."

She checked for the nurse again. The hall was still empty. "Like *me?* What do you think you need to offer? I'm not looking for a meal ticket."

"Then what are you looking for? A guy who's been in prison for fourteen years?"

"You have no control over what your mother and uncle—"

He refused to let her interrupt. "Or is it my gang connections you find appealing? What if I can't break free of The Crew, Peyton? What if, because of your association with me, they come after *you?* Caring about me puts you in danger. Don't you understand?" He lowered his voice, as if he spoke the next words grudgingly. "And it gives me so much more to lose."

"You're not afraid of losing me. Not like that. You're afraid to care in the first place."

"I *can't* care. Not right now."

She remembered the tenderness with which he'd touched her on Saturday night. Maybe he didn't *want* to feel anything, but he did. He was as susceptible to love and fear and pain as any other man."

"Nice try." Even if his statement was true, she didn't know what to do about it. She felt drawn to him, and that desire wasn't going away. No matter how sudden, inexplicable or ill-timed it was, she wanted to be with him. His past didn't change what she felt. Because logic had no place in this.

Footsteps behind her indicated that the nurse had returned with the doctor. Crossing to the sink to wash her hands, she motioned for them to take over as if she'd merely been helping out in the nurse's absence.

The doctor worked on Virgil for several minutes while she watched, but when he began to suture the hole in Virgil's stomach, she had to turn away. It made her feel faint, even though she wasn't usually queasy around blood. "Will he be okay?" she asked, finally asking the question that burned in her mind.

Dr. Pendergast continued to stitch while he spoke. "He'll be good as new."

"You're sure?"

"I'm sure. Tell your friend she can rest easy. He'll have another scar to add to all the rest, and he'll probably wind up in the SHU for fighting, but he'll live."

She folded her arms. "He's not going to the SHU. No one starts a fight that's four on one."

"He did almost as much damage to them as they did to him," the doctor pointed out.

"Doesn't matter. He didn't start the fight. And he wasn't the one with a weapon."

The blood covering Dr. Pendergast's gloves seemed at odds with his cavalier attitude. "That's not what the others are saying. They're saying he started the fight, that they took the shank away from him."

Because the one with the weapon would get into more trouble than the others. They had good reason to make the claim.

Peyton didn't argue. This wasn't any of the doctor's affair. She'd handle the situation herself.

"I'll get to the bottom of it," she promised. Then she left to see what had happened to Weston and the other two. Apparently Buzz hadn't sustained more than a few bruises. If he'd caused this fight, he deserved more, but she felt somewhat vindicated once she visited his pals. Westy had a busted nose, a fat lip and a cut on the eye that required a couple of stitches. Ace Anderson, Westy's cell mate, cradled a swollen hand in his lap. And Doug Lachette had what he swore were broken ribs as well as the more obvious bloody mouth and lost tooth.

"Way to hold your own," she murmured, silently applauding Virgil as she left the infirmary. But she knew the next time a fight broke out, someone might be carried to the morgue in a body bag.

And that someone could just as easily be Virgil.

23

Wallace's car was sitting in her drive when Peyton returned home. After the day she'd spent, he was the last person she wanted to see. Especially since she'd already made it clear that she preferred he go back to Sacramento. Why hadn't he gone? What made him think he could hang out at her place indefinitely?

The fact that he was still here felt like an invasion of privacy. But she knew he wouldn't understand why. She'd left him and Virgil alone in the house when she went to work as if she was fine with it—but she was more fine with Virgil being in her space than Wallace.

That she preferred Virgil seemed crazy, even to her. She knew Rick better. And Rick didn't have a past.

"God, what's going on with me?" she moaned. Then she collected her briefcase and purse from the car and took a deep breath before heading to the house. She was tempted to march up to Wallace and demand he pull Virgil from the prison. But Virgil would never forgive her if she did. He'd blame her if he was brought up on charges and sentenced to another prison term, or if Laurel ended up getting hurt. He preferred to handle this his own way and, while she respected that, she felt torn about his methods.

So what should she do? What *could* she do? Let Operation Inside run its course? Allow Virgil to continue risking his life? Or bring it all to a stop—and leave Crescent City without a job?

She wished the warden would play the heavy, take the decision out of her hands. He had more power than she did. But there wasn't any chance of that. Fischer had decided to support the CDCR and was doing it with his eyes closed.

"Here we go," she muttered as she climbed the stairs to her deck.

Rick was pacing in her living room. He was on the phone, in the middle of a heated argument, and barely turned to look at her when she came in.

Other than giving him a short wave, she ignored him, too, and went into the kitchen, where she dumped her belongings on the counter before opening the freezer. What was she going to have for dinner? She wished she'd gone out. If she'd known her company hadn't left, she would have, if only to delay her return.

"You stupid bitch!" Rick yelled. "You *can't* leave California! Don't you dare! I'll fight you every step of the way! Those are my kids, too."

Flinching at his language and his anger, Peyton rolled her eyes. She shouldn't have to put up with this. What was it he'd said about his divorce being less acrimonious than his parents'? That didn't seem likely. And, lucky her, she got to hear this latest battle....

Unable to tolerate it, she shut the freezer and snatched up her purse. Rick didn't even notice when she left. He had only one thing on his mind—verbally destroying his soon-to-be ex-wife.

Head down, she hurried to her car and peeled out of

the drive. She told herself she was going to Michelle's. She needed a break, a chance to think about something else. But she didn't actually go to her friend's. She went into town to purchase a veggie burger. Then she turned around and drove right past Michelle's house—and all the way to the prison.

The sound that woke Laurel in the middle of the night wasn't very loud. Just a creak, really. And yet...it roused her from a deep sleep.

It's the marshal. Every night when she retired, Jimmy Keegan, the U.S. marshal who'd been staying with her since Rick Wallace left, called his wife, watched another hour of TV, then retired. They'd only been together for three days, but they'd already established this routine. Probably because there wasn't much else to do. It wasn't as if they could go anywhere. Although Keegan slipped out occasionally for very brief periods, to buy them a treat or some more milk, he wouldn't even let the kids play in the yard because it was too risky. He was that strict.

Laurel didn't mind. She felt safe for the first time in a long while. Vigilant as he was, she couldn't imagine anyone getting past him, so she disregarded whatever had disturbed her and allowed her eyes to drift shut.

Shuffling, coming from the direction of the laundry room, made her eyes snap open again. *What was going on?*

A sliver of moonlight filtered through the blinds, falling over her son, who was sleeping on the twin bed against the wall. Mia curled against her in the double bed. Her daughter's warmth was reassuring. Both Jake and Mia were fine.

But *something* was wrong....

What time was it?

Late.

Careful to move very slowly so she wouldn't wake Mia, she reached over to the nightstand to get her cell phone. The rental house in which they were staying had been furnished when they arrived, but very sparsely. No clocks or pictures hung on the walls. Only the furniture had been provided—the kitchenette set, the sofa, recliner and TV in the living room, the beds, dressers and nightstands in the bedrooms.

Sure enough, it was 2:30 a.m. Late, as she'd thought.

Creak...

She caught her breath. That had to be Jimmy, didn't it?

Of course. If The Crew had followed her and Rick Wallace that first night, they would've struck before now. They had no reason to wait. But the noises she'd heard were all wrong. There wasn't just *one* person moving around. There were two.

She broke into a cold sweat. Jimmy would never invite someone in during the night, especially without telling her. He wasn't even from this area. Like her, he didn't know a single soul.

Her lungs burned from lack of oxygen as she held her breath again and listened. What was that? It sounded like whispering....

Adrenaline hit her, making it hard to get up, but she managed to climb out of bed, creep across the room and open the door slightly so she could peer out. It was too dark to see anything. But she heard a man cursing about getting blood all over him. Then her legs nearly turned to rubber.

Blood? *Whose* blood? But in her heart she knew. She

wasn't sure what had happened to the marshal, but she was fairly certain he wouldn't be able to help her.

If he was dead, or even incapacitated, she had mere seconds. Did she spend those seconds trying to call the police? Or did she get her children out of the house?

Ultimately, she had no choice. She had to go for the children. They'd have a much better chance of survival if she attended to them immediately. And they were what she cared about most.

Wishing she had the marshal's gun or some other weapon to defend herself, she closed the door and locked it as quietly as possible. Then she woke Jake with a warning not to say a word. But of course, he did. He was too sleepy and confused to understand, let alone obey.

"What's the matter, Mommy?"

At least he'd followed her lead and whispered. "Don't talk," she breathed in his ear. "There are strangers in the house and they might be dangerous. Just do exactly as I say. I'm going to help you through the window. Run next door and ring the bell until someone answers. Tell them to call the police. Then stay there until I come for you."

Worry pinched his small face. "What about Mia?"

Mia was beginning to stir.

"She's going with you. Hold her hand the whole way and keep her safe. But you first."

He got up as bravely as any man and put on his shoes and coat without her having to ask.

Footsteps came down the hall as she cranked open the window. Then the doorknob turned. *Click, click... click, click.*

Oh, God...

A man's voice carried to their ears, even though he

was talking to someone else. "I don't give a rat's ass. Kick it in."

Fortunately, the screen gave her no trouble. It was warped, barely hanging on to begin with. She shoved it out, but the old pane would swing open only so far. Would Jake fit through?

"Come on," she whispered.

As he climbed onto the bed, Mia sat up and rubbed her eyes. "Where are you going?"

Laurel put a finger to her lips. "Shh."

Her daughter's eyebrows bunched together. "Why do I have to be quiet?"

"You're going outside with your brother, okay?" She pulled Mia into her arms. "Stay with him. I'll be there in a minute."

"But it's cold outside!"

"Be quiet!" Laurel snapped.

Someone hit the door at the same time, frightening Mia into silence. Eyes huge, she threw her arms around Laurel and clung tight.

Another blow to the door seemed to shake the whole house. Laurel had no idea what these men would do once they managed to get in, but she didn't want her children to be there when it happened.

She gestured to her son, who was standing on the bed, staring at her in a terrified trance. "Hurry! Let's go, Jake."

Praying that he'd be able to fit, she guided his feet through the opening. Once he was halfway out, she realized he was going to make it, but that brought little relief. She couldn't tell how much longer the door would hold.

She hung on to Jake until he dropped to the grass. "Mia, now you." Her cell phone lay tantalizingly close, just beyond her daughter on the bed. She'd call for help just as soon as Mia was out, even though she knew there was almost no chance the police could arrive in time....

"What about you, Mommy?" Mia asked, refusing to let go.

"I'm coming. Go with Jake."

"No! I want you!"

There was no time to be gentle. Yanking her daughter's locked hands from around her neck, she grabbed her face. "Yes, go! Now!"

The shock of her response caused Mia to cry.

"Don't!" Laurel gasped. "They'll kill you!"

Tears slipped down the girl's round cheeks, but she made no sound.

"Open this door or you're dead!" someone screamed from the hallway.

Laurel felt certain it was the man with all the tattoos who'd threatened her before: Ink. The Crew had found her.

"Mommy?" Mia whispered in panic.

Safety. That was all that mattered. She pushed her daughter through the window and, fortunately, Mia didn't put up a fight.

Laurel watched her children only long enough to see Mia's feet touch the ground and Jake clasp her hand. Then she closed the window. She didn't want Ink to know she'd let them into the yard. She hoped he'd be so focused on her he wouldn't notice their absence until after they got away.

Because of her terror, she lacked the physical strength to close the window tightly enough to latch it. But she did the best she could so they wouldn't guess it'd been opened. Then she dove for her phone.

She had it in her hand, was already punching in 9-1-1, when the door splintered and crashed against the inside wall.

"He *what?*" Peyton gaped at Regina Murray, the nurse who'd replaced Belinda Rogers at the shift change.

Regina's size and mannerisms had always reminded Peyton of the nurse in Stephen King's *Misery*. But hard as Regina was to like, Peyton tried to treat her as cordially as possible. "The dumb cluck insisted on being taken back to his cell," she said, and gestured toward the empty room where Peyton had seen Virgil earlier.

Apparently he'd left shortly after she did, because the room was already clean and ready for the next occupant. "But it's only been a couple of hours since he was here."

Regina hugged the chart she held. "I know. I can't quite figure it out. Most guys will say they're sick when they're not just to get in here. It gives them a break from the tedium and a little female attention."

It wasn't female attention they wanted as much as prescription painkillers. And Regina was no attraction. Instead of whistling or admiring her, like they did with Belinda, they made unkind comments. *I'd rather sleep with my own grandmother....*

Peyton was infinitely glad Regina didn't seem to pick up on that behavior, since there was no way to stop it. At least she tried, by denying privileges to the men who persisted. When she'd first started as a C.O. there was one inmate who'd masturbate in front of her at every opportunity without fear of reprisal because the warden refused to punish him. *That's what you're gonna get inside a maximum security prison,* he'd tell her. Prison officials weren't quite as accommodating of women sixteen years ago. Most believed they had no place in corrections. There were some who still felt that way.

"But…this fella didn't want to stay," Regina was saying. "He claimed to feel just fine."

What he *said* didn't matter. Virgil needed the rest, the safety. "Why was he so set on leaving?"

"Who knows? As soon as the doctor stitched him up and X-rayed his hand, he hopped off the table and that was it. We don't make them stay here against their wishes, not unless it's imperative to their health."

Momentarily distracted by mention of the X-ray, Peyton asked, "Is his hand broken?"

"No. Sprained but not broken."

Was she crazy to have worried so much about him? There'd been all that blood.… *"Anything* broken?"

"Nothing. He's tough as nails, that one. He hurt the guys he was fighting as bad as they hurt him," she added with a chuckle.

That, Peyton had seen for herself. But it made her more apprehensive than happy. Would the Hells Fury launch another attack in an attempt to get even? Had Virgil started a war? Or was he making the kind of inroads he'd set out to make?

It could go either way.…

Wishing he'd stayed, at least for the night, she glanced at the empty bed again. "He had a stab wound. That alone should be reason to keep him for a few days."

Interpreting that comment as criticism, Murray drew herself up to her full five feet ten inches. "Fortunately, the wound wasn't all that deep."

"What about the risk of infection?" Peyton pressed.

The chain on her glasses swung as she shoved them higher. "He's on antibiotics. If he stays out of trouble, he should be fine."

But Peyton had no confidence Virgil would even *try* to stay out of trouble—and she definitely didn't want him getting into another fight while he had such a serious wound. He shouldn't be in too much of a hurry to get what he wanted or it might backfire. And there'd be no second chance.

"What about Weston?" she asked.

Murray sniffed. If it wasn't so hard to get and keep medical help, Peyton would've replaced her long ago. The inmates were prickly enough. "Went back to his cell, too. They all did. Mr. Anderson left last because he had to wait for Dr. Pendergast to cast his hand."

So there was one broken bone as a result of the fight. At least it wasn't Virgil's.

"Fine. Thanks."

Dr. Pendergast stopped her on the way out. "Chief Deputy?"

"Yes?"

"I'm glad to see you. I think we might have a problem."

She already had a problem. Several of them. Wallace camping out at her house was one. Virgil injured in a cell with the man who'd caused it was two. The delicate balance she had to maintain in order to squeak through the coming weeks while keeping everyone safe and retaining her job was three. "What kind of problem?"

He motioned for her to join him and together they walked into the inner office. "I heard Weston Jager talking to Doug Lachette."

"And?"

"I think they're going after the new guy again."

"Did you tell Bennett? Did you warn him that he'd better stay here?"

"I tried. I told him he shouldn't fight again or it'll rip

out those stitches. But we would've had to physically re-strain him to keep him here, and that didn't make much sense."

"That's it," she said. "Weston just won himself a ticket to the SHU." She wanted to send Virgil there, too, where she knew he'd be safe. But Wallace and Fischer would override her if she did. Segregating him would defeat his whole purpose.

John hadn't been in the dining hall earlier when the fight broke out, but he'd heard details from several people in the five hours since. The C.O.s were all abuzz, talking about how one guy, a new transfer, had just about kicked the shit out of three seasoned gang-bangers. He might've come out the clear winner if they hadn't shanked him. John wished he could've been there to witness it, especially once he learned that Westy had been involved. He didn't think Westy had ever come out on the bad end of a fight. Westy stacked the deck, if he had to.

Apparently he hadn't stacked it high enough when he picked a fight with this man.

John tried not to reveal the satisfaction that knowledge gave him as he waited outside Westy's cell. He'd just received orders to leave Ace in gen pop but move Westy over to the SHU. Good news all around. Once Westy was in segregation, he'd need John's help more than ever to carry messages and smuggle contraband, which meant prices would go up.

"So what happened?" he asked as Westy gathered his stuff.

Westy glowered at him but didn't respond.

"I heard that dude can fight."

Ace Anderson was lying on his bunk, staring at the

fingers dangling out of his new cast. He'd been Westy's cell mate for…John couldn't even remember. A year, at least. "Doesn't Westy's face tell you that?"

When he chuckled at his own joke, Westy threw a balled-up shirt at him. "Shut the hell up! At least I didn't break my damn hand!"

Ace pulled the shirt from his face. "That con has a hard head."

"So what's this guy's name? Where'd he come from?" John couldn't wait to get a look at him. He had to be as big as a house, judging by the way everyone was talking about him.

"Who cares?" Westy took back his shirt. "He's gonna be a dead man soon. That's all I know."

"You don't have enough enemies with the blacks and the Mexicans?"

Westy paused to glance at him. "Don't be telling me how to run my business."

John shrugged. "I'm just sayin'."

"I don't want to hear what you have to say. We clear?"

"I wish we'd done some homework before we messed with him," Ace admitted. "We could've been more prepared."

"How do you get more prepared than four on one?" John knew this comment would make Westy angry, but it was a jab he couldn't resist.

"It was three on one, okay?" Westy said. "Buzz's got a month left. He don't want to fight so you're not gonna get much out of him. And we weren't all that serious. We were just messin', givin' him a little initiation to the joint."

Sure, John thought. But he didn't say it.

"Now I know why he didn't come in on the bus," Ace said. "That boy's one bad dude."

John had been biting a hangnail, but at this he dropped his hand. "What do you mean he didn't come in on the bus? All the transfers came in on the bus."

"Not this asshole," Westy grumbled, packing his stuff again.

"He came at the same time as the others, but he was driven up here by two uniforms," Ace explained.

"How do you know?"

"DeWitt was at the sallyport. He, uh, had a package to deliver to me—" he grinned meaningfully "—and mentioned that some badass had come from Corcoran by personal transport. *Has* to be this guy."

Why would two officers handle a transfer when they had the bus coming the same day, with at least ten other cons from Corcoran? That was a waste of time and gas. Unless…

"What's he look like?" he asked.

Westy had finished gathering his belongings. "'Bout six-four, two hundred and twenty pounds. Blond hair, military cut. Blue eyes. Has *love* and *hate* tattooed on his knuckles."

"Dude's been liftin', you can tell," Ace added, but John scarcely heard him. That was the guy his sister had described to him! She'd seen him having dinner with Rick Wallace.…

John's heart began to jackhammer against his chest. He'd solved the mystery. He'd put the pieces together and figured out what Rick Wallace and Peyton Adams had been hiding. They had a plant inside the prison. One who could, apparently, hold his own among the gangbangers and other dangerous losers. Maybe that was how they expected him to stay alive.

They were taking a hell of a risk, which was why they'd needed to keep it secret.

John smiled. He had what he wanted, and it was every bit as good as he'd hoped.

In a hurry now, he smacked the wall. "Hey, let's get going, huh? This doesn't need to take all day."

Westy gave him a look that said he'd just as soon rip his head off as obey, but John wasn't worried. Westy would forgive him soon enough.

"Let's go," he said again.

Ace came to his feet. "Dude, I'm gonna miss you," he told Westy. "I wonder who else they're gonna stick in here to pester my ass."

Westy didn't even bother to respond. He was too angry, too dejected.

John kept his mouth shut until they were out on the grounds. But he was too excited to wait any longer. "I've got something for you," he murmured. "Something big. But you're going to have to pay for it."

Westy didn't hear him. He was somewhere inside himself, nursing his resentment. John had to give his arm a jerk to catch his attention.

"You do that again, and I swear—"

John repeated what he'd said.

"What is it?" Westy was suddenly alert, hopeful.

"Money first."

"What, you think I can pull a wad of cash out of my ass? Fat chance. I don't even know what the hell you're talking about."

"Trust me. It'll be worth a lot."

"How much?"

"Five grand."

"Are you *crazy?*"

"I'm telling you this is worth it!"

"I'll be the judge of that."

"So we have a deal?"

"If what you give me is that valuable, I'll pay. I'm not committing until I hear."

Could he be trusted? He'd always been dependable before. Cooley paid him, not Westy. "Fine. That dude you were fighting?"

"Yeah?"

"He's a plant, a snitch."

Westy stopped dead in his tracks. "What?"

"He's a *cop*."

"No..."

"It's true."

"Can't be. I can smell a cop a mile away."

"He's some kind of mole working with the authorities."

Skepticism etched deep grooves in his face. "What are you talking about?"

"Shh..." John got him walking again.

"If you're yankin' my chain—"

"I'm not yankin' anything."

He lowered his voice still further. "How do you know it's true?"

"My sister saw him having dinner with Wallace just last week."

"No fucking way."

"It's true." Another C.O. approached. Only when they were well past him did John explain.

"You could be making this up," Westy said when he was through. "Maybe you just don't like the guy. Maybe you want us to take him out."

"I don't want him in here any more than you do," John told him. "Who knows what he'll tell the warden?"

Westy started to laugh. "Oh, I get it. He could rat

on you as easily as me so you want me to pay you five grand *and* kill the bastard."

"If he rats on me, who'll smuggle in your dope?"

Unable to argue with that, Westy sobered. "I'll need more than what you've told me."

"Like what?"

"Some way to be sure. I don't want to get Deech involved in this, have him risk his ass by ordering a hit if this is all some bullshit you've dreamed up to make a quick buck."

They'd reached the SHU. "I'll see what I can do."

Westy stopped before it was too late to talk. "Wait a second…"

"What?"

"It's gonna be easy."

John held the door. "What's gonna be easy?"

Westy tapped his head as if he'd just had the most brilliant idea in the world. "Do as I say and we'll know whether he's a snitch within twenty-four hours."

24

After leaving the infirmary, Peyton had returned to her office. She'd been too unsettled to go home and face Wallace and had needed a place to relax for a few minutes. But then she'd started going through the stack of items awaiting her attention and wound up working another two hours. Fatigue weighed heavily as she packed up to leave.

Her phone rang. Curious as to who would even know she was here, besides the skeleton medical staff working graveyard and the people she'd passed coming and going from the prison, she checked caller ID. It was an internal call.

"Hello?"

"Chief Deputy? It's Sergeant Hutchinson."

Peyton made a face. McCalley had given John the word that he was no longer under disciplinary action. He'd left her a voice mail notifying her that it had been handled. But she didn't feel good about it, so she didn't want to talk to John. "Yes?"

She wondered if he could hear the dislike in her voice.

"I just transferred Weston Jager to the SHU as you requested." He sounded like the old John, the one who'd tried so hard to befriend her. But she didn't understand why he felt he had to call *her* to report this. He had a line supervisor.

"Thank you. How does his face look?"

He chuckled. "Like he's been hit by a train. That new guy, he really packs a punch."

Peyton thought of Virgil's knife wound. "I think he sustained his share of damage."

"Still, for three on one, he handled himself pretty good."

Irritated without fully understanding why, she clenched her teeth. "John, I've got to go. I'm exhausted. I was about to leave."

"I'll let you get some rest," he said. "I just called to tell you that Weston passed me a note as I was moving him."

"A *note?* What'd it say?" She covered a yawn. "That we have the wrong guy?"

"To ask you to come see him in his new cell as soon as possible."

She didn't want to go back inside the prison. "Did this note say why?"

"It said he has something very important to tell you."

"Then why didn't he share it with you?"

"I can't say. Maybe he didn't want me to hear. He was trying to keep his request to see you on the down low, as if he didn't want anyone else to find out. I don't know if it makes any difference to you, but I got the impression it might be worth your time."

"Don't tell me the prospect of spending the rest of his sentence in the SHU has caused a change of heart about his gang activities."

"That's possible. Maybe he's ready to debrief."

She doubted it. Things were never that easy. Not with someone as hardened as Weston. "I'll believe that when I see it," she said. "But I'll stop by before I go. Anything else?"

"Nothing, just a quick thank-you."

"For...?"

"Agreeing to waive disciplinary action," he said. "I'm really not the kind of person that whole thing made me out to be. And I want you to know I'm going to do everything I can to prove it."

She felt too guilty taking any of the credit for his reprieve, or even letting him believe she'd been in agreement with it. "I'm afraid that wasn't me, John. That was Fischer. He overrode my recommendation."

"I see." The stilted John was back. "Well, however it came down, I'm grateful."

"You caught a break. Make it count, huh?"

"Thanks for your faith in me," he said.

The sarcasm in his parting words echoed in her head long after she hung up. There was something about him she didn't like, although she couldn't put her finger on exactly what. But maybe she was being too hard on him. He'd tried to be nice to her. And anyone could make a mistake, especially in the heat of the moment.

She just hoped a simple mistake was the extent of it. Because, inside a prison, mistakes like that could cost lives.

Skin's sister was the spitting image of him. And that only made what Pretty Boy had to do harder. He couldn't believe he was finally coming face-to-face with her and it had to be under *these* circumstances. Over the years, he'd imagined their meeting so differently. Since his own family didn't give a damn about him, Skin had been generous enough to share her letters and pictures. Pretty Boy felt as if he knew her, and he would've liked her even if she wasn't attractive, simply because he admired Skin so much. There'd even been a time when he'd thought maybe, just maybe, they'd wind up together someday. The idea of becoming Virgil's brother-in-law, of helping take care of Laurel and her children, made him feel useful, as if he belonged.

And now he was going to *kill* her? It'd only been eighteen months since he and Virgil were cellies in Tucson. Shortly after he was paroled, Virgil was transferred to Florence and talk of his exoneration began to swirl. Pretty Boy remembered how eagerly he'd embraced the possibility because it meant they'd be able to see each other more often. The future had looked bright—until everything reversed itself. Now no amount of wishing would change it back. Skin had betrayed The Crew— betrayed *him*. He had to believe that or he couldn't do what had to be done. The others believed it, didn't they? Duty, loyalty, the oath he'd given demanded he retaliate. And if he didn't follow through, he'd be the next to die. Or he'd have to go on the run and ramble around America with no friends, no support group, no job— always looking over his shoulder for fear someone from his past would catch up with him.

If only he'd been able to see this coming.…

"Oh, boy, look what I found." Ink squeezed past him to get into the room. "Pretty, ain't she?"

Laurel shrank into the corner.

"You gonna tell me you haven't heard from your brother *now?*" Ink sauntered closer. "He's obviously up to somethin' if you're hangin' out with a *U.S. marshal.*"

"Wh-where is the marshal?" she stammered, shaking.

"Where do you think?" Ink responded.

Terrified though she was, she glared up at him with the same stubborn defiance Pretty Boy had seen so often in Skin. "He's *d-dead?*"

"Yep." He dusted off his hands. "Pointblank made sure of that."

"And the l-loss of a man's life means n-nothing to you?"

Ink grinned. "Nothing at all. One minute he was creeping out to check on a noise. The next…" He whistled as he drew an imaginary line across his throat.

What little color there was in Laurel's face drained away. "You're an animal, you know th-that? You make the p-perfect argument for c-capital punishment."

Pretty Boy resisted the urge to intercede as Ink yanked out his gun and strode forward. He told himself to let this happen, to get it over with so they could go back to California and he could try to forget. His situation gave him no other choice.

But Ink didn't fire. He paused, glanced at the beds, then looked in the closet. "Where're the kids?"

Hugging herself, she drilled him with another malevolent stare and refused to answer.

"I said, *where are the kids?*"

She must've gotten them out of the house, because they'd been here at some point. The bedding was rumpled; there were impressions on all three pillows. She definitely hadn't been sleeping in this room alone. How she'd done it, Pretty Boy didn't know. The windows didn't look as if they opened wide enough, but maybe they did.

Good for you. He could only hope Mia and Jake were well away from this house. He couldn't tolerate seeing Ink kill a couple of kids, especially *these* kids.

He'd watched them grow from babies via Skin's pictures. Witnessing what Ink did to Laurel would be bad enough.

The veins bulged in Ink's neck. "Answer me, bitch!"

"If you th-think I'll tell you anything, y-you're crazier than I th-thought!" Ducking her head, she covered up with her arms as if she expected that to be the last thing she ever said.

Ink grabbed her by the hair and dragged her up against him, placing the gun to her temple. "Tell me, or I'll splatter your brains against the wall."

She was hyperventilating, but she wasn't pleading for her life. She wouldn't give Ink the pleasure.

Virgil would be proud....

Ink struck her with the gun. "Tell me!"

"N-never!" she said, and surprised them both by spitting in his face.

"You're gonna pay for that."

Before Ink could make good on his threat, Pointblank poked his head into the room. "You're not done? Come on, ladies, let's finish up and get the hell out of here, huh?"

"The kids are gone," Ink complained.

Pointblank had wiped off the blade of his knife, but the marshal's blood still stained the handle as well as his fingers. The artery he'd cut when they lured the guy outside had spurted like a geyser, spraying Pointblank's T-shirt and face, too. Now the marshal's body was being used as a doorstop as the ever-widening puddle of his blood fanned out on the back porch. "So?"

"So Shady said to do them all."

Pointblank grimaced. "They're just kids."

"Kids who are related to Skin! We didn't come this

far to do half a job, did we? How do you think that'll go over with Shady? Besides, this bitch just spit in my face. She deserves to see them die."

With a curse, Pointblank sheathed his knife. "Fine. They can't be far. I'll find them. But don't make a production out of this."

"What does that mean?" Ink called after him.

"Kill her now and be quick about it. Who cares if she spit on you? This is a job."

That was the difference, Pretty Boy realized, the reason he put up with other members of The Crew but not Ink. Violence and crime weren't a means to an end for Ink. He *enjoyed* inflicting pain on others.

To make sure Pointblank didn't find those kids, Pretty Boy started into the hall. But before he could reach the door, Ink thrust the gun he'd been waving around into his hands.

"What the hell?" Pretty Boy tried to give it back. "I've got my own weapon." He hadn't taken his semi-automatic from where he'd shoved it in the waistband of his jeans, and that was telling, but he'd spoken the truth—he did have one.

"Hold it for me."

"What for?"

Ink was lifting his shirt and undoing his pants, which made his intent clear.

"Come on, man. Don't be a loser."

"She deserves this. And I want Skin to see it. Take out that fancy-ass phone of yours and video it."

"Oh, that's smart. If the video falls into the wrong hands, they'll put your ass back in prison and throw away the key."

He whirled around. "And who's going to give it to the wrong people? *You?*"

"I'm just saying you don't create shit that can prove you're guilty of a crime like this, man."

"Which is why you won't get my head in the frame, jackass!"

"Fuck you! Here, take your damn gun." Once again Pretty Boy tried to return Ink's pistol, but Ink wouldn't take it.

"Film it!" Throwing her on the floor, he started pulling up her nightgown.

Laurel wasn't going down without a fight. She was frantic—scratching and clawing and biting—but she didn't scream. She was probably afraid that would draw the children to her, if they were still within earshot.

Pretty Boy felt just as horrified, enraged and helpless as she did. No way was he filming this. He'd seen a lot of sick shit in his life, could tolerate almost anything—except a man beating up on a woman or a child. Being part of The Crew wasn't supposed to be like this. In prison, they targeted rapists and child molesters, punished them for their actions. Now they were becoming just like them?

"You getting this?" Ink grunted. She'd hit him, connected with his stomach, but it didn't really faze him. He ripped her panties while trying to get them off her.

Pretty Boy opened his mouth to try and talk Ink out of what he was doing, but before he could make up his mind about what to say, Pointblank yelled from the front door.

"Found the little bastards!"

Crying filled the house. Pointblank was coming through the living room, bringing the kids to the bedroom—probably so Ink could do the honors. Pretty Boy didn't believe Pointblank wanted to hurt those children any more than he did. But Pointblank had a better position in The Crew, greater authority, and he'd follow any kind of order before he'd lose that.

"They were standing out on the neighbor's porch, shivering," he explained with a laugh as they came closer. "No one was home, but they didn't have the sense to go somewhere else. They just kept pushing the doorbell."

What'd he expect? They were kids, man. *Little* kids.

God, he was in the middle of some messed up shit.

A bead of sweat rolled from Pretty Boy's temple, stinging his eyes. He couldn't let this happen, didn't want any part of it or the kind of people who could do this. Ink and Pointblank—neither of them could measure up to Skin, no matter what Skin had done since being released from the joint.

Ink didn't seem to care whether or not Pointblank had found the children. What Pointblank said, all the crying, none of it seemed to register. Now that he had Laurel's panties off, he was too busy trying to force her legs apart to care about anything else.

From what he'd seen so far, Pretty Boy thought Ink should thank him for *not* filming. Ink was too stoned to do much more than punch and fumble.

"It'll hurt less if you quit fighting," he panted, and began to choke her.

She did what she could to free herself, but it was no use. In another second Ink would be pumping away—

A child's voice, full of fear, broke through the melee. "Mommy? Mommy!" And that was the last thing Pretty Boy heard before he pulled the trigger.

His right arm jerked with the recoil, his ears rang from the blast and the smell of gunpowder burned his nose and throat.

Trying to convince himself that he'd really shot Ink

and not just imagined it, he blinked several times to clear his vision. There was no blood, nothing like when Pointblank used his knife on the marshal, but Ink lay slumped over Laurel, motionless.

Pretty Boy expected to feel instant remorse, or maybe fear for what his actions would set in motion. Instead, he experienced a rush of satisfaction, a sense of resolution that put the conflict tearing him up to rest. He'd made his choice. Maybe he'd regret it later, but he didn't regret it now.

"That's what you get," he muttered to the inert Ink. Ink was no better than all the other scumbags who'd been in the hat while he was in prison.

Pointblank came charging into the room, dragging the children behind him. "What's going on?"

There was more blood on Laurel, who was shaking and crying, than on Ink. Pretty Boy wasn't sure how that'd happened. The bullet must've gone all the way through him.

It took Pointblank a second to realize that the gunshot he'd heard had resulted in *Ink's* death. When Laurel managed to escape from under his limp body, Pointblank did a double take. Then he gaped at Pretty Boy. *"What did you do?"*

"What I had to do." Somehow Pretty Boy felt calmer, more like himself, than he had in weeks. But that calmness disappeared when Pointblank released the kids, who'd been tugging to get free and ran crying for their mother.

"Are you *crazy?*" His voice ominous, Pointblank went for his knife. "Shady will kill you for saving her. He'll kill me, too!"

Pretty Boy hadn't thought this part through. He liked Pointblank more than Ink. No doubt Pointblank knew it. Maybe he was counting on their friendship to save him, because it didn't make much sense to come at him with a knife when he was holding a gun. Or Pointblank understood that he'd better do what he could to defend himself because, after this, Pretty Boy had no choice but to fire. Not if he wanted to save Laurel and the kids. And not if *he* wanted to get safely away. "Then I guess I should do him a favor and take care of this myself," he said, and pulled the trigger twice.

The children screamed. Laurel scrambled to her feet but was so unsteady she fell again. Still, she tried to pull her children behind her, to shield them. She didn't understand why he'd done what he'd done, whether he'd kill again. She'd never met him before. For all she knew, he was on some murderous rampage....

Raising one hand to tell her it was over, he shoved Ink's pistol in his waistband next to his own. Tears streaked Mia's and Jake's faces, but they were too terrified to cry. They'd seen more than any kids should have to see. But at least the blood staining their mother's clothes wasn't her own.

"I don't understand," she whispered. "You—you were with *them*. Wh-why did you—?" At a complete loss, she stopped talking but her meaning was clear.

Hesitating in the doorway, he glanced back at her. "Virgil was once my best friend," he said. "As far as I'm concerned, he always will be. You see him, tell him Pretty Boy sends his best."

"Pretty Boy?" she repeated.

"Rex McCready," he corrected. He wasn't Pretty Boy anymore. That was the nickname he'd been given by The Crew.

She gulped for air and dashed a hand across her

wet cheeks. "Why d-did you come here w-with them if—?"

"Just be glad I did," he broke in. "And whatever you do, don't stay in Colorado. Take your babies far away, and if you want to be safe, don't ever come back."

25

It was nearly one in the morning. Except for some hushed talking, the occasional flush of a toilet or the jangle of keys, the Security Housing Unit was quiet this late at night but it wasn't dark. It was never completely dark. The lights dimmed at 2200 hours after the first-watch shift change, but that was it.

Peyton's heels clicked as she walked down a corridor fronting eight cells. From inside one of these "pods," the SHU appeared smaller than it was in reality. Not in terms of building size—the structure was two stories and had a central command post that sat high above both tiers—but in housing capacity. One of the largest and oldest isolation facilities in the country, Pelican Bay's SHU housed more than twelve hundred men in gray cells made almost entirely of concrete—the bed, the chair, the desk, everything except the stainless-steel combination toilet and sink. There were no bars on these cells like in old prisons. Painted bright orange, the doors were solid steel, except for round nickel-size cutouts and a slot for the meal tray.

Most inmates in this unit lived alone, but thanks to overcrowding more than a few had cell mates. Depending on the cell mate, sometimes it was better to be alone.

Peyton couldn't imagine spending twenty-two and a half hours a day locked in such a small space with the same person for years on end. She wondered how many marriages—even happy ones—could withstand that kind of close, unrelenting contact.

But going without human interaction wasn't easy, either. Pelican Bay was designed with no windows except a narrow vertical slit in each cell. The convicts couldn't see trees or earth or sky, or at least no more than a few inches of it. They couldn't see the outside of the building where they were being held or other inmates because no two cells lined up directly across from each other. Twice a day corrections officers brought trays of food. Every three days they delivered soap, shampoo and toothpaste in little paper cups. Beyond that, SHU residents had very limited contact with officers, and rarely received visitors. For one thing, family and friends had to call ahead, set up an appointment and get clearance, which made it a hassle. For another, Pelican Bay was too remote. Most of the inmates came from L.A., a two-day drive. Even when they did get a visitor, they had to sit in a booth separated by Plexiglas and speak via telephone. There were men in here who hadn't received a visitor in years.

Some mental health professionals claimed such extreme isolation pushed men over the edge, drove them insane. Pelican Bay was often the target of this kind of criticism. After what she'd witnessed, Peyton wouldn't argue with that. At a minimum, she believed years in the SHU couldn't be healthy, that it would do nothing to make these men less angry or less violent. Just the opposite was true. But she didn't have a better option for curtailing gang activity. As soon as the government provided one, she'd be more than happy to implement it. That was actually one of the things she hoped to achieve in the foreseeable future. She wanted to incorporate more consistent and effective rehabilitation programs to see if that might lower the recidivism rate for Pelican Bay offenders; if so, other prisons might adopt a similar approach. The entire system needed a massive overhaul. Just for starters, Peyton felt the state should provide a structured integration program for offenders who'd be leaving conditions such as these to go back onto the streets. A whopping ninety-five percent of the twelve hundred who called the SHU home were eligible for parole, meaning they'd be free one day.

Weston didn't have a cellie. Peyton preferred he be alone to reflect on the actions that'd landed him in the SHU. She hoped removing him from gen pop would isolate Buzz, shift the paradigm of power enough that Virgil could make some headway. Weston belonged in the SHU, anyway. This wasn't a place one was sent by a judge. Only those who acted up on the inside or joined a gang came here.

Clearing her throat, she stopped at his new cell. "Sergeant Hutchinson said you had something to tell me?"

The holes in the door darkened, indicating that he was standing on the other side. "Why you doin' this to me, boss?"

His voice sounded far more nasal than usual, due to the swelling of his nose. Peyton couldn't help feeling a bit smug that he hadn't gotten away with the one-sided beating he'd no doubt intended when he and his three buddies ganged up on Virgil.

"You know why you're here."

"No, I don't!"

She adjusted the goggles she'd donned to protect her eyes, a necessary precaution since so many inmates created homemade projectiles they launched with the elastic taken from the waistbands of their underwear. Although the missiles could be dangerous in their own right, she was less worried about the pointy end of such objects than what might be smeared on them. The inmates used feces, urine, semen, anything they could to spread hepatitis and HIV. She wore a knife-proof vest for the same reason. It not only protected her from blow darts, it covered her vital organs in case someone tried to stab her by shoving a shank through one of the holes in the door. "Come on. You started that fight in the dining hall."

"Who says it was me?" A flash of white told her Weston hadn't bothered to dress for this little interview. He was wearing boxers and a T-shirt—standard apparel. Residents of the SHU hardly ever wore the yellow jumpsuits they were given, even in the daytime. What Weston had on now, together with a pair of flip-flops, was pretty much what he'd have on tomorrow. There wasn't a lot of incentive to dress when you never saw anyone. Some of the men in the psych ward refused to wear anything at all.

"You tell her, Wes!" someone shouted.

With so little sensory input, the inmates became very sensitive to any change in their surroundings—and eager for the smallest distraction. No doubt the man who'd just yelled wasn't the only one listening in. Peyton didn't have to worry about Detric Whitehead overhearing, though. She'd been careful to put Weston in a different pod than his fearless leader. But that didn't necessarily mean Detric wouldn't hear about what Weston had to say, especially if it was at all out of line. "You're telling me it wasn't? You *didn't* start the fight?"

"No, ma'am. It was that new guy. Bennett."

She couldn't see his face, couldn't even see both eyes at once, but she sensed that he was scowling. "Bennett picked a fight with you—*and* your three friends?"

"Yes! I'm not lyin'!"

But, of course, he was. That was what he did whenever it suited him. "On his first day inside, when he doesn't know who you are or what you can do or what the consequences might be? I find that a little difficult to swallow."

"Then swallow this!" someone yelled, and several others laughed, the sound of it echoing off the concrete walls.

Just as she'd thought she would, Peyton regretted coming. If not for Virgil, she wouldn't have bothered. "I don't know very many guys who want to walk into something like that."

"Because other guys can't fight like this dude can! He's not scared of anything. You saw what he did to me, what he did to Doug and Ace."

Peyton sighed. "You brought me all the way down here for *this?* So you can whine and complain?"

"To tell you this ain't fair! Why am I the only one being punished?"

"You're the ringleader."

"That's bullshit!"

Growing impatient, she said, "It's late and I'm exhausted. Do you have anything to tell me or not?"

"Like what? What do you wanna hear? What did you think I was gonna do? Turn traitor? Snitch?" He sounded convincingly belligerent, but his eye suddenly disappeared from the hole while he slipped a folded piece of paper beneath his door.

"You're gonna make me go J-Cat in here," he continued, probably for the benefit of the men on either side of him. "This here is the bowels of hell."

J-Cat was prison slang for "crazy." "You'll survive."

"I'm claustrophobic," he insisted. "I can't handle doin' this kinda time."

She retrieved his note and put it in the pocket of her skirt. "Then I suggest you curb your violent tendencies."

"That's all you got for me? That's it? Oh, man, this is jacked up," he complained, but when he shuffled back to his bunk, she knew his real message was in her pocket.

Virgil wanted to get some sleep. The painkiller the doctor had given him had made him sleepy. And he needed the rest to help him heal so he could cope with whatever came along tomorrow. But he wasn't about to close his eyes while his little rat of a cell mate kept scurrying around, pacing and muttering. After what had happened in the dining hall, Virgil doubted Buzz would challenge him, not while they were alone. But if the Hells Fury told Buzz to shank him in his sleep, Buzz would have to do it whether he was scheduled to be paroled next month or not. Buzz had access to the gang's new enemy, which put him in a tight spot. If he didn't follow through, his buddies would kill him before he ever got the chance to walk out of Pelican Bay. If he did as they ordered, the authorities would charge him with murder and he'd be looking at another long stay, this time in the SHU. But that was what it meant to belong to a gang. The welfare of the group came before the welfare of the individual.

To ease the pressure on his stitches, Virgil rolled over

as Buzz made another pass between the toilet and the door. "What's your problem?" he asked at last.

Buzz's eyes darted to him, but he didn't stop pacing. "I don't have a problem."

"Then you're tweaking, because you haven't quit moving since I got back. Why don't you lie down and get some sleep before you make yourself sick?"

"I have a lot on my mind."

"Think about it lying down."

He kicked the toilet. "It's not that easy! Havin' you here isn't good, man. I can feel it. And I'm sittin' on four weeks, just *four* weeks, until I get outta this shit hole."

Virgil shrugged. "So what's the worst that can happen?"

"You act like you don't care about your own damn welfare, but you know what? You're gonna care when they come for you. You got my man sent to the SHU. For that, he's gonna have you strung up by your balls."

"I think he already tried."

Buzz ran his fingers along the wall. "You ain't seen nothin' yet."

"What, he'll bring eight guys next time? How many of you pussies does it take to get the job done?"

"Man, you got a death wish!" he cried. Then he surprised Virgil by chuckling and shaking his head as if he couldn't believe Virgil had actually called the HF pussies.

That was the slight softening Virgil had been hoping for. "If what I saw in the dining hall is the best you got, I'm not afraid of you or your friends," he said. "Anyway, maybe by the time you come after me again, I'll have some support of my own."

Buzz quit laughing. "What's that supposed to mean?"

"You're the one who told me to clique up. You guys

want to cause me trouble? I'll clique up with the NF and give *you* trouble."

Uncertainty flickered in his eyes. "That gang's for Mexicans. They won't want you."

"You sure?" Virgil felt fairly confident he could convince them. He made a better friend than he did an enemy—at least, that was what he hoped to convince Buzz of. "I could always say I have Mexican blood on my mother's side."

Buzz started fidgeting again. "Do you?"

"As long as I'm willing to do what needs to be done and I'm loyal, it won't matter, right?"

"You'd be loyal to those spic assholes?"

"As long as they were loyal to me."

"What the hell? What sort of white supremacist are you?"

"One who'll fight as hard as necessary to come out on top. Nobody in here's going to push me around, I can tell you that. Not even my own kind. *Least of all my own kind.*"

Buzz brooded on that for a few minutes, then said, "What if I talked to Weston? See what he has to say about recruitin' you for the HF?"

A quick yes would be too suspicious. Virgil had to resist, put up a fight. "Hell, no. Your boys just shanked me."

Buzz didn't try to talk him out of his refusal. But he climbed up on his bunk as if he'd finally thought of a solution to his problems, which gave Virgil hope that the pain he was suffering because of that fight in the dining hall wouldn't be wasted.

Remembering what Peyton had said when she came to visit him in the infirmary, he let himself drift toward sleep. *All I know is that I can't stop thinking about you. Every time I close my eyes you're there.*

No matter how this ended, at least he had that.

Wallace was still up, looking annoyed as he used *her* remote to scan through the television stations on *her* TV. Peyton couldn't help resenting his presence even more now. Why wasn't he gone? Or at the motel?

Telling herself to be diplomatic—she or Virgil might need Rick's support as they navigated the next few weeks—she tried to bear up under the stress of having him around, in addition to what Weston Jager had said in his note, and forced a smile as she walked in.

"Hey, what's going on?" she asked, her tone friendly.

He dropped the remote and leaned his elbows on his knees. "I've been waiting for you. I felt bad I was tied up when you came home earlier. Didn't mean to chase you off."

"You didn't chase me off. How's it going with your wife?"

"You know how it is with relationships," he said. "One minute everything's fine and the next…" He clicked his tongue. "She's coming up with all these stipulations and demands."

"Divorces are never easy."

"She wants to take the kids out of state so she can live near her parents. Can you believe that? They moved to a small town in Wyoming a couple years back and she's trying to convince me it'll be the perfect place to raise the girls. It might be perfect for *her,* because she'll never have to deal with me, but I'll never get to see my kids."

"She doesn't care about that?"

"She says I'm so busy I don't see them, anyway. She doesn't understand the pressure I'm under, never has."

"It's hard to understand unless you live it," she said, but she suspected his tendency to put his own needs, wants and desires first was more to blame than his job. "Just a sec." She went into the kitchen to set her purse on the counter and plug in her cell phone.

"Give me an update," he called. "How'd it go with Skinner today?"

"Not as smoothly as I'd hoped. Can I get you a glass of wine?" she called back, but a quick glance in her fridge told her he'd already availed himself of the beer John had left behind when he'd brought dinner.

"No, thanks."

She poured herself a splash of chardonnay and carried it into the living room.

"So?" he said. "What happened?"

"Virgil's already been shanked," she announced.

His eyebrows shot up. "That didn't take long. How badly is he hurt?"

She sat across from him because she couldn't bear to sit any closer. "He'll be okay, but the injury required twenty-six stitches." After kicking off her heels, she tucked her feet underneath her. "Four men jumped him in the dining hall."

"*Four?* He's lucky to be alive. How'd he do?"

"He put three of them in the infirmary. They have to be impressed." Which was what Virgil was hoping, of course. "Whether or not the damage he inflicted makes them want to kill him or recruit him remains to be seen."

Wallace whistled. "We're off to a running start."

"There's more."

He was wearing the clothes he'd had on yesterday,

but he'd removed his tie, if he'd ever had it on to begin with, and rolled up his sleeves. "I'm all ears."

"Weston Jager passed me a message."

"Weston is…?"

"A high-ranking member of the Hells Fury."

"Right. I've heard you talk about him before."

"He's also one of the men who went after Virgil."

"Any chance you could call him something else?"

"Like…?"

"Skinner or Bennett. Every time you say Virgil, it's as if…as if you consider him our equal."

This was what he focused on instead of asking about Weston's message? "He *is* our equal! Why do you always have to put him down?"

"Why do you always have to defend him?"

She dropped her feet and scooted to the edge of the couch. "I should never have told you what happened between us. You can't get past it."

"I could if you didn't give away your true feelings every time you mention his name! Was he *that* good in bed?"

He was amazing, the best, but not because he was so skilled at pleasure. Their night together, before she'd spooked him into throwing up his defenses, was the most honest sex she'd ever had, the first time she'd made love with a man whose soul was as bare as his body. Their night together had meant a lot to her. "You're making too big a deal out of it," she muttered.

"I am?"

"Yes!"

"Fine. I just—" he pinched the bridge of his nose "—maybe it's him. I don't like the way he looks at you."

"I don't know what you're talking about."

"This morning? At the table? There was so much raw desire coming off him it felt like he was making love to you right there in front of me. And he didn't care whether or not it bothered me."

Why would he care how it affected *Rick?* Wallace thought the whole world revolved around him. What was going on between her and Virgil had nothing to do with anyone else. It didn't have anything to do with what Virgil was trying to accomplish or what she had dreams of doing, either. It was just…there. Unexpected, inconvenient, frightening in ways, but inescapable.

To avoid an argument, she attempted to redirect the conversation. "Can we talk about what really matters?"

"I'm in the middle of a divorce, Peyton. I'm trying to let you know that I'm interested. And all you can do is obsess about someone who'd be terrible for you. Do you realize that getting with a guy like that would ruin your whole career?"

She wanted to ask *how* Virgil would ruin her career. As long as they waited until after the investigation, it should be fine. But Rick hadn't qualified his statement. If she chose Virgil over him, would he try to sabotage her position with the CDCR?

She suspected he might, which was shocking and insulting and only made her dislike him more. But Virgil's stint in the infirmary was too fresh for her to forget the danger he was in. Maintaining the peace with Rick would create a far more stable foundation from which to help him. Anything unrelated to getting him out as quickly as possible could be dealt with later. "I just told you that Weston Jager passed me a note. Aren't you the least bit curious about what it said?"

"What'd it say?" he asked, but she could tell he was still preoccupied with his jealousy.

She removed the torn paper from her pocket and handed it to him.

"'Get me out of here, and I'll get your man in.'" He glanced up at her. "What the hell?"

"I put him in the SHU because of the fight. I didn't want to give him and his pals the chance to gang up on Virgil again. I felt the others would be much less likely to attack if Weston wasn't there to give the go-ahead. Even if they did, Virgil would have one less opponent, right? But Weston's scared of spending too much time in the SHU, blames his buddy's stay there two years ago for sending him to the psych ward for good. So he wants out and he's offering us a deal."

"Then he knows?"

"That's the odd part. I don't think he does."

"But this note…"

"Weston would *never* turn. He's too strong right now, too angry. And if he knew, he would've gone after Virgil in a different way. It would've been serious from the beginning."

"Getting shanked isn't serious?"

"It started as a fight. They were just feeling him out, seeing what he had. Virgil admits he sort of provoked it."

"You're guessing that Weston's fishing."

"Based on the behavior he's exhibited, yes. I've worked in corrections long enough to have a good feel for these things."

He tossed the paper on the coffee table between them. "That's quite a gamble."

Weston's chicken scratch stared up at her, making her doubt her conclusions. "He's feeling us out, too.

There are all kinds of murmurings and conjectures at the prison. The slightest change or even rumor sets off a chain reaction, and the men are always pushing, testing boundaries, seeing what they can get away with. Maybe our trip to the library on Friday caused some speculation. He hears something's up, meets this new guy who can fight and gets suspicions."

"You're that convinced he's bluffing?"

"I am. Otherwise, I would've pulled Virgil out. Weston didn't know when he fought Virgil in the dining hall, or that incident would've gone down very differently. That he'd find out within hours is…unlikely, especially when he spent most of that time isolated in the infirmary."

"I think you're wrong," Rick argued. "He knows. It says so right there!"

"He couldn't. We've told only a handful of people, trustworthy people who have nothing to gain by seeing this fail."

"So how do you suggest we react to this?" He gestured toward the paper. "Leave him in the SHU?"

Would that create more or less danger for Virgil? She wished she could say with one hundred percent certainty.… "Yes. We laugh and tell him he's crazy. Even if he does know, I think it would make him question whatever information he's received." At least that was the conclusion she'd come to at the prison while pacing in her office, weighing every detail in her mind. She'd thought it through carefully and decided to trust her intuition and the experience she'd gained working with men like Weston. Then she'd forced herself to drive home even though she was terrified to leave Virgil behind.

Rick crossed his legs, folded his hands in his lap and

leaned back. "*I* think you should set up a meeting with Weston."

She jumped to her feet. *"What?"*

"Don't get upset. Just listen. If we can enlist his help, Virgil will become a validated member of the Hells Fury in no time. This other guy you've mentioned—this Buzz who's his cell mate—he's small potatoes by comparison, right?"

"Yes, but—"

"And Buzz's about to be paroled. Weston would be the better sponsor. He's more credible. And he's giving us an opportunity. I say we take it."

"No." She shook her head. "If Weston learns Virgil's a snitch, Virgil's dead."

"We don't have a crystal ball, Peyton. This was a risk from the start. You pointed that out pretty emphatically. Enlisting Weston's help will advance our goals the quickest."

"You're not listening."

"What I'm hearing is that you don't know for sure either way."

"It *smells* wrong. I work with these men every day. Weston would've handled this differently if—"

"If you make a mistake, you could be signing Virgil's death warrant!"

"I understand that. But I can't trust Weston. I just can't do it."

A muscle began to twitch in his cheek. "Are you saying you *won't?*"

The challenge he'd issued gave her pause. He was pulling rank.

"You're not going to respond?" he said.

"I don't know what to do."

"Then do as I say. Last I checked, I was still calling

the shots for this operation." He cracked a smile, but she knew there was no levity in his words.

"What if you're wrong?"

"Then I'll take responsibility. I'm a big boy. I can deal with it."

But if anything happened to Virgil, could *she?* "Fine. I'll meet with Weston in the morning," she said.

26

Peyton slept badly all night, then woke before her alarm could go off and lay in bed trying to convince herself that the nightmares she'd had about Virgil weren't a bad omen. He was okay. If he'd suffered a setback or been injured again, someone at the prison would've called her....

Grateful that the long night was finally over, that she could go back to work where she'd at least be close to him, she got up, turned off her alarm and crept up her curving stairs to the kitchen. Wallace was sleeping in the guest room, which she had to pass, and she didn't want to wake him. She preferred to have this time alone.

Thinking of the conversation they'd had last night, she smothered a groan. Was she really going to cut a deal with *Weston Jager?* She couldn't. But if she refused, Wallace would go to the warden and they'd proceed without her. He wouldn't let her opinion override his.

Her cell phone buzzed as she was reaching for the coffee grounds. Surprised to be getting a call so early, she grabbed it, didn't recognize the number, but walked out onto the deck. When she heard the voice of her caller, she hurried down the steps and into the forest.

No way did she want Wallace to know she was talking to Virgil.

"Oh, my God," she gasped. "Tell me you're okay."

"I'm okay."

"Good. Now that I can breathe… Everyone's in their cells this time of the morning. How are you calling me?"

"I promised Buzz fifty bucks if he let me borrow his cell."

Buzz had a cell? As a prison administrator, she wasn't too happy to learn that. But hard as they worked to stop the smuggling, it went on. And personally, she couldn't be happier that Virgil had found a means to contact her. "Where'd you get fifty dollars?"

"Where do you think?"

His gate money. They gave parolees two hundred dollars when they released them.

"I told him I needed to call my girlfriend," he added with a chuckle.

She smiled at the admission. "So…*am* I your girlfriend?"

There was a slight pause, as if he wasn't sure how to respond. Then he said, "You're the only one I dream about."

Remembering his kiss, reliving it in her mind, she moistened her lips. "That would probably be more flattering if you had access to other women."

"All I care about is getting access to *you*."

This was a far different Virgil, one who was showing his tender side. His injuries must be getting the better of him, or he was feeling fatalistic or depressed. "Is that the pain meds talking?" she asked. "Because the last time we chatted, you were pushing me away."

"The meds can't change how I feel, but…maybe

they're changing what I'm willing to say. I shouldn't be telling you that you matter to me. I'm a fool for even wanting you."

Spinning in a tight circle, she savored the smell of the forest around her and knew she'd never forget this moment. "Then we're both fools because I want you, too."

"You can't be serious."

She couldn't deny it. "I am."

"See? Now that's going to make me even crazier. Because I can't be with you. And how long can I expect a woman like you to wait?"

The solidity of his medallion, which she'd put on before bed last night, reassured her as it hung between her breasts. She wrapped her fingers around it, glad that she had something tangible, something that belonged to him. "I can't imagine I'll be going anywhere. I've never met anyone who makes me feel the way you do."

The tone of his voice suddenly became wary. "Someone's coming. I gotta go."

But she hadn't broached the subject of the note from Weston yet.... "No, wait! I need to talk to you."

"I can't. I just...I wanted you to know—in case something happens to me—you've already been the best part of my life." Those words came in a rush; then he was gone.

Tears rolled down Peyton's cheeks as she stared at her phone. He'd risked his life to tell her that. If Buzz called back to see who he'd been talking to and got her voice mail—or she answered and he recognized her voice—Virgil would be exposed.

But the fact that she meant that much to him made her care about him all the more.

She caught herself. *Care* about him? Her feelings

were stronger than that. She s pretty sure she was falling in love.

Taking a few minutes to change her voice mail to a computerized response instead of a personal message, just in case, she hurried back to the house.

"You seem to be in a much better mood," Rick said as he walked into the kitchen and found Peyton smiling over a bagel and her second cup of coffee.

Clearing her throat, she made an effort to rid herself of the goofy expression. "Yes, I'm, um, feeling better," she managed to say.

He watched her curiously. "You must've slept well."

"Well enough. You?"

"Like a rock."

"Glad to hear it." She added cream to her coffee. "What are your plans for the day?"

"I'm heading home. I didn't pack enough clothes."

"Things at work are probably piling up, too, huh?" She feigned interest in the paper, as if she was absorbed in an article. But she'd been trying to read it since she sat down for breakfast and couldn't seem to comprehend a single word.

"I'm actually dealing with my workload. I handled quite a bit via the internet yesterday. Computers are great, aren't they?"

Not if you preferred that he get back to the office.... "Mmm-hmm."

"Where'd you get that?"

Peyton had been toying with Virgil's medallion. When Rick asked about it, she slipped it under her blouse. "Oh, I picked it up at a flea market in San Francisco a long time ago. Why?"

He shrugged. "It's sort of masculine, isn't it?"

"Maybe a little." She got up and turned away. "What would you like for breakfast?"

"A cup of coffee will do. I've got a lot of driving ahead of me. I'll pick up a breakfast sandwich on the road."

"Okay."

She was handing it to him when he said, "I'll be back tomorrow."

The cup rattled in its saucer, but she covered her reaction by pretending to cough as he rescued his drink. "You're coming right back?"

"Yeah. It'll be more convenient to work here for a few days."

"At *my* place?"

"If you don't mind."

She did mind. That was asking way too much. But she figured they could go over that when he returned. Right now, she didn't want to give him any excuse to stay. "Mercedes doesn't want you to…you know, get your things and move out?"

"There's no rush. We're going to break it to the girls tonight. Next weekend will be soon enough to pack." He put a hand on her shoulder. "I'd rather be here to support you in what we're trying to pull off. I know the anxiety isn't easy for you."

She didn't challenge him on that, either. She was just happy he was leaving, for even a short period of time.

Her smile was strained. "I hope it goes well at home."

"There's not much chance of that, I'm afraid."

Peyton felt genuinely bad about his acrimonious divorce, but she didn't understand why he had to make *her* life miserable, too. "Hopefully, we'll have everything down to a routine by the time you come back."

"I don't have to rush off. Would you prefer I came to the prison with you this morning? We could meet with Weston together."

He seemed eager for any diversion or excuse that would keep him from facing the crisis waiting for him at home, but she wasn't about to go for that. "There's no need. It'll be simple."

Sighing, he poured some coffee into one of the foam cups she'd put on the counter. "You're not going to let me in, are you."

She began to wash up. "What are you talking about?"

"You're completely closed off. You're not even giving me a chance."

"This is a stressful time, Rick. We've already discussed it. I'd rather leave it for now, okay?"

He lifted his cup in a small salute. "You're right. Everything will be different once Virgil's out of the picture. Then you won't need to worry about him anymore. He'll be off somewhere, living his own life, and things around here will get back to normal."

She felt relieved that he'd been willing to accept such a flimsy excuse. "Right. First things first."

"Call me after work," he said, and surprised her with a quick kiss on the mouth before gathering his briefcase. "Think about *that* while I'm gone."

As soon as he'd picked up his briefcase, grabbed his coffee and headed out, she wiped her mouth. She didn't care if it was childish. Then she collected her keys and hurried to Pelican Bay.

When a stocky young C.O. came to get him from his cell, saying the chief deputy warden wanted a word with him, Virgil was told it had to do with the fight. Buzz believed it, but Virgil knew better.

"What's the matter, man?" Buzz said. "If she was gonna put you in the SHU she would've done it already."

Virgil realized he was scowling. It wasn't that he was unhappy about seeing Peyton; it was that he wanted to see her too badly. He'd let himself fall into the very trap he'd been trying so hard to avoid.

"Tell her I'm busy," he said in a last-ditch effort to save himself.

The C.O. brandished his extendable baton. "Get going, and do it n-now," he stammered.

Had that been anything close to a believable threat, Virgil might've refused and let the poor kid go to the stress and trouble of physically removing him. Why not? There wasn't anything this guy could do that would be worse than what Virgil had in store for himself. He might as well tear his heart out as fall for the chief deputy warden of Pelican Bay. Even if she thought she wanted him in return, it couldn't last.

But this poor C.O. had to be a new hire. He was so scared Virgil couldn't make him use his baton.

Cursing his own stupidity instead, he allowed the guard to shackle his hands and feet to a belly chain and moved out of the cell.

The trek through the prison took longer than Virgil expected—because once he knew he was going to let himself see her, he couldn't wait.

When they finally reached an office that had the name Joseph Perry, Associate Warden, on the door, Peyton was sitting behind the desk. She wore a suit similar to the one she'd been wearing on Friday, and he felt his chest constrict as she looked up. He'd never seen such a beautiful woman.…

She ordered the guard, Officer Dean, according to his nametag, to leave. Then Virgil understood why she'd sent such an inexperienced C.O.

"But…Chief Deputy," Dean responded. "This man doesn't have a good attitude."

Virgil cocked an eyebrow at that. He considered himself to be on his best behavior. If he really wanted to, he could disarm the kid in a heartbeat, even with his shackles on.

Peyton gave him a look that indicated she'd handle it. "I've got someone else coming for him. In the meantime, I have an alarm box right here." She pulled it out of her pocket. "Besides, I was a C.O. for years. I can handle him."

Dean was only about two-thirds Virgil's size, but he was still bigger than Peyton. He shot Virgil an uncertain glance before asking, "You're sure you don't want me to wait until—"

"I'm positive," she broke in. "I want to make it easy for him to talk, if he chooses to do so. You understand."

"Oh…" He nodded. "I get it."

When he acquiesced, Virgil nearly grabbed him and told him that he should never, under any circumstances, leave her alone with any of the other cons, even if she insisted on it. In his view, having him do so today didn't set a good precedent. Just because *he* was safe didn't mean any of the other men in Pelican Bay could be trusted.

"I hope you don't do this with regular cons," Virgil said after the boy had left.

"I'm not dying to be alone with any of the other inmates." She came around the desk to lock the door.

"Who's Joseph Perry and why are we in his office?"

"He's one of the associate wardens. My office is outside the fence, so this was my best option, unless I wanted to use a conference room."

"What if he comes back?"

"He won't. He's gone for the day. Let's get you out of those for a minute." She removed a key for his handcuffs and belly chain from her briefcase, but she wouldn't catch his eye while using it. She seemed nervous. For some reason, he was, too.

"Why am I here?" he asked, his voice a low murmur.

"I need to show you a note Weston sent me, see what you think we should do."

The scent of her perfume clouded his ability to think. He could remember it so clearly from when he was running his lips over her skin last Saturday. Which led to the memory of her smooth flesh against his in the bed, her breasts bare beneath him in the moonlight....

"What'd you say?" His body had reacted to his thoughts, left him hard, every muscle rigid.

When she raised her eyes to his, she must've realized that he was too busy drowning in desire to comprehend anything else, because she didn't try to talk to him about the note.

"God, it's good to see you on your feet," she said, and then the shackles dropped and his hands were free to touch her.

Peyton couldn't stop kissing Virgil. He was safe, for the moment, and in her arms, and that was all that mattered. She knew there were concerns, dangers, and that they were very real, but they floated somewhere beyond them, beyond that locked door.

"I want you," he said, his hands already pulling her skirt.

She caught them. "We can't. There isn't time."

"But I may never see you again."

She gazed into his troubled eyes. "Don't say that." She couldn't bear the thought of it. "You're going to be fine. We'll get through this."

"Just let me touch you."

Closing her eyes, she threw back her head as his fingers slipped beneath her panties and his lips moved down her throat. She had to say no before this went too far, but she wasn't sure she could. She'd never felt anything this exquisite before. Her whole body ached for him—

But then he stepped back. "Why?" he asked, those blue eyes of his as piercing as ever. "Why me?"

He couldn't trust anything, couldn't accept even positive attention without examining it for danger. He'd been forced to defend himself for so long he didn't know how to stop. He reminded Peyton of a wounded animal that both wanted attention and snarled at anyone who tried to provide it.

Cupping his cheek, she ran her thumb over his bottom lip. "Because you're so much more than you know."

His hands found what he wanted as he rested his forehead on her shoulder. "I'll clean up my life," he promised. "I can make something of myself. I swear it. Then I'll take care of you."

"You don't have to take care of me. And you don't have to convince me of your potential. I believe in you already. Just worry about protecting yourself so I can sleep at night while you're in here."

He kissed her gently, moving his tongue so leisurely against hers she got the impression he was memorizing the taste of her, savoring every second. And then his fingers grew more intimate and slid inside her.

Clenching her hands in his hair, she moaned into his mouth and felt his muscles tense. This was crazy, foolhardy; they had to stop. But her skirt was already up around her waist and with his free hand he was doing his best to unbutton her blouse.

"Virgil, if we're caught—"

"I just want to see it," he whispered.

"See what?"

"My medallion hanging around your neck."

A smile tugged at her lips. "It's there."

When he grinned back at her, she couldn't help laughing. He had such an exultant expression on his face, as if he'd just won the greatest prize imaginable. But before he could kiss her again, a timid knock sounded at the door.

"Chief Deputy?"

"Oh, no," she whispered. Dean hadn't left.

"No one else has shown up yet," he called. "And... I'm getting worried about you. Is everything okay in there?"

"Everything's fine." She brushed her lips across Virgil's one last time before righting her clothes and scrambling to get the cuffs back on him.

"We need to talk about what to do with Weston," she murmured as she dropped the key to those cuffs in her briefcase. "He's acting as if he's found out you're a plant. He wants to make a deal with us. He says if we let him out of the SHU, he'll get you inside the HF."

"Can he *know*?"

"My gut tells me he can't, that he's bluffing...."

"Then don't do it."

She nodded in agreement. How she'd get around disobeying Rick's orders, she wasn't sure, but she didn't have time to worry about that right now. There was another knock.

"Excuse me, um, Chief Deputy Warden?" the C.O. called out.

"Coming!" She hurried across the room, but before she could reach the lock, the handle jiggled.

Assuming it was Dean, she turned the button. But the voice that came from the anteroom didn't belong to the guard. It was Wallace.

27

Rather than offer an immediate excuse, Peyton pretended the fact that the door was locked held no significance. "What are you doing here?" she asked. "I thought you were heading home."

Wallace didn't answer. His eyes moved to Virgil. Virgil looked as if the guard had just led him in, but Peyton doubted Wallace would be pleased to see them together in Perry's office.

"You can go back to work now," he told Dean, his voice clipped.

Obviously relieved, Pelican Bay's newest C.O. responded with a dutiful, "Yes, sir," and strode down the hall.

Silence settled, thick with disapproval, while Virgil and Rick glared at each other.

Peyton cleared her throat. "Would you like to come in?"

"Will you send him out and lock the door if I do?"

Ignoring the insinuation, she perched on the edge of the desk. "No one purposely locked the door, Rick. The button must've been accidentally pushed."

"Right. I'm pretty sure it got pushed just before you took off your clothes." He laughed, but there was no humor in it. "Or maybe your hair's mussed because there was a sudden windstorm in here?"

She tucked the fallen strands behind her ears and raised her chin. "It comes loose now and then."

He walked in and kicked the door shut. "Why are you doing this? Why are you risking my investigation?"

"*Your* investigation?"

"It was *my* baby, *my* idea."

And his glory if it worked. She'd understood that from the beginning. "This isn't about professional success, Rick—getting a promotion or a raise or impressing our superiors. This is about *lives*. And not just Virgil's. A lot of people could be hurt if this turns into some kind of war."

He threw up his hands. "Everything would be fine if you could just leave him alone! But you're acting like a bitch in heat."

Virgil's hands curled into fists, and Peyton quickly stepped between the two men. She had to defuse this situation right away.

"You need to calm down. You don't know what you're saying."

He yanked on his tie, loosening it. "Yes, I do! I've told you what I can offer you. And I'm not just talking about a good living and professional success. You're right—this isn't all about our jobs. Would you *really* rather be with him than me? You're *that* interested in screwing around with this murderer?"

Tension rolled off Virgil like a tsunami, making her fear where this might end. She grabbed his arm while she tried to placate Rick. "Let's leave all the personal stuff out of this, okay? I called Virgil in here because I wanted to discuss Weston's note. It's his life on the line, not yours. He has a better feel for what's happening, what the Hells Fury might do. He knows what to expect from gang members." With her free hand, she gestured toward Weston's note, which she'd set out on the desk before Virgil arrived. "I just wanted to show him what Jager gave me. See what *he* thought we should do. There's nothing wrong with that."

She thought he'd rant about the risk of exposure and blowing the whole operation, but he didn't. "So you figured you'd start by showing him a little titty?"

Virgil jerked away from her. "That's enough!"

"Stay out of this," Rick said. "You have nothing to do with it."

"You'll see how much I have to do with it if you keep this up."

They circled Peyton while she struggled to keep them apart. "Look, you're both acting…crazy, okay?"

"I'm not acting crazy at all," Rick said. "I've asked you both not to let your personal feelings interfere with the operation."

"But it's okay if *your* personal feelings interfere?" Virgil said.

Rick turned to her. "You had no good reason to bring him in here. You didn't need to discuss that note with him. I'd already told you what to do."

She couldn't claim he hadn't been clear because he had. "I was gathering *more* information. I want to be sure we're making the right decision."

His gaze dropped and she realized that her top button was still unfastened, partially exposing her bra—and Virgil's medallion. "So it's dangerous men who excite you, Peyton? That's the secret? You'd rather whore for prison trash than have a legitimate relationship with an upstanding citizen? How many of the others guys in this prison have you done?"

Virgil's chains rattled as he tried to circumvent her, but Peyton grabbed him again. She didn't think he'd have much trouble punishing Wallace, even with his sutures and his hands cuffed. It was the consequences he'd suffer that she hoped to avoid. "No," she told Virgil. "Don't you see what he's doing?"

Once again, he jerked loose of her grasp, but he didn't advance on Wallace. "Of course I see it. I'm not going to hurt the little prick, even though he deserves it. What I *am* going to do is give him exactly what he wants."

This seemed to surprise Rick. "Which is what?"

"The man who ordered the hit on Judge Garcia. And I'll do it without making any deals with Weston Jager."

That slowed Rick down. "Even if he can help you get inside?" he asked.

"If we trust him, it's all over."

"You can get in on your own?"

"That was the plan from the beginning, wasn't it? I'm making progress with Buzz. I'll get you the evidence to bust the HF for that judge's murder. All you have to do is keep Laurel and the kids safe and leave Peyton alone."

Rick gave him a dirty look. "Peyton is none of your affair."

"Then unlock these." Virgil held out his cuffed wrists. "I'll find another way to protect Laurel and start a new life."

Peyton was hoping Virgil *would* quit the operation. She reached into her briefcase and got the key, but Wallace stopped her. He'd already lost his marriage. He had to realize by now that he wasn't going to get her. Why not hang on to what he'd originally hoped to accomplish with Operation Inside? Considering how much he cared about his career, that was better than nothing.

"Fine." He shoved a hand through his hair, standing it upright, which made him look as crazy as he'd been acting. "Maybe you're right. Let's…let's not be too hasty. We need to think this through."

"*I* don't need to think it through," Virgil said. "I know what I want."

Rick gestured to Peyton. "And what you want includes her."

"If you can't accept that, say so now, and we'll make changes."

A tense silence gripped the room. Virgil and Rick glared at each other; Peyton waited, holding her breath.

Finally Rick stretched the muscles in his neck as if he had a headache. "No, let's finish it. That's all we can do at this point."

Virgil wasn't quite so quick to agree. "There'll be no second chances. You do or say *anything* to Peyton that I don't like, and it's over, you understand? I may be prison trash but I take care of my own."

"If you think your relationship with her will last, you're deluded," Rick scoffed.

Virgil glanced at her. She detected a trace of uncertainty—he feared Rick was right—but he was determined not to betray how he felt. "You let me worry about that."

"So we leave Weston in the SHU?" Rick clarified.

"That's exactly what we do."

The associate director smiled as if he couldn't wait for everything to blow up in their faces. "Fine. Have it your way."

Virgil grinned back at him but there wasn't an ounce of amiability in it. "That's how I like it."

"Don't be *too* sure of yourself," Rick warned. "Your pals in The Crew tracked Eddie Glover down and shot him three times."

Virgil's muscles went taut. "No..."

"I wouldn't lie about that."

"Is he dead?" His voice sounded strangled.

"No. He's going to make it."

"Then The Crew must know where Virgil is," Peyton said. "And you were aware of it."

Rick lifted a hand as if asking her not to leap to conclusions. "Eddie swears he didn't tell them where you are."

"Then he didn't," Virgil said. "He wouldn't hang me out to dry."

Rick didn't back off. "But there's something else you should know."

"And that is...?" With his eyelids half-closed, Virgil's expression revealed the contempt he felt for Rick.

"The Crew found your sister, too. Last night."

Virgil's face went blank. He didn't move. He made no sound. And yet Peyton could sense the intensity of his reaction.

"Are Laurel and the kids okay?" She was afraid of what Virgil would do if they weren't.

"They're a little shaken up but otherwise fine," Rick said. "I wish I could say the same for the U.S. marshal who was with her."

Peyton's stomach knotted. "He's dead?"

Rick's eyes grew even cooler when they shifted to her. He seemed to feel she'd let him down, that she'd *owed* him some debt of gratitude and commitment just because he'd wanted her. "That's right." And because he knew it would upset her, he seemed almost happy to add, "They slit his throat."

This was exactly the type of thing Peyton had feared. She covered her mouth as she tried to absorb this news.

Virgil's nostrils flared. "You're sure Laurel and the kids got away? Because if you're lying to me—"

Wallace pulled out his cell phone and showed Virgil the text he'd received. "See for yourself. They've been moved out of Colorado and are in protective custody again."

Virgil stared at the floor for several seconds before speaking. "How'd they get away?"

"There were three men who came to the house. One ended up turning on the others."

Confusion drew his eyebrows together. "*Who* turned?"

"You can't guess? You were one of them."

Virgil didn't appreciate Wallace's smirk. "I don't even know who was there."

"Pretty Boy, Pointblank and Ink. You recognize them by their nicknames, don't you?"

"Pretty Boy."

"That's right. He told Laurel he was your best friend." Rick looked at Peyton. "You have yourself quite a man here. He keeps company with the crème de la crème."

"Are you trying to *completely* ruin my opinion of you?" she muttered.

"Why not?" he replied. "You've ruined mine of you."

If Virgil heard their exchange, he didn't react to it. Was he regretting his decision to leave The Crew? Was he tempted to put an end to all of this by returning to the gang? Had Rick convinced him that he was reaching too far by wanting more than he had, by wanting *her?*

Virgil was so hard to read; it was difficult to say. But Peyton knew she ran the risk of losing him to The Crew as much as anything else. He was a good man, but he was still a product of his past. Changing his life *that* drastically was almost impossible. Everyone he knew, everything he'd done, even the people he met now—people like Rick who judged him by his past—worked, like gravity, to hold him in place. And if he went back, those he loved would no longer be at risk. That had to be the biggest draw of all.

"Where's Pretty Boy?" he asked.

"If we knew that, we'd have him arrested," Rick said.

A muscle jumped in Virgil's cheek. *"For saving Laurel's life?"*

"For killing the marshal."

Virgil stared down his nose at the smaller man. "Too bad *you* weren't still standing guard."

His meaning was too clear to miss. Rick's cheeks grew mottled. "Pardon me?"

Virgil didn't bother repeating it. "What about Pointblank and Ink?"

Rick's voice was sulky. "Pointblank's dead. Ink's in the ICU, with two police officers guarding him."

His mind filled with God knew what, Virgil squared his shoulders. "Does it look as if Ink will recover?"

How much did he care about Ink? Peyton wondered. And what about Pointblank, who'd died? Those men had been his friends. What he was feeling couldn't be pleasant. People he'd once cared about had shot someone named Eddie, who seemed important to him, and tried to do the same to his sister. The casualties were mounting....

"Who can say?" Wallace replied. "Right now he's hanging on by a thread." To add more emphasis to what he was about to say, he stepped closer. "So does this change where we're at? Do you still want to play it without bringing Weston Jager into our confidence?"

Peyton didn't appreciate the challenge in his tone. "Wait a second. You can't expect him to go back inside after learning that Eddie—"

"Eddie didn't tell them," Virgil interrupted. "And if I give up now, Eddie's pain, my sister's fear, that fight in the dining hall, what Pretty Boy did...it'll all be for nothing."

"But even if Weston didn't know about you before, he probably does now," Peyton argued. "Maybe Eddie didn't tell them but they found your sister *somehow*. There has to be a leak."

"It's a gamble we've got to take."

She shook her head. "No, it's not. The odds have gotten worse. Much worse."

He brushed off her concern. "I'll just have to be more convincing." Chains rattling, he gestured toward the phone with his cuffed hands. "Call for an escort. I'm going to my cell."

It wasn't easy to concentrate. Virgil was playing chess with Buzz on the tier, trying to keep up appearances, but his wound hurt and his mind kept returning to Peyton and what had occurred in that conference room. He had so much to worry about—and yet she overshadowed it all. Was Rick Wallace right? Would he be able to keep her? Considering their circumstances, he had little faith in that, and yet…he couldn't stop wanting her, couldn't stop hoping.

At least thinking about her helped him escape the guilt that plagued him. Pretty Boy had done him the biggest favor in the world, had saved the people he loved most, and by doing so had put himself in a terrible position—all for the sake of a friendship Virgil couldn't even maintain. Where had Rex gone after leaving the safe house? He didn't have anywhere *to* go, did he? He couldn't go back to The Crew. They'd be looking to put a bullet in him.

I've made a mess of the lives of everyone around me, everyone I care about. But there was no way to tear himself from the fabric of The Crew without making a hole. Had he been wrong to accept the government's offer? He'd justified it by telling himself he *should* put Laurel ahead of his brothers in The Crew. He'd never believed in their ideology. He didn't want to be like them or continue to associate with them. But that didn't mean he didn't care about certain members. Pretty Boy had been part of his life for *fourteen years,* Pointblank for six. It wasn't as if he saw them as bad people. In prison the line between good and evil blurred too much, especially in that length of time.

He'd believed that certain sacrifices would be worth the reward waiting on the other side, or he wouldn't have done it. Now he wasn't sure he or Laurel or Rex would even make it to the other side. By grasping for a better future, he'd let his loved ones down. And they deserved more. Rex was just as decent as Eddie, only he came from a shitty family that had basically driven him away, and he'd fallen in with a gang instead of going to college and getting a job.

Virgil pictured Peyton again. Would he let her down,

too? At the very least, he suspected Rick Wallace might go after her job because of him.

He should've left her alone. He'd known that all along. But just the taste of her made him feel drunk....

"Hey, you gonna move or not?" Buzz asked.

Did he care about the game? No. Buzz wasn't much of a challenge. But goaded into action, he slid his queen down the diagonal and took Buzz's rook.

"Oh, great. *Thanks.*"

Virgil had no sympathy for him. He couldn't allow himself to like his cell mate or anyone else he met inside Pelican Bay, couldn't form any bonds. He'd already learned that lesson the hard way by growing attached to people he'd had to turn his back on. "You don't want me to take it? Protect it."

His cell mate slid his own queen over to shield his bishop. "Someone's in a piss-poor mood."

"How do you know I'm not normally like this?"

"Because you weren't like this last night, even after the fight."

"Maybe I like to fight."

"Four on one? You're jokin', right?"

"Nope." Virgil summoned a cocky grin, but it was all a front. He was feeling worse by the minute, could feel rivulets of sweat pouring down his back.

Buzz shook his head. "Dude, you're crazy."

Several members of the Nuestra Family hung out on the fringes of the tables, eyeing them and talking in loud voices. "One-on-one, he would've pounded all their asses!" "I'd like to see him go at it with White-head himself." "If he was smart he'd clique up with us, you hear what I'm sayin'? This here's a gang that can appreciate that kind of talent."

"You're not listenin' to them, are you?" Buzz

grumbled. "That bullshit you were spoutin' before, you wouldn't really consider it."

Virgil shrugged. "I'll consider whatever serves my purposes." Knowing the HF already suspected him made it impossible to act interested in joining *them*. His only choice was to play hard to get, to force *them* to pursue *him*. If they would. This route would take more time than he'd hoped to be inside this hellhole. But from what Virgil could see, the only way to convince the HF that he was legit was to turn away the very thing they'd expect him to want.

Buzz lowered his voice. "I told you. I'm gonna talk to Westy. I'm gonna get you in."

Fortunately, Buzz didn't seem to be as suspicious of him as Weston was. That gave Virgil hope. "Westy's in the SHU, man."

"Don't matter. I'll get a message to him. Or Detric. Deech is the one who'll decide, anyway."

"How will you communicate with him? He's in the SHU, too."

His eyes flicked to two guards who were talking in the corner. "How do you think? I'll hire a little help."

Virgil needed to learn which guards could be trusted and by whom, so he ignored the growing pain in his gut and paid close attention. "Those guys will help you out?"

"For the right price. They don't do it 'cause they like us."

Since they weren't close enough for him to read name tags, Virgil memorized their faces. "Good to know, in case I change my mind."

"So you're interested?"

"Not right now."

Buzz's face fell. "*What?* You can't be serious! You're

gonna need a posse in here. So what if you can fight? No one wants to be friendless."

"If you think I'm willing to stab guys for the Hells Fury you're crazier than I am."

"It's better than stabbin' guys for the NF! You said you like to fight."

"I like to fight when I have a reason."

He leaned forward. "Look, I know you're no green recruit. You've got experience, and you'll be treated with respect."

Virgil allowed his surprise to show. "What does that mean?"

"It means you won't be a grunt."

"No initiation?"

"I'm not sure about that, but I'll suggest it. I'll see what I can do."

Virgil rolled his eyes. "You'll *suggest* it? Talk to me when you've got some authority. Maybe then I'll consider what the hell you're offering. By the way, you suck at chess. I'm done with this." Leaving the game half-finished, he got up and went back to his cell. He needed to lie down, was afraid he'd pass out if he didn't. The doctor had told him to rest, but he'd done the opposite. He'd had no choice, not this afternoon. He had to come across as if he was impervious to pain and injury. That was part of the psychological warfare he hoped would ultimately keep injuries to a minimum—especially his.

Someone was coming up behind him—he could hear footsteps—but whoever it was didn't move fast, so he didn't turn. He didn't want to act paranoid. With the stories circulating about him, he didn't think anyone else would be willing to take him on. At least, he hoped not—because if someone attacked him now, there wouldn't be a damn thing he could do to save himself. He'd never felt so weak. The shank he'd taken to the gut had shocked his system and he couldn't seem to recover....

"How you feelin'?"

It was the blond C.O. who'd been conferring with the other guard in the corner.

Virgil didn't want to be perceived as friendly to the C.O.s. He knew that wouldn't help his cause. And he needed some space, some privacy to deal with the way he was feeling. So he gave the guy a look that told him to piss off. "You must be bored, because I can't imagine you're really concerned."

He didn't react like Virgil expected. The guy stepped inside his cell, something most C.O.s avoided without backup, and whispered, "You're doin' great, making it all very believable."

A shot of adrenaline alleviated some of Virgil's lightheadedness. "What are you talking about?"

"If I didn't know better, I'd think you were legit."

"What?"

"Peyton sent me. She wanted me to tell you that if you ever have any info to pass along, you can trust me. I'll handle it for you."

Could that be true? Peyton hadn't mentioned taking a C.O. into her confidence. And Buzz had just indicated this guard could be bought. But if *she* hadn't told him, who had?

Virgil wanted to admit he needed a doctor, but Buzz's words of a few minutes ago stopped him. He couldn't trust this guy. "Get outta here," he said with as much attitude as possible. "You got the wrong guy."

The C.O.—Hutchinson from his name tag— glanced over his shoulder before continuing. "See?"

he whispered, eyes alight with excitement. "You're so damn believable! I think this was a great idea!"

Virgil waved him away. "You're nuts, man. Certifiable. I don't even know who Peyton is."

"Right." He winked. "I'll be around if you need me."

As the C.O. wandered off, Virgil tried to figure out what the hell had just happened. But spots danced before his eyes. The dizziness had returned, all the worse for that momentary reprieve. He had to steady himself with a hand against the wall so he wouldn't sink to the floor.

While he was standing there, gathering his strength, he realized that his wound was bleeding again. He was staring at the blood when he heard Buzz talking to someone as he approached the cell.

Turning so his cell mate wouldn't see the growing red stain on his shirt, he dropped onto his bunk rather than lowering himself as gingerly as he was tempted to do. Then he paid the price for showing off. Pain burned deep, like a ball of fire, so intense it made him nauseous.

Was his wound getting infected? Prisons weren't the cleanest institutions in the world....

He knew he should see the doctor.

He also knew he wouldn't even ask.

28

Rick sat on Peyton's deck, his chair pushed close to the house so he could be sheltered by the eaves. A steady drizzle had begun a few minutes earlier. Wearing his heavy overcoat with the collar turned up, he stared out at a gray, churning sea, tapping his foot on the wood planking. Waiting…waiting…waiting. He'd spent most of the afternoon in meetings with the warden on various issues, going over CDCR mandates, but they had no more business to conduct, so there was no excuse to stay over another day. As soon as the warden left for the night, Rick had climbed into his car to head back to Sacramento and made the mistake of answering a call from Mercedes. They'd screamed at each other about their children, their house, their assets and who was at fault for the failure of their marriage until he couldn't tolerate the sound of her voice any longer and had hung up—only to hear from his mother immediately afterward. He'd answered *that* call hoping she'd have some sympathy for him. She and Mercedes had never been close. Instead, she expressed sadness for his girls and pleaded with him to fight for his marriage, to seek counseling, to hang on at all costs.

Mercedes is a supportive wife and a good mother.

You don't throw away a woman like that. Where do you think you're going to find someone more devoted to you and those kids than she is?

He didn't want to hear it, didn't want to learn how badly she regretted her own divorce, either. It was too late for him to change course. He hated Mercedes with a passion, felt he must've hated her for years and never known it. When he pictured her face, her body, he cringed. How could he have been so blind? Why had it taken him so long to consider Peyton as a viable alternative instead of an extramarital temptation? If only he'd realized sooner, before she'd met Virgil....

He'd gotten seventy-four miles down Highway 1, as far as Trinidad, before turning back. As much as he wanted to see his girls, he couldn't bring himself to go home. He knew how nasty it would get with Mercedes. He also knew, if he left town now, he'd lose Peyton for good, which pretty much took care of his dream of coming out of this mess better off than before.

He wasn't willing to live with no. He'd never had an honest chance with Peyton. Surely, now that he was cutting himself free of everything that'd held him back, he could beat out a thug like Virgil Skinner. Virgil had nothing to offer a woman, except beefcake.

"It won't last," he muttered aloud. She was just acting out some kind of captor fantasy. Maybe she was even punishing him for leaving her lonely for so long. And he'd made the situation worse by handling it with less sensitivity than he should have.

He hoped to make it up to her. He wished she'd come home so they could talk. Every minute that passed made him fear she was having sex with Virgil again, and that whipped him into a jealous frenzy. Why was she so attracted to Skinner? He was arrogant and uncouth and hard to know. He didn't have two nickels to rub together. He had a terrible past. He couldn't trust anyone, would never open up.

Maybe Virgil was well-endowed. Maybe he was such a good lover she couldn't resist him.…

Quit it. That was insecurity talking.

He checked his watch. Nearly nine o'clock. Would Peyton stay at the prison all night?

He was thinking he might have to drive over there to see what was going on when his cell phone rang. The area code told him the call originated in L.A., but he didn't recognize the number.

"Hello?"

"Is this Rick Wallace with the CDC?" A voice as unfamiliar as it was raspy grated in his ear.

"Yes…"

"Good, because I'd like to make you an offer."

"Who is this?" he asked in confusion.

"I could be your best friend. Or I could be your worst enemy. Your choice."

Oblivious of the rain that had bothered him just a few minutes earlier, Rick got to his feet. "I have no idea what that means."

"Maybe this will help. We want Virgil Skinner. Tell us where he's at, and we'll make it worth your while."

"You're from The Crew?" He'd never anticipated *this.*

"I've obviously reached the right person."

They knew he was involved. How? *Where* were they getting their information? "Who gave you my number?"

"The little girl I just spoke to at your house. For security reasons, you really should get an unlisted number."

When he chuckled, Rick imagined one of his daughters reciting all seven digits of his cell number to whoever asked, so proud that she could remember it. The people who'd killed Laurel's babysitter, the men who'd attempted to kill Eddie Glover, had just contacted one of his *children!*

Nausea made him gag. "You better not have—"

The man on the other end cut him off. "It was just a call. For now."

What did *for now* mean? Was his family in danger? Would The Crew make him and those he loved a target? He'd never dreamed they'd be that bold. He was on the *administration* side of corrections. He never dealt with actual convicts, not on a day-to-day basis. And he'd certainly never been threatened. "What, exactly, are you saying?"

"I'm telling you we're going to find Virgil Skinner one way or the other. If you make it easy for us, we'll throw you a few Gs for your trouble and you'll never hear from us again."

Blinking against the rain, Rick held a hand to his chest as if he could slow the beating of his heart. "Why do you think *I* can tell you where he is?"

"Come on! We're not playing games."

Lying wouldn't work. They already knew too much. And it was a waste of time to ask this man to divulge his source, because he wouldn't.

"What do you say, Mr. Wallace? You like your comfy life, don't you? You like feeling safe at night."

Rick remembered how The Crew had terrorized Laurel before he got her out of Florence. How they'd managed to track her down even after she was in protective custody. The gang was a lot more organized and resourceful than he ever would've guessed. And now, after killing Trinity Woods and Marshal Keegan, wounding Eddie Glover and attempting to murder Laurel and her kids, they were at *his* house!

Operation Inside had seemed like such a good solution when he'd first come up with it. He'd considered it a creative way to make a name for himself, felt it would be a stepping-stone to bigger and better things. Now he was afraid of where it all might end. Peyton had tried to tell him, but he hadn't listened. It'd been a mistake to bring Virgil here. Maybe, given enough time, Virgil would be able to provide the evidence to convict whoever had ordered the hit on Garcia, but there were no guarantees. And that chance wasn't worth risking the lives of his girls. Or spending the rest of his life looking over his shoulder. Or losing Peyton to a man who wasn't worthy of her.

Even if she wouldn't have him, he didn't want her to be with Virgil.

"I need an answer," the guy pressed.

Rick squeezed his eyes closed. With just two words— *Pelican Bay*—Virgil would no longer be a problem to him, and the threat posed by Virgil's low-life friends would be gone. It'd almost be as if he'd never gotten involved in this.

"Five Gs, Mr. Wallace. Think of the kind of family vacation that can buy."

"I don't want your money," he snapped. And it was true. That would only create a tie between him and The Crew, a tie others might discover. If he simply gave this man what he wanted, who would be the wiser? Then everything that'd gone so wrong since he started this whole thing would instantly improve.

He didn't have any option, he told himself. They'd find Virgil, anyway. It would be better if it happened before anyone else got hurt. Virgil was the one who'd joined The Crew in the first place. He'd understood the risks: *blood in, blood out.*

"He's in Pelican Bay."

"What's he doing there?"

This answer was more difficult. Rick knew what it might mean. The Hells Fury would have a greater chance of reaching Virgil than The Crew....

But remembering Virgil standing in Peyton's office, tall and proud despite his cuffs and chains, and knowing that he was taking what Rick had warned him *not* to take was too much. Rick had the chance to strike back, and he took it. "We put him there to investigate the Hells Fury, to tell us who killed Judge Garcia in Santa Rosa," he said, and hung up.

If he's such a good fighter, let him fight his way out of that....

Shady smiled as he punched the end-call button on his phone. "We've got him!" he announced to Horse and Meeks.

Don "Meeks" Mechem sat in the converted garage across from Horse. An older member of the gang, still physically fit but already gray at forty-five, he'd mostly gone legit. If not for Pointblank's death, he probably wouldn't have requested a meeting. He didn't show up at regular events. But Pointblank had been like a kid brother to him, and he wasn't taking his murder lightly. "And now Skin's going to pay," he said.

Horse held up his drink in a toast. "For Pointblank."

"And Ink," Shady added. Although no one particularly liked Ink well, he'd become as much a reason for revenge as Pointblank. In some ways, Pointblank had been the luckier of the two. According to Ink's doctors, he wasn't going to come out of the hospital the same as he was before being shot. He was currently on a respirator with tubes going in every direction, had nearly died twice. If he survived, he'd be unable to walk. And to top it all off, once he healed, he'd have to stand trial for what he did to those prostitutes, as well as answer for his part in all the other violence. That meant he'd likely get a life sentence. Or two or three.

What had happened at the safe house was a bad deal. But there were some positives that'd come out of it, at least when they looked at the big picture. The Crew hadn't seen this much solidarity in two years. Shady could feel the members rallying behind him, as their leader, while he worked to avenge their fallen comrades—and he loved every minute of it. *Everyone* was on the hunt for Virgil and Pretty Boy; *everyone* was putting out feelers, checking contacts and reporting because they were all determined to make Virgil and Pretty Boy pay for turning on them.

"How do we handle it?" Horse asked, after draining his glass.

Shady wished he could blow Virgil's head off himself. He knew nothing would make him look better to the rest of the gang than that. But Skin was in prison, which meant Shady couldn't get access to him. Someone else would have to do the honors, someone on the inside. The question was, who?

"We drive up to Crescent City, meet with Detric Whitehead and form an alliance with the HF," he said.

"Shit, do you know how far that is?" Horse complained. "It's like...fourteen hours!"

"You're worried about your *time?*" Meeks growled.

"When Ink's in the hospital and could die at any second? And Pointblank's being buried this week?"

Horse's gaze dropped to the floor. "I didn't mean it that way. I'm in. Of course I'm in."

"There's no need for all three of us to go to Crescent City," Shady said. "Someone's gotta take care of things around here. And we still have to find Pretty Boy. He'll probably come to L.A."

Stretching out his long legs, Horse crossed them at the ankle. "So you want me to stay?"

"Yeah. Find him while we're gone."

"I'll do what I can."

"When do we leave?" Meeks asked Shady.

Slamming his empty glass onto the table, Shady scooped up the keys to his truck. "What's wrong with tonight? We play our cards right, we can get there before visiting hours tomorrow afternoon."

Meeks heaved himself to his feet. "Who we gonna see?"

"Detric Whitehead," Shady replied. "Like I said."

When Peyton spotted Rick's car in her drive, she felt her temper rise. This time she was going to tell him, in no uncertain terms, that he had to go. She didn't care what it meant for her job. No boss had the right to do what he was doing. She'd sue him for sexual harassment, if necessary.

But before she could reach the deck and confront him, he hurried down the steps and brushed past her with a comment about having to get home.

"You're leaving for Sacramento?" She shaded her face from the rain. "This late?"

Ducking his head, he unlocked his car and tossed his briefcase inside. "Yeah, listen, I waited around for a bit, hoping to talk to you. I know I've been acting like an ass lately. And I'm sorry. Truly. We'll have a conversation on the phone tomorrow. I just remembered that... there's something I've got to do."

"No problem." She was so eager to have him gone she didn't question his rush—until after he'd driven off. Then she wondered what he'd been doing for the past four hours. She knew he'd left the prison shortly after the warden because that was what the C.O. at the guard shack had told her. She'd thought he'd already left town, as well; that was why it had come as such a surprise to find him at her house. But if he wanted to drive back to Sacramento, why didn't he get an earlier start?

She had no idea, but she didn't really care.

Breathing a huge sigh of relief at *finally* having her house to herself, she ran up the stairs to let herself in. She'd grabbed a bite to eat on the way home. Now she craved a nice long shower and a good night's sleep. She wasn't sure she could manage the sleep part—she was on edge, worried about Virgil and probably would be the whole time he was inside—but she knew she had to try.

Her cell phone buzzed on the bathroom counter while she was standing beneath the hot spray. Normally, she would've ignored it, returned the call once she got out. But it was late for a sales call or anything like that, and the memory of Virgil using a contraband cell phone had her getting out dripping wet.

Sure enough, this call was from the same number.

"Hello?" she said, breathless with hope and anticipation.

No one answered.

"Hello?" she said again.

"Who is this?" a voice responded.

Buzz! Her heart nearly seized in her chest. Fear urged her to hang up, but she couldn't. That wouldn't be doing Virgil *any* favors. Getting back in the shower with the water running, she closed the door so the noise and echo would help camouflage her voice and pretended to be someone much coarser and bolder. "Who's *this?*" she snapped back.

Her answer got no response, but Buzz was still listening. She could sense him on the other end of the line.

"Where's Simeon?" she asked.

"Sleeping," Buzz said, and then he was gone.

Peyton stood shaking in the shower long after Buzz hung up. Had he fallen for her act? Or had he recognized her voice?

What was he going to do?

Rex had no answers. He'd returned to Los Angeles because that was the only city he could call home, but he couldn't go to any of the houses or bars that were familiar to him. The Crew owned or frequented those places, and he knew what would happen if he showed his face. No doubt they'd already put out an order to shoot him on sight.

He did have one thing going for him. He hated his family and everyone knew it, so it was unlikely that gang members would threaten them. Virgil was his only family, really, and The Crew had been after Virgil *before* Rex defected. What he'd done wasn't going to affect anything.

Maybe it was time to go legit, he mused. Should he try to change his life? He'd flirted with that idea for years, wished he could figure out how. That had to be what Virgil was doing. But Virgil had the advantage of a clean slate. Rex did not. Beyond that, he had no way to make a legal living. He was driving a stolen car. He'd just killed two men from his own gang. And he was probably wanted as an accomplice in the marshal's death in Gunnison, as well as the Eddie Glover shooting—thanks to Ink. From what he could see, he didn't have a chance of cleaning up.

Which was why, once it grew late, he found himself driving past the illegal club Horse operated at Sixtieth and Vermont. It wasn't the drugs, prostitutes, slot machines or illegal firearms that attracted him. It was the sheer familiarity of the turf. He'd felt so alone since Gunnison, so adrift. And that made him just a little reckless. He kept thinking about walking into Horse's club, confronting him and anyone else who was there. He knew he wouldn't make it out alive. Everyone inside would be packing heat. But at least he'd go down like a man. Maybe he'd open fire, take a few of those bastards with him. He sure as hell didn't want to run for the rest of his life.…

He was sitting at the curb across the street, letting the engine of the stolen Sentra idle while he wondered who might be inside and whether or not he had the balls to do what he'd been contemplating, when a Honda Civic pulled up and Shady's girlfriend stumbled out. Rex recognized Mona instantly. He'd always felt sorry for her. Shady kicked her around, passed her off to his friends, called her the most terrible names.

The driver of the Honda didn't seem to realize he was there. He was too busy screaming that Mona better not have given him herpes or he'd come back and take his twenty bucks out of her hide. Then he tossed her panties out on the street, along with her money, and sped off.

Teetering on high heels, she tried to collect the cash but fell over when she reached down and didn't get up.

She sat in the middle of the road, her tight skirt too short to hide her bare ass, staring up at the black sky as if she wished it would swallow her. And then she started to cry.

Shady had turned her out. She wouldn't be down here, hooking for Horse, if he hadn't. But she wouldn't last long here, either. She was too much of an addict to make a good prostitute.

She'd hit rock bottom. It was the most pathetic sight Rex had ever seen, and he'd seen a lot of sad things in his life. He told himself he had no business watching her. That he should drive off and forget all about Mona, Shady, Horse and the others. But her sobs were so gut-wrenching he couldn't bring himself to leave.

Leaning out the window, he whistled to catch her attention.

Her head popped up and, hiccuping as she looked over at him, she made a weak attempt to pull down her skirt. "You should get out of here," she warned when she recognized him. "Horse'll kill you if he sees you."

Apparently she'd heard about his situation. "I know."

She wiped her face. "So…why are you here?"

"Same reason you are." He had nowhere else to go. It was the story of his life. He'd been scrabbling around, looking for a place to belong, since he could remember.

"What do you want?" she asked, curious enough to be distracted from her heartbreak.

To start over. To get out. Like Virgil. If only he knew how.… "Climb in. I'll take you to a shelter."

She raised her chin. "What if I don't want to go to a shelter?"

"You have to go somewhere, right? You won't survive here much longer."

She knew it, too; he could tell. "I have a sister," she admitted after a lengthy silence.

"Will she help you?"

"Maybe. I haven't ever given her the chance."

"Then don't you think it's time you asked?"

Slowly she climbed to her feet and came around the car.

"Where we headin'?" he asked once she'd strapped herself in.

She toyed with the twenty her last john had paid her, the only thing she had to show for her years with The Crew—besides a debilitating drug habit and possibly, likely, an STD or two. "Beverly Hills."

He felt his eyebrows go up. "No kidding?"

She grinned at him. "No kidding."

They had some trouble with the address. She got confused and couldn't remember it right. But eventually they located her sister's house and he waited while she went to the door. When the woman who answered hugged her, Rex knew it was going to be okay. At least for now. He was about to take off when she came hurrying back to the car.

"Do you want to stay here for the night?" she asked. "My sister'll let you crash on the couch."

"No, thanks." He preferred to remember her at this moment, didn't want to stick around in case her situation didn't look quite as good in the morning, when she needed a fix.

"You're sure?"

"Positive."

"Okay, well, I appreciate the ride."

"Good luck." He shifted into Drive, but she didn't step away.

"You know, I'm not sure whether to tell you this." She fiddled with her skimpy, bralike blouse. "I've been thinking about it for the whole ride, but…"

"What is it?" he prompted.

Her chest lifted as she drew a deep breath. "They found Skin."

Rex almost couldn't believe his ears. *"What did you say?"*

"It's true. I heard Horse talkin' about it earlier."

"How?"

"Some big muckety-muck inside the CDC ratted him out. Rick Walrus or something like that. They were all laughing about how fast he offered Skin up."

The bastard… "So where *is* Skin?"

"Pelican Bay. He's informing on the Hells Fury. No one knows why. The cops cut him some sort of deal, I guess. But whatever he was hopin' to get out of it… it won't happen. Shady and Meeks are on their way to Crescent City right now." She shivered. "I know it can't be good news for you, considerin' what they're gonna do. I've heard you talk about Skin, and I can tell you respect him. But…I thought you might wanna know."

"Thanks," he said. No words could convey the depth of feeling that engulfed him when he pictured Virgil locked inside Pelican Bay with no clue that one of the "good guys," whom he was supposed to be able to trust, had just sold him out.

29

Rick Wallace hadn't been picking up his cell phone or returning the messages she'd left, so Laurel wasn't expecting it when he answered.

"Mr. Wallace?" she said, startled by his hello.

"Yes?"

She cleared her throat. "This is Laurel Hodges."

She got the impression he wasn't happy to hear from her. "Who gave you this number?"

"*You* did. Don't you remember? You said if I ever needed anything to give you a call."

"Oh, right. That night in Gunnison." He sighed loudly enough that she could hear. "That seems so long ago."

He sounded stressed. She felt guilty for bothering him, but she couldn't believe that he was dealing with any more than she was. And this wouldn't take more than a second. "Not to me," she said. "I feel as if a tornado's picked me up and is still whipping me around. I have no idea where it might drop me, or when." Although two men from the U.S. Marshal Service had taken her to a different safe house, this one in Albuquerque, New Mexico, the man who'd stayed with her had told her it wasn't a permanent location. The government was still working on the details of her new identity, which made everything even more difficult for her because she couldn't settle anywhere. They'd left her waiting on pins and needles. And with no work, no friends, nothing except her children to distract her, she was going crazy, especially during naptime when the house was quiet. The marshal spent most of his time in his bedroom.

"I'm sorry, but I'm late for a meeting." He didn't seem to care about her plight. "What can I do for you?"

"I'm calling to check on my brother. If you won't give me any way to reach him directly, you have to at least give me periodic updates. I'm in an unfamiliar house in an unfamiliar city. The Crew killed the last marshal, and I saw one man gun down two others. I think it's understandable that I'd be a little rattled and need some reassurance to help me adjust to all this upheaval."

"Well, I don't know what to tell you. You can't call me every day. I'm busy. I've got a lot going in *my* life, too."

Was he joking? Could it be anything close to what she was going through? Was someone out to kill him and his family? She doubted it. "Then give me another number. Someone I can talk to now and then. That's the only way I can get through this. If I know Virgil's okay, I can go on. But when I'm not sure—"

"We'll let you know if anything happens to him," he broke in. "No news is good news, as they say."

Judging by the curtness of his voice, he was hoping to brush her off, but she wouldn't have it. "That's not good enough, Mr. Wallace. If I can't hear from Virgil himself, I have to hear that he's making progress so… so I can believe he'll put an end to this for all of us."

"I'm not at the prison," he said. "I have no idea

what's going on there. I'm not as involved in this as you might've thought."

"Then who is? Will you give me the warden's number? There can't be any danger in that. How hard could it be for him to tell me that my brother's fine?"

"You don't understand. I can't—"

She tightened her grip on the phone. "Don't say that, *please*. You don't know how frightening it is wondering if I'm really as alone as I feel! If I have to, I'll call you day and night until—"

"Stop. I get it." He grunted in frustration, but when he spoke again, she was glad she'd pushed. "Call Peyton Adams. She's at Pelican Bay State Prison."

That was where they'd taken Virgil? Wallace had just told her? She hadn't expected him to give her that much. "And the number?"

"Wait, scratch that. Whatever you do, don't call the prison or speak to the warden. Let me get you Peyton's cell phone. Hang on." She didn't get a chance to ask who Peyton was. She didn't care as long as this person was close enough to Virgil to keep her informed.

"I should never have gotten involved in this.… I'll be damn glad when it's over," she heard Rick mutter. Then he recited ten digits and hung up.

Peyton had never dreamed she'd hear from Virgil's sister. When the call came in, she'd just gotten out of a budget meeting and only answered because she hoped it was Virgil. She had to warn him that the HF was doing what it could to check him out—at least, she thought that was what the call from Buzz signified. And because Buzz's phone probably wasn't the only one in the prison, Virgil could be calling from any number, even numbers with area codes from faraway places. There were pay phones on the tiers, but the men had to sign up in order to use them, had limited access and every conversation was monitored.

"Who are you?" Laurel asked once she'd identified herself and was sure she had someone named Peyton on the phone.

"I'm the chief deputy warden."

"Oh, now I get it."

Peyton wished *she* did.

"Is Virgil okay? I've been going crazy worrying about him. I just…I need someone to tell me that everything's fine."

Peyton ducked into the women's restroom. She'd been walking through the bull-pen area, wasn't quite at her office, and didn't want to pass Shelley. She was afraid something in her conversation would pique her assistant's interest. Shelley had already been watching her a little more closely than usual today. As hard as she strove for normality, her agitation would give her away.

At least the bathroom, which was empty, afforded her a small amount of privacy. This late in the day, most of the support staff were packing up to head home. Shelley would be going, too. Hopefully soon.

"He's fine," she told Laurel. "Well, as fine as can be expected." She considered mentioning his injury but decided to put it off for the moment, in favor of satisfying her own curiosity. "I have to admit I'm surprised to hear from you. How did you get my number?" Last she'd heard, they weren't revealing Virgil's whereabouts to anyone, even Laurel.

"Rick Wallace gave it to me," Laurel said. "I hope that doesn't upset you. He didn't want to. But I wouldn't take no for an answer. He doesn't know what it's like waiting and wondering. I'm not even in a familiar place, you know?"

"I know." Peyton tried to imbue her voice with understanding. She certainly sympathized with Laurel and was well aware she'd been through hell. But her mind wasn't on what she was saying. Virgil had made it clear that he didn't want Laurel to know where he was, that he didn't want any link between them. He was afraid The Crew would exploit it in some way. So why had Wallace suddenly coughed up this information as if he was no longer worried about that? And why hadn't he returned her calls today? She'd wanted to talk about getting some information on The Crew. The police must have a few details about the leaders, at least. Maybe they even had pictures. After what had happened to Laurel, Peyton thought it might be wise to learn a little more about Virgil's adversaries. That could help protect him. At a minimum, they should send descriptions to the local police, tell them to be on the lookout. It was such a simple thing to do and as far as she was concerned, should've been done already. She'd said as much in her last two messages to Rick, but she'd received no response. It felt almost as if he was…avoiding her.

Was he embarrassed about the way he'd behaved? He should be. But he wasn't that hard on himself. More likely, he was wrapped up in his divorce.

Why did he have to split up with his wife *now?*

"Virgil's my only family," Laurel was saying.

"He's worried about you, too," Peyton told her.

"I know. Can you tell him I'm okay? I mean…I'm not *really* okay. Some days it feels like I'm losing it." She chuckled awkwardly. "But I'll hang on. I've managed this long."

"How's the marshal treating you?" Peyton asked.

"Fine. He doesn't say much. He does routine checks every hour or so but spends the rest of the time in the bedroom, watching movie after movie."

"Why does he go to the bedroom?"

"Because I don't want my children to see the violent movies he watches, especially after what they've already seen."

Peyton stared at herself in the mirror above the sink. "How are Jake and Mia? Are they okay after witnessing the shootings?"

"You know their names?"

"Yes. I've seen their picture, too. They're beautiful children."

"They're coping. I've told them what they saw wasn't real, just some actors pretending. They're young enough to buy it. I think. They also believe we're on vacation for a few weeks. That's the only thing I could come up with."

"This will all be over soon, okay?" She wished there was more she could say to comfort Laurel, but there wasn't.

"Do you *know* that?" Laurel asked hopefully. "Or are you just saying it?"

"Like you, I'm praying for it. We have to have faith, right?"

"Right. I get it. Okay. Will you do me a favor?"

"I'll do anything I can."

"Tell Virgil I love him. I—I didn't tell him on the phone when we talked. I…couldn't."

"I can do that. Sure."

"And…can I call you again? Just to check in and make sure everything's fine?"

"Of course. Call whenever you feel you need to."

"Thank you," she said, and they hung up, but Peyton

didn't immediately go to her office. She leaned against the sink and tried to imagine what would make Rick Wallace tell Laurel where Virgil was.

"Wow, you're working late again?"

Shelley stood in the doorway. Peyton smiled as pleasantly as possible but she resented the interruption. "I won't be here much longer." She'd just found some fabulous information online about The Crew. A cop in Los Angeles had posted a website dedicated to L.A. gangs, their signs, colors, philosophy, known leaders, even a bit of their history, and he'd included a whole page on The Crew.

"Okay, well, I'm heading out," Shelley said. "But before I do, I thought I'd see if you wanted to deal with this."

"With what?" Peyton asked.

Shelley walked in and plopped a stack of messages on her desk.

Peyton shoved away from her computer. "What're those?"

"They're all from the same guy. Rosalee delivered them to me before she left for the night. She said he's been trying to reach the warden all day long."

Rosalee was the warden's assistant. "And Fischer wouldn't talk to him?"

"He's been too busy. And let's face it. This guy's probably a family member of one of the cons, all in a tiff about how we're violating his constitutional rights by not serving enough pudding for dessert." She laughed. "But he said it was urgent and he was so insistent, Rosalee asked me to see if you'd be willing to talk to him the next time he calls."

Peyton wasn't particularly interested. She had too

much going on already. Virgil and his safety took precedence over everything else. But Shelley's comment about talking to this guy *the next time he called* struck her as odd and made her look through the messages. There were at least ten slips in the stack, but not one included a telephone number.

"He wouldn't leave his contact information?"

"Said he doesn't have a phone. He's calling from *pay phones*." She rolled her eyes. "Isn't that pathetic? He's probably on drugs. Everyone has a phone these days."

If he was on drugs, wouldn't he have given up after two or three attempts? Peyton glanced at the times the calls had come in. Almost once an hour all day long. That was too regular, too consistent, for someone who was high and not thinking straight. "Did he say what it was about?"

"No. Wouldn't give her any idea. What a nutcase, huh?"

"Rex McCready." Peyton read the name aloud. She didn't recognize it. Or...did she?

Swiveling back to her computer, she scanned the webpage she'd just pulled up and, about two-thirds of the way down, spotted the name—Rex "Pretty Boy" McCready. *Pretty Boy.* The man who'd saved Laurel and her children. The name must've registered even though she'd barely had time to skim over what she'd found before Shelley interrupted.

Holy hell... What did he need? Why was he so determined to get hold of the warden?

He wouldn't have called unless he had a good reason. He was a wanted man.

He obviously knew Virgil was here. Why else would he call? And if *he* knew Virgil's whereabouts, so did The Crew. Was that what he was trying to tell them?

If so, it was okay for the moment. The Crew wouldn't be able to reach Virgil while he was inside.

But gangs sometimes formed alliances, if it was in the interests of both groups. And The Crew would know Virgil's name wasn't Simeon Bennett. They'd know he wasn't a legitimate con here because he'd been exonerated and released from ADX Florence. All they had to do was share that information with the HF, and together with what Weston already suspected, they'd *all* know the truth.

Pulse racing, Peyton dropped the messages and looked up at Shelley. "What's today? It's Thursday, right?"

"Yeah, it's Thursday," she said, nonplussed. "Is something wrong?"

Yes, something was wrong. Thursday was visiting day for the SHU. *Shit!* What were the chances?

"I need you to do an errand for me before you go."

Shelley didn't seem happy to hear this. She had her purse on her shoulder and her car keys in her hand. "What?" she asked hesitantly.

"Go over to visitation and get me a list of everyone who came to the prison today. Ask specifically if anyone requested a meeting with Detric Whitehead or Weston Jager."

"That'll be a pretty short list. Can't you just call over there?"

Peyton didn't have time for any argument. An inmate was most vulnerable when he was in the yard or the dining hall. And it was the dinner hour. "I want a list of *all* visitors, and I want you to get it and bring it to me *now*. If you don't move your ass, you can find yourself another job."

The sharpness of her response made Shelley's eyes

flare wide. "Okay, jeez. I wasn't saying I *wouldn't* do it. I was just saying, if you're only looking for a list of SHU visitors, there probably aren't more than two or three," she grumbled as she trudged off.

Peyton didn't respond. Her mind was racing through possibilities, hoping it wasn't already too late to pull Virgil out of the dining hall, if necessary. She would've sent word to the C.O.s in gen pop to get over there, but she was afraid her concern was making her imagine danger where there was none. She didn't really know what Pretty Boy wanted to impart; she was guessing at all of it.

But she was pretty sure she'd guessed right when Shelley returned. She didn't recognize any of the visitors on the list Shelley slapped down in front of her. None of them matched the known gang members mentioned on the website, either. She'd been scrolling through it and doing internet searches, looking for other names affiliated with The Crew. But the fact that none of the names matched didn't bring her any relief. Visitors for men in the SHU had to get clearance, which meant The Crew wouldn't send someone who was likely to be rejected. They'd send someone who didn't have a record.

What *was* significant was that, after going God knew how long without any visitors at all, Detric Whitehead had a man by the name of Donald Mechem visit him about five hours ago.

30

Virgil thought he was running a fever. He kept breaking into a cold sweat and he felt nauseous. But he wasn't about to let the Hells Fury know he wasn't in good shape. Not when they were huddled over in the corner like they'd been the night they attacked him.

Something had changed. He wasn't sure what, but even Buzz, who'd been promising gang sponsorship, wouldn't come close to him. Several members of the Nuestra Family had sauntered over to invite him to join them, but he could tell that the HF was looking for any excuse to jump him again and he didn't want that to be the trigger. He didn't feel well enough to be up on his feet, let alone swinging his fists.

After telling anyone who approached to leave him the hell alone, he moved his food around his plate to make it look like he was eating and hoped to survive dinner without an altercation. He had no chance out in the open. He didn't even think he could handle Buzz if it came to a fight in the cell. His arms and legs seemed to weigh a ton, and his head kept spinning and pounding. As much as he didn't want to admit it, he needed to see a doctor.

He'd just decided that he'd ask to visit the infirmary

when that guard who'd approached him in his cell—
Hutchinson— came up. "Hey, big guy, how ya doin'?"
he asked, popping his gum as he talked.

Virgil drew a deep breath. *Steady. Hang on.* "Not so
good," he said. "I think my wound's infected."

"That'll knock your legs out from under ya."

The C.O. seemed to be speaking too loudly, but Virgil
thought that might be a misperception caused by his
fever. When he didn't respond, Hutchinson leaned down
and whispered, "You want me to notify Peyton? She
can get you out of here, you know. Get you to a decent
hospital. The doctors at the infirmary suck. And it's no
wonder. If you were a talented physician, would you
want to work here?"

Virgil pushed his tray aside. "Are you going to take
me there or not?"

"You're an arrogant bastard, aren't you?" He straightened. "Sure, I'll take you there. When everyone goes
back, you just stay put and I'll escort you myself."

Virgil didn't argue. He didn't realize he should've ob-
jected until the dining hall began to clear and he wasn't
the only one who lingered behind. One of the other
C.O.s waved to get the Hells Fury up and moving, but
Hutchinson said, "I got the trailers, no worries, Greg."
"Greg" turned away and headed out with the rest of the
prisoners.

Then, as beleaguered and dimwitted as Virgil felt, he
knew he was in trouble even before Hutchinson snapped,
"If you're gonna do it, do it now and make it good. Because this time he can't come out of it alive."

Peyton felt a measure of relief when she called the
guard station at Facility A and was assured that the
dinner hour was over, all had gone smoothly and the

men were on the way back to their cells. She figured Buzz might try something once he and Virgil were alone. But she doubted that while Virgil was awake Buzz would take him on. If he did, Virgil stood a good chance against only one man.

That didn't mean she was willing to risk his life by leaving him vulnerable to a surprise attack, however. She was going to get him out of Pelican Bay as soon as possible. Now that The Crew had most likely found him, there was no point in trying to continue the operation, not if his cover had been blown. She just hoped to extract him without causing too much of a scene. She knew Fischer wouldn't like it if the staff discovered what they'd been up to. Because the C.O.s hadn't been told about Virgil's true identity and purpose, they'd feel distrusted; they might wonder if *they* were being targeted by the investigation, too. And keeping up morale was key to running a prison successfully. So was avoiding any unexpected developments or the chaos they could create. She needed to handle this as quickly and quietly as possible.

"Please bring me Simeon Bennett," she told Sergeant Hostetler, who was still on the phone with her. "I need to talk to him."

"Is there a problem?" he asked.

The worry clawing at her gut must have seeped into her voice. Closing her eyes, she tried to calm down. "No, nothing serious. Just…some rumors I need to address."

"You bet," he said. "Or…wait just a sec." A moment later, he came on the line again. "Looks like he's not back in his cell yet. I'll bring him over as soon as I see him."

Peyton glanced at the clock. Most of the men were

back from dinner by six. They were given only so much time to walk from the dining hall to the cell block. Why wasn't Virgil there? She didn't want him lingering behind...*ever.* "Don't wait. Go look for him."

"*Look* for him? He'll show up any second. There isn't anywhere for him to go."

The emergency in her voice had confused Hostetler; she'd just told him what she wanted wasn't serious. But this time she didn't try to cloak the fear that was rapidly turning into panic. *"I said go look for him!"* she yelled, and slammed down the phone. Unable to trust the C.O.s to move fast enough—they didn't understand what was on the line—she hurried around her desk to race across the yard and into the prison herself.

I'm going to die, Virgil thought. Thanks to an infected wound, a dirty C.O. and three gang members, one of whom included his cellie, he wouldn't make it back from the dining hall, let alone walk out of Pelican Bay with a new chance at life.

He'd known that accepting the government's offer would put his future at risk. He wasn't surprised by this attack. He'd felt it coming long before he'd noticed the unrest during dinner. This was how he'd expected to die back when he first went to prison at eighteen. All the other stuff—the exoneration, meeting Peyton, *loving* Peyton—that was what really surprised him. And now that brief flash of hope was about to be extinguished.

What would Peyton think? She'd fought so hard against this. And what would happen to Laurel and Mia and Jake?

"You bastard." Buzz held a shank, the handle of which appeared to be a ballpoint pen, the sharp end a nail. But he hadn't struck yet. Virgil could sense his reluctance. He was so close to being free; he didn't want to bury himself under another prison sentence. That partially fueled his rage. He blamed Virgil instead of the leaders of the Hells Fury for forcing his hand. "I was plannin' to get you in, help you become one of us!" he growled, keeping his voice low.

The others acted as a wall to block the view of anyone who might glance back.

"You sure you want another ten to fifteen for murder?" Virgil breathed.

"I do what has to be done." He pounded his chest with his free hand. "I'm loyal! I'm HF!"

Virgil struggled to remain on his feet. "And you think Detric Whitehead would sacrifice a decade or two of his life for *you?* That's the lie, man. He doesn't care about you. He doesn't care about anyone but himself. He's *using* you."

"Get it over with," Hutchinson barked. "We only have a few seconds. You get me in trouble again and *I'll* tell the cops who killed that judge."

Eyes shining with adrenaline-fueled fury, Buzz lunged forward.

Virgil managed to sidestep the first jab. He had almost no energy, but his own adrenaline had helped him that much. Then he went for the guard. The C.O. was his only hope because he wasn't expecting to be attacked. No one else expected him to go after the C.O., either. But the guard had a can of pepper spray on his belt. If Virgil was going to use the last of his strength to do something, he needed it to be effective against more than one person.

Buzz thrust again just as Virgil reached for the pepper spray, but Virgil saw the shank coming and, in a motion born more of instinct than intent, pulled John in front of him.

The C.O. stumbled, nearly fell, then jerked and cried out as the shank went into his neck.

Virgil didn't have the strength to bear John's weight. He had to let go of his human shield as the others pressed forward to finish what Buzz had started.

Another guard came running, screaming for the cons to stand down. Virgil could hear the pounding of his feet, the shouting of the other men, and yet it all seemed to be coming from a distance. Even if that C.O. was closer than he thought, Virgil doubted he'd act quickly enough to help. The guard didn't know what was going on, would need to take precious seconds to assess the situation.

Fumbling to get hold of the pepper spray before it was too late, Virgil grabbed the canister despite John's thrashing around on the floor. He pulled it from the C.O.'s belt and sprayed—but not before someone got him from the side.

When Peyton arrived at the dining hall and found Virgil lying on the floor, her panic turned to anguish. She was too late. Judging by the blood on his shirt, he'd been stabbed again, this time on his right side.

Was he dead? He wasn't moving....

John Hutchinson lay next to him, writhing in pain. A shank protruded from his neck. He gasped for breath while the C.O.s who'd responded when the alarm sounded herded Buzz, Ace Anderson and an inmate by the name of Felix Smith against the wall.

"Medical personnel are on the way," Hostetler told her. His manner was matter-of-fact, businesslike. He'd handled this situation by the book. But this wasn't just another violent episode that they had to process according to a set of rules. One of the people affected by this incident meant everything to her.

Images of what it must've been like for her father, dying in much the same way, ran through Peyton's mind as she sank to her knees. Had she lost someone else? After all the years she'd worked in corrections, trying to make a difference?

Succumbing to tears, she reached for Virgil's hand. It'd taken her thirty-six years to fall in love, and then she'd done it against her better judgment and in only a matter of days. Was it over before it had really begun?

"Virgil?" she whispered, cupping his cheek. She could feel the surprise and attention of the others. Their eyes bored holes in her back, but she didn't care.

There was no response, but he was warm. Praying that meant there was still a chance, she pressed two fingers to his throat—and found a faint pulse. He was alive! She didn't know how long he'd last, but she clung to the slim chance implied by that barely perceptible movement.

"Virgil, can you hear me?" she asked. "I'm with you."

"She knows him?" someone muttered.

"Looks like it…"

The medical team that rushed into the room behind her tried to pry her away, but she refused to let them. As long as she could touch him, she felt she could lend him some of her strength, her energy, the determination and spirit to keep fighting.

"Chief Deputy." The doctor's voice was filled with reproof when she resisted.

She shot him a defiant look. "I won't get in the way, but I won't leave him, either," she said.

She was glad she'd refused when they lifted him onto the stretcher and his eyes fluttered open and focused on her.

"Don't cry," he mumbled with a tender smile.

By the time Peyton had Virgil removed from Pelican Bay and admitted to Sutter Coast Hospital it was another late night. The doctors said he had a systemic infection and needed stronger antibiotics, as well as more stitches. They weren't making any promises that he'd survive. He wasn't in good shape. Apparently he would've wound up in the hospital—or dead—even without another shank wound. But she was cautiously hopeful. At least he was out of Pelican Bay and getting the best medical help available. And she no longer had to pretend she didn't care about him. Too many people had seen her reaction to his injury. That removed a weight.

She was dozing in a chair next to his bed when he began to stir. Fighting the exhaustion tugging her toward unconsciousness, she forced her eyes open so she could make sure he was okay, and found him staring at her in the half light streaming from the hallway.

"Hey, you," she said, getting up so she could move closer.

"Hey," he responded. "What's going on?"

She bent down to lean her elbows on the edge of the bed, which put her face only a few inches from his. "You're pretty sick, in case you haven't noticed."

"My shank wound is infected."

"You knew that before this happened, didn't you?" She took his hand. "The doctors said it must've been going on for twenty-four hours or longer."

"I suspected."

She frowned. "And yet you said nothing."

"There was too much riding on what I was trying to do. You know that."

"It doesn't matter. Sooner would've been better, Virgil. Now it's gone into your blood."

He gave her a wry smile. "Does that mean I'm going to die?"

"Quit being so glib. You could!"

"Come on, I'm going to be fine."

She kissed his knuckles. "You're so reckless," she murmured.

"You are, too," he said. "Or you wouldn't be hanging out with me. What are you doing here?"

"What do you mean?"

"It's late, for one thing."

"So?"

"We've been over the rest of it before."

She gestured for him to stop returning to that old territory. "Don't bother giving me another list of your shortcomings. I've made up my mind."

"You have?" He sobered, studied her. "And what have you decided?"

"That unless you're secretly a selfish bastard who's nothing like what you seem, you're exactly what I want."

"I'm afraid to count on us lasting," he admitted.

"Yeah, well, getting together is a risk for both of us, right?"

"One you're willing to take? Have you *really* thought about it, Peyton?"

"In the past few days, I haven't thought of much else."

He raised his other hand, ran a finger down her cheek. "For your sake, I wish I could talk you out of it. But for mine… See? Maybe I am a selfish bastard."

"You have a right to be happy." She laid her head on his chest and could hear his heart beating. He smoothed her hair. "Are you worried that I might not be able to have children?" she asked at length.

"We're talking about *children?*"

She lifted her head to see his face. "If you want kids, it's something to consider."

"Are you prequalifying me for marriage?" he asked with a laugh.

"Just confirming a few things before we go any further."

"You don't think it's a little too soon?"

"Given your projected life span? We have to keep things moving." She wiggled her eyebrows at him.

"I want kids. But if it doesn't work out, we'll have each other."

"You're sure?"

"I'm sure." He fell silent again but continued to stroke her hair. Then he said, "Do you know if Laurel's okay?"

"I'm positive she's fine, but I'll check on her in the morning, just to be safe. She called me earlier."

"How?"

"Wallace."

"He gave her your number?"

"She insisted on getting some word about your welfare."

"Still, what a bastard. I told him she wasn't supposed to have any information."

Clearly Rick had been exasperated and hadn't wanted to deal with her. And there was his divorce, which seemed to be making life difficult for him. But…it was almost as if Rick knew Operation Inside was coming to a close before they did. "Laurel's missing you. She told me to tell you she loves you," Peyton said.

"I'll be glad when I don't have to worry about her anymore. What happened to Buzz?"

"He's in the SHU. So are his friends. They'll all be charged with attempted murder."

"He can kiss his parole goodbye."

"At least he gets to be just like his hero."

"Detric Whitehead?"

"Who else?"

He toyed with her fingers. "What about the C.O.?"

"John Hutchinson? He's here in the hospital, in even worse shape than you are. Last I heard, they were still fighting to save his life."

His eyes closed briefly, then reopened. He was too tired, too sick for this, and yet he kept talking. "He's dirty. You know that, right?"

She'd suspected it. Shortly after she'd arrived at the hospital, she'd received a call from Rosenburg who was investigating the latest incident in the dining hall. He said the C.O.s who were there when it happened, especially one named Greg Mortenson, felt there might've been some deal between Hutchinson and the HF that'd facilitated the whole thing. "I'll look into it. He certainly won't be *working* at the prison anymore. But whether or not he becomes an inmate will depend on what we can prove."

"He set me up."

She should've had John fired when everything didn't add up the last time he'd caused trouble. She'd been trying to give him the benefit of every doubt. And she'd had the warden taking his side, too. But he could've cost Virgil his life. "Then you'll testify against him. If he survives."

"I—"

"That's enough talking for now. Get some rest, okay? I'll be right here."

He couldn't seem to rest; he was too intent on making sure she heard what he had to say. "He can tell us who killed the judge, Peyton."

She sat up. "How do you know?"

"He said something about it when he assumed I wouldn't live long enough to share the information."

John... The thought of what he'd done disgusted her. What a hypocrite! She'd expected so much more from him. "I'll make the police aware of it. If I know John, he'll be willing to cough up any information he has if it means they'll go easier on him as a result." She gave Virgil's hand a squeeze. "Come on, now, get some rest."

"Wait, there's one more thing..."

"Nothing matters more than you taking it easy."

"But I don't understand how it happened. One minute, I could feel that everything was, for the most part, okay. Buzz was still trying to recruit me. The HF seemed tentatively open to the idea. And then, suddenly, it was as if a cold front had moved in."

"It was The Crew," she explained. "Somehow they found out where you were and paid a visit to Detric Whitehead to alert him."

"How?"

She remembered his friend, Rex McCready, who'd called so many times, trying to warn them. But she didn't mention him. Virgil was already too riled up. He was even trying to sit when he needed to let his body heal.

"What are you doing?" she asked, pressing him back.

"If The Crew knows where I'm at, we've got to get out of here."

"But you can't leave—you'll die!"

He grabbed her arms. "You don't understand. They won't quit, Peyton. It's a matter of pride for them. Their leader, Shady, has always felt threatened by me. He'll come after me again and again, to prove his superiority, if for no other reason. And if they know you're with me, they'll try to get to me through you."

Peyton thought about the cell phone Virgil had used to call her from inside Pelican Bay. It would be so easy for someone in the HF to use that phone or another one to contact Donald Mechem, the man who'd met with Detric Whitehead, and let him know that Virgil was out of prison and in the hospital. Maybe they'd already done that. And everyone knew she cared about Virgil beyond what she felt for any other inmate. She'd made that clear when he was lying on the floor of the dining hall. No doubt news of their relationship had spread through the entire prison by now. That was too juicy a rumor not to create a huge stir.

"I'll make sure the police post a guard at the door," she said.

Too ill to keep fighting with her, he slumped back. "Fine, but then you can't leave my side. I've got to know where you are *all* the time, that you're safe."

"I won't leave," she said. It was the only way to get him to relax. But she knew it was a promise she couldn't keep. She couldn't stop living her life. She had to go home, shower, change and go to work. And she had to do it just a few hours from now.

31

It was seven in the morning when Peyton's cell phone went off, waking her from a deep sleep. Afraid the noise would disturb Virgil, she slipped past the two uniformed guards she'd called for three hours earlier, and answered. Rick Wallace. *Finally.* Her last attempt to contact him had been a text message telling him Virgil had been attacked—again.

"Where've you been? I tried to reach you at least a dozen times yesterday," she complained.

"I've been busy. I'm going through a divorce, remember?"

How could she forget? "Did you read my text? Operation Inside is over."

"I got it. That sucks."

"Virgil was attacked again," she reiterated when he didn't ask after their "informant's" welfare.

"Is he okay?"

He didn't seem to care one way or the other. "Barely."

"Shit happens, I guess. It's not like anyone was to blame."

There was definitely someone to blame. The HF, The Crew and whoever had given them information. And *shit happens?* Virgil had almost died. Not only that, Wallace was the one who'd pushed so hard for this. She hadn't even told him John Hutchinson had information on the judge's murder and that, provided he'd talk, the whole thing might not have been a complete waste, and yet he was shrugging it off?

"You're acting…unlike your usual self," she said. "What's wrong?"

"I've told you. I'm going through a divorce! Anyone would be acting unlike themselves. Divorces aren't any fun, in case you haven't heard."

Neither was being attacked, but his problems were always worse than anyone else's.

She stepped aside to allow a nurse to hustle past her. "I suppose. But we can't wash our hands of this quite yet."

"What are you talking about?"

"I think we have an informant in the department."

Silence. Then, "No…"

"Yes! How else did The Crew manage to keep stride with us? Someone's been talking."

"Maybe so. But there's no way we'll ever be able to prove it."

"How do you know? Just because it might be tough doesn't mean we shouldn't try. Whoever gave Virgil up has blood on his or her hands."

"Don't be melodramatic, Peyton. There are a lot of ways The Crew could've found him."

"Without inside information? Name one."

"I don't know! They have a huge network."

"Well, whoever's helping them has caused a real problem. Now that they know where Virgil is, they won't back off."

"Then he needs to get the hell out of town."

As much as Peyton didn't want to see Virgil go, Rick's suggestion was the safest alternative. "He needs to go into the program as soon as possible," she agreed. Once he was well enough to travel, anyway. But what would they do to keep him safe until then? She didn't want to think about how easy it would be for someone with a gun to come into the hospital and shoot up the place. Neither did she want to consider what WITSEC for Virgil would mean for her.

"I'll set it up as soon as his doctor gives the okay," Rick said.

"Have everything ready before then."

"I think I know how to do my job," he snapped, and hung up.

He didn't like the fact that she was so concerned about Virgil. But his lack of concern bothered her just as much. *Shit happens...* That was easy to say when it happened to someone else!

Going back into Virgil's room, she retrieved her purse while he continued to sleep. Then she blew him a kiss and hurried out again. It was time to get ready for work. She couldn't leave everyone in the lurch by not showing up.

"I can't believe it!" Shady cried. "How'd they miss him? It was three on one, they had the help of a stupid HACK, and they still couldn't get the job done? Who said the HF are bad? They're pussies—that's what they are!"

Don motioned for him to keep his voice down. They were walking down the pier, next to a string of boats bobbing in the water. For the most part they were alone because it was cold, even at midday. But there were a few people up by the tackle shop who might be able to overhear. "Calm down, man. He's a lot sharper than the average con."

Shady had his hands in the pockets of his baggy jeans and was stalking toward the end of the pier, but at this he pivoted and came back toward Meeks, who'd been trailing after him. "Don't say that shit to me! This guy isn't any better than we are. He's a traitor. That's what he is. And for that I'm gonna gut him."

Still worried about attracting attention, Meeks glanced behind them. "We'll have our chance, huh? But you really got to calm down. All that speed you been doin' has you messed up, man. You should sleep. We'd be smart to have some patience."

"Patience, my ass. This is gonna happen, and it's gonna happen soon. I didn't drive all the way up to sea-coast Siberia just to turn around and head home. You hear me? I didn't spend all of last night sleeping in my truck just so I could crawl back to L.A. with my tail between my legs. What would I tell Horse and everyone when we got back?"

"That it's not over, because it isn't."

Shady shook his head. "No, they're waiting to hear that I got the job done, and that's exactly what's gonna happen. I won't let Skin make me look like a fool to my own men." Swinging back around, he braced against the salt air sweeping in off the sea and started toward the water again. He had too much anger and adrenaline flowing through him to stay put. He knew his agitation would be apparent to anyone who saw him, so he was trying to keep his distance from others, but it wasn't easy to go unnoticed in this place. They didn't fit in with all the clean-cut correctional officers, retired loggers, hopeful shopkeepers and Obama-loving artisans.

"I think you're taking this too personal, Shade,"

Meeks warned. "And it's gonna get your ass in trouble."

"Don't tell me my business!"

Meeks raised his hand in a placating gesture. "I've been down this road before, bro. You need to listen."

"You've been out of the race too long, that's all. You've lost your edge. I'm tellin' you I'm not leavin' here until Skin is six feet under."

Meeks's jaw tightened at the disregard Shady showed for his advice, but Shady was so worked up he didn't care. He hadn't slept more than a few winks in three days but the drugs made him feel powerful. Fearless. He *was* powerful. And while he felt no fear, he'd dare anything.

"You're acting crazy."

"Maybe I *am* crazy!" Spittle sprayed from his mouth but he didn't wipe it off. "Virgil Skinner's laughing his ass off right now because he's making us all look like idiots. We have an entire gang against him—*two* gangs—and we haven't been able to touch him."

Meeks nudged a fallen leaf into the water with his foot. "I don't think Skin's laughing. The HF dude who called me said he didn't look too good when they carted him away. He's in the hospital. That tells us something."

"They'll bring him back from the brink if we let them. We gotta take him out while he's weak."

"And how do you suggest we do that, tough guy? They have armed guards at his door! I saw them myself when I tried to get in there this morning."

"There has to be a way to reach him," he fumed. "We've got nothin' so far. Thanks to Pretty Boy and what he did in Gunnison, we've got *less* than nothin'."

Meeks's cell phone rang. Eyebrows rumpled in frustration, he pulled it from his pocket. "'Lo?" Head down, he began to walk away. Shady got the impression he'd walk all the way to L.A. if he could. But he wasn't getting out of this. He'd wanted to be a part of it; he'd follow through or suffer the same fate Shady had in store for Virgil.

"Who told you that?" Meeks said. "When?…No kidding.…What does she drive?…When does she usually leave?…Right. We're on it."

"Who was that?" Shady asked once he'd ended the call.

"A messenger from the Hells Fury."

"What do they want with us now?"

"They want Skin as much as we do."

"They should. So what'd they have to say?"

Meeks slid his phone back into his pocket. "You're determined to find a way to hurt Skin?"

"Yeah."

"Now we've got it."

Shady felt cautiously hopeful. "Through a woman?"

"The chief deputy warden herself."

"No…" He couldn't believe it. Someone like that would be too far up the food chain to take any interest in a con. Except that Virgil didn't look like the average criminal and technically wasn't one. He'd switched sides. And he'd always had a way of making people admire him.…

"How'd he meet her?" he asked skeptically.

"Who knows? Probably through whatever deal he did with the CDC. The warden and maybe a few others would've had to be involved, right?"

"But he's only been here a week or so."

"Maybe she's butt-ugly and he was desperate, but there are rumors going around that she was crying when he got hurt. And before that, she asked a C.O. to leave them alone in an office. Those rumors have to be based on *something.*"

Or not. As far as Shady was concerned, it was a long shot. How much could Virgil care about this woman if he'd just met her?

But killing her would let Skin know they wouldn't give up, wouldn't go away. And they had nothing better to do while they waited for the opportunity to get to him. "How do we find her?"

"There's only one road leading in and out of that prison. We watch for a white Volvo SUV with a woman behind the wheel to drive by and then we follow her home."

At last. Something they could do that would siphon off some of his anxiety. "Then let's go."

As soon as they climbed into the truck, Shady crushed another meth crystal and snorted it. He preferred to be flying high when he met the chief deputy warden. He'd never done a woman before, not like he was going to do this one.

He wanted his encounter with her to leave an impression that Virgil would never forget.

It'd been a difficult day, one in which Peyton didn't accomplish nearly as much as she normally did. Her time was taken up with putting to rest everything that'd happened during the past week. She'd spent an hour first thing with the warden and Investigator Rosenburg going over every detail of the dining hall incident, what John Hutchinson might know about Judge Garcia and how they were going to get Virgil out of Crescent City. After that they'd had a conference call, including Rick Wallace, to confirm their plans for Virgil to go into

WITSEC and to talk about the leak, but that hadn't lasted long. Once again, Rick had acted distracted and eager to get off the phone. Only at her insistence did he stay on so they could call Laurel as a group and let her know the situation.

Like Peyton, Laurel was relieved that Virgil was out of the prison mostly in one piece. At least, she sounded that way. Probably because if he healed as well as expected, she might get to see him soon. Peyton was now confident he *would* heal. Her discussions with his doctor, at noon and again at three, had reassured her. She'd been told he was responding very quickly to the antibiotics. He should be fine in a few days—provided they were able to keep The Crew and the Hells Fury away from him.

If Virgil entered WITSEC, Peyton had no idea what it would mean for her. Despite her teasing about marriage, she didn't know him well enough to make any permanent decisions. She needed to figure out what she was willing to sacrifice and what she wasn't. And yet, if he moved on without her, she was quite certain that would be the end of their relationship. He'd experienced too many terrible things in his life to believe something as good as what they felt for each other could survive. She could easily see him treasuring their brief time and yet letting it go. He'd justify that in his own mind by saying he didn't want to risk ruining the memories they'd created.

There were *so* many questions that had to be answered. About her and Virgil. About her job, too. She'd confessed her involvement with Virgil to Fischer. The warden had been careful to reserve judgment, had merely told her to take the next two weeks off as paid vacation. He said she needed the rest. But she knew it was because he wanted some time to reflect on her behavior and decide whether or not it warranted a reprimand.

And then there were the less personal questions, not the least of which was how The Crew had managed to find Virgil, especially so fast. No one was supposed to know where he was. Even Fischer hadn't been told his real name and true background, not until today. There had to be someone inside the department who'd leaked the truth. How else would they have found him—and Laurel, too?

Although Rick Wallace hadn't been too concerned about ferreting out the identity of their traitor, she definitely wanted to see the department pursue an investigation. Whoever had assisted The Crew was guilty of almost getting Laurel, her children and Virgil killed. And they had caused other deaths. A U.S. marshal and one Crew member were dead, with another on life support.

She thought Rex McCready might have information that could help explain everything. Too bad after all those calls to the warden yesterday, he hadn't called back. But she'd worry about all of that and the rest of it later. Right now the most pressing thing on her mind was seeing Virgil again. He hadn't been happy that she'd left him when she said she wouldn't. He'd just threatened to walk out of the hospital if she didn't return immediately. But she'd already planned to go back there as soon as she'd cleared off her desk.

Stifling a yawn, she glanced at the clock on the dash. Not quite five. She'd managed to get away early, which was good. She didn't want to miss dinner with Virgil and still had to stop by her house to change. She also needed to pack an overnight bag, since she'd be spending the night. Fortunately, she'd have tomorrow to recover lost sleep. Her vacation started immediately.

Maybe she'd go with Virgil when he left Crescent City, at least until her vacation ended. Two weeks might tell them both what they needed to know....

Turning up the music, she began to sing along. On the whole, life was looking up. There'd been no incidents at the hospital today to make her fear The Crew would try to reach Virgil before they could get him away. Nothing of note had happened at the prison, either. Virgil would be well soon and then he'd go somewhere his past would never catch up with him.

And, for two weeks, they'd be together.

With that happy thought in mind, she turned into her drive, left her purse in the passenger seat since she was coming right back and hurried up to pack and change.

"Now's our chance," Shady said. They'd parked down the street on a dirt road off the highway, but they'd already passed the cabin where the woman they'd been following had turned in and knew where it was.

"I'll wait here, keep a lookout," Meeks said as Shady got out.

Shady jerked around to face him. "What'd you say?"

"This is your deal, man. I'll help you kill Skin, and I'll help you kill Pretty Boy. They broke their oath to the gang, and they deserve to be punished. I'll even get your back while you're inside. But I don't do women."

What was this? More pussy talk like, *Have some patience...calm down...let's think about it?* He'd been right when he said Meeks had lost his edge. The guy was as weak and pathetic as those Hells Fury fuck-ups who'd ruined their opportunity to finish Skin off. But why argue? If he was going to do this, he might as well do it while he had a good buzz going.

"Fine. I don't need you."

Meeks called him back. "What about this?" He held out one of the guns they'd hidden under the seat. But Shady didn't plan on using a gun. A gun made it too fast and easy on the victim. This was for Virgil, which meant it had to be special.

"Everything I need is right here," he said, and took the knife from the sheath he kept strapped to one calf.

"But there's no one out here to hear the shot. You could use a gun, no problem."

"I'd rather slit her throat."

It wasn't easy to climb the stairs to the chief deputy warden's door without making any noise. The deck had a tendency to creak, but the wind was blowing, which set her wind chimes dancing. He took each step slowly, listening for any sounds beyond the tinkle of those chimes, and knew she hadn't noticed anything wrong when he found the door slightly ajar.

A wall of windows made it plain that she wasn't in the central kitchen, dining or living room area. She'd probably gone to her bedroom to change.

If that was the case, he figured he might as well let her know there wasn't any reason to get dressed.

Every minute seemed like an hour while Virgil was waiting for Peyton. Although he'd spent the day sleeping, too out of it to think much about anything, ever since she'd called to tell him she was on her way, and he knew she was leaving the protection of the prison, he'd been nervous. She didn't understand what The Crew was capable of, how determined Shady would be....

Adjusting his bed so he could reach the phone, he called her cell. But she didn't pick up.

When she didn't answer his second attempt or his third, he began to worry even more. She knew how concerned he was. Why wasn't she answering?

Was it because she couldn't?

Just the thought of Shady getting his hands on her sent terror charging through him. He didn't want to cause the destruction of the one beautiful thing he'd found in his life. That was the reason he'd been so hesitant to get involved with her. He didn't want to taint who or what she was, didn't want to drag her down with him if The Crew ever found him.

He was about to call the police and ask them to look for her, or try to send the officers at his door, when the phone on the table beside him rang. Assuming it had to be her, he relaxed and answered, but the person on the other end of the line wasn't Peyton.

"Skin?"

Pretty Boy. Virgil couldn't believe it. When he'd left Florence, he'd prepared himself never to hear from his best friend again. But he should've known it couldn't end that way. "Hey, man. How are you?"

"I'm surviving. You?"

"I'm still around."

"I hear you're in a bad way."

"Not so bad anymore. Where are you?"

"Here in Crescent City." He groaned. "Only you could make me drive those winding roads for hours on end. I had to pull over and throw up *twice*."

"What a kid," he teased.

"I came to help. I'm not sure what I can do, but when the damn warden wouldn't take my calls I just kept driving. Next thing I knew…here I was. I figured maybe I'd show up on his doorstep, *make* the bastard listen. But everything went down before I could get here."

"It was close there for a second. So...how'd you find me? How'd you learn I was in the hospital?"

"The whole town knows you're in the hospital. What happened at the prison is on the front page of the *Daily Triplicate*. Article says you, going by the name 'Simeon Bennett,' and a C.O. were in an 'altercation' last night and that you're now in intensive care under armed guard. Intensive care," he repeated. "I read that shit and I thought maybe you weren't going to make it."

"So you just called me up."

"I wasn't sure what name you were admitted under, so I told the operator, 'That guy who almost got killed at the prison last night.'"

"And she put you through?" Virgil asked with a laugh.

"I told her I was your brother."

Until now, Virgil hadn't realized how badly he'd missed Rex. God, it was great to hear his voice, to feel his support. Rex had pulled him through those early years in prison. Their friendship had made the past four-teen years worth living. "I owe you for what you did for Laurel and her kids."

"Don't mention it. I never liked Ink, anyway."

But he'd liked Pointblank. He was trying to shrug it off, but Virgil knew what protecting Laurel had cost him. His entire life had changed. "You gonna be okay without The Crew?"

"I don't need The Crew. I've got you, right?"

Virgil grinned. "Yeah, you got me."

"Good. Then it won't be so fuckin' lonely anymore. I'd come see ya right now, but those armed guards sound a bit off-putting. I wouldn't want to have to kill them, you know? That wouldn't be in keeping with my new stand-up life."

"No need to get yourself in trouble. I'll be out of here soon enough. We'll catch up then." His thoughts returned to Peyton and the worry simmering in his gut. "But could you do me a favor while you're here?"

"Anything."

"You got a car, right?" He had to have some type of transportation; he'd mentioned driving.

"I have *borrowed* a vehicle, yes, Mr. Skinner."

Virgil couldn't help laughing. Stealing a car was a hell of a way to go legit, but he knew Rex didn't have many options, and if he gave the car back when he was done with it, maybe they wouldn't add that to the list of charges against him if he was caught. What he'd done at the safe house had been done to protect a woman and two children. If he wasn't the one who killed the marshal, he could probably clear up his legal troubles without having to serve too much time.

"My...woman hasn't shown up here and I'm getting worried that—"

"Your *woman?*" he interrupted. "Damn, you move fast."

"Just making up for lost time. Will you check on her for me?" he asked, and gave Rex directions to Peyton's house.

32

Peyton wasn't sure exactly what drew her attention. One minute she was happily stuffing a change of clothes into a small overnight case, eager and excited to see Virgil. The next she felt a trickle of fear slide down her spine like a cold, wet hand, leaving goose bumps in its wake. It might've been a creak or a rustle that didn't sound like the usual settling noises. Whatever set her off hadn't been big because she couldn't identify it. She just had the impression that she was no longer alone.

Standing over the bag she'd been packing, she listened more carefully. She was imagining things, wasn't she? Virgil had been frightened for her, hadn't wanted her to be out by herself. But surely The Crew wouldn't be able to find out where she lived and come after her *this* fast.

Or maybe they could....

She glanced at the bed, the nightstand, the floor, searching for her cell phone, even patted the pockets of the jeans she'd just pulled on before remembering—she'd left it in her purse out in the Volvo. At least she had the home phone. She hurried around the bed to the nightstand and dialed 9-1-1, but before the operator could come on, footsteps, moving on the floor above her, nearly made her pee her pants. She didn't want to be trapped in her bedroom, with nowhere to run and no way to defend herself. There wasn't even a door to the outside down here, or a window that opened. She'd either have to break the glass overlooking the sea and figure out how to scramble through it, or she'd have to get out the way she'd gotten in—by the stairs.

Then she heard a different sound, this one much closer, and realized the stairs weren't an option. Someone was already coming down them. She could see a man's tennis shoes and denim-covered legs just before a tatted hand came into view gripping a giant knife.

"Emergency Services. Can you give me the nature of your emergency, please?"

She gulped for enough air to be able to talk. "There's a man in my house!" she screamed.

The second he found her, Shady grabbed the handrail and used it to support himself so he could jump the rest of the stairs. He was hoping to reach the chief deputy before she could get the door shut, but he didn't make it. Dropping the phone, she darted forward and managed to slam and lock the door as he landed. Which only enraged him. Now he wanted to kill her just for *trying* to resist. And he would. He had her cornered. All he had to do was get through one flimsy barrier.

"Hey, Virgil sent you a surprise," he called out. "He wants me to show you what it feels like to be raped in the ass like some of those stupid bastards in that prison you run." He'd been one of those bastards once. Years ago. The "jocker" who'd used him actually looked a lot like Virgil, but the similarities ended there. Shady had never known Virgil to have a homosexual relationship. Somehow, he'd always managed to defend himself even though he'd gone to prison at a younger age than Shady had, and that made Shady hate him all the more.

Spurred on by his desire to outdistance those memories, he hit the door again. This bitch thought she could keep him out? She was crazy. He'd get in. The door was already beginning to splinter. She didn't understand who she was dealing with, didn't know that he was obliterating Virgil when he obliterated her. And, fortunately, he could batter the door all day because he didn't feel any pain.

"The police are on their way!" she shouted. "Get out of here—unless you want to spend the rest of your life in prison."

Briefly, his mind flashed back to *Where the Red Fern Grows,* a book given to him by his fifth-grade teacher and probably the only one he'd ever read from start to finish. In it, the boy caught a raccoon by putting a shiny piece of tin or something—he couldn't remember exactly what—in a homemade trap. When the raccoon reached in to take the object, he couldn't get his hand out. The animal could escape if he let go of what he wanted, but he wouldn't....

Was he making the same mistake? Maybe. But he wouldn't be able to live with himself if he walked away at this point; his self-esteem couldn't tolerate such a defeat.

Lowering his shoulder, he crashed into the door yet again and heard a loud pop as it gave way.

When Rex found Peyton's cabin, her car was parked in the drive. Everything looked fine. Skin was probably worried about nothing. But as long as he was here, he might as well let her know that Virgil was concerned about her, that he'd been trying to reach her. Maybe her cell phone had died and she'd forgotten to charge it....

He pulled in behind her car and got out. But just as he reached the stairs, he heard a woman scream from inside.

Son of bitch! Yanking his gun from the waistband of his jeans, he took the steps two at a time. But before he could get to the landing, a gunshot rang out from the forest.

Shocked, he crouched low and peered through the slats of the handrail, hoping to see who was out there, when another shot went off. And this time he felt a searing pain in his chest and the hand that held his gun went numb.

Two gunshots sounded outside, seconds apart, making Peyton wonder if she really wanted to escape the house. What was going on? Were the police having a standoff with The Crew? If so, she didn't want to walk into the middle of it. She couldn't get out, anyway. She'd thrown everything she could at the window with little success. Anyone who was here to help her would have to come inside. She'd managed to crack the safety glass in a few places by swinging a lamp at it, but she hadn't had enough time to actually make a hole.

She still held the lamp—which was her only weapon—but as soon as the door broke open she had to turn and face her intruder. It was Shady, The Crew leader Virgil had told her about. His name was tattooed on his arm.

Although briefly tempted to make a mad dash for the small bathroom attached to her bedroom, that door didn't have a lock. It wouldn't take a man more than a few seconds to force it open. And if she allowed him to corner her in there, she'd have no room to maneuver, wouldn't even be able to swing the lamp. Her only hope was to get around him and up the stairs—but she couldn't imagine how she'd do that when he stood in the doorway, blocking her path.

"What a pleasant surprise." He gave her an appreciative smile. "You're not butt-ugly, after all."

Chest heaving with fear and adrenaline, she held the lamp at the ready. "Stay away from me!"

"Leave it to Virgil to get himself a piece of that." He licked his lips as he looked her up and down. "You can't say he doesn't have good taste."

"I don't know what you're talking about."

"You're not puttin' out for Skin?"

She couldn't admit to the relationship. "No, of course not! You're wasting your time."

He waved toward her chest. "Then why you wearin' his coin?"

The medallion! That The Crew might recognize its significance hadn't even crossed her mind. She normally wore it under her clothes, but when she changed she'd pulled it out over her turtleneck sweater. "He gave it to me as a…a bribe."

"*Sure* he did." The blade of the knife in his hand gleamed against the fading light. The sun was setting, creating a spectacular display of various shades of purple outside her window. It would soon be dark. Would she live to see another day? Or would this be her last sunset?

"We can make this easy, or we can make it hard." He winked. "The easy way would mean you put down the lamp."

"Go to hell." There was another gunshot outside. That gave Peyton hope, especially when Shady cocked his head to listen. She could tell he was as curious about those shots as she was. They made him nervous enough that he stopped toying with her and moved in close, eyes glittering with intent.

"Sounds like we might have to skip the foreplay and get right to business."

Her throat as dry as parchment, she swallowed and stepped back until there was nowhere to go. "And that business would be…?"

"Saying a permanent goodbye to you."

Screaming as he darted forward, she swung the lamp with all her strength, but he ducked, and when it didn't connect, the momentum knocked her off balance. He took advantage of that by grabbing her makeshift weapon with his free hand, wrenching it from her grasp and throwing it aside at the same time he thrust with his knife.

Pain exploded in Peyton's arm. Dazed, she stood staring at the blood pouring from the wound. Her mind urged her to continue fighting. He was about to thrust again. She could see the knife coming. But she could no longer use her right arm, which had far more strength and dexterity than her left.

At the last second, she tried blocking his knife with her other arm. This time he attempted to hit a more vital area and missed altogether when she jumped to one side.

He was finally out of her path to the door, so she made a dash for the stairs. Getting out was her only choice. But she tripped on the lamp and stumbled, and he managed to grab her by the hair. She felt sure he'd stab her in the throat or maybe the stomach or chest, but there wasn't anything she could do to stop him. She was completely vulnerable.

"Virgil will kill you for this," she said, and braced for the worst. But a fourth gunshot went off, this one so loud it made her ears ring. Then Shady dropped like a stone to the floor.

Shaking and crying, she scrambled away from him as fast as she could. She wasn't sure if he was dead and didn't want to risk being stabbed again. She also wanted to see who'd shot him.

The man who staggered into her bedroom used the wall to prop himself up. Blood soaked his shirt, his right arm hung limp at his side and the other held a gun. With his tattoo sleeves and unusually pale face, he looked almost as scary as Shady. But he was far handsomer, and she knew everything would be okay when he closed his eyes, drew a deep breath so he could speak and said, "Don't be…afraid. I'm…Virgil's best friend."

Epilogue

Eighteen months later...

Virgil watched Peyton as she got up from her lounge chair to go inside the house and get more drinks. They were close to the baby's due date and that made him worry about her. He'd asked her to request some time off work—he'd received his $700,000 settlement and his own business was going well enough that they didn't need the income. But she'd refused. She said she was still too new at the federal correctional institution in Cumberland, Maryland, and that she had two months before she'd need to take maternity leave. She didn't want to be a weak link. And there was no talking her out of it.

At least she was working with medium-security offenders now; she seemed to enjoy her job, and she insisted that she felt great. She certainly looked good. But as far as Virgil was concerned, that had always been the case. As the pregnancy progressed, she complained about water retention and getting fat, but he knew how excited she was to be able to have this baby, and all he saw was the woman he loved.

Rex pointed to the article Virgil had found online this morning and printed out to show them. "So Rick Wallace has finally been sentenced."

"All thanks to Mona," Virgil responded with a chuckle. "What were the chances?" If she hadn't told Pretty Boy—Rex—how Shady had learned of Virgil's whereabouts, he probably would've gotten away with what he'd done.

"Took them long enough," Rex said.

Virgil picked up his beer. His sister, Laurel, and the kids were in the yard, playing with a kiddie pool. They'd come for the party, but he saw her often. She lived just down the street. "Losing his job and spending five years behind bars won't be easy on him. But it's too bad he'll be doing time at a medium-security prison instead of the kind we used to know."

Rex scowled. "In my opinion, he deserves more than he got. Why do you think they went so easy on him?"

Virgil squinted against the sun as he glanced at the barbecue, where he had some chicken and burgers grilling. "He had no prior record and wasn't the one who gave up Laurel's whereabouts, so he got off easy. Unless you count Meeks and Shady, no one actually died as a result of his actions. If they could've blamed the marshal's murder on him, it would've been a different story."

"I wish they could figure out who told them how to find Laurel."

"So do I. But it looks as though it won't happen."

Rex's gaze once again strayed to Laurel, who was refilling the pool.

Virgil nudged his foot under the table.

"What?" he said.

"You could be a little less obvious, you know."

His friend scowled. "I don't know what you're talking about."

"You're kidding, right? You drool every time my sister comes within ten feet of you."

Rex lifted his beer to shield his mouth from Laurel and lowered his voice. "Shut up! She'll hear you."

"Seriously, it's been a year and a half since you first met. You should ask her out."

"She'll let me know when she's ready."

Virgil got up to check the burgers. "After what she's been through, she might not recognize when she's ready," he murmured. "Make your move."

Rex whistled under his breath. "She's something else, isn't she?"

"She's a handful. I wouldn't wish her on my worst enemy," he teased. "But I already know you're a glutton for punishment and won't listen."

Rex stretched out his legs so he could cross them at the ankles. "Come on, what're you saying? You'd give your life for her."

"I know. That's why I'd like to see her with someone like you."

His eyebrows shot up. "You mean an ex-con? I've never been exonerated...."

"Stop feeling unworthy. You've turned your life around."

"And if our past catches up with us?"

"The Crew won't ever find us here. We have brand-new identities and we're living on the opposite side of the country."

"If we could get used to our new names, Charles Pembroke."

"We're getting there, Perry Smith. Ask her out."

"Nah."

Virgil rolled his eyes. "For a tough guy, you're sure a chickenshit."

"Maybe when I have more to offer."

"What more do you need?" Virgil wanted to know.

"You've wanted her since before you even met her, and our business is doing great. That's plenty to offer." As a matter of fact, Ex-Con Protection, a bodyguard service, had grown much faster than either of them had expected. By next year, they'd each be making more than Peyton. And it wasn't hard to make more than Laurel, since she couldn't seem to settle into any one thing. Virgil worried about her. Although their uncle was finally in prison serving a fifteen-year sentence, their mother had settled down with yet another man in L.A. and their lives had become considerably calmer, his sister still seemed restless. He wasn't sure she'd ever be able to forget everything that had happened, but he knew from experience that it would help her heal if she could find someone special to love.

"You're perfect for her," he said.

"I don't know, man." Rex rearranged the appetizers on his plate before risking another glance at Virgil's sister. "What if she shuts me down?"

"Then she shuts you down. What have you got to lose? She's not in your bed at night as it is."

Rex blew out a sigh. "Oh, what the hell. I've had just enough beer to let you talk me into this." Taking one last swallow, he crushed his can, tossed it in the recycle bucket and walked over to talk to Laurel.

Peyton returned to find Viril watching Rex and Laurel while he flipped the burgers and Mia and Jake splashed in the pool. "What's going on?" she asked.

He took her hand and kissed her knuckles, then jerked his head toward Laurel and Rex. "I think he's finally going to ask her out."

* * * * *

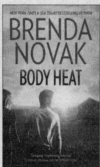

The chilling Krewe of Hunters trilogy from
New York Times and *USA TODAY* bestselling author

HEATHER GRAHAM

SOME SECRETS REFUSE TO STAY BURIED...

| Available now | On sale August 2011 | On sale September 2011 |

Available wherever books are sold.

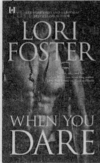 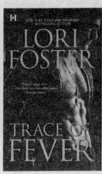 

Check out all three *THE SEARCHERS* books
by *New York Times* and *USA TODAY* bestselling author

SHARON SALA

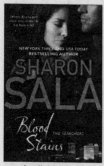

Available now! Available now! Coming October 2011

The truth will set you free—
if it doesn't get you killed.

Available wherever books are sold.

www.Harlequin.com

MSSTRI11

REQUEST YOUR FREE BOOKS!

2 FREE NOVELS
FROM THE SUSPENSE COLLECTION
PLUS 2 FREE GIFTS!

YES! Please send me 2 FREE novels from the Suspense Collection and my 2 FREE gifts (gifts are worth about $10). After receiving them, if I don't wish to receive any more books, I can return the shipping statement marked "cancel." If I don't cancel, I will receive 4 brand-new novels every month and be billed just $5.99 per book in the U.S. or $6.49 per book in Canada. That's a saving of at least 25% off the cover price. It's quite a bargain! Shipping and handling is just 50¢ per book in the U.S. and 75¢ per book in Canada.* I understand that accepting the 2 free books and gifts places me under no obligation to buy anything. I can always return a shipment and cancel at any time. Even if I never buy another book, the two free books and gifts are mine to keep forever.

191/391 MDN FEME

Name	(PLEASE PRINT)

Address	Apt. #

City	State/Prov.	Zip/Postal Code

Signature (if under 18, a parent or guardian must sign)

Mail to the **Reader Service**:
IN U.S.A.: P.O. Box 1867, Buffalo, NY 14240-1867
IN CANADA: P.O. Box 609, Fort Erie, Ontario L2A 5X3

Not valid for current subscribers to the Suspense Collection
or the Romance/Suspense Collection.

Want to try two free books from another line?
Call 1-800-873-8635 or visit www.ReaderService.com.

* Terms and prices subject to change without notice. Prices do not include applicable taxes. Sales tax applicable in N.Y. Canadian residents will be charged applicable taxes. Offer not valid in Quebec. This offer is limited to one order per household. All orders subject to credit approval. Credit or debit balances in a customer's account(s) may be offset by any other outstanding balance owed by or to the customer. Please allow 4 to 6 weeks for delivery. Offer available while quantities last.

Your Privacy—The Reader Service is committed to protecting your privacy. Our Privacy Policy is available online at www.ReaderService.com or upon request from the Reader Service.

We make a portion of our mailing list available to reputable third parties that offer products we believe may interest you. If you prefer that we not exchange your name with third parties, or if you wish to clarify or modify your communication preferences, please visit us at www.ReaderService.com/consumerschoice or write to us at Reader Service Preference Service, P.O. Box 9062, Buffalo, NY 14269. Include your complete name and address.

SUS11

BRENDA NOVAK

32993	INSIDE	___ $7.99 U.S.	___ $9.99 CAN.
32905	STOP ME	___ $7.99 U.S.	___ $9.99 CAN.
32904	WATCH ME	___ $7.99 U.S.	___ $9.99 CAN.
32903	TRUST ME	___ $7.99 U.S.	___ $9.99 CAN.
32902	DEAD RIGHT	___ $7.99 U.S.	___ $9.99 CAN.
32886	DEAD GIVEAWAY	___ $7.99 U.S.	___ $9.99 CAN.
32885	DEAD SILENCE	___ $7.99 U.S.	___ $9.99 CAN.
32831	KILLER HEAT	___ $7.99 U.S.	___ $9.99 CAN.
32803	BODY HEAT	___ $7.99 U.S.	___ $9.99 CAN.
32795	WHITE HEAT	___ $7.99 U.S.	___ $9.99 CAN.
32724	THE PERFECT LIAR	___ $7.99 U.S.	___ $8.99 CAN.
32725	THE PERFECT MURDER	___ $7.99 U.S.	___ $8.99 CAN.
32667	THE PERFECT COUPLE	___ $7.99 U.S.	___ $8.99 CAN.

(limited quantities available)

TOTAL AMOUNT	$ _____
POSTAGE & HANDLING	$ _____
($1.00 for 1 book, 50¢ for each additional)	
APPLICABLE TAXES*	$ _____
TOTAL PAYABLE	$ _____

(check or money order—please do not send cash)

To order, complete this form and send it, along with a check or money order for the total above, payable to MIRA Books, to: **In the U.S.:** 3010 Walden Avenue, P.O. Box 9077, Buffalo, NY 14269-9077; **In Canada:** P.O. Box 636, Fort Erie, Ontario, L2A 5X3.

Name: _____

Address: _____ City: _____

State/Prov.: _____ Zip/Postal Code: _____

Account Number (if applicable): _____

075 CSAS

*New York residents remit applicable sales taxes.
*Canadian residents remit applicable GST and provincial taxes.

MIRA | HARLEQUIN®
www.Harlequin.com

MBN0711BL